ESSEX GIRLS

Laura Ziepe was born in E̶̶̶̶̶̶̶̶̶ here for all of her life. ̶̶̶̶̶̶̶̶̶̶̶̶̶̶̶ first series of *The Only* ̶̶̶̶̶̶̶̶̶̶̶̶̶̶̶ in front of the camera ̶̶̶̶̶̶̶̶̶̶̶̶̶̶̶ ch preferred the dram ̶̶̶̶̶̶̶̶̶̶̶̶̶̶̶ on her laptop! When she's ̶̶̶̶̶̶̶̶̶, she loves to read, travel, cook and spend time at home in Essex with her fiancé and two Chihuahuas, Dolly and Dusty.

Cardiff Libraries
www.cardiff.gov.uk/libraries

Llyfrgelloedd Caerdydd
www.caerdydd.gov.uk/llyfrgelloedd

ACC. No: 03128190

LAURA ZIEPE

Essex Girls

AVON

This novel is entirely a work of fiction.
The names, characters and incidents portrayed in it are
the work of the author's imagination. Any resemblance to
actual persons, living or dead, events or localities is
entirely coincidental.

AVON

A division of HarperCollins*Publishers*
77–85 Fulham Palace Road,
London W6 8JB

www.harpercollins.co.uk

First published in Great Britain by Judy Piatkus (Publishers) Ltd in 2000

This edition published in Great Britain by HarperCollins*Publishers* in 2013
1

Copyright © Laura Ziepe 2013

Laura Ziepe asserts the moral right to
be identified as the author of this work

A catalogue record for this book is
available from the British Library

ISBN-13: 978-0-00-748646-5

Set in Sabon LT Std by Palimpsest Book Production Limited,
Falkirk, Stirlingshire

Printed and bound in Great Britain by
Clays Ltd, St Ives plc

All rights reserved. No part of this publication may be
reproduced, stored in a retrieval system, or transmitted,
in any form or by any means, electronic, mechanical,
photocopying, recording or otherwise, without the prior
permission of the publishers.

MIX
Paper from
responsible sources
FSC C007454

FSC™ is a non-profit international organisation established to promote
the responsible management of the world's forests. Products carrying the
FSC label are independently certified to assure consumers that they come
from forests that are managed to meet the social, economic and
ecological needs of present and future generations,
and other controlled sources.

Find out more about HarperCollins and the environment at
www.harpercollins.co.uk/green

For my special and much loved Nan, Eileen.
I know you would have been so proud.

Biggest thanks to my lovely agent Hannah Ferguson, editor Caroline Hogg and Avon editorial director Claire Bord for all their hard work; I'm incredibly grateful that you've made my dream become a reality. Also to the fantastic team at Avon and everyone involved in making this happen. Thank you so much!

I would also like to thank my parents; the most supportive, selfless and loving people I know. One of my best and oldest friends, Claire Honey; thank you so much for encouraging me to write this book and for offering advice and help when I needed it. You always believed in me!

CHAPTER 1

The irritating sound of the alarm was instantly switched off.

Jade stretched lazily in bed and turned to her boyfriend, Tom, who was about to get up.

'Oh, stay a bit longer,' she pleaded. 'Please.'

Tom sighed, glancing at the clock on the wall. 'I'd love to, but you know I can't be late.'

As he pulled himself up, she tugged at his arm playfully and he collapsed beside her, laughing. 'Okay, you win. Just for a minute though.'

Cuddling under the covers, Jade began to kiss his neck.

'Oh no, not my weak spot,' he groaned. 'You know I'll never leave and I *have* to.'

Jade held on to him tightly until he pulled away from her warm embrace, reluctantly.

'I'll be back before you know it. Keep the bed warm, gorgeous.' He winked at her and then left.

It was the same every Saturday morning. They would spend Friday nights together, Jade would stay at Tom's parents' house and then he'd have to get up early to coach a kids' football team. He didn't really need to as he had a full-time job in a bank, but he loved it. Jade had always thought it was really sweet. She could picture him running around in the back garden with their own future sons, teaching them how to play. Though of course she didn't tell Tom that; she didn't want him to get scared and run a mile.

Jade tried to doze back off to sleep, it was far too early to get up. Besides, she had nothing to do until he returned. Thoughts of Tom were keeping her awake though; she was so happy with him. She'd been worried when she first started university three years ago. It was a massive change in her life – and leaving her best friends Kelly and Lisa in Essex for a life in quiet Bath hadn't been easy. Embarrassingly, she'd even cried when she waved goodbye to them and saw their sad faces through the window of the car.

'Sugar Hut won't be the same without you,' they'd shouted. 'Don't forget about us!'

Of course she hadn't, and at first she went home to Essex every other weekend. But when she met Tom the visits home decreased. She still managed to rack up an eighty-pound phone bill from time to time, often going over her free minutes allowance because she was talking to her best friends for too long. Her friends were happy she'd met Tom; Jade had never had a serious boyfriend until she'd met him, and now to her delight they were planning on renting a flat together in Bath. As much as Jade loved her home town Chigwell, she also loved how different Bath was. The people were friendly, a lot more down to earth and low mainte-nance, and though it had taken her a long time to get used to it, she had to face the fact that fake tan just wasn't an option here. When she'd first arrived on campus, the other girls had looked at her like she was from another planet. She'd had her nails done and a spray tan for her first day; after all, she'd been single and on the lookout to meet some new hot men, and surely there was no better place than university, swarming with gorgeous guys in football and rugby shorts? To this day, she could have sworn the girls singing the *Oompa Loompa* song were aiming it at her. Okay, so she did look a few shades darker than everyone else, but she most certainly was not orange. She'd only had one spray, not her usual two, and the colour was called 'Bronze Beyond'. She'd made friends quickly enough and realised it was probably better to fit in with the pasty crowd, despite the fact she preferred her sunkissed look. It took some getting used to, and she always de-tagged every photo put up by her university friends on her Facebook page, just in case someone from Essex saw her looking as white as a ghost, but Jade had grown to love the carefree nature of the city. She didn't have to make as much effort when she went out, just a light layer of make-up and a brush of the hair like everyone else. Simple, quick and a nice change from the two-hour preparations she would have gone through back in Essex. Tom was always saying he loved the natural look and fancied her most when she was bare-faced, though deep down Jade just assumed he wanted her to believe this so she wouldn't go out dressed to the nines and catch the eye of another bloke. In her opinion she looked like Worzel Gummidge first thing, especially after a night out.

Yes, Bath was a lovely place to live and Jade had fallen in love with it. Before she moved in with Tom though, she needed a job, and for the past two weeks she'd done nothing but send her CV off to agencies and various companies. So far, she hadn't heard a thing, so she guessed what she'd been told was true; getting a job after university wasn't always easy. It was likely she was going to get a 2:1 grade in Psychology, as her results from her second year had only been a few marks away from a First and she felt she'd done just as well on this year's exams; the main problem was that she didn't actually know what she wanted to do with her degree. If she was honest with herself, she was worried that she'd cave in and end up getting a job as a teacher, which everyone else she knew seemed to do. But deep in her heart she knew she didn't want to do that. The thought of trying to teach a class of pubescent teens terrified her – she'd had a bad enough time at school herself, and there was no way she could go back there. Her senior school in Essex had been so bitchy; it was all about what shoes, bag and coat you had, with girls constantly bragging and showing off. If it hadn't been for Kelly and Lisa, she would have hated it. When the three of them were together they felt invincible and it helped that everyone had loved Kelly, because she was so ditzy. She often had the class in stitches with her ridiculous answers to the teacher's questions. Jade had always enjoyed her school work, not that she'd admitted it; saying you liked writing essays on *Pride and Prejudice* would have been social suicide. She could always teach younger kids, but the thought of snotty noses was enough to make her gag.

At first, she'd loved having the free time to think about what she wanted to do with her life, whilst waitressing part time in Café Rouge. With no alarm to wake her up after late nights and no coursework it seemed perfect, but only a few weeks later Jade was starting to get bored of doing nothing. Sitting in her pyjamas until three in the afternoon searching for jobs online had definitely lost its appeal.

Jade got out of bed and grabbed Tom's cosy dressing gown. Now would be a good time to really think about different job roles she could take on. She searched his bedside drawers for some paper and a pen. There was no time like the present and she was adamant to work out what she wanted to do with her life today. She had no luck finding any paper in the drawers on her side of the bed, so she moved across to the other side where Tom slept. In the second drawer she found a large notepad and some pens and lifted them out. She froze. Underneath the notepad was a mobile phone she had never seen before. Jade couldn't describe why, but she had a sudden feeling of dread. Why did Tom have another phone? Telling herself it must be an old handset, she tried to calm her suddenly fast heartbeat. She picked it up, hoping with all her might that it would have a flat battery and wouldn't switch on. When it did, her hands began to shake and her heart began to hammer so hard that she felt the blood rush through her ears. It's nothing, she told herself when the welcome message appeared; an old phone that she shouldn't even be looking at. *Breathe.* She opened the messages folder and felt physically sick when she saw countless texts from a girl called Louisa. Hands shaking, she clicked to read the latest one. Please be a really old message, she thought, please.

So nice being with you last night baby. Miss you xx

She clicked down, shocked at what she was reading. When was this? Please say it was way before he met me? All her happiness, hopes and dreams with Tom came crashing down when she saw the date: June 16th 2011. That was a month ago! How dare he? Her heart raced even faster, and she had to force herself to breathe slowly and deeply. Tears formed in her eyes. She wanted to stop herself from reading the texts, but it felt like someone else had taken over her body and she simply had to see more.

Glad you like the pic of my boobs, loved your one too! Makes me want you again, badly. When will I get to see you again Tom? ;) Love your kisses. I'm at uni on Tuesday for my theatre class, so any day apart from then is good for me.
June 15th 2011

Hey sexy, thanks for the flowers. Got them this morning. You're so cute xx
June 11th 2011

Baby, one afternoon with you isn't enough! My bed is too big and cold without you :(Wish you were still here
June 11th 2011

Jade couldn't read them all; it was far too painful. She'd seen enough. She sat with her head in her hands and tried to breathe. Her heart was still pounding and she realised her happy life as she knew it was now going to change forever. Why? Why was this happening to her? She hadn't so much as looked at another man since she'd been with Tom. They were happy. She wasn't deluded; it wasn't one-sided, she knew he was happy too. She started to pace up and down his room, thinking about what she should do next. All of a sudden, anger rushed through her veins and out through every pore of her skin. The two-timing, lying scumbag! How long had he been seeing this other stupid bitch for? What an arsehole! Just who the hell did he think he was? How could she have been such a fool? But she had been. She sat down on the bed and began to sob. She'd believed everything he'd said, no questions asked. She loved him. He was her first boyfriend; her first true love. She'd understood what love truly meant when she met Tom. Now though, he had broken her heart. Jade put her hand to her heart and collapsed back on the bed, her heart honestly feeling as though it had been torn in two. It was a physical, deep aching pain inside. Without even thinking about what she was doing, she picked up her own phone and called Kelly.

'Hello?' Kelly answered after the fourth ring, in a sleepy voice.

6

'Hi Kel,' Jade sniffed. 'Sorry to wake you. It's only me.'

'What's wrong babe? Are you crying?'

'Mmm . . .' The huge lump in Jade's throat prevented her from being able to talk.

'Oh no. What's up hun?'

'I'm at Tom's. He's gone football coaching, like he does every Saturday and I went to get something from his drawer and found another phone.'

'I don't like the sound of this,' Kelly said concerned. 'Go on.'

'There are all these messages from another girl called Louisa, who I think goes to my uni because she mentioned something about theatre class,' she sniffed again. 'They're really bad; he's been seeing her behind my back.'

'Oh my God, shut up! You're joking?'

'I wish I was,' Jade answered sadly.

Never afraid to speak her mind, Kelly answered, 'What a fucking bastard!'

'I know. I'm still at his place now. What shall I do? I'm so upset and shocked. I feel sick.'

'He's an arsehole, babe. What did the messages say?'

'There were loads. I couldn't even face reading all of them. She was texting him things like "my bed is cold without you", so clearly he's been sleeping with her. This was only a month ago. She texted him on the 11th June about the bed thing and now I keep racking my brains, wondering what I was doing at that time.'

'Wasn't that when you had your last exam, hun? I asked you to come home a few times, but you were always studying.'

'Yes, you're right. I kept apologising because I couldn't spend as much time with him as normal. He was probably glad, so he could see *her*. I bet he was with that bitch when he was off work and supposedly ill; she said something about being "with him" in the afternoon. And there was me feeling sorry for him, what a mug! He's a disgusting little rat. I'm so pissed off. I was so happy. How the hell could he do this to me?'

'He doesn't deserve you. You're gorgeous and the loveliest person ever, he's just another wanker bloke.'

'I know.' Tears rolled down Jade's cheeks without her even realising. 'It just hurts so much. Two and a half years I've wasted on him. How do I know this is the only girl he's slept with? He could have given me something for all I know.'

'Get checked, babe, in case there were more girls than just her. I know it's hard, but you can't think about what he was doing or might have been doing, when and where. All you need to think is that he is a wrong 'un and you deserve a hell of a lot more. At least you found out before you moved in together.'

'I hate him. I hate him so much.' She couldn't hold back her tears.

'Please don't cry, Jade. I hate to hear you sad when I'm so far away. Now do me a favour and listen, okay?'

Jade nodded, forgetting her friend couldn't see her, and wiped her tears away.

'Get everything you own from his house and get out; don't leave anything behind as he'll use it as an excuse to see you later. Are you listening?'

'Yes,' she sniffed.

'Go back to yours and then when you can, pack your bags and come home to Essex.'

'I don't think I'm ready to leave just yet.'

'Oh babe, I know it's going to be hard, but you have to stay strong. You can't stay there alone and heartbroken. You need to get your life back on track.'

Rage surged through Jade as she thought about Tom and Louisa once again. 'I know what I need to do, and that's to get even.'

'What do you mean?'

'I want revenge. I'm not allowing that bastard to get away with it. He's going to pay.'

'I'm liking this idea. What are you going to do though?'

'I'm not sure just yet, but I'm going to humiliate him like he's humiliated me.'

'Well, be careful and let me know what you decide. Will you come back to Essex afterwards?' Kelly asked hopefully.

'Yes of course. I miss you so much. Especially now. But I better go; I have some plotting to do.'

'Call me if you need to – and book your train back asap!'

'I will. Thanks, Kel.'

'Any time. I'm sorry he's done this to you, but you will find someone ten times better than that dickhead.'

Jade laughed, despite her unhappiness. 'Speak soon.'

She hung up and sat on the edge of the bed with her head in her hands, trying to think of how she could get him back. What could she do? It needed to be something good. Jade told herself she wasn't going home to Essex until she taught him a lesson. Yes, the most mature thing would be to walk away with her head held high, but embarrassing him somehow would make her feel a whole lot better. She got his hidden phone and called her mobile so she had the number. She then went down his contact list and deleted Louisa's number, changing it for her own, but keeping the name Louisa. When Jade texted him he would think it was this other woman. She placed his phone back in the drawer where she'd found it, and got her things together to leave.

She knew that Tom thought the majority of Essex girls were dumb airheads judging by the comments he'd made in the past. Well, he was certainly going to regret the day he ever messed with this one.

*

Tom climbed out of his car and walked towards the football pitch, where most of the boys had already arrived and were kicking footballs to each other. He looked up at the shining sun; it was going to be a great day. Maybe he would suggest going for a picnic this afternoon with Jade, he thought to himself, envisaging a nice lazy day lying in the sun with his girlfriend. He loved spending his weekends with Jade; they always had such a good time together.

He'd fancied her the moment he first clapped eyes on her a few years ago, even though he did think she was wearing too much make-up. It hadn't surprised him in the slightest when she said she was from Essex. You could tell an Essex girl a mile off, he mused; they were all hair extensions, orange tans and fake eyelashes. It wasn't long before he'd persuaded Jade to tone it down and in his opinion she now looked so much better. She was naturally pretty and didn't need any 'war paint'. Fake-looking girls definitely didn't appeal to him; Tom was much more a Keira Knightley fan than a Katie Price one. He was glad Jade's Essex accent was becoming more subtle too. He often corrected her speech, and could sometimes see the hurt in her eyes when he pulled her up for sounding like a working-class fishwife, but he told himself it was for her own good.

He would never move to Essex – it certainly wasn't the place for him he'd realised, after visiting Jade's home a few times. He'd only ever been to Chigwell and Loughton, but everyone had seemed so vulgar and false. They'd gone to one nightclub called Faces and he couldn't believe his eyes when he saw tables of people, some even 'Z' list celebrities, ordering bottles of champagne with sparklers, trying to show the world that they had money. In his eyes, they had absolutely no class. Jade's friend Kelly was awful too; such a typical Essex girl, common, and as thick as two planks. The other one, Lisa, was okay, as she seemed a bit more intelligent and was very pretty too; he definitely wouldn't mind spending a night with *her*. He knew there must be parts of Essex that were less brash, but seeing where Jade lived had put him off the county for good. It was convenient that Jade liked Bath, because he intended to stay there for the long run. It was where he had lived all his life and was where he always wanted to be.

Life was going well at the moment, he thought to himself, whilst getting the equipment for the coaching session out of his car. It looked like he would soon be promoted at work, he had an amazing girlfriend who he would soon move in with, and even had a bit on the side with a girl who adored him. He knew it was wrong, but what man didn't cheat? So long as Jade never found out, which he was sure she wouldn't, it didn't do any harm. Besides, he was going to finish it soon, as Louisa was becoming far too clingy for his liking, demanding to know when she would be seeing him again, and he definitely wasn't up for that; he already had a girlfriend, one he had no intention of leaving. He'd been out one night with his friends when he'd met Louisa, and to start with, seeing two women at the same time had been a thrill. She had a fairly pretty face, nothing amazing, but a body to die for and she was always so eager to please. She made him feel good about himself, and he'd enjoyed boasting to the lads that he was worn out by the demands of two girls. But he hadn't planned on seeing Louisa for long; love them and leave them was his motto when it came to a cheeky bit on the side. He loved Jade a lot, but wasn't entirely sure he could ever commit himself to just *one* person, whoever she was. There was too much temptation in the world, especially for someone as good looking as he was. Plus, he'd turned down lots of girls in the past because of Jade, so really this whole thing with Louisa was nothing compared to what he could have done.

The loud shrill ringtone of his mobile interrupted his

thoughts. He smiled when he saw Jade's name flashing across the screen.

'Hi Jade.'

'Hi.'

'What's up?'

'Nothing really. Kelly just called me and said she's coming to Bath for the day to see me. She was on the train when she rang. She's feeling down about something and wants cheering up so we're going out for the day. Just thought I'd let you know as I won't be able to see you today or tonight and I know we were going to do something.'

He was disappointed. 'Oh right. Why didn't she tell you she was coming beforehand?'

'Something has happened and she's really upset. It wasn't planned. Sorry,' came the curt reply.

He sighed. 'Oh well, it can't be helped. Why don't you stay at mine and wait for me to get back before you leave to meet her? You got me all worked up this morning and I'd love to get back under those covers with you.'

'I can't. She's not going to be much longer so I'm leaving your place now,' Jade replied breezily.

Tom was irritated. 'Fine. Tell Kelly that in future you need a bit of notice. You can't just be there whenever she decides to come down. You do have a life.'

'Tom, my friend is upset and needs me, so I'm going to be there for her. Look, I need to get going so perhaps I'll see you tomorrow.'

'Fair enough. Bye.'

Tom felt well and truly put out. How inconvenient that Kelly had just decided last minute to visit Jade. Did she not think that Jade may have made plans? She was supposedly feeling down about something, Jade had said. Perhaps she'd broken a nail, Tom sniggered to himself. Didn't she have any other bloody friends in Essex to whine to? He had no plans for the rest of the day now as all his friends had gone

12

away for the weekend. Maybe it wasn't such a good idea to finish with Louisa just yet. Perhaps he'd see what she was up to? She was always game for anything – and he certainly wouldn't be getting any sex from Jade today, after all.

He called the boys over and started the warm-up session.

*

Jade was amazed how calm she had been on the phone to Tom. She had really wanted to scream at him the minute she heard his voice, but knew that wouldn't get her anywhere. Who did he think he was, telling her to inform Kelly she needed to give more notice next time? Had he always been like that – or was she only just seeing him now for who he truly was? The more she thought about it, the more Jade realised he was always trying to control her.

She calmly collected her things from the flat, making sure she hadn't left anything behind.

Jade wished deep in her heart that the whole thing was just a huge mistake; that they could carry on normally and forget any of this ever happened. What she would give for that feeling of utter happiness and complete contentment that she'd had only forty minutes ago. She always thought she was so lucky to have Tom, but now she could see she wasn't at all; *he* was lucky to have *her*. She wasn't perfect, she knew that; she snored a little (so she'd been told), she often sat in her pyjamas all day and no, she never felt quite herself without her fake eyelash extensions. But she was loyal, honest and trustworthy and had truly loved him. She would never betray someone she loved and she would have done anything for him. So, *he* was the loser. He was welcome to that tart.

Jade closed the front door behind her quietly and ran

13

to her car. She thanked her lucky stars she'd hadn't bumped into Tom's mum on the way out, as she would probably want to chat for ages and ask her where she was going. It was clear that his mum never thought she was good enough, so the last thing Jade needed was to run into her. Jade had had to bite her tongue on more than one occasion, especially when she commented that perhaps Jade should consider a cookery class so she could feed her son 'decent' meals, after she'd cooked Tom a Marks and Spencer meal deal one evening. What was wrong with a meal deal? It wasn't as though she'd cooked him a Pot Noodle or something! Jade started the ignition, her mind working overtime, wondering what she could do to get her revenge.

When she walked through the front door to her flat she noticed a leaflet on the welcome mat about a *Sleeping Beauty* theatre performance that evening at the university. *I wonder if his little bit on the side is performing?* Jade wondered as she eyed the cast list avidly. As soon as she saw the name 'Louisa Dalton' written as the main part of Sleeping Beauty the idea came to her. If it worked, it was the perfect way to show Tom up. The perfect way to show him that, actually, she was in control. Jade couldn't wait.

*

Tom pulled into his drive and suddenly realised how hungry he was. His mum would be up by now and he couldn't wait to eat one of the legendary bacon and cheese baguettes that she made every Saturday. He would miss his mum spoiling him when he left home. Jade had already said outright that she would not be waiting on him hand and foot, especially when they were both working. Women and their bloody equal rights these days, Tom thought, infuriated. Maybe he'd suggest that she paid for meals out equally too, see how she liked that!

He was the only one still living at home, as his older brother had moved out a long time ago, and his mum loved nothing more than to fuss over him. He certainly wasn't complaining. Jade often told him he should help his mum out more and that she shouldn't be still ironing his clothes, but she liked doing it and besides, what did Jade know? It made his mum happy to be there for him, it made her feel needed. He didn't have a clue how to iron and if he was honest, he didn't *want* to know how to either. As far as he was concerned it was a woman's job.

He walked through his front door and the smell of bacon came wafting towards him, much to his delight.

'Morning Tom,' his mum said, handing him a baguette wrapped in a napkin.

'Morning Mum.' He took a huge, hungry bite.

'Think I heard Jade leave earlier. She didn't say goodbye though.'

Tom could see she was offended. 'I wouldn't take it personally, Mum. She was in a rush as her dopey Essex friend is upset about something and has just turned up to see her.'

'Still, she could have at least called out that she was leaving to me. So what are you doing today then?'

'I'm not sure yet. About to make plans,' he said, as he walked out the kitchen, chewing a delicious mouthful of bacon. He was humming as he kicked his shoes off and made his way upstairs. His mum was very particular about not wearing shoes on her cream carpets. She was extremely house-proud, exactly how women should be, he thought fondly. Tom sat on the bed, annoyed that Jade hadn't even bothered to make it for once, which was unlike her. Too worried about meeting up with that bimbo, he thought. He reached into his drawer and searched for his phone, hidden under a few large notepads. He switched it on and wasn't surprised to see a text message sent a few minutes earlier from Louisa. God, she was keen, he thought arrogantly.

What are you up to tonight? Want to fulfill a fantasy of mine?

This was more like it, Tom thought as he read the message. Maybe Jade had done him a favour blowing him out in the end. A night of fulfilling fantasies had to be better than a picnic and perhaps the dull cinema later on, surely? He texted back, wondering what Louisa had in mind.

Sounds good to me. What time and where shall we meet?

Hopefully it was a threesome and she had another hot friend; that would be the best night ever! How his friends would be jealous if he told them that was how he'd spent his Saturday night. A text pinged back almost straight away.

Meet me at the university theatre at six tonight. It'll be empty, I've checked and the doors are always open. I've always wanted to do it on the stage. Every time I see it, I picture us together on it. Take all your clothes off and wait for me. It'll be dark in there and I'll meet you. Promise I won't be late xx

Was she being serious? The university theatre? What if somebody saw them? Then again, who would be at the university theatre on a Saturday night? The whole campus was usually dead at weekends because people went home, and she did say she was sure it was empty. Plus, who cared if a cleaner or caretaker got a cheeky glimpse? Knowing someone could be watching them might even even be a turn on. If there were loads of people around he would just meet her outside and tell her they had to go somewhere else; maybe they could do it in his car in the car park? His phone beeped again.

I hope you're not going to be a chicken? Come on, I want to get dirty with you on the stage . . .

He sighed. How could he refuse that? He'd look like a complete loser if he turned her down. Maybe she wanted to boast to all her theatre friends that she'd done it on the stage with him; she was obviously up for it so why shouldn't he be? The worst thing that could happen was that someone would see them and it might get back to Jade, but that was a risk he was willing to take – the thought of doing it somewhere different was just too much of a thrill to turn down. Louisa might not be the love of his life, but she sure as hell could be fun at times. She wasn't even asking to be taken out for dinner beforehand like she normally did, so it seemed that finally she was getting the picture it was only ever going to be just sex between them.

Okay, you're on. Wear that sexy black underwear set I love. See you at six then xx

Jade felt sick when she read his reply, hands shaking with adrenaline and anger. Her sexy black underwear? Did she ever actually know Tom at all? Right now, it didn't seem like it. He'd been with her last night in his bed and now he was happily meeting up with some slag offering herself on a plate to him! It had been so easy getting him to meet too; he didn't seem to hesitate for a moment. At least her plan was working, she told herself, looking for the handcuffs he'd bought her last Valentine's day and placing them in her bag. The fact that he'd agreed to meet Louisa without a second thought made Jade certain that he was about to get what he deserved.

At five thirty that evening she made her way to the university theatre. Luckily there was no one around. The performers and staff wouldn't be there for about another hour or so, so she had plenty of time to make sure her plan ran smoothly.

The stage was already filled with props, which included a single bed for Sleeping Beauty, made from wrought iron. She tested the handcuffs, satisfied that they would go round the posts of the bed. Now all she had to do was sit in the darkened wings at the side of the stage and wait for him. She switched the lights off and waited.

Twenty minutes later she heard the door open, and Jade's heart was thumping so loudly in her chest that she couldn't breathe. What if it wasn't him? What if someone had arrived early for the performance tonight? She heard the footsteps coming closer to the stage.

'Louisa?'

It was Tom.

'Yes,' she whispered, trying to disguise her voice. It was pitch black in the room and she could roughly make out the outline of his body.

'Come here then,' he said, his voice thick with lust as he removed his belt, the buckle making a loud bang as it hit the floor. She could hear him removing his t-shirt and then his jeans. Then she knew he was silently peeling off his boxer shorts. She peeked carefully, and saw Tom lying on the bed.

Jade felt a mixture of emotions. She was angrier than she'd ever been in her life, but nervous at the same time. She knew any feelings she had ever held for him had gone. Here was her long-term boyfriend, who she was planning on moving in with, stripping off naked for another girl. She made her way over to the bed, terrified that he would know immediately it was her and not Louisa. She was almost there; her plan couldn't go wrong now.

'Come here, sexy,' he pleaded as she approached the bed, concealed by shadows.

'Close your eyes,' she whispered. 'I have a surprise for you.'

'Mmm . . . I like surprises,' he said in a husky voice. 'They're closed.'

She walked over to him, took his arms and handcuffed each one to the posts of the bed.

'Kinky,' he said. 'I like it.'

She stifled a giggle and began to pick his clothes up off the floor.

'Come here, babe. What are you doing? Where are you going?'

Jade spoke loud and clear in her own voice. 'I thought you liked surprises?'

'Who is that?' Tom asked in a panicky voice, trying to get up and yanking his arms, frustrated that he couldn't move.

'Oh, it's only your girlfriend. Remember me? Mind you, you're probably too busy shagging other girls to actually give a shit.'

'Jade?'

'Well at least you haven't forgotten my name,' she said sarcastically.

'What the hell are you doing here? Take these handcuffs off me now. Let me explain! Just let me out!'

He sounded terrified now and Jade was ashamed to admit she was enjoying it.

'Why should I do anything you ask me to? You're a lying, cheating arsehole and I never have to do anything you say again.'

'What are you talking about? I've never cheated on you, I swear. Please Jade, listen to me. Let me go and I'll explain everything.'

'Are you kidding me? You're still going to deny it? I saw your phone you idiot – and all your messages to Louisa. I changed her number to mine and you've been texting *me* all day. You're here to have sex with her so don't even bother trying to lie!'

His voice was shaky. 'Jade, I know this looks bad. W . . . worse than bad, it looks bloody terrible. Please,' he sounded almost close to tears, 'I love you.'

'You don't love me, Tom. You wouldn't do this to someone you love. I would never, ever do this to you. I've done nothing but love you. I've had other men come on to me, you know, but I'd never go behind your back. I've never wanted to. You're enough for me but I'm obviously not enough for you. Who is she? How long have you been seeing her for?'

His voice still sounded utterly panicked. 'She's just some girl that practically stalks me. I don't like her and I've never met up with her before. I was just drunk once and stupidly gave her my number. She means nothing to me, I promise. This would have been the first time I met her and I wouldn't have gone through with it. I was just messing around! You're the one I love. I've never cheated on you. You have to believe what I'm saying.'

His pathetic lies almost made her laugh. 'Stop lying to me. I'm not stupid!'

'You can't leave me here like this. I know you're not that out of order.'

'You've been sleeping with another girl, Tom! Do you want to bet that I won't leave you here?'

'I can't believe this is happening.' Tom's voice was small as the reality hit him that she wasn't going to let him free.

'Well, believe it,' she said, walking away with his clothes.

'Jade! Please! You can't do this to me! Just let me go and we'll talk about it! You can't leave me like this!'

It was hard not to enjoy how distraught he sounded. He

20

deserved everything he got. What they had had was special, but now he'd gone and spoilt everything. She would never and could never forgive him. Now she knew everything had been a lie, and no longer thought of him as the same amazing boyfriend who she could trust with her heart. She was so angry she could scream.

'Goodbye Tom,' she said, drawing the curtains on the stage.

She could hear him violently trying to pull the handcuffs off the bed and break them. The metal rattled but didn't give way.

'Jade! Let me go! Let me explain! Please, it's really cold! You can't do this!'

She opened the doors to the theatre and walked out, leaving them wide open. She threw his clothes in a dustbin in the car park, satisfied he wouldn't find them there. It was over. Now he too would feel as humiliated as she had. The feeling of guilt was gnawing away at her, so she forced herself to think of *why* she'd done it, and started to smirk as she imagined how people were going to find him in his sorry naked state. Tom certainly wouldn't be pulling off the role of Sleeping Beauty anytime soon.

All her plans were over, finished. There was no way she would stay in Bath now. There were too many memories and besides, who would she even live with? Her closest friends had all moved out of their shared house and gone back home a month ago, straight after their last exam, which is why she had moved in two sociology students who had just left halls and were going into their second year. She hardly even knew them and hadn't bothered making much conversation because she thought she'd be moving in with Tom soon. Jade's lease was up soon so the best option was to move back home. But Jade felt as though Bath was her home now – that was the problem. Bath, with its beautiful countryside and stunning architecture. Jade never would have even thought about things like that when she lived in Essex. She'd changed; could she really go back? Being in Essex was like her part-time life now, and this was where she lived.

Jade got into the driver's seat of her car and cried. Her anger had melted away and now she just felt a raw emotional pain. She had loved Tom. But now he'd ruined it all.

CHAPTER 2

After a day of moping about and feeling sorry for herself, Jade looked out of the window and saw her dad's car pull up outside the flat. She looked around, sadly. She'd packed up her whole life in Bath in boxes, bags and suitcases and was ready to leave.

Yesterday had been one of the toughest days of her life. Tom was still the only thing she could think about. She had been with him for two and a half years and still couldn't believe what had happened. Jade had been willing to change herself and her life to please him and he'd done nothing but lie and cheat in return. She'd already heard what had happened to him in the theatre; he'd been found by the cast of the play. Apparently someone had taken a photo on their mobile of him running away in a dress and it was going around Facebook. She thought that by publicly humiliating him it would make her feel better, but now she just felt nothing but sad.

She was tired. Tired of thinking about him and nothing else. Tired of only caring about her heartache and not having any interest in doing anything. It was as though nothing in her life was important. She felt so emotional about everything. Even an advert about animal cruelty had made her cry. She knew it had only just happened and she was bound

23

to be upset, but she wondered; how long would she go on feeling like this? She was a complete mess, and didn't want to talk to anyone, apart from Kelly and Lisa.

Tom had bombarded her with messages begging her to forgive him, insisting he'd never do it again, saying that despite what she had done to him, he still wanted to be with her. Jade had replied just once, to say that if he'd ever cared about her at all he'd leave her alone and let her get on with her life. Hopefully he would.

*

Jade opened the door to her dad before he knocked. He smiled at her as he walked along the path.

'Hi Dad,' she said, hugging him and kissing his cheek as he stepped through the door.

'Hello love,' he replied, wiping his feet on the welcome mat. 'How have you been?'

'I've been okay,' she lied.

'So is this everything?' He pointed at her things on the floor, all ready to go. 'You don't need help with the packing then? That's a bit of luck,' he joked.

'Yeah, I've done it all already. That's everything.'

'So, you've broken up with Tom? I thought it was all going well.'

Jade shrugged. 'Things change.'

He laughed. 'Just when your mum and I thought we'd got rid of you, eh?'

She managed a weak smile. Her dad wasn't very good in these situations. He hated talking about feelings and even though she knew he loved her immensely, he'd never been particularly affectionate. He was a man's man, as her mum always said.

Her father looked at her, concerned, and put his hand gently on her shoulder. 'Are you sure you're alright, love?'

'I'm fine,' she said, brushing him off and turning round to face the boxes. She couldn't talk to her dad, she'd just get upset and she didn't want him to see that. She just wanted to go home. 'Right, shall we start to pack the car up then or did you want a cup of tea first?'

'That's alright. I stopped on the way for petrol and got some lunch and a coffee. Let's head back shall we, and hopefully we'll miss the traffic.'

'Thanks, Dad. I really appreciate you helping me,' Jade replied, and started to pick up the boxes to take to his car. There wasn't enough room for everything to be put in her Mini, but she felt bad making her dad drive all the way down to Bath to help her. She sat in her car waiting for her dad to pull away so she could follow him.

As she drove down the road, a tear slid down her cheek and she quickly brushed it away.

This was really it. After three years in Bath, she was now going back to Essex for good. Back to the same old haunts she used to go to, seeing the same old faces she hadn't seen in a long while. She didn't even know if she'd fit in any more. It sounded silly, but she really had grown up. She was different. Her once bright blonde highlighted hair was now toned down with caramels and chocolate browns, her bras were no longer filled with gel and her make-up was subtle to the point of being almost non-existent. Would it be easy to fit right back into where she left off? Or would she be the odd one out now? The outsider? It was a scary thought. At least she had her two best friends, who would love her no matter what.

*

Jade's first night at home felt strange. Her mum had fussed around her, made her favourite meal of roast chicken, and even her older brother Simon came to visit with his wife

25

and two sons. Jade put on a brave face and pretended she was fine, that she was happy to be home. Playing cops and robbers with her nephews had actually taken her mind off Tom for once. She'd last seen them six months ago, and was amazed by how different they looked now. They had grown so much, even though they were only just four and six. It was nice that her family were happy to see her and have her back home. After feeling nothing but pretty rubbish about herself, heartbroken at what Tom had done to her, it was lovely to feel wanted again, even if it was also weird climbing back into her old bed, knowing this was where she would live for the time being. As much as she loved her parents, it would be hard to get used to living under their rules again. There would be no going back to Bath in a few days like normal. This was it.

Jade had woken on the first morning at five a.m., and it took her a while to remember where she was and why. She was sick to death of crying, but couldn't help it when she realised the reality of her situation. She preferred to sleep, where she was happy in her dream world. Why did she have to wake up? She missed Tom already. She hated herself for it after what he'd done, but she knew she was going to miss everything about him. Their long chats for hours about nothing, his silly jokes, his amazing body. Would she ever meet someone she loved as much again? After all, in all her twenty-one years, Tom was the only person that had made her knees go weak. What if she never got that again? She had to get over it, Jade told herself sternly. Had to stop crying all the time and move on with her life. He'd cheated. Tom wasn't the person she thought he was – she had to keep thinking of things she hadn't liked so much about him rather than all the good things. Like the way he and his friends often made fun of her Essex accent.

'You alriiight babe, you look branna today than last

week, you been on a sun bed?' they'd mocked her at times. 'I'm just gonna go to Saffend in me eye-eels.' Then they would all burst into laughter.

'Ha ha,' she'd usually replied, not really finding it at all funny and feeling self-conscious every time she spoke. They made her feel ashamed that she was from Essex and she hated to admit it to herself but, looking back, she realised she was always trying to impress Tom and be the person that he wanted her to be.

He hadn't been perfect and she had to stop believing he was.

After four hours of tossing and turning, Jade sleepily dragged herself out of bed, had a shower and got dressed into her black skinny jeans and a short leopard print blouse. She studied herself in the mirror, satisfied that her outfit could pass for both day and night. Today, she was going to make an effort with her appearance for once. She straightened her long hair with her GHDs, which she normally just left wavy, and applied her make-up carefully, adding a lot more bronzer than usual – after all, she was back in Essex, you could never wear *too* much. She felt better already. She packed her bag with make-up so she could touch up later if she went out with the girls. She couldn't wait to see Kelly and Lisa. Spending the day with them was going to be great; it didn't matter that they had no idea where they were going yet. If anyone could make her laugh right now it was them.

*

Kelly was in her dressing gown, relaxing on the couch in the lounge. Her hairdresser, Amy, had already been this morning and as usual, had blow-dried her hair to perfection, so all she had to do was apply her make-up and she was ready for the day. Amy was the only hairdresser she trusted to get her hair just right and she had her

27

round to the house at least twice a week; she didn't know what she'd do without her. It was all about the big hair, Kelly thought as she caught sight of her reflection on the mirrored coffee table. She'd made Amy backcomb for England this morning and was very pleased with the outcome.

Her mum's chihuahua, Lord McButterpants, jumped up at the sofa and she scooped him up and placed him on her lap, much to the dog's delight. He was a gorgeous little thing; he had long, soft, creamy-coloured fur and was no bigger than a kitten. Her mum was out today and Kelly promised she'd look after him. He hated walking because his tiny legs got tired so quickly, so she would take him out in her mum's Louis Vuitton dog carrier, she decided as she spotted it on the floor in the hall.

She was so glad her best friend was finally back in Essex – she'd missed her more than she'd ever realised. Going out was never the same without Jade. Yes, she always had a good time on nights out, but not in the same way she did when Jade was there. She did go out with Lisa sometimes, but she was always with her boyfriend, Jake, which was a bit annoying, so Kelly usually had to resort to going out with some girls from her salon.

She had been gutted when Jade had told her she was going to university, especially when she said it was all the way down the country in Bath. She felt like she'd be left behind and forgotten about. Then Jade had said she was going to live in Bath for good with Tom, and Kelly had seriously thought she'd lost her friend forever. Secretly, Kelly had never been too keen on Tom, as he seemed to look down his nose at her, and Kelly also believed he was the reason Jade was changing so much. Jade always wanted to impress him and never did things she thought he wouldn't approve of. It was hard to watch your best friend changing for someone else, especially when you thought they were pretty much perfect just the way they were.

There was no way that *she* could ever have gone to university – she hated writing essays and had barely passed her GCSEs. Kelly was certainly not academic and had decided a beauty course was definitely the thing for her. She loved making people feel better about themselves and their appearance and it was amazing how a spray tan could really lift your mood and make you feel a hundred times better. Everyone should have them in her opinion; even men, and her male client list was getting longer by the day.

She went up to her room to start on her make-up and wondered what Jade would be wearing for their day out. She'd almost given her a heart attack when she went out last time she was back in Essex, as she was only wearing mascara and no fake tan! For Jade's last birthday, Kelly had bought her a St Tropez gift set, hoping she would take the hint, but to her surprise she still went out looking as white as a sheet. She just looked so different and even sounded strange too; her normal accent was slowly fading away. She felt like all her friend's Essex traits were disappearing and if she'd have been with Tom any longer, he would have made sure they were gone for good. Jade would be back to normal soon, Kelly told herself, it wouldn't take long; she'd make sure of it.

She was just finishing applying her Benefit lip gloss when the doorbell rang and she jumped up excitedly. As she answered her front door she screamed. 'Ahhhhh! My Essex girl is home!'

She hugged Jade tightly.

'Hi, Kel.'

'Come in, babe. Lisa will be here soon. It's so nice to see you! I'll put the kettle on.'

Kelly glanced at Jade. She was wearing bronzer, so that

was a good start. Still no fake tan or eyelashes though. There was only one thing for it; she needed an Essex make-over.

*

Jade followed Kelly into the kitchen as she went to make the tea. It only seemed like yesterday that they were in here, gossiping and laughing after a night out, eating one of Kelly's mum's amazing fry-ups. Kelly's parents were a lot more relaxed than her own and Lisa's were so strict they were a nightmare, so the girls had always stayed at Kelly's house after nights out.

'Lord McButterpants!' Jade squealed happily, picking up the little dog who was wagging his tail frantically with excitement. She'd missed Kelly's mum's dog; he was utterly adorable. She remembered the first time Kelly told her what they had decided to name him and she thought it was a joke.

'Don't laugh, Lord McButterpants will hear you!' Kelly said with a stern expression as she covered the dog's ears.

Jade had soon got used to the unusual name and had to admit, it actually suited him. Lord McButterpants was exceptionally confident and walked around the house with his head held high, full of self-importance. He went crazy over peanut butter treats, which is where the word 'butter' came from in his name. Jade thought his name was hilarious – and so did everyone else when Kelly called him in the park.

Jade studied her best friend. She hadn't altered one bit in three years. She had lovely blonde hair, which was thick and wavy, and the most amazingly large blue eyes she'd ever seen. Despite the fact she had long eyelashes anyway, she was never without her false ones and today was no exception. Her tan was clearly false as she hadn't been away since the previous summer, but always flawless, even if it was too dark to be natural. Jade always got Kelly to do her tan, as she was a full-time beautician and a very good one too. If it was anyone else they would have been resentful of the extra work, as Jade used to have a fake tan every weekend they went out, but Kelly was so lovely natured and generous that she enjoyed making her friends happy.

Jade had never met anyone else like Kelly. To look at you'd assume she was arrogant, because of her stunning looks, but that was far from the truth; she had a heart of gold. She wasn't the sharpest tool in the box, but she knew this, didn't care and even made fun of herself. In fact, she often played up to it in front of men and they all seemed to love her. Whoever Kelly set her sights on she seemed to attract. She made it look so easy.

Kelly turned to her, looked her up and down and smiled. 'Hun, do you mind if I do you a tan and a make-over before we go out? I want to try this new instant tanning lotion I've just bought and I'm getting tested on make-up next week at college.'

Jade eyed her suspiciously. 'But you finished college years ago?'

Kelly faltered. 'Errr . . . yeah, but I'm doing this new evening course in make-up. Did I not mention it?'

Jade shook her head. Kelly was definitely lying, she just knew it. Kelly couldn't even look her in the eye, which was a sure sign that her friend had just made up a load of rubbish.

'Kelly, tell me the truth. What's wrong with my make-up?'

'Nothing.'

'Kelly . . .' Jade folded her arms across her chest.

Kelly hesitated, wondering whether to say it or not. 'Okay, but promise you won't take this the wrong way? I'm only saying this because I'm your best friend and I love you.'

'No, I won't take it the wrong way.'

'You're pale!' Kelly blurted, as soon as Jade had finished her sentence. She took a deep breath. 'And not just a little bit pale, we're talking Vicky Jenkins pale.'

Jade gasped in shock. Vicky Jenkins was a girl from their old school who everyone used to laugh at because she was so white and hated tans. The colour of the make-up she used to put on in the school playground was the colour of talcum powder! 'I think that may be the worst thing you've ever said to me.'

'It's only because I care,' Kelly smiled sweetly.

'Okay, what else?'

'You really want to know?'

'Yes. I can handle it,' Jade said bravely.

'Your hair,' Kelly shook her head looking at it. 'It's like the flattest hair in the whole of Essex. It's almost stuck to your head! You need volume, waves, backcombing. You have hardly *any* make-up on. I don't think I can even see any eyeshadow, your eyelashes are non-existent and don't even get me started on your chipped red nails. Which, by the way, is so last season's colour.' Kelly exhaled a deep breath as though a weight had been lifted off her shoulders.

Jade was shocked. She'd actually made an effort today, and here was Kelly telling her she looked all wrong.

Kelly was worried she'd upset her. 'Babe, you're stunning and you always look nice. But, come on, you're not in Bath any more. You're in Essex now, where you belong.'

Jade sighed. 'You're right. I'm so used to Tom criticising me about wearing make-up and dressing up that I don't remember what I used to be like before. Help me. Please?'

Kelly beamed and practically danced round the room. 'I've been dying to get my hands on you for the past two and a half years! Right, clothes off. You can't have a spray tan seeing as we're going out tonight and it takes hours to develop, but I have some really good instant tan we can

32

use. I'll run up to my room and get everything. We can use the mirror in the kitchen.'

Five minutes later, Jade was standing in just her underwear while Kelly worked her magic, applying layers of thick brown tanning cream to her legs.

'So how have you been feeling, babe?' Kelly questioned.

'Not the best, I won't lie. Still really pissed off about the whole thing with Tom. I feel slightly better today though.'

'I can't believe what you did to him. How funny. I was telling loads of girls from my old beauty salon about it and we were all in stitches! I would've loved to have seen his face when he realised it was you and not her!' Kelly smiled.

'I know,' Jade grinned. 'It *is* pretty funny. He asked for it though.'

The girls chatted about Tom, and Jade explained how he'd contacted her since they'd split up and how she'd told him to leave her alone.

'It must be hard, hun,' Kelly sympathised. 'He seemed quite nice when he came to Essex. I don't think he liked me though.'

'Of course he liked you!' Jade fibbed. 'He *was* nice – when he wasn't lying to me that is. Well, I thought he was anyway. I can see now that it's for the best we're not together. I loved him. But I never felt like I was good enough for him.'

Kelly gave Jade a dressing gown to sit in while her tan dried, wiped her make-up off and applied some tanning lotion to her face. Then she got out her nail varnish case which was full of hundreds of glossy varnishes, in every colour of the rainbow.

'I love that colour,' Jade pointed to a deep red.

'No babe, it's all about pink for summer. Trust me; this is the colour for you,' Kelly said pulling out a hot pink bottle of OPI varnish. 'I'm going to bling your nails up too

33

with some little crystals, because personally I think they look better with a bit of sparkle.'

An hour later and Jade couldn't believe her eyes when Kelly handed her the mirror.

'See,' Kelly said. 'Much better. You look like the old Jade!'

'Oh my God!' Jade said with her mouth wide open. She looked incredible. Her eyes were covered in a gorgeous smokey black MAC eyeshadow, lashings of eyeliner and huge false eyelashes. She had nude glossy lips and her cheekbones looked amazing because of the Bobbi Brown blusher and highlighter Kelly had applied. Even her eyebrows, which she never usually touched, looked perfect. Best of all though, she had a tan! Just looking at herself now made her realise how she'd missed it.

'What do you think of the hair?' Kelly grinned, pleased with her work

'Fantastic!' Jade said, swishing her backcombed locks happily. 'I feel like I finally look like I belong back in Essex.'

'Totes! I've got some clip-in hair extensions you can use too, babe. I'll put them in before we go. If we'd had time, I could have given you HD brows, but I'll have to do that another day.'

Jade was baffled. 'HD what?'

'HD brows, hun. Haven't you heard of them?' Kelly looked surprised as she re-applied some more Dior lip gloss to her lips in the mirror. 'All the celebs have them. They're totally in right now. You get the perfect arch on the eyebrow and pluck, tint and thread them until they look beauts.'

'Next time I'll have them then. Thank you, Kelly.'

'Any time. You look gorgeous. Just remember my motto and you'll always look unreal: "Keep your heels, hair and head held high."'

Jade laughed and Kelly walked over to boil the kettle and make another cup of tea. She picked up her mobile with a concerned expression. 'Oh no! There's something wrong with my mobile. It's been charging for ages and still has no battery. I'll have to go and get it fixed or something today.'

Jade's eyes followed the charger lead to the plug and noticed it wasn't even switched on. 'Errr, Kelly.'

She looked up, her eyes wide with anticipation. 'What?'

'It might help if you switched it on.' Jade gave a throaty laugh and Kelly joined in.

'So, do you know the other girl that Tom was with?' Kelly asked, as she sat at the table with her mug of tea.

Jade shook her head, still unable to take her eyes off her new appearance in the mirror.

'Facebook?'

'What about it?'

Kelly was shocked. 'Haven't you even looked her up?'

Jade shrugged her shoulders casually. 'No.'

'Check his friends list. That's if you want to.'

Jade smirked. Kelly was clearly dying to see what the other girl looked like and she didn't blame her. If she hadn't felt so heartbroken it was normally the first thing she would have done. She was always secretly nosing around people's profiles and even sometimes ended up looking through albums of people she didn't even know.

Kelly continued, 'Have you not even been on there since you broke up?'

'No,' Jade shook her head again, picking up Lord McButterpants and stroking him. 'I didn't want to go on there to be honest. I know it sounds ridiculous, but I'm dreading seeing what he's up to and changing my relationship status so everyone can see we're over. It's so embarrassing. I may just delete myself.'

'Don't be so silly. You shouldn't delete yourself. *You* never did anything wrong.'

'You're right,' Jade agreed. She felt stronger already

talking to Kelly. 'Do you still have your laptop? I'll change my status now. That's if he hasn't already done it.'

'He won't have,' Kelly assured her, jumping to her feet and hurrying out the room.

A minute later, Kelly returned with the laptop. Jade signed into her Facebook account, apprehensively. She was slightly relieved when it still stated she was 'in a relationship with Tom Noble' on her profile page. She wanted to be the one to change it, not him. She clicked and checked the single box. Done. She then checked his page and was relieved to see he didn't have any updates in over two weeks, indicating he hadn't been online. Clicking on his friends list, she searched the name 'Louisa'. Her heart was hammering in her chest as she knew she'd be on there. A plain-looking blonde girl appeared on the screen.

'I've found her,' Jade told Kelly as she shifted in her chair.

'Let's see,' Kelly replied, turning the laptop round to face her. She gasped. 'She looks fat!'

'Do you think?' Jade said hopefully, knowing full well she wasn't. She appreciated Kelly's attempt though; slagging the other girl off was what friends did, it was completely understandable. Louisa was definitely not drop-dead gorgeous, just your average everyday type, but by no means was she fat.

'She looks like she's been eating far too many pies in her profile picture. Damn, that's the only one we can see, she's set it to private. She has two chins for God's sake, what on earth was he thinking?'

'Do you not think she's at all pretty?'

'Jade, take a look in the mirror and now take a look at fatty on Facebook. You win, hands down. Tom is an idiot!'

They were interrupted by the sound of the doorbell; Lisa had arrived. Jade reached up to hug her friend.

'Hi,' they both chorused happily.

Jade had forgotten how amazing Lisa's figure was. Wearing her skin tight wet-look leggings, her long legs looked phenomenal. She looked like a supermodel. She was five foot nine and it always made Jade laugh when she walked next to Kelly, who was only five foot one. The two of them usually made her stand in the middle.

After discussing how vile Louisa was and updating Lisa on the situation, Jade was well and truly finished with the subject.

'So you two, how are your love lives going? They've got to be better than mine.' She turned to Lisa. 'Are things still all good with you and Jake?'

Jake was Lisa's long-term boyfriend. They'd been together since they were sixteen after meeting at an under-eighteens nightclub, and were practically inseparable. Jade and Kelly both really liked him; he was like one of their own friends.

'Yeah we're good, the usual.' Lisa beamed, unable to hide her happiness.

'You two will be married soon,' Kelly teased. 'Let me be bridesmaid, remember?'

'You'll both be my bridesmaids, but give me a break, I'm only twenty-one still.'

'You're lucky to have a decent man like Jake. My love life is crap. Can't find anyone I fancy,' Kelly moaned. 'All the blokes round this way are either ugly or love themselves. I'm so bored of it all. I wish I could go somewhere else. I don't want much. Just a nice man, preferably older and more mature, good looking and maybe rich too. '

Jade and Lisa laughed.

'I'm not being shallow but he'd have to be. I'm not going to be a millionaire beautician, am I?'

'Maybe you should put the prices of your spray tans up,' Lisa joked. 'You *are* good.'

Kelly giggled. 'Can you imagine if I said I'd had lots of good feedback, was the best in Essex and put them up to fifty quid? My clients would have a heart attack.'

'Well at least you have a job,' Jade complained sulkily. 'I still don't even know what I want to do with my life.'

'I can always see if they need people at my place?' Lisa offered.

As much as Jade appreciated her looking out for her, Lisa worked at a television company, something that didn't really interest her.

'Thanks, but I'll be okay. I'll find something soon hopefully.'

Kelly squeezed Jade's hand gently. 'Cheer up Jade. I know you've been feeling down lately but today is going to be a good one now you're with us, I promise. You can't buy happiness, but you can buy clothes – and that's close enough.'

They laughed and Jade decided she was going to make an effort to brighten up now she was back with her friends.

'Where are we going today anyway? Shopping I take it?' Lisa asked, running her fingers through her long dark hair.

'After I've sorted my face out and you've told me what outfit looks best – I've got three options – I was thinking shopping in Loughton, lunch, then The King William pub and Nu Bar for old times' sake?'

Jade and Lisa both agreed with Kelly. This was just like the old days.

*

The girls teetered down Loughton High Street in their heels and sighed as they were stopped by yet another group of girls wanting to stroke Lord McButterpants.

'How do you get anywhere with this dog?' Jade asked Kelly as the gushing girls finally walked off in the other direction. 'We've been stopped about ten times already!'

Kelly looked down at the dog proudly. His little head was curiously poking out her brown and beige Louis Vuitton

38

dog carrier. 'Ahhh, he can't help it that he's pure beauts, can you Lord McButterpants? He's a babe magnet, especially in his cute little leather jacket I've dressed him in today. Totes brings out the colour in his eyes.'

'He sure is cute,' Lisa agreed, slowing down as a white dress in the window of a boutique caught her eye. 'Let's go in here, girls.'

'Are you sure you don't want to go in there instead?' Jade joked pointing to the baby shop next door and nudging Lisa teasingly. 'You and Jake will be having kids before you know it. You may as well get started on a wardrobe for them.'

Kelly's face lit up. 'Oh, please let me be godmother! And you can't use the name Evangelina for a girl or Parker for a boy; they're my baby names.'

Lisa wrinkled her nose. 'Evangelina and Parker? It'll be hard not to pinch those two,' she laughed playfully. 'What are you two on about anyway? I don't want kids for a long time. I want a career and to travel before even thinking about becoming a mum. That's years away in my opinion.'

'What about Jake?' Jade asked, as they made their way into the boutique. 'He loves kids, doesn't he? It wouldn't surprise me if he'll be wanting them soon. Probably as soon as you move in together.'

Lisa hesitated. 'Well, he does talk about kids and that he doesn't want to be an old dad, but I'm just nowhere near ready. The thought freaks me out a bit so I just change the subject every time Jake mentions it.' She pulled out a navy dress from the rail. 'What do you think of this?'

'Stunning, hun. Your legs will look unreal in that, and the colour will compliment your dark features. You have to try it on, it would be rude not to,' Kelly said, eyes sparkling with excitement as she made her way over to the shoes.

After lunch in The King William, they dropped Lord McButterpants back to Kelly's mum's house, re-applied their make-up and made their way back to Loughton. Seeing as it was a Saturday night, Nu Bar was packed and the girls were feeling tipsy after two bottles of wine. Jade glanced around her, memories flooding back from previous nights spent there before she went to university. It was like a different world. Girls were preened to perfection, with either perfectly straight hair or immaculate curls, not a strand out of place. Jade caught glimpses of designer bags by Gucci and Dolce and Gabbana. Their killer heels were gigantic and their skirts minuscule. False, long eyelashes were fluttering everywhere and there wasn't a pale person in the whole bar. It was like a competition for the most tanned person; and that included the boys. Thank goodness Kelly had given her a make-over otherwise she definitely would have been the palest! Or the most normal, whichever way you wanted to look at it. The boys had made the same amount of effort as the girls. Their gelled hair was swept over, faces glowing, trousers tight and smart shirts tucked in. Oh yes, Jade was definitely back home.

'Shots!' Kelly shouted above the music, as the shot girl wearing tiny hot pants and a matching top made her way over to them.

'I'm crap with shots,' Jade worried. 'Honestly, I'm always sick. I never did them at uni, I just couldn't.'

'Oh come on,' Lisa said. 'Live a little!'

Okay, Jade thought, one shot won't hurt. She downed the sambucca in one and gagged, passing the glass back to the girl. I would rather drink my own urine than this, she thought. Never again. To her horror Kelly was passing her another.

'Why are we doing another? What's this? I've just downed one.'

'It's on me, babe. A welcome home shot.'

Not wanting to look boring or ungrateful, Jade downed it on the count of three along with Lisa and Kelly.

'Cheers babe,' Kelly said to the shot girl, handing their glasses back. She complimented her, 'Reem outfit.'

'Thanks. This is one of the more boring ones; we get to wear all different sets.'

'Oh my God, shut up! I'd love to dress up like that while I was working.'

'You should get a job with the company I work for, the money is great,' the girl suggested. 'Look online. The company is called Sexy Shots.' She walked off to some men calling her.

'Oh please one of you get a job as a shot girl with me,' Kelly pleaded, smiling. 'It looks so much fun and I could do with the extra money so badly. Come on Jade, you need a job?'

'Why not?' Jade replied, thinking it would be great to get a fun part-time job while she was searching for a career. 'So long as I don't have to drink them. It has to be better than serving miserable customers in Café Rouge.'

'Count me out,' Lisa answered. 'Jake would go mad if I was dressed like that and walking round bars chatting to men. I am a tad jealous though; my friend's mate does it and on good nights makes over two hundred pounds.'

'You're kidding! In one night? Me and you will definitely look tomorrow then,' Kelly said to Jade.

After a couple of hours, Lisa, who had been texting on her phone for the last thirty minutes, decided to call it a night.

'I'm off, girls. Jake is picking me up and I'm staying at his.'

'I'm so jealous, you cow. You're getting your lovely boyfriend to come get you and leaving us surrounded by these creeps,' Kelly sulked, looking around at the unappealing men left in the bar.

Jade agreed, silently. She'd had an excellent night with the girls, but seeing the men she had to choose from now she was single was depressing. No one here was as good looking as Tom, not even close. She kept looking at her mobile, wishing he'd text again, but knowing it was best if he didn't. She just needed to be reassured he felt as miserable as she did, wherever he was at that precise moment. She was drunk, but not drunk enough to make the mistake of contacting him though, so she pushed the thought from her mind.

'Go on. Go have sex with your gorgeous boyfriend and leave us moping about our pathetic love lives in here.'

Lisa smiled, cheekily. 'I may just do that. He's just texted saying he's outside, so I'm off. Bye girls.' She kissed them both on the cheek. 'See you soon.'

Jade watched as Lisa walked off and saw some of the men eyeing her up on the way out. She was naturally very pretty. She was half Spanish and had beautiful long dark hair, which was glossy and shiny because it had never been touched with hair dye; it was the envy of every woman. She never went over the top with make-up, because with her dark, olive complexion and coffee-coloured eyes, she didn't have to. Personally, Jade thought she looked prettier without any make-up on anyway.

They decided it was time to go home, so waited for a taxi outside. Kelly seemed a bit bored.

'Honestly, I just feel fed up with it here. As much as I love doing beauty, I'm always skint. I had to save for like, two months to get my new Marc Jacobs bag and I'm sorry, but that's just not on. I know everyone wherever I go and can never find a man I'm interested in. I feel like I just need to get away somewhere,' Kelly explained in the queue.

'We could always go away somewhere new for the weekend. What about Brighton? Or Newcastle, somewhere up north?'

'Nah, never understand their accents, babe.'

'What about Brighton then? People in Brighton don't have accents,' Jade said.

Kelly thought for a moment. 'You sure?' she asked, doubtfully.

Jade shook her head and laughed. Most people would think Kelly was joking, but Jade knew her well enough to know she was being serious. Kelly paused and thought for a second, then a smile slowly crept up on her face.

'Oh my God, babe, I've got the best idea ever,' she said, excitedly.

'What? Where are we going?'

'Marbella! I went last year on holiday and loved it. But I only went for a long weekend and it wasn't long enough.'

Jade looked at the floor sadly. 'I remember. I couldn't go because I went to France with Tom.'

'You'll love it, it's brilliant. But I was thinking, instead of just going for a week, why don't we work there? I saw so many girls last year working in clubs and that and they looked like they were having the time of their lives. It'll be so much fun – imagine our tans! We could stay for a few months. It shouldn't be too hard to get a job in a bar or something and we can save up some money for flights by doing shot work. What do you think?'

Jade thought about what Kelly was asking her. It was perfect timing to do something like this. She didn't have a full-time job yet and when she did, she would never be able to work away for the summer. Was this her last chance to do something spontaneous and fun? She wasn't happy thinking about Tom all the time, so surely working in Marbella would take her mind off things? It would be great. She could see herself now, sunbathing all day and getting a gorgeous tan, chilling out over sangria and then off to her fun bar job in the evenings. It sounded perfect. Jade started to get excited.

'I think it's a great idea! Let's do it!'

*

Lisa snuggled up to Jake in his huge warm bed and thought about how lucky she was to have him. It was so nice to go out with her friends, without the worry of looking for a boyfriend; knowing that she already had the perfect one. Jake was different to most men they knew. For one, he was mature and wanted to settle down, even though he was only twenty-two. She thought about poor Jade and how Tom had cheated on her. She couldn't imagine how painful that must have been. If Jake ever did that to her she would fall apart. She trusted him one hundred per cent, and genuinely didn't feel like there was a chance of that ever happening.

It was so nice to have Jade back home, to have the three of them back together again. If she was honest, it took the pressure off her always having to go out with Kelly. Lisa loved going out, but not every single weekend, and she felt guilty when she had to let Kelly down. Sometimes she just wanted to spend her free time with Jake. Jake worked around the clock as a carpenter and she worked long hours for a TV company so any free time they had was precious. Plus, as she wasn't looking for a man, she usually preferred just going to the cinema or for a meal, but Kelly always insisted they went to a bar or club.

'You okay babe? Can you not sleep?' Jake asked, when she cuddled up close to him.

'I'm fine,' she said, finding his lips in the dark and kissing him.

'Good,' he said, drawing her closer. 'I forgot to mention something to you actually, so I'm glad you're awake. You know the other day when you were talking about getting a new car? Well I was thinking, instead of us both getting cars, why don't we just buy one between us? I'm sure we'll be moving in together soon and let's face it, seeing as you'll only be needing the car at weekends, it works out perfectly. It's silly us both getting cars, especially when I already have my work van too. That would mean we'd have three vehicles between us.'

Lisa thought for a moment, considering what he was saying. He was right; three vehicles between two people didn't make any sense. Jake had a work van already, but wanted to buy a nice car to drive round in when he wasn't working. Her heart was set on getting a Range Rover though, and she knew he hated them as he was often saying how common they were in Essex and how bad they were for the environment. She'd also been looking forward to having her own freedom and being able to go and see her friends as and when she liked. If they shared a car, she'd always have to ask permission and vice versa. She yawned. 'I'm not so sure, Jake. You know how much I've been looking forward to getting a Range Rover.'

'Yes, but it makes so much more sense for us to *share* a car. I'm sure there's one we can both agree on. What about a Golf? We won't need a big car and it'll save us money. When we move in together, we're going to need to watch what we spend. We'll have bills to pay, council tax, food shopping; the list is endless.'

Lisa wrinkled her nose at the thought. She didn't want a Golf. She wanted a Range Rover, and had done for ages. The thought of saving money and being careful with every penny she spent sounded so grown up and tedious. Bored of the conversation, and deciding not to discuss it further she rolled over onto her front, away from Jake. 'Let's just talk about it another day, yeah? I need to sleep.'

'Okay, well think about it. Night. I love you,' he said.

'I love you too, Jake,' she said sleepily. 'More than you know.'

CHAPTER 3

'Would you like any drinks?' the pretty air hostess asked them.

'A Diet Coke please,' Kelly asked.

'Will you be paying in Sterling or euros?'

'Can I not just pay in pounds?' Kelly asked, scratching her head thoughtfully.

The air hostess looked confused.

'Sterling *is* pounds,' Jade told her, stifling a giggle.

'What? Really? I've never even heard of it,' Kelly replied, completely miffed as she searched through her purse.

An hour later the pilot announced they would be landing and Jade was relieved. She hated flying with a passion. The fact that they had bought the cheapest flight was partly to do with it, as they'd had to be up, washed, dressed and out the door by four thirty a.m. Jade tried to stretch in the confined space in her seat. Honestly, these seats were made for children, not adults with legs longer than a metre. She looked beside her at Kelly who had just dropped off into a sound sleep. She was so lucky. Jade could never sleep on planes at all, even if she'd only slept for four hours the night before; it was impossible. The three men laughing and talking loudly a few rows up weren't helping either. How the hell did they have so much energy? She rolled her eyes when she heard one of them ask for a beer from the air hostess. Seriously, at this time in the morning? Probably their first stupid lads' holiday.

However, Jade's mood improved when she felt the warm sunshine through the tiny windows on the plane. Three months of glorious sunshine beckoned and it couldn't come quickly enough. For the first time in a long while she actually felt excited about meeting new men too. She wasn't in a rush for a serious relationship, but a bit of fun wouldn't kill her. In fact, she craved it.

Jade thought back to the last month. Becoming shot girls had actually worked out perfectly. It had given them a taste of what to expect in Marbella and Kelly's friend had given them the details of the manager of TIBU nightclub, Joe. They'd contacted him and he had agreed to hire them both; they'd squeeze in a one-week holiday to relax before they started. Jade just hoped the money was as good as shot work as some nights they had made up to one hundred and fifty pounds, and it had been fun working together with Kelly and chatting to men, convincing them to spend their cash getting drunk. It hadn't exactly been hard. Then they'd met Stephen, a nightclub promoter who had asked them to be nightclub hosts, which basically meant hosting a table with a load of men, getting them to buy bottles of drink and getting paid for it. Of course, they'd agreed. They'd really enjoyed it at first as it just felt like partying for free, but after a while constantly dealing with sleazy drunk men started to get annoying. Despite that, Jade had enjoyed herself; being single wasn't as bad as she had first thought. She had met some men that were quite nice and had cheekily snogged a couple like a teenager at the end of the night. Even though she couldn't honestly say she was over Tom one hundred per cent, she was getting there. He had texted her once asking how she was, but she'd ignored him. It had made her feel stronger, knowing that she had the power to not reply like he had probably expected her to. She was ignoring *him* – not the other way round.

The captain announced they were landing and Kelly stirred.

'Morning sleepy head!'

Kelly groaned as she tried to stretch. 'What time is it? Are we there yet?'

'Only about thirty minutes away.'

Forty minutes later they were leaving the plane. Kelly pointed to a girl in front with dark brown hair scraped up on top of her head.

'I know that girl,' she whispered.

The girl turned as if she had heard her and caught Kelly's eye. She smiled and waited for them to catch up as they disembarked.

'You alright Kel, babe?' She hugged her. 'How are you?'

'Really well, hun. Haven't seen you for a long while. Oh my God, you look tanned already!'

She was right, Jade thought to herself. Kelly's friend had a lovely dark tan and was wearing tiny denim hot pants to show off her slender legs.

'Yeah, I only went home for five days. I've been working out here in TIBU club for the last month. I'm back now to do the rest of the summer.'

'Oh shut up!' Kelly gasped ecstatically. 'We've got jobs there, and we're out here for three months now.'

Her mouth opened wide. 'You're joking babe! Cool. You'll love it here, it's so much fun and you can earn alright money as well.'

Kelly nodded and then introduced Jade to her. 'Jade this is Adele. Adele, Jade.'

Adele said hello and then started to walk off. 'Go to Plaza Beach today and I'll meet you there. It's where everyone goes.'

Kelly waved her off. 'I remember that from last year. Cool hun, we'll see you there.'

Adele disappeared and Jade asked Kelly about her.

'She seems nice, how do you know her?'

'I did a beauty course with her. I've always thought she was okay, but loads of girls hated her and said she was a bit of a bitch. Don't see why though.'

'Well at least you know someone we're working with already. I'm a bit nervous about it,' Jade replied, as they made their way to the toilets to freshen up.

'Hun, trust me, we'll be fine. We're only going to be waitresses; all you have to do is host tables like in Essex and serve their drinks. But let's not even worry about working until next week. Firstly we have a week's holiday to do nothing but sunbathe!'

'You're right,' Jade agreed. 'Let's just enjoy it.'

*

Adele walked over to the baggage claims searching for her case, which had a huge pink bow on so she'd find it easily. Much to her disappointment it wasn't there already, so she waited, getting her phone out and texting Lee, her new boyfriend, to say she'd landed safely.

She was glad Kelly was working in Marbella too. She didn't know her that well, but she'd always seemed quite nice at beauty college. She'd been out with her once before on a night out, she recalled, and couldn't help but feel slightly jealous when she uploaded her photos on Facebook and received messages from loads of blokes asking who Kelly was. She wasn't *that* pretty, Adele told herself. She looked just as good as Kelly when she was done up with her false lashes and hair extensions, surely? Plus, Kelly was really photogenic, so she looked better in pictures. Adele did like her though; it was hard not to,

49

seeing as she was so friendly. Kelly's friend, Jade, seemed nice too. She was also attractive, Adele thought, a little bit resentfully. She could tell they were best friends and thought how nice it must be to go away and work with someone you were really close to. Adele had never really had a best friend. If she was really honest, she preferred the company of men and always thought it must be because she had three brothers. Sure, she had girl mates, but no one she liked the best particularly.

Adele took a mirror out of her bag to check her appearance. Her hair was a bit of a mess and her new hair extensions were actually really hurting her head. She'd had weaves put in this time instead of glued ones because it was cheaper and quicker, and they'd done nothing but give her a headache so far. Her eyelash extensions looked good though. They were as thick as spider legs, just how she liked them. She needed to get back to her apartment, let her hair down, put a bit of make-up on and she'd be ready to go to Plaza Beach to sunbathe.

*

Kelly and Jade arrived at PYR Hotel in Puerto Banus, which they had booked after being told that this was one of the most fun places to stay. They were just about to leave reception to go to their room when a loud group of boys, who were obviously over-excited about their holiday, stopped them.

'Alright girls?' one of them said in a Welsh accent.

'Yes thanks,' Jade replied, too tired to make conversation.

'Where you from?'

'Essex,' Kelly replied.

'Oooh Essex girls,' he said happily to his mates, as though he'd won the jackpot.

'Seriously, do blokes still get all excited when you say

50

you're from Essex?' Jade whispered to Kelly, irritated that Essex girls had a name for being 'easy'. What a load of rubbish. Did they also think they wore white stilettos and danced around their handbags too?

'Where are you from then?' Kelly asked.

'Cardiff,' he replied. 'You should come visit me when you get back home,' he said, trying to impress his mates.

'No thanks, Scotland is miles away,' Kelly replied, dismissively.

'Scotland?' the boy asked, confused.

Jade tried not to laugh. 'Come on Kelly, let's go,' she said taking their keys from the receptionist and walking away.

Kelly followed, confused – Jade could hear the blokes laughing that Kelly had thought Cardiff was in Scotland.

'Cardiff *is* in Scotland isn't it?'

'No, you dope. It's in Wales!' Jade answered laughing as they reached the lift.

They were happily surprised with their room. It was basic, but very large; they had plenty of space and even a small kitchen. They unpacked their suitcases as quickly as they could. Despite being so tired, Jade was excited to see everything and get in the sun.

'Right babe, what bikini are you wearing today?'

Jade didn't really have many bikinis with her. She absolutely hated shopping for them, as there was nothing worse than stripping off in the changing room mirrors and seeing a body you didn't exactly love staring back at you. She was happier not looking. She'd dropped a dress size when she first split up with Tom, feeling far too sad to eat; whenever she was stressed in life she lost her appetite. Luckily it hadn't taken too long to get it back though; spending time with the girls had soon cheered her up and now she was back to her healthy size ten figure. She wasn't by any means big in any way, but in her opinion her boobs were too small, hips a little too big and she hated her bum, which she wished was more toned, although everyone told her otherwise. She pulled out a plain black and white striped one she'd bought from Primark last year from her drawer.

'I'll probably just be wearing this,' she said, showing Kelly.

Kelly nodded, her face impassive.

Jade looked down at her bikini and then back up at Kelly. 'Why, what bikini are you wearing?'

'I'll wear my least dressy one if you're wearing plain black and white, so I won't look out of place.'

Jade frowned. '"Least dressy"? What do you mean? Show me what you've brought.'

Jade's heart sank as Kelly pulled out an array of colourful bikinis. The bed was soon a mass of sequins, beads, diamantes and tassels. Jade had never seen anything quite like it. She lifted up a white, all-in-one, cut-out swimsuit with beautiful coloured gems encrusted round the centre, off the bed. 'Kelly, are you kidding me? What's this?'

'That's a monokini, babe. You can borrow it if you like.'

Jade couldn't hide her shock. 'Where did you get all these from? They're amazing!'

'Mostly online from America. I did say Marbella was dressy and to bring your best stuff.'

'Best stuff? I've never seen anything like this,' she said, pulling a hot pink tasselled one from the bed admiringly. 'I thought you meant at night, not for the beach. All mine are bloody Primark and H & M. They're all plain and boring,' Jade said sulkily.

'You can borrow mine. Honestly, any one you want, just take.'

'Thanks,' Jade said, knowing that she wouldn't and couldn't fit into Kelly's double D cups even if she wanted to. 'I'll just wear this plain one for now.'

Kelly could sense Jade was a bit gutted. 'I think there are a couple of shops that do really nice dressy swimwear here. We can look there before we go to Plaza Beach if you like?' she offered.

Jade perked up a bit. 'Really? Okay, sounds good. Let's definitely do that then, as otherwise I'll be plain Jane for the summer if this is the sort of thing people wear.'

'I remember seeing Sonia Lopez here last year; remember her from our old school? She bought one that was gorgeous and showed me where the shop was.'

Jade thought back. Sonia Lopez was the girl with the mega rich parents at her old school. Didn't she once have a pair of Gucci shoes that cost her £500 just to wear to school?

'Are the prices reasonable?' Jade enquired, completely clueless.

Kelly hesitated, and turned back to her suitcase to unpack. 'Errr . . . I don't think it's too bad. It's really good quality and you have to remember, you get what you pay for.'

Jade watched Kelly parade around in a gorgeous two-piece white bikini with diamond straps and silver chains to fasten the bottoms; it was amazing.

'Kelly, what are those diamond crystal things stuck on your skin?' she asked bewildered, as she noticed a pattern only half covered by her bikini bottoms.

'It's a vajazzle, babe. Don't say you've never heard of them?' She pulled her bottoms down lower to reveal the pattern of a star.

Jade shook her head, agog.

'Where have you been for the last few years?' Kelly laughed, as if having a vajazzle was the most normal thing in the world.

'In Bath. And I definitely did not see or hear of anyone having a vajazzle there!'

'You *have* to let me do you one right now. You can't go out without a vajazzle to the pool!' Kelly gasped, horrified at the thought. 'I've brought loads of patterns with me in case mine comes off. Look . . .' She reached into her suitcase and pulled out several different designs. 'You can have a fairy, star, flower, cherry, butterfly . . .'

'I'm not so sure I want one,' Jade said, a bit confused as to why people would want one.

'You *don't* want a vajazzle?' Kelly looked at her like she was crazy.

'Errr . . . well maybe I will then,' she agreed. They were quite pretty after all, and if everyone else was going to have one then why should she be the odd one out? She opted for a flower and Kelly put the crystals on her perfectly. She'd have felt embarrassed if it was anyone else lowering her bottoms to stick tiny crystals on her skin, but seeing as she'd known Kelly for years and she had a way of making people feel comfortable, Jade felt totally relaxed.

'You can't go in the water today now though in case they wash off and the last thing you need is a patchy vajazzle,' Kelly said. 'Though I'll doubt you'll want to anyway, as it messes your hair up.'

Jade pulled her bikini bottoms down to observe Kelly's work. It actually looked good. 'I love it!'

Kelly's face was beatific. 'I knew you would. You won't be able to live without a vajazzle in your life now, trust me. They're reem.'

An hour later, they were standing outside the swimwear shop that Kelly had told Jade about.

Jade gasped. 'Wow! These bikinis look amazing!' She felt her spirits lift as she piled up about ten to try on. 'I love them all!'

'See, I told you there was a nice shop,' Kelly said, looking pleased with herself.

Jade's grin dropped when she saw the price of one – the pile of the bikinis she was holding was so high it came up right under her chin. 'Kelly, it's two hundred and fifty euros for this one!'

'Really?' Kelly tried to remain positive. 'Maybe that's just a special expensive one or something? You know, like a limited edition or something? Remember, they'll last for years too, because they must use the most expensive material.'

Jade glanced at the prices of the others – there wasn't even one under one hundred and fifty euro. 'Kelly, I'm not spending that amount. I just can't. It's ridiculous.' Feeling hot, despite the air conditioning, and now embarrassed in front of the snooty store assistant at having to put all the bikinis back, Jade left the store, disappointed. 'Let's just go and have a nice chilled day sunbathing. It's exactly what I need.'

As they made their way to Plaza Beach, Jade was surprised at hearing loud music blaring out. 'Is there a nightclub open in the day or something?' she said looking round to see where the noise was coming from.

Kelly stifled a giggle. 'That's Plaza Beach, babe, that's where we're going.'

Jade was confused. She'd never been to a beach where they played music. Maybe one where there were some annoying teens with an iPod and speakers blaring out, but that's about it. As they turned the corner, she was in shock. Men with six packs and bronzed bodies were everywhere. Girls wore make-up and looked gorgeous, slim and toned. Some were even walking around in five-inch heels and wedges. There were huge upholstered cream sunbeds with groups of about eight people on each one, lounging in the sun with huge cushions as pillows. It was unbelievable. It was like a beach version of Essex!

'I never knew it was going to be like this!' Jade said to Kelly.

'I did try to explain it, babe,' she replied, peering over the top of her Miu Miu sunglasses.

Jade felt completely out of place. Her plain swimwear now felt even more plain and dull. This place was like battle of the bikinis! She also felt as white as Casper the friendly ghost. She eyed up Kelly, who looked tanned.

'Kelly, how come you're not as white as me? Did you put fake tan on?'

'No, don't be silly, not for holiday. I had a few sunbeds before I came out here, I got a cheap course. I had to, I was *sooo* white.'

Probably the same colour as me, Jade thought, annoyed that she hadn't considered the same thing.

'Don't worry hun, you'll catch the sun in no time,' Kelly smiled.

They found two free sunbeds, which was surprising as the place was packed, and Jade relaxed as she lay down and felt the warmth of the sun on her skin. Thank God she had her vajazzle; at the moment that was the only thing making her feel like she belonged there. She was going straight back to buy one of those bikinis without a doubt, and she was waking up every day for a week at nine thirty to sunbathe, even if it meant she had to set her alarm. If only she had known Marbella was going to be like this. She would have made much more of an effort. She'd only ever been away once with her friends to Greece, and stupidly assumed it would be the same.

Jade sat up and rested on her elbows to take a look around. She had already spotted a couple of good-looking men, although some of them were wearing sunglasses and she knew it might be a different story when they took them off. It was amazing how important the eyes were when it came to fancying someone. All in all, this place looked like it was going to be fun. Pretentious maybe, but fun.

'Three o'clock, hun,' Kelly nodded to her right at two men standing by some sunbeds, chatting.

'Three o'clock?' Jade answered, dumbfounded. 'Surely it's not *that* late already?'

'No, silly,' Kelly giggled. 'Turn to three o'clock. Hot men.'

Jade glanced at them. Nice bodies, yes, but not really her type. It was weird really, as she didn't have one particular type, unlike some people, who only liked dark hair and blue eyes. Jade just knew her type when she saw him. She sat up and looked out to the sea which looked an amazing deep blue, and clear turquoise in places. A fair-haired man in red shorts was walking out of the ocean and Jade had to prevent herself from gasping. Wow, now *he* was her type! His hair had obviously been highlighted by the sun, and he had a mahogany tan and the most beautiful face she'd ever seen on a man. Simply gorgeous.

'I think I'm in love,' she whispered to Kelly.

'What?'

Now understanding the clock time signal, Jade muttered, 'Twelve o'clock.'

Kelly sat up, gazing at him secretly through the black lenses of her sunglasses. She nodded approvingly and smiled. 'Very nice.'

Jade watched as he walked past. His body was to die for. He definitely worked out to get abs like that! His eyes were a striking green colour. He was perfect. She was annoyed that she didn't look better herself. He didn't even look in her direction and she couldn't blame him. There were so many pretty girls around!

Her thoughts were interrupted by Adele shouting out Kelly's name. They sat up and both crossed their legs so Adele could sit at the end of their beds.

'Alright, girls?'

'Good babe, you?' Kelly asked, re-applying some sun lotion.

Jade was amazed at how different Adele looked compared to a few hours ago. She had a lovely purple embellished bikini on, which looked very expensive, her hair was wavy and loose and she was wearing mascara. She wasn't beautiful, and she was a bit too masculine to be pretty, but quite attractive. Jade smiled, feeling a bit shy and out of place.

'Yeah good. Boiling,' Adele said with a giggle, wiping her forehead. 'Have either of you got a mirror?'

Kelly handed her a compact which had a small mirror inside. Jade had to hold back from laughing as she watched Adele coat her lips in gloss and pout at her reflection. She looked completely in love with herself. Kelly caught Jade's eye, bit her lip and turned away, also finding it funny to watch.

'Where you off to tonight?'

'Where's good to go?' Jade asked.

'Think everyone is starting at Sinatra's bar tonight, so go there first. Luckily I have a night off before I start work again.'

They chatted for a while and Jade decided that Adele seemed really nice, which was good as they were going to be working alongside her. She offered them both a cigarette and they declined, as she lit her own.

'You both single?' Adele asked.

They nodded.

'There are loads of nice blokes this season. I've just started seeing this guy called Lee, from Glam nightclub,' Adele said. 'I really like him, met him when I first got here last month.'

'Ah that's good,' Kelly said. 'I well wanna meet some nice new guy while I'm here. I've been single for *ages*.'

Adele took a drag from her cigarette, exhaled and said, 'You seen anyone you fancy yet?'

'Nearly everyone here!' Kelly giggled. Then she looked over at Jade. 'She's already in love, this one.'

Jade felt embarrassed. *Thanks a lot, Kelly*, she thought.

'Come on, spill the beans. Who do you like? You've only just got here,' Adele laughed, flicking the ash from the end of her cigarette. 'You two are worse than me.'

'I don't like him, I don't even know him. I only just saw him for one second!' Jade protested.

'Don't be shy, babe, show her who you fancy,' Kelly giggled looking round to see if she could spot him again.

Jade hesitated, feeling as though she was in a school playground discussing her first crush. 'I just think the bloke over there,' she looked back quickly to check where he was, 'the one at the bar with the red shorts on and blondy hair, is quite nice.'

Adele's jaw dropped. 'Oh my God. What, Sam?' she asked, looking over at the two men.

'Why, do you know him?' Kelly questioned.

She nodded and exhaled another puff of smoke. 'He's my ex.'

Jade felt her heart sink. How embarrassing. She felt extremely uncomfortable and unsure what to say. Adele, obviously knowing that she felt awkward, added, 'We went out for a year, ages ago, babe. He's a nice boy, but we just used to argue about anything and everything.'

Jade smiled and began to backtrack instantly. 'I just thought he looked nice, that's all. I only saw him for a second.'

'We're still mates,' Adele continued, wiping her forehead with the back of her hand. 'I'll put in a good word for you, if you like?'

'No, don't be silly, that's fine.' Jade flushed beetroot, feeling completely weird about the whole situation.

'Oh babe, that's so nice of you, definitely put in a good word for her,' Kelly said. 'And while you're at it, set me up with him,' Kelly said, pointing at a man with the biggest muscles Jade had ever seen. They all giggled.

'Flipping hell,' Adele said as she stubbed out her cigarette with her white Havaianas flip-flop, covered in purple Swarovski crystals to match her bikini. 'He'd eat you for breakfast!'

He looked over and Adele waved at him as if she knew him. He waved back, baffled, and the girls sat there laughing. *She is so confident*, Jade thought, enviously.

Adele looked at Jade's bikini and she wasn't sure if she was imagining it, but it looked like she was smirking. She then turned to Kelly.

'Lovely bikini, babe. Where's it from?'

'Thanks hun,' Kelly replied adjusting the straps. 'It's from this online boutique in the States. They had amazing ones on there.'

Adele grinned and raised her eyebrows. 'Did you know that there's another girl wearing the exact same one over there?'

Kelly's jaw dropped. 'Shut up! Please tell me you're joking?'

Jade turned to look and then tried to make her feel better. 'She's sitting really far away, don't worry. Plus, you look so much better in it.'

'Anyway girls, I'm going to head back to my sunbed and soak up the sunshine,' Adele interjected, looking pleased with her work and standing up.

'Like you need it, Del, you've got the best tan ever,' Kelly complimented her.

'You can never be too tanned,' Adele pointed out. She paused before she left and turned to Jade. 'Seriously babe, I'll put in a good word for you. It's been ages since I was with Sam and I'd love to see him happy with a nice girl. I'm happy with Lee, so trust me; you've nothing to worry about.'

'Honestly, it's fine,' Jade protested shaking her head.

'Okay hun. Well if you want me to, let me know. See you tonight girls,' she said walking away.

'Bye,' they chorused.

'Right quick, we need to go somewhere else,' Kelly said hastily, as soon as Adele was out of earshot.

'What? Why?'

Kelly's voice shrilled as she jumped up, stuffing the sun lotions in her bag. 'Babe, did you not just hear that there is another girl wearing this bikini? We can't stay here now! People will see!'

'Don't be so silly. Just forget about it,' Jade replied as she stretched lazily, too relaxed to want to move again.

Kelly looked down at her, her head blocking the sun much to Jade's irritation. 'Come on, we have to go. I searched far and wide for the most amazing, unique bikinis and now someone has the same one. I can't believe it! It's *sooo* embarrassing!'

Knowing her friend wasn't going to give up, Jade exhaled loudly, stood up and put her shorts on reluctantly. 'Come on then, let's go.'

*

Adele walked back to her sunbed and glanced at Sam, who was sitting by the bar. She could see why Jade fancied him; he was exceptionally good looking and she couldn't believe her luck when she'd managed to get with him a few years back. When Adele wanted something, she always got it, and Sam had been no exception. If she was honest, when they had first met she knew he wasn't overly keen on her. She was the one that always had to text and call him first, otherwise she doubted their relationship would have ever happened. Secretly she guessed it was because at the time, every one of his friends had girlfriends and the lads' nights out had stopped, so Sam just thought he'd do what everyone else was doing, which was get a girlfriend and have quiet nights in. Adele didn't care though; she'd had exactly what she wanted. Their relationship had lasted a year in the end, longer than she'd even expected. Eventually, they'd both decided to end things. They were too young for anything serious, and Adele had guessed that Sam had wanted to be single. Adele had never felt completely secure in their relationship and had often snogged other men behind his back. He'd never found out, he would have hated her for it. Not that she ever would have been stupid enough to get caught, she mused, she was an excellent liar and always managed to twist things round with ease. The closest he'd ever come to finding out was when someone had uploaded a photo onto her Facebook page of her with her arms around a guy she'd met at a club. She made the person delete it immediately and luckily Sam had never seen it.

She saw Jade walk past with Kelly. She was prettier than she even realised. One of those annoying girls who didn't have to try too hard to look fantastic. So she liked Sam did she? Adele had a niggling feeling, and she couldn't quite put her finger on what it was. She didn't like the idea of Sam and Jade together. Jade was really nice and she'd bet that Sam would like her too. Well, not if she had anything to do with it. She didn't want to be with Sam herself, as she really liked Lee, but she definitely didn't want Jade with him either. She had no choice but to put a stop to it.

*

After they left Plaza Beach, Jade stopped and bought a bikini from the store they'd been in earlier that day. She'd realised that she kind of needed it, and if she missed the chance then someone else might buy it and she'd be left with her rubbish cheap bikinis. Plus, they'd saved money on their cheap flight, so it was fine. She'd wear it all the time, on every holiday she had until she was thirty-five. Plus, two hundred euro spent on a bikini wasn't that bad, was it? She decided on a pretty lemon embellished òne. Definitely Marbella swimwear Jade thought happily, as they walked back to the hotel. How annoying that she could only afford one though, after all, she couldn't wear it every day because people would notice. It was amazing how expensive they were, especially when it didn't even look that hard to make. The thought struck her like lightning.

'*Oh my God*. I have, like, the best idea ever.'

'What?' Kelly peered at Jade excitedly.

Jade was so enthusiastic that she couldn't get the words out quick enough. 'We could make our own swimwear! Customise them so they're different to everyone else's. Design our own patterns! Create our own styles! There must be a market or shop around here somewhere where they sell cheap crystals and sequins or something? Then we can sew them on. It'll be fun!'

'That's such a good idea, babe! We'll have the most reem swimwear in the whole of Marbs!' Kelly agreed animatedly.

'Exactly! We just need to know when the market is on and head down there.'

'Let's ask at the hotel,' Kelly said, walking faster.

'What are you wearing tonight?' she asked Kelly.

'Dunno, babe. Maybe my white strapless dress with nude Gina heels.' She thought for a second. 'Actually, no, I'll save white for when I'm more tanned. I might wear my black lace Alexander Wang dress, you know, the one which makes my boobs look massive.'

'Kelly,' Jade giggled, glancing at her naturally huge chest. 'Every dress makes your boobs look massive!'

CHAPTER 4

After two and a half hours, the girls were finally ready for their night out and decided to sit on the balcony and drink the vodka and orange they had bought earlier. It was a beautiful evening and Jade felt a wave of happiness wash over her. What was it about sunshine and warmth that made you feel so much better? Though she did have to admit she'd overdone it with the sunbathing on her first day; she always did. She'd never learn that putting on factor twenty just once for the whole day was not enough and now she felt a bit sore in the places she'd missed, like the very top of her stomach, just under her bikini.

'This holiday is gonna be amazing, babe, I can feel it,' Kelly said, joining Jade who was sitting at the table on the balcony reading a magazine. 'Six more days of chilling out before we start work.'

Jade smiled at Kelly, who looked beautiful in her black dress and lightly tanned face. 'It's a shame Lisa couldn't come too.'

'She'd miss her lover boy Jake too much,' Kelly giggled. 'I'd say Marbs is more of a single girl's place.'

'Yeah, you're right,' Jade replied. Her gaze was fixed on the beautiful sunset. 'I can't believe the sun is still out, even at this time.'

'I know, babe. The Spanish sun is so much hotter than the English one. Wish we could swap,' Kelly said as she held her hands up and admired her nails.

'What do you mean?'

'I wish we could have their sun instead so it was always hot,' Kelly said with a nod, as though she knew what she was talking about.

Jade was bemused. 'But we do have the same sun. There is only *one* sun.'

'Shut up! I thought there was a sun in every country. So you're telling me there is only one in the world?'

Jade laughed, 'Kelly, I do hope you're winding me up.'

Kelly laughed, throwing her head back, her hair blowing in the breeze. 'Actually come to think of it, that does ring a bell. I remember something about that in Mr Gregson's science class. But, what about in other countries, like, I don't know, Africa or somewhere, where it's like the middle of the night or something and there's no sun at all?'

Jade's mouth curved into a smile. 'For starters, it's not the middle of the night in Africa, which isn't even that far from here. Secondly, it's all to do with the world turning round. Countries closer to the equator are usually the hottest too.'

Kelly looked mesmerised. 'God, you're so intellectual,' she said seriously. 'I don't even know what an equator, or whatever you just said, is. You were always so good at science.'

'I'm seriously not that clever at science.' Jade couldn't help but let out a short laugh. 'I only got a C at school.'

Jade sipped her drink and winced at how strong Kelly had made it.

Kelly burst into laughter.

'Are you trying to kill me or something?' Jade said with a grimace, swallowing the liquid reluctantly.

Kelly held the palms of her hands up. 'I didn't put that much in, honestly!'

After a good few drinks, Jade already felt tipsy. They made their way to Sinatra's bar, which was absolutely packed with people. Wow, Jade thought happily, this place was a lot classier than the dingy bars in Greece. She'd even spotted a few soap stars on their way there, how exciting. Maybe one of the hot male actors would fall in love with her and she'd be on the cover of *Heat*!

Kelly stood on her tiptoes and peered through the bar, spotting Adele and waving. She was sitting with another girl and two boys. She gestured for them to come over and they both kissed her hello.

'Evening girls,' Adele pouted. She turned to her other friends standing next to her and introduced them. 'This is Gary, Lee and Sophie. This is Kelly and Jade.'

They all said hello to each other and Jade couldn't help but notice Adele had once again managed to get another good-looking bloke. Lee was tall, with dark hair and stubble, and striking hazel-coloured eyes. How did she manage to get these men?

'That's my Lee I was telling you about,' Adele whispered, checking that he couldn't see.

'Babe, he's well fit,' Kelly said eyeing him up sneakily without him noticing. 'Absolute sort.'

'So funny as well,' Adele smiled, glancing in his direction.

They bought drinks and sat down beside them.

'I feel smashed already,' Adele said with a giggle and a hiccup. 'The drinks here are so strong; the measures are a joke, just to warn you. The shots are definitely larger than at home.'

'They can't be any worse than Kelly's!' Jade laughed, explaining about the strong drinks they'd started their night with.

'We're going to TIBU after here, you girls coming? I'll introduce you to Joe, who manages all the waitresses and staff.'

'Ah thanks honey, it will be great to meet him before we start.'

*

The girls walked up the staircase to enter TIBU. Adele kissed the security at the entrance and also the snobby-looking woman with the clipboard, eyeing the rest of them up suspiciously.

'Alright Alice, they are with me. These guys are workers,' she said in a poised manner, as she pointed to Lee, Sophie and Gary, 'and these will be starting work here soon.' This was aimed at Jade and Kelly. 'We were just going to have a few drinks and introduce them to Joe.'

Alice nodded and stamped their hands, allowing them all in for free. This was great, Jade thought!

'We'll get free drinks as well,' Adele boasted, as she waved at and kissed all the waiters and waitresses and walked around the club confidently, chin lifted proudly. The outside bar was heaving, with every table packed, but before they knew it, space was being made for them at a table and a waitress appeared with glasses of champagne.

'I love it here,' Jade whispered to Kelly.

'This is Marbs, hun!' Kelly winked.

They chatted to the others, who all seemed nice enough, though Jade noticed Lee wasn't as perfect as she previously had thought, as he seemed a bit arrogant and full of himself. They were briefly introduced to Joe, who seemed really busy, and Jade watched the waitresses at work to see what she would be doing in a week's time. They were all slim and attractive, wearing tight red tops with the gold TIBU symbol. They looked really glamorous and once again, Jade felt as though she really needed to top up her tan and make an effort to look nice, in order to fit in. It was hard work trying to look amazing all the time in Marbella! Her

67

make-up-free days in Bath seemed like another lifetime now. Kelly interrupted her thoughts by nudging her.

'Is that the bloke from earlier?' she asked, pointing discreetly to a man serving behind the bar.

Jade's heart missed a beat. It *was* Sam, and he looked even better than she remembered. His tan looked darker, making his gorgeous green eyes stand out and as he laughed, she saw a smile that could have been from a Colgate advert. Wow. However Jade tried to play her thoughts down, worried that Kelly would say something in front of the others. 'I think it's him, not sure.'

'Yes it's definitely him,' Kelly stated, staring.

'Okay, well stop staring, Kelly!' Jade hissed, afraid he was going to notice.

A little later the bar had quietened down and Lee and Gary had gone inside the club to chat to some people they knew, so it was just the girls left on the table. Adele spotted Sam and to Jade's horror, called him over. If she says anything, Jade thought, I'll just die, I know I will.

As if reading her thoughts, Adele whispered, 'Don't worry hun, your secret is safe with me.'

Once again, Jade tried to play it down, embarrassed. 'I only said he was good looking. Honestly, I don't want to be set up with him.'

'Hey.' Sam kissed Adele on the cheek as he walked over.

Jade quickly glanced at him. She could feel herself go hot and couldn't even look for long in case he saw her staring.

'How's it going? Busy night?' Adele asked, in her distinctively husky voice.

'Yep, Saturdays are always busy though. Take it you have a night off?'

'No, I just always sit here drinking when I'm working,' Adele teased, pouting her lips and flicking her long dark hair over her shoulder. 'Of course it's my night off! Where you going tomorrow daytime?'

68

He shrugged his toned shoulders casually. 'Don't know. Plaza Beach probably, that's where we always end up. How come?'

'This is Kelly and Jade,' she introduced, waving a hand in their direction. 'You should come to the beach tomorrow with us, they're going to be working here too next week. Bring some of the other boys as well?'

He smiled at Kelly and Jade and said hello, then looked back quickly in the direction of the bar. 'Sounds good, I'll BlackBerry message you. Better go, bar is getting busy again. Bye girls, nice to meet you.'

'Bye,' they chorused.

Jade watched him as he made his way back over to the bar. He was tall, just over six feet she guessed, with fairly broad shoulders and an amazingly toned body. She imagined how safe and protected she'd feel if he wrapped his strong arms around her. His white TIBU top brought out the colour of his striking, stunning emerald eyes. His fair hair had streaks of gold running through it, highlighted from the sun. Somehow he reminded her of Leonardo DiCaprio in *Titanic*.

'He *is* good looking,' Kelly said when she noticed Jade glancing over at him.

'Very,' Jade replied dreamily. 'He reminds me of Leo in *Titanic*.'

'Deffo, babe. Oh my God, I loved that film so much. Do you remember we used to watch it over and over?'

'Yes, it's such a good film.' Jade smiled at the memory. When they'd discovered the DVD they were hooked, and used to watch it eating Monster Munch crisps and Doritos with dips as they blubbered throughout the ending.

'I'm not being funny, but whoever made that story up must have such a good imagination. They must be so intellectual. I'd love to be that talented.'

Jade laughed, almost spitting her drink out. 'No one

made it up, Kelly! It actually happened. The *Titanic* really did sink!' She laughed even harder at Kelly's incredulous expression.

'Are you joking babe? Oh my God, shut up! I thought it was all made up! The *Titanic* really sunk? What about all those poor people?' Kelly's eyes were wide with amazement.

'It's a well-known tragic story and it was made into a film, silly.' Jade wiped her eyes, which had started to water because she had been laughing so hard.

'I just can't believe that,' Kelly shook her head, completely bewildered. 'Poor Rose! Poor Jack! Whatever happened to her in the end? She didn't marry that horrible bloke she was supposed to, did she? I mean, I know that necklace was pure beauts but he was just nasty!'

Jade burst out laughing again as she explained the characters were actually made up even though the story was true, leaving Kelly even more dumbfounded.

A few drinks later, she caught Sam's eye and he smiled at her, making her heart somersault. It was official. Jade was in love.

*

Sam went back to the busy bar and thought about how much he loved his job. Hot girls everywhere, good money and baking sun every day; there was no other place he'd rather be. He looked over at Adele and the others. She was an odd one, Adele, wanting to spend the day together when he'd seen her with her new guy, Lee, several times. He doubted that Lee would be happy knowing Adele was going to the beach with her ex. It had been a long time since they split though, Sam justified to himself, and they were very young when they had dated. It wasn't like there was any chance of any romance happening between them again anyway, no way. He couldn't believe he'd gone out with Adele in the first place. She seemed to have become more full of herself recently and her looks meant everything to her, something that didn't interest him. It was all about what you looked like, what shoes you had and how much your designer bag cost as far as Adele was concerned. She was a typical Essex girl, he decided, but he'd only been twenty-one when they'd met and if he was honest, he didn't even know what he was looking for at the time. All his friends had started to date girls and Adele just came along, then before he knew it, they were a couple. They'd been more like friends really and he knew the relationship would never last from the first day. They still spoke when they bumped into each other at home, but that was about it. Then he'd seen her on his first day in Marbella and couldn't believe it. He wasn't bothered about her being there either way; they were still on friendly terms. Still, he was glad she was with Lee now and hopefully she would find the happiness she was after.

Sam wasn't looking for any kind of relationship. Not while he worked in Marbella anyway. This was a place to be single, not loved-up with someone. He never understood girls that were constantly on the hunt for their Mr Right. It was like they felt pressure to settle down and meet 'the one', especially the girls he met over the age of twenty-five. He'd been on a few dates at home recently with older girls and it seemed all they wanted was a serious relationship. Their constant questions about whether he wanted kids in the future, and did he see himself married within the next five years drove him mad. It felt more like an interview than a date at times! His view on love was that it would happen when it happened, and in the meantime, he might as well have as much fun as possible.

The two girls Adele had just introduced him to seemed nice, especially Jade. She was very pretty too, which was a bonus. The beach should be a fun day tomorrow, he thought, as he poured glasses of champagne for two blondes who were eyeing him up.

*

Jade woke up the following morning with a dry mouth and pounding head. She needed a drink desperately and winced when she opened her eyes and realised they hadn't bought any water the day before. Big mistake. She glanced over to see Kelly texting on her phone.

'Morning babe.' Kelly looked over when she heard her move. 'I'm just texting Lisa and told her about our first night. She said she misses us already and told us to be careful with our drinks. Bless, she's such a worrier.'

'My God, my head,' Jade groaned. 'We forgot to buy water.'

Kelly smiled. 'There are taps in the bathroom you can drink from, silly.'

'What? You didn't drink from them did you?'

'Yes, why?' Kelly answered, bewildered.

'Kelly, you can't drink water from the taps in Spain!'

'Why?' Kelly was bemused, her smooth forehead creased up.

'They give you an upset stomach; just don't drink from them, okay?'

'Okay,' Kelly said frowning even more. 'Whatever you say. I always have though and I've always been fine. I've got paracetamol, but nothing to drink it down with if you can't drink the water. Don't worry, we'll get ready quickly and then go for breakfast. Then we can quickly go to that market and head to meet the others.'

Jade agreed, forced herself out of bed and went to the toilet. She glanced at herself in the mirror and cursed herself for not being more careful in the sun yesterday. She had a red nose and had burnt under her eyes. She always burnt there, when on earth would she ever learn? She had a shower and promised herself that firstly, she wasn't going to burn and look like a stupid patchy weirdo and secondly, she was going to try to make herself look amazing today, especially if the most gorgeous man on earth was joining them at the beach.

Jade came out the bathroom and Kelly went in for a shower.

'Take your time by the way,' Kelly called out. 'It's only nine. No one will even be up yet.'

'Okay,' Jade called back, glad she had time to make herself look half decent.

Jade looked at herself in the full-length mirror. She wasn't what you would call 'skinny', especially since she'd got over her heartbreak and was back to eating slabs of Galaxy, but she was very slender. She had always wished she had bigger boobs like Kelly, and when she had the money she was definitely going to get her boobs done. It was so common in Essex that it was almost odd to have real ones! Kelly also had the curvaceous bum she wished she had, instead of her flat, saggy one, but she definitely would only go as far as a boob job, nothing ridiculous like bum implants! Overall her figure wasn't at all bad though; going to the gym twice a week at university had paid off. She decided to wear her new lemon jewelled bikini and was pleased with how she looked in it. It was quite padded so gave the impression she had *some* boobs and the bottoms were stunning, with tiny encrusted jewels along the top. She'd never seen swimwear like it. She had to admit though, the colour would look better with a tan. Maybe she could put some fake tan on? Just until she got a proper one? She quickly got out her St Tropez set and quickly but artfully applied some. She just wouldn't be able to go in the sea in case it came off patchy. She

73

applied her sun lotion on top carefully, making sure she didn't miss any part exposed to the sun. There, she looked better already. Now she just had to do something with her hair.

'What shall I do with my hair today? It's so boring,' she moaned to Kelly as she came out of the bathroom wrapped in a towel.

Kelly looked up with a sparkle in her eye. 'I'll curl it for you if you like?'

'Do you think it'll look okay curly? I don't want to look like I've got a poodle perm.' Jade only ever wore her hair straight or left it to dry naturally, which gave it a slight wave.

'I know what I'm doing, trust me. I'm a professional.' Kelly took the curlers out of her drawer and plugged them in.

'Thank you. I'll put a bit of make-up on while they're warming up.'

Jade didn't want to look overdone; she somehow needed to look natural, yet amazing. She plucked her eyebrows carefully and coloured them in with her pencil from Benefit. She brushed sparkly tan Barry M eyeshadow on her eyelids and coated her lashes with mascara. Then she put bronzer on her face and cheeks as well as blusher on her cheekbones, and finished with a clear lip gloss.

'Does my make-up look okay?' she asked Kelly, who was tying up the straps on an amazing purple glitter bikini.

'Perfect. Not too much and not too little. You look gorgeous. Sit down and I'll do your hair.'

Jade knew it was ridiculous. Curling your hair just to go to the beach? She would never have dreamt of doing this in her wildest dreams a few months ago, but there was just something about Marbella and the people there that made it acceptable. She had to admit, Kelly did a good job and her hair looked very glamorous and bouncy. Kelly then backcombed all the back and sides. Wow, she was good. Her hair looked huge. She'd even give Cheryl Cole a run for her money. Jade then went over her make-up as she waited for Kelly to get ready.

Kelly came out of the bathroom and Jade was stunned. She looked drop-dead gorgeous. Her make-up looked perfect and her hair beautifully thick and wavy. Her figure looked to die for, especially her enviable bust.

'Kelly, you look like you've just stepped out from the pages of *FHM*!'

'Ah thanks hun,' she smiled happily, slipping into the highest wedges Jade had ever seen.

Jade's eyes were firmly fixed on Kelly's feet. 'We're going to the market, remember. You're going to have to walk in those things.'

'Babe, I one hundred per cent don't do flats. I'll be fine.'

Jade nodded as she put on her plain white flip-flops. If only she'd thought of bringing wedges. Kelly looked so glamorous and pretty. Perhaps I should add just a touch more lip gloss and eyeshadow, she thought, reaching for her make-up bag.

*

The market was packed and the sun seemed to be getting hotter by the minute. Jade glanced at Kelly who looked hilarious, walking unsteadily in her ginormous wedges and huge oversized Dior sunglasses through the crowds of people. They stuck out like a sore thumb, and Jade couldn't wait until they found what they were looking for and could head to the beach.

'Oh my God,' Kelly said as they neared a haberdashery stall. 'This is a million per cent our stall!'

There were rolls of every kind of material in any colour, boxes of buttons, sequins, ribbon, diamantes, feathers and beads. It was perfect. Better than Jade had even imagined.

'Our bikinis are going to look amazing!' she said excitedly, eyeing up everything on the stall.

'I want these pink feathers on my white one,' Kelly said, hunting through the boxes. 'Oh and these silver jewels to add to my hot pink one with bows!'

'Oh my God, how nice would this look on my black Primark one?' Jade beamed, holding up a gold sequin and lace mesh trimming.

Kelly was breathless. 'Everything is so cheap too!'

'I just love this diamante bow brooch. This will look amazing!' Jade said, dangling it in front of Kelly's face.

The girls made a huge pile of what they were buying. It was going to be trial and error with what looked good, and a whole lot of fun finding out too, Jade decided. She couldn't wait to get back and start sewing. They bought two sewing kits on the same stall and made their way back.

Thirty minutes later they met Adele and Sophie at Plaza Beach at the bar.

'Hey girls,' Adele said giving them a kiss on the cheek. She looked them up and down inspecting their outfits. 'Wow, you two look gorgeous. Just waiting for the boys to arrive. Think Sam is bringing quite a few of his mates; loads of them work at TIBU so it'll be good for you to get to know them.' She noticed their carrier bags. 'Where have you been – shopping?'

'Yeah, we went to this market not too far away.'

'I'm not really a market kind of girl, myself,' Adele said snootily, wrinkling her nose. 'Buy anything nice?'

'We just went to buy loads of nice bits to sew on our bikinis,' Kelly said, pulling some out to show her. 'It's a lot cheaper than buying expensive ones and at least I won't have to worry about having the same bikini as anyone else now. How embarrassing was that?'

'Suppose so,' Adele said, looking through the bag with interest. Jade noticed her mouth was smiling, but her eyes told a different story. Or was she imagining it?

'No Lee?' Kelly asked, surprised as she looked round.

Adele waved her hand dismissively. 'No, not today. His parents are visiting so he's spending the day with them.'

Ten minutes later, the boys arrived and Jade instantly felt her shy side kick in. If only she was more like Adele and Kelly. They were so confident. Then again, Kelly and Adele didn't have a huge crush on Sam. Plus, Adele knew them already so she didn't really count.

'Hey girls,' Sam said and caught Jade's eye. She smiled and felt her heart flip. *Hold it together,* she thought, angry at herself.

'Hi,' she managed.

They were introduced to his two friends, Steve and Dean, and she could instantly tell that Dean had a soft spot for Kelly. His eyes practically fell out of their sockets when he saw her, and he only looked at Kelly when he spoke to the both of them.

'Where you girls from?'

'Chigwell in Essex. You?'

'I'm from Kingston in Surrey, but the others are from Essex too,' he said pointing in Sam's direction, much to Jade's delight. 'I met Steve at uni and I visit him quite a bit and go on nights out there, it's great. How long have you two been here?' Dean asked. He was quite handsome, with dark hair and blue eyes.

'We got here yesterday,' Jade answered.

'You both working at TIBU?' he asked, still only looking at Kelly. Seriously, men were just so transparent when it came to fancying someone. Plus, it was slightly rude to not even acknowledge she existed. Jade gave up even trying to join in the conversation, and feeling slightly annoyed she left the two of them to talk.

'Have you girls got drinks on you already to take down the beach?' Sam asked her.

Jade tried to look him in the eye, but could only do so for a few seconds. He was so gorgeous. 'No, we haven't got anything yet. Have you?'

'No. We need to go to the shop. Coming?'

'Yes, I'll come,' Adele said, overhearing their conversation. 'We need drinks too. The others may as well wait here. What does everyone want?' Adele shouted in an abrasive voice above the conversations around them. After taking the orders, Adele, Sam and Jade made their way to the local shops while Kelly, Sophie, Dean and Steve stayed behind.

I hope this isn't awkward, Jade thought, as they walked away from the others.

'How long are you here for?' Sam asked Jade as they made their way to the shops.

'I think we're staying until the end of the season,' Jade replied. 'What about you?'

'Yeah, same,' Sam answered. 'Feel like I've been here forever already, as I got out here early May.'

'Do you remember when we went away to Cyprus together and John got really drunk and stripped off naked and ran down the beach?' Adele interjected loudly, touching Sam's arm, her lips pouting. 'That was *so* funny!'

Sam grinned and raised his eyebrows. 'Yeah, I'd forgotten about that.'

Adele continued. 'And then we stitched him up and drew all over his face and took photos . . .'

Sam laughed, remembering.

'Do you still speak to John?' Adele asked Sam as they reached the shop.

Jade walked off to get some drinks while Adele followed Sam to get a newspaper, still chatting about their holiday in Cyprus. *Just because he was talking to me, she had to butt in*, Jade thought crossly. Then she cursed herself for being so silly. Adele had offered to set her up with Sam in the first place, so there was no way she would be bothered about them chatting. She was just laughing about an old memory, that's all.

She met Adele and Sam at the till and they made their way back. Adele continued to bring up old memories, but Jade didn't mind. It was good that they were still friends after a finished relationship; it showed that Sam was grown up and mature. Plus, they'd obviously finished on good terms, which was more than she could say for her and Tom.

*

Adele was glad she had just interrupted Sam and Jade's little conversation. Jade looked far too pretty today for her liking, and had obviously made a huge effort to impress him. She was so perfect with her big bouncy hair and pretty little yellow summer dress, which matched her bikini underneath. Well, she would soon show *her* who was in control. She could get Sam back if she liked and she wanted Jade to know that. Adele truly believed she could get anyone she wanted. She didn't know why the thought of the two of them bothered her so much, as she certainly didn't want to get back with Sam, but it just did. Today, she would flirt like mad with him and show Jade that she was boss. She'd told Lee it was a girls-only day today and he was fine about it. If he happened to see them all, she would talk herself out of it like she always did; maybe just say that they'd bumped into them. Lee had no idea that Sam was her ex-boyfriend because she lied when he asked who he was, saying he was just a bloke that went to her old school. Men were so gullible at times. All she had to do was act all innocent and they hung on her every word.

What a good idea Kelly and Jade had had, buying

79

jewels and beads to sew on their bikinis – if only she had thought of that first. Some of the pieces looked really pretty and she imagined once they were sewn on, their bikinis would look just as good as some of the ones she bought for an absolute fortune. It would be too embarrassing to admit she wanted to go to the market to buy some bits too. She'd have to ask them where it was and would look like such a copy-cat. Adele had far too much pride for that.

She adjusted her top and pushed her boobs up even more in her aqua Victoria's Secret bikini, which made her tan look sensational. Adele had also made an effort today, knowing that the other two girls were going to be joining her. She knew they were competition in the looks department, but Adele always enjoyed a challenge.

*

Adele, Sam and Jade met the others and made their way to a quiet spot on the beach. There was only one sunbed, so they decided to put their things on it instead of any of them using it. If Jade was honest, lying on a sandy towel with the uneven, lumpy sand beneath her was her idea of hell, but she didn't want to look like a spoilt brat, and no one else seemed to mind so she didn't say anything. Kelly placed their bags from the market underneath the sunbed and lay down on her Ralph Lauren towel. Sam laid his towel in front of hers and lay down, rubbing lotion into his body.

Adele lay next to Jade and then turned to her, resting her chin in her hand as she leaned on her elbow. 'Where you going out tonight?'

'We're not sure yet,' Jade said as she glanced at Kelly, who shrugged her shoulders.

'Well I'm working, so come to TIBU and I'll hook you

up with some free drinks and get you on the free guestlist,' Adele offered, kindly.

'Ah thanks,' Kelly said, then mouthed to Jade secretly, 'She's so nice.'

Jade nodded. Yes, Adele was really nice going out of her way to help them, she was glad they had met. Jade would just have to put that tiny bit of annoyance she felt to the back of her mind.

'Flipping hell, Kelly, are your boobs real?' Adele questioned as Kelly took her top off and revealed her sexy one-piece, which pushed her boobs up to the maximum.

'Sure are, hun!' Kelly stated proudly, with her head held high.

'She's so lucky isn't she?' Jade said, consciously looking at her small ones and at Adele's obviously cosmetically enhanced ones.

'I thought they were fake!' Adele answered, completely shocked.

'What's this about boobs?' Sam asked, not surprisingly interested.

'I was just saying I couldn't believe Kelly's boobs were real,' Adele said again.

Sam eyed Kelly up and smiled. 'Good set.'

'Thanks,' Kelly answered, confidently.

'I've never been a massive fan of fake tits,' Sam continued. 'Personally I don't care if a girl has smaller ones, just prefer them natural.'

Jade felt better. *Mine are real, Sam!* she wanted to say. *I'm all natural!* Not that he'd ever doubt it with *her* two fried eggs. Maybe she wouldn't get a boob job after all.

'You never used to complain about mine being fake,' Adele reminded him, flicking a bit of sand on his towel.

'Didn't want to hurt your feelings,' Sam teased, throwing a handful of sand back. The sand went in Adele's hair.

81

'I'm going to kill you, Sam!' she laughed, standing up and heading over to him with two handfuls of sand.

'Don't you dare!' he warned as she held her hands above his head. 'Adele, think very carefully about this. If you drop that sand, this means war. I mean it . . .'

She opened her hands out and the sand went all over his hair and stuck to his oiled face and body.

'Right, that's it!' Sam warned, grabbing her round the waist as Adele screamed, and headed towards the sea.

'No please don't, Sam! It's freezing in there! Please! Help girls!'

Jade looked at Kelly and rolled her eyes. What was Adele doing? Purposely flirting with Sam to make her jealous? It was weird, especially seeing as she was with Lee.

They watched as Sam threw her in the sea and laughed as she screamed even more.

'I hate you!' she yelled with a smirk.

Sam made his way back and lay down again. 'You'll never win against me, Adele! Always remember that,' he yelled, as she made her way back, soaking wet.

Jade noticed the way Adele swung her hips and flicked her hair seductively because she knew they were all watching her.

'I'm not talking to you, Sam,' she said, with a babyish pout.

Oh please, Jade thought, *flirt a bit more, why don't you?*

*

It got to about five and they decided to head back to get ready for the night out. The boys said goodbye and went in the opposite direction to their apartment.

'So Jade, do you still like Sam?' Adele asked her as they picked their towels up and shook the sand off them when the boys and Sophie had left.

Jade didn't entirely know how to answer. She felt so awkward, but didn't want to lie. 'He's really nice, but if you still have feelings for him or there is something between you then that's cool. It's not like I know him . . .'

'Babe, please,' Adele interrupted, as she ran a brush through her tangled hair. 'Me and Sam are *so* three years ago. We're friends, nothing more. I'm really happy with Lee. I'll put in a good word, trust me.'

Jade shook her head quickly. 'No, don't do that. If anything is meant to happen then I'm sure it will. Please don't say anything. I'll be so embarrassed.'

'Ahh bless,' Adele replied, staring at her reflection in a mirror on the handle of her brush. She looked up and finally spoke. 'Okay, I won't say.'

'Right, we're going to go get something to eat if you want to come?' Kelly asked Adele, who was now sunbathing alone.

Adele stretched her limbs lazily, folded her arms and rested her head on the palms of her hands. 'No babe, that's fine. I'm going to catch the last few rays and then I'll meet Sophie and we'll probably get something.'

'Okay, if you're sure,' Kelly said with a raised eyebrow. 'See you tonight, girls. Say you're on my list at the door!'

*

Adele was so glad they'd finally left her alone. She could see their bags from the market still underneath the sunbed, which they'd forgotten to take. What a pair of ditzy idiots, she laughed, looking into the distance to make sure they had gone. She'd been hoping all day they were going to forget them, and had even slyly kicked them further under the sunbed so that they were out of sight. She picked the bags up and placed them into her own Juicy Couture beachbag. The idea of customised swimwear was such a good one, it was a surprise that *they* had come up with it. Obviously she'd have to wait a week or so before she started adding some of the lovely bits they'd bought to her own bikinis. It would be too obvious otherwise. It had been so simple; like stealing candy from a baby.

*

An hour later when Jade and Kelly were leaving Wok Away restaurant, Kelly froze on the spot, her mouth a perfect 'O'.

'Oh my God!' she gasped, lifting her hands to her cheeks. 'Euston we have a problem! We've left the bags with all the bikini accessories at the beach.'

'Oh no!' Jade said, quickly checking they hadn't left them where they were sitting. 'Hopefully they'll still be there, let's not panic just yet.' Then she giggled, recalling the words her friend had just used. 'Did you just say "Euston we have a problem"?'

'Yeah, babe, it's a saying or something,' Kelly muttered as she marched quickly in the direction of the beach.

'It's *Houston*, not Euston!' Jade burst into laughter as she tried to keep up with her.

'That's what I meant,' Kelly grinned. 'Now come on, let's get there quickly.'

*

'They're gone, I can't believe it!' Jade cried as they reached their sunbed five minutes later, only to find the bags they had left were no longer there.

'We're so stupid. How did we forget them?' Kelly replied, cursing herself.

The beach was still busy and Jade assumed someone had picked them up and taken them themselves. How annoying. Now they'd have to go back to the sweltering

84

market another day! Some of the pieces she'd picked had been the only ones on the stall too, she remembered, disappointed. There had been only one diamante bow brooch! She'd never be able to get the exact same patterns or bits of fabric.

'Don't worry, hun. We're still going to have the best swimwear ever. We'll just have to go back to the market on Wednesday when it's on again.'

'You're right,' Jade replied, trying to stay positive. 'Now let's go get a cocktail to cheer ourselves up.'

CHAPTER 5

A week later, and Jade and Kelly were both getting ready for their first night at work. Jade was reading a text from Lisa as she waited for Kelly to finally finish styling her hair.

Missing you two loads! Weather in England is rubbish. Jake has seen some flats he wants us to look at. I'd rather have a small house though, so trying to convince him it's a better idea! Lisa xx

Hurriedly, Jade texted back.

It's boiling here! We're missing you too. Good luck with house hunting. You'll never be able to fit all your shoes in a flat! Tell him extra room is needed for the Jimmy Choos. Jade xx

Jade gave herself one last glance in the mirror and picked up her bag.

'Ready?'

'Yeah, let's go,' Kelly answered, walking to the door.

They had just moved in to a new, very small apartment, which consisted of two beds, a chest of drawers, small wardrobe and a tiny bathroom. Two Essex girls staying in such small accommodation was asking for a mess – their room already looked like a bomb had hit it. However, the room was cheap and the girls knew they would spend hardly any time there anyway, so it wouldn't matter. They'd had a great first week and it had been nice getting to know people and just relaxing with no worries, but they couldn't stay there any longer without making some money. Marbella was a lot of things but cheap definitely wasn't one of them, even with some of their drinks being on the house. After a week of getting to know Adele, Jade secretly wasn't sure if she was as nice as she made out. Despite Kelly firmly telling Jade on more than one occasion that Adele and Sam were only friends, Adele's constant flirting with him was really winding her up. It was as though Adele waited for her to walk by before grabbing Sam's arm and bursting out laughing, flicking her long dark hair in the process. Kelly interrupted her thoughts.

'So, what did you think of Jonny last night?'

'Kelly, I'm not going to get with Billy's mate just because you like him!'

Kelly laughed realising that Jade had guessed her plan straight away. 'He's not that bad! They wanted to know if we wanted to go for dinner with them one night this week? Oh, please say you'll go?' she whined.

They had met Billy and Jonny late the night before and Kelly and Billy had instantly hit it off, leaving Jade with his friend, Jonny. Jade had kind of hoped that was the last they would see of them, so was gutted when Billy told them they worked in Marbella too and it was their night off. Jade had a sneaking suspicion that Kelly would end up wanting to spend all her time with him. She supposed that was the problem going on holiday in a two. She hadn't minded speaking to Jonny for an hour the night before, but seriously, going to dinner on a double date? Not fun.

'Kelly, he's definitely not my type. Why don't you two just go?'

'Oh don't be stupid. As if I'm going to go on my own and leave you. It's just dinner, you don't have to marry him for God's sake.'

Jade sighed, knowing she'd just have to take one for the team. Kelly would do the same for her.

'Okay, but just the once.'

*

Kelly couldn't stop thinking about Billy. She had clicked with him straight away and really felt a connection. She wanted to meet him again soon, but was very aware that if she did she would be leaving her friend on her own. It was a tough one. She hadn't met someone she'd actually liked for a very long time and it was so exciting. Just the thought of him gave her butterflies inside. He had lovely blue eyes, rimmed with long black eyelashes that girls would kill for, sleek dark hair which he wore in a side parting, and he dressed immaculately; very much the perfect Essex boy in her eyes. He lived close to her at home in Essex too, in Buckhurst Hill. It was amazing that they'd never bumped into each other before; there was no way she'd miss a face like that wandering round Nu Bar. The thing she liked most about him was the fact that he wasn't a typical flash Essex boy. He was really down to earth and she could imagine he would more likely be spotted in Topman than Gucci. Billy obviously didn't need designers to look good. She was very impressed with his clean-cut, preened style and was secretly looking forward to getting home and going on a shopping trip to Bluewater with him. They matched each other perfectly, Kelly thought; they both made an effort with their appearance and clothes and Billy was only five foot nine, so he wasn't too tall for her, unlike most men.

He was friendly, likeable and keen on her too; she could just feel it.

Kelly found that she was excited about work tonight. This was a million times better than touching scabby old women's feet and giving them a pedicure. Maybe after work they could meet up with Billy and Jonny? The boys worked for a bar nearby and would be finished earlier than they would, so they could wait for her and Jade somewhere. She was sure she could talk Jade round.

Jade and Kelly arrived at TIBU, feeling nervous. Some of the bar staff were already cleaning and organising glasses, including Sam. Joe met them at the entrance and sat them down to explain what would happen. He was fairly attractive, about forty, Kelly guessed, with a good physique and lovely olive skin.

'Hi girls, you ready for tonight?'

'Sure am,' Kelly said with a cheeky grin as they followed him to a table and took a seat.

'Right, great. Okay, so you're both going to be waitressing for me in the outside bar. I need you here for nine on the nights you're working to set up the tables. Basically you'll need to just put a candle and drinks menu on each, ready for when people start to arrive. There is a minimum spend on each table and you'll both be serving the customers, pouring drinks and things like that. Obviously you have to be friendly, welcoming and make sure they have a good time and are looked after. You'll be allocated six tables to deal with each.' He looked at them both to make sure they understood.

The girls nodded. It sounded fine so far.

'That's pretty much it.' He sat back in his chair and folded his arms. 'We're only open three nights a week so the rest of the time is yours. Pay is fifty euros a night, plus tips. Any questions?'

'All sounds fine to me,' Jade said and Kelly agreed.

'Excellent. At the end of the night I'll ask someone to deal with the tips and split it between the staff and the rest will clean up,' Joe announced firmly, rubbing the stubble on his chin with his fingers.

'Okay, that's fine,' Kelly said confidently.

'You already know Adele, so she's in charge of telling you which tables you'll be working on. Any problems with anything, come straight to me. We have security here as well so just be aware, you know, in case a fight breaks out or something.' He made a face. 'It doesn't normally happen but on the odd occasion you'll get a couple of drunken twats who start throwing punches.'

'It's always men that can't handle their drinks,' Kelly claimed, clearing her throat.

'Exactly,' Joe agreed. He stood up, looked round the bar and then back at them. 'Right, if you're both fine about everything, feel free to get started setting up the tables.'

'Thanks Joe,' Jade said, and they both stood up to get to work.

*

To begin with, it seemed like a lot of standing around and waiting for people to arrive. Joe obviously hated seeing them doing nothing though, and soon asked them to clean some glasses in the bar inside.

The glass dishwasher was full, so Jade filled two sinks with hot, soapy water to clean by hand with Kelly.

'Urgh,' Kelly grimaced, turning up her pert little nose. 'This one still has bright pink lipstick on and it's not coming off. I've tried wiping it too.'

'Put some elbow grease into it,' Jade advised as she tackled a champagne glass. 'It'll soon budge.'

Kelly started to look in the cupboards underneath the sink and without saying anything, walked off to the other bar.

'Where did you just go?' Jade asked, confused, as Kelly made her way back over.

'I've been looking for elbow grease but I think they must have run out. Shall I tell Joe?'

'What? No, Kelly, elbow grease isn't a real thing, silly! It's just an expression!' Jade's mouth twitched and she burst into laughter.

Kelly scratched her head, baffled. 'Oh, I thought you meant it was something you put into the water to clean the glasses.'

After they cleaned the glasses there wasn't much else to do until people arrived. Not that the girls minded, as that meant they could chat. Adele was talking to Sam and laughing as usual, Jade noticed. Adele caught her eye and called them over.

'Sam reckons I look a bit like Megan Fox. What do you think?' she boasted, with her trademark pout. *Seriously*, Jade thought, *as if you would announce that, even if you were Megan's double! Talk about loving yourself!* Plus, she looked absolutely nothing like her.

'Yeah, Megan on a bad day,' Sam teased.

'You dick!' she laughed, throwing an ice cube at him, which smashed on the floor when he dodged out the way.

'I can't really see it that much,' Jade said, getting annoyed.

'Maybe a bit,' Kelly said, trying to be nice.

'Well *you* don't look like any good-looking celebrities,' Adele said to Sam, flicking his arm flirtatiously.

'Well I can't be that bad if you used to fancy me,' he said, cockily.

'Not any more, you're not my type. You're Jade's though,' Adele said, looking at her with a hawk-like stare.

Sam's eyes locked with hers, and Jade's mouth flew open but nothing came out. She felt herself blush crimson, her head pulsing with blood, and she wanted the ground to swallow her up. *God*, she thought, *you absolute cow.*

91

Somehow she laughed it off and walked away, pretending she noticed a table which needed tidying. Kelly followed her.

'You okay, hun?' she asked, knowing how embarrassed she must be.

Jade wiped a table even though it was already clean. She exhaled sharply, her voice a bit shaky. 'No, not really. Adele is a right bitch and has made me look like the biggest idiot in the world. She knew I didn't want her to say anything!'

'I don't think she meant it, but that was out of order, I agree. Don't worry about it, honestly.'

'I'm never going to be able to look him in the eye again,' Jade sulked.

Adele walked over, obviously aware that Jade was upset. 'Babe, sorry if I just upset you then. I didn't even mean to say it, it just slipped straight out my mouth!'

'Don't worry, I'm really not bothered anyway,' Jade lied, feeling awkward.

'Good,' Adele gave a fierce smile. 'He said he thinks you're pretty by the way.'

Jade's heart skipped a beat, but she just shrugged, still feeling embarrassed. *Did he really say that?* she wondered. *Or is it just Adele making things up as she feels guilty for blurting it out?* She decided to just try and forget the whole thing. *I suppose at least he knows I fancy him now.*

*

Sam felt bad for Jade, who was clearly exceptionally embarrassed about what Adele had just said. She shouldn't be, he thought wryly, as he was massively flattered. She seemed like a lovely girl, exactly the type he usually went for and now he knew she liked him, he would definitely be trying to get to know her better. Jade wasn't overdone like the majority of Essex girls; he liked that she didn't have those stupid hair extensions and wasn't bright orange. He would never understand why girls thought it looked better to have loads of hair. Seriously, did they not realise how off-putting it was, running your hands through your girlfriend's hair and finding out half of it was stuck on with glue? The extensions were so deceiving too nowadays, blending in with the exact colour of their hair; you could never tell if it was real until you felt it. Plus there were the tans. They were all so brown they looked like they'd been rolling around in mud all day. What happened to looking natural? Then again, Sam thought, he did live in Essex – how could he expect to find many natural girls there?

That was a bitchy thing for Adele to do, Sam sighed. What was wrong with her? He thought she was friends with Jade and Kelly. He was glad she'd told him, as he would never have guessed Jade fancied him, but she should have pulled him to one side and told him without poor Jade knowing. What was with Adele's flirting and sudden interest in him too? She was up to something that one, he was sure of it. He hadn't seen her behave that way since they'd been a couple; maybe she still had feelings for him? Sam grinned to himself; he certainly didn't need to worry about not having enough girls that liked him, that was for sure. He didn't want Adele to get the wrong idea though; he definitely had no romantic interest in her.

*

The girls were tired after their first night at work, but decided to go to a club anyway with everyone that worked at TIBU. Jade overheard Sam say he was going too, and thought maybe she'd try and speak to him if she got the chance.

'I don't know what's wrong with me when it comes to him,' she said to Kelly, on their way to the club. 'I just

93

really fancy him and get ridiculously shy when he's around. It's like when I first met Tom I suppose. I just think he's amazing. Seems like a really nice boy too, when he's not flirting with Adele.'

'Well maybe it's a good thing Adele said what she did,' Kelly said, cheerfully tilting her head. 'I know it's embarrassing but now he knows you like him, who knows what will happen?'

'I can't see how he'd ever like me though, not when he's *that* good looking.'

'Babe, he went out with Adele. She's not drop-dead gorgeous. Quite pretty, yes, but not as nice as you are.'

'I'm not so sure,' Jade said glumly, hunching her shoulders.

'Well if not, there's plenty of other fish in the sea.'

'I only want that fish though,' Jade exhaled loudly. 'I saw you talking to Billy and Jonny at the end of the night. Are they going out to the same club?'

'Yeah, they said they were. They finish work earlier than us, lucky things. They'd been finished for an hour and we were still working! Oh well, I quite like our job so I don't mind.' Kelly linked arms with Jade as they walked.

'Okay, well I don't mind talking to Jonny for a bit while you flirt madly with Billy. But not all night though.'

'Okay, though you might make Sam jell if he sees you talking to Jonny.'

'Jell?' Jade replied, bewildered with her choice of words.

'Short for jealous, silly.'

'I doubt very much he'll be jell of Jonny.'

Kelly defended him quickly. 'He's a nice boy, don't be so harsh.'

'Okay, I'll talk to him for you, but only because you want me to.'

They were interrupted by Sam and his friend, Steve, who also did bar work at TIBU, coming up behind them.

'Alright, girls?' Steve asked. They'd got to know him more since the beach day and Jade really liked him. He made them both laugh so much their stomachs ached.

'Yeah, you?' Kelly said, slowing down so they could catch up.

'Bloody tired, but Sam has convinced me to go to this club with you lot,' he said, clapping Sam on the back.

'Yeah, you're so hard to convince, Steve. I asked if you were coming and you said yes!' Sam laughed jovially.

Steve smiled. 'I don't like being left out of things, what can I say?'

They walked together and followed some other workers up ahead. Apparently it was only a five-minute walk, but in her sky scraper heels, which were beginning to pinch her toes, Jade felt like they'd been walking for ages. Somehow Steve ended up walking alongside Kelly, and Sam next to Jade. She tried her best to act casual and forget Adele's earlier comment.

'How was your first night?' Sam asked her.

Her insides turned to jelly when his arm brushed hers as they walked. 'It was really good, thanks. I really enjoy working there so far. Can't believe we took home one hundred and twenty euros in tips too!'

'Yeah, it's good money and we only work three nights, which is great compared to some places. It's just enough to survive on to live here. Though I sometimes do a bit of bar work in the day in another bar too, for some extra cash. I worked out here last year too.'

'You've been here since May, haven't you?'

'Yep, long time.' He looked into the distance thoughtfully.

'Now I know why you're so tanned!' Jade said, glancing at his dark, muscly arms.

He turned to her and held his arm out comparing tans. 'You two have almost caught up with me though, and you only arrived a little while ago!'

'Not quite,' Jade grinned, secretly pleased with how tanned she had managed to get in the last week.

They were silent for a few seconds, but it seemed like minutes. *Think of something interesting to say,* Jade thought, annoyed with herself. Sam broke the silence.

'What are you two planning to do on your nights off? Just go out to bars and clubs?'

Jade gave an insouciant shrug. 'Yeah I suppose so. Haven't really thought about it.'

'I always start by going out all the time, but after about four weeks of working and going out, I start to feel it, you know; the drinking and late nights get too much. I sometimes have quiet nights in and just watch DVDs on my laptop.'

'Oh really?' Jade stared at him. 'That's a good idea. Shame we didn't think to bring one.'

They were almost at the entrance of the club and Kelly and Steve had stopped and got into the small queue ahead.

Sam hesitated. 'Well, maybe one night if you don't fancy going out drinking, you might want to come watch a film with me?' he said, shyly.

Before Jade could answer, Steve interrupted them and called out at the top of his voice, 'Come on you two! My ninety-year-old nan walks faster than you!'

Jade spotted Adele waiting in the queue also, eyeing her and Sam suspiciously.

'I'd like that,' Jade replied, but unsure whether Sam had heard as he walked off as he spotted someone else he knew in the queue, shaking his hand and speaking to him. Jade joined the others, bursting with happiness inside. Maybe he liked her too then? He must do. You wouldn't want to invite someone round to watch a DVD if you didn't, would you? And he hadn't mentioned Kelly or anything.

She whispered to Kelly what Sam had said, and she looked just as happy as Jade did.

'Did he?' Kelly beamed broadly, revealing her dead straight teeth. 'Ahh, that's so sweet! I knew he'd like you a hundred per cent. He's totes in love with you!'

Jade noticed Adele watching them, and when they walked through the club entrance she was waiting for them.

'Hi girls,' she said, with what Jade could only describe as a fake smile. 'What are you both so happy about?' she asked accusingly, her eyes narrowed into slits.

'Nothing,' Jade said quickly, making it clear to Kelly that she didn't want her to say. 'Just news about one of our friends at home.'

'She's pregnant,' Kelly lied, 'with triplets. It's a dream come true for her.'

Jade elbowed her without Adele seeing. She didn't want Kelly to say anything else and make it obvious they were lying. She'd already said triplets, which wasn't exactly common.

'Sounds more like a nightmare,' Adele sniggered with a suspicious expression, unsure whether to buy their story as they walked into the club, which was packed.

'I need a drink so badly!' Jade said, turning to Kelly. Adele had stopped to talk to some other girls she knew and Jade grabbed Kelly's arm to pull them away so they weren't stuck with her all night; she didn't want to be around her. They made their way to the bar and someone squeezed Jade's hip cheekily. She looked round and was delighted to see Sam.

'Drinks are on me, girls. What you having?'

Jade adjusted the strap on her white Topshop dress nervously. 'A vodka and orange for me if that's okay. Kelly?'

'Same. Thank you.'

Sam got served at the bar, then handed them their drinks.

'Babe, I've just spotted Billy. I'll leave you two to talk and will just be there.' Kelly pointed to where Billy was. 'Come get me when you need me, okay?'

'Okay,' Jade said, excited that she would be spending more time alone talking to Sam.

When Kelly left and Sam had received his change from the bar, he turned to speak to her.

'What do you do for work back home?' he asked, sipping his drink.

'Well I've just left university, so need to get a full-time job when I'm back. I'm not sure what I want to do just yet. You?'

'I was working in the City, but hated my job so I left. I'm in the same boat; need to get a job when I get home.'

They chatted for a while, getting to know each other, and Jade felt herself really relax. He was really easy to get on with and when he spoke to her, she felt like the most special girl in the world.

'I like you,' he said staring into her eyes and moving a bit closer. 'And I'd like to get to know you more.'

She laughed it off, embarrassed and ecstatic at the same time. 'I like you too. Obviously you already know that though, because Adele told you.'

He smiled and his eyes suddenly glinted. He took a deep breath and studied her. 'I'm glad she did.'

Not wanting to seem too keen and also needing to see if Kelly was okay, she said she'd catch up with him in a bit and go find her.

'Okay,' he said, looking for his friends. 'Don't be gone too long though.'

He kissed her on the lips. He tasted delicious, just as she knew he would. She never wanted to pull away.

'See you soon,' Sam said.

*

It didn't take long to find Kelly, whose lips were locked with Billy's by the DJ booth.

Jade pinched her bum jokingly and Kelly looked round with a smile.

'Alright, hun?'

'Yeah all good, just thought I'd come and find you and check you were okay, which clearly you are,' she laughed.

'I really like him,' Kelly said in her ear, so Billy couldn't hear.

It must be serious, Jade thought; for Kelly to say she actually liked someone was a huge deal. She never liked anyone and hadn't had a boyfriend for about three years. Jade was pleased for her, though slightly dreading being left alone for some of the holiday while Kelly fell in love. Kelly kissed Billy on the lips and then said something to him Jade couldn't hear.

'Let's get another drink,' she suggested, reaching for the lip gloss in her bag and applying some to her lips. 'I'm going to let Billy spend a bit of time with his mates so we should get a drink and then go dance.'

Jade nodded and followed her.

'Nice chat with Sam?' Kelly asked over her shoulder as they headed in the direction of the bar.

'Yes, he said he liked me,' Jade gushed, slowing down and leaning closer to Kelly so she could hear her over the loud music. 'I was really embarrassed, but basically wanted to scream with happiness from the rooftops.'

'Did he? Maybe we should go on a double date one night with Billy and Sam then? How good would that be?'

'One step at a time,' Jade said, cautiously, knowing Kelly often got a bit carried away.

*

Sam was feeling good. He'd spoken to Jade and she was lovely. They had lots in common and he could certainly see them spending more time together in future. She'd

99

been to university, and he liked that; beauty and brains was a winner as far as he was concerned. Hopefully she knew he liked her now as well, he thought, as he went to the bar where Steve was standing and bought another drink. He was starting to feel quite drunk already; he knew he should have eaten more earlier on. That was the problem with working abroad and having to fend for yourself, he never made time to eat; and when he did it was just junk food. He cared a lot about fitness and liked to stay in shape. Some mornings he went for a run on the beach, worrying that he would start to become flabby. It was hard work, especially when the burning sun started to rise, but that was the whole point; no pain, no gain. He went to the gym every morning before work at home, in fact he found it quite addictive and he always felt really guilty if he didn't go. He'd rather be addicted to that than something like smoking, he decided; he'd take fitness any day of the week.

He bought himself and Steve a shot of tequila, as well as their drinks. 'Quickest one to down it for ten euros?' he dared him.

'You're on,' Steve replied without any hesitation.

'After three, ready? One, two, three . . .'

Sam was quickest so Steve bought another one, not wanting to be beaten by his friend.

'Double or nothing?' Steve challenged.

'Go on then,' Sam agreed, fancying his chances.

Sam won again. Four shots later, he was forty euro richer, but feeling a lot more drunk.

Steve shook his hand and clapped his back. 'You won fair and square,' he admitted. 'God knows how you down them so quickly, mate.'

Sam laughed and walked off, coming face to face with Adele as he did so.

'Alright, babe?' she said, touching his arm.

He nodded. 'Enjoying your night?'

'I've lost the girls I was with,' she said with a sulky pout. 'Stay with me for a bit.'

'I'll help you find them if you like. I was going to look for Jade, have you seen her?' He looked behind Adele through the crowds to see if he could catch a glimpse of her.

Adele's face dropped. 'Jade? Ah babe, you don't like her do you? I've just seen her over the other side of the club snogging the face off of about three different blokes.'

'What, Jade?' Sam said, incredulous. 'Are you being serious?'

'Yeah,' Adele lied, enjoying his shocked reaction. She played with her hair sensuously as she spoke. 'Nice girl, but I think she gets about a bit, if you know what I mean. I heard she had a threesome with two blokes that work for Ocean Club as well.'

'But, she doesn't seem like that at all,' Sam answered, aghast.

'Don't worry about it,' Adele said casually. She leant forward to kiss him like it was completely normal, and he kissed her back. He was annoyed by what she'd just told him, and also drunk and not really thinking properly. He felt her wrap her arms round his neck and waist. At that moment in time, it felt good to be wanted. He knew in the back of his mind he shouldn't be doing it but, for some unexplained reason, continued anyway.

*

Jade and Kelly walked through the club to the bar. Despite temperatures being high outside, the club was actually quite cold due to the blasting air-con, and Jade shivered. They got their drinks and stood near the dance floor. The club was packed with people. Stunning girls with long hair and short dresses were everywhere. She could see why people loved Marbella; it was a different world, where only preened and beautiful people existed. It was hard keeping up with everyone and Jade believed looks were certainly not everything, but it was a great experience being here and she loved every minute so far.

She looked amongst the hundreds of people in search of Sam. Where was he? She could see Steve at the bar, but Sam wasn't near him. All of a sudden a group of girls moved from the dance floor and Jade spotted him and gasped. There, on the edge of the dance floor, was Sam, his hands round another girl's waist. As the girl pulled away from his kiss, to Jade's horror, she realised it was Adele.

Jade felt her face burn and she held her hands to her cheeks. 'Oh my God, Sam is kissing Adele.'

'*Oh. My. God,*' Kelly said, agog, her hand flying to her open mouth.

'I knew she had an issue with me liking him, I just knew it.' She watched as Adele wrapped her arms around Sam's neck and kissed him again, eagerly. He tried to pull back a few times, but Adele forced his face forward to hers and in the end he gave up and let her kiss him. Jade was stunned and had no words. What on earth was Adele playing at? Could she not stand that Jade liked him and he might like her too? Was she seriously that insecure she had to run and snog him, just to show that she could? Jade finally spoke, exasperated. 'I'm so pissed off with her, what a complete cow. I thought she was with Lee, as well?'

'She was a hundred per cent jell that he liked you,' Kelly said putting her arm round her gently. 'Are you okay?'

'Not really. He couldn't have liked me that much, could he? They're both welcome to each other,' Jade replied feebly, swallowing hard.

Kelly stroked her arm tenderly. 'Come on babe, don't get

upset. I know she's been out of order, but she clearly wasn't over him. He's just a typical bloke who can't resist someone coming on to him. There are so many fit men here, don't worry about Sam. Let's just get another drink and have a laugh together.'

It was ridiculous, but Jade felt like crying. She was too humiliated to show even Kelly this, but couldn't pretend she was okay enough to act like nothing was wrong and go on enjoying herself whilst Adele and Sam were snogging.

'I think I just want to get back and get some sleep to be honest. You stay and be with Billy. Honestly, I don't mind. I'm just not in the right frame of mind now and I feel really pissed off.'

'Don't be silly. Please stay?' Kelly pleaded hastily, her eyes opening wide.

Jade felt slightly annoyed with Kelly, who was clearly only bothered that if Jade left she would be expected to leave too, when she wanted to be with Billy. 'I'm not saying *you* have to leave, Kelly. You can stay here with Billy. We only live a few minutes away, I'll be perfectly fine, don't worry.' She downed her drink and put her glass on a table nearby.

'I'm coming with you. Don't be ridiculous, it's fine. But please just let me quickly tell Billy we're leaving?'

Jade nodded and followed her back to Billy, who was near the DJ booth.

'He's going to walk us back,' Kelly told her, after talking to him.

Jade was a little disappointed; she just needed to be alone and the last thing she wanted was to walk back with two lovebirds.

There was no sign of Sam and Adele as they walked out of the club. Jade wondered if they'd gone back together, then pushed the thought from her mind. It had nothing to do with her and she no longer cared. Adele had made her look and feel stupid. She vowed to keep her at arm's length in future, and thought back to how she'd had a bad feeling about her when they'd first met. Her initial suspicions had been proved right; Adele *was* a bitch.

Billy was a little drunk and kept stumbling on the way home, making Kelly giggle like a schoolgirl. They reached the apartment, and Kelly stopped outside.

'I'm just going to say goodnight to Billy, babe. You go up and I'll see you in a bit.'

'Okay, night,' Jade said, turning on her heel, glad she'd have a bit of time alone.

She got back in the room and couldn't believe the heat, their apartment was like an oven. Just another thing to top off her rubbish night. Jade wiped the beads of sweat away from her forehead, which formed again almost immediately. They'd bought two little fans which they had placed either side of their unmade single beds, but they made absolutely no difference at all and were about as effective as someone blowing in the air. Jade changed into her summer pyjamas, which were little lilac shorts and a vest, brushed her teeth, took off her make-up, and then lay down on her bed and gave a theatrical sigh. It wasn't so much that she really liked Sam and he'd been kissing someone else. He was single and owed her nothing. Yes, he said he liked her, but he was on holiday and there were pretty girls everywhere. Unless they'd been spending lots of time together and agreed to only be with each other, there was nothing she could say about a kiss. She did think he could have at least considered her though; he knew she was in the club and liked him. It certainly wasn't nice to see him with someone else, especially when they'd just been talking moments before. The thing that annoyed her the most was the fact that Adele, who had pretended to be their friend, had purposely gone out of her way to show her that she could still have Sam if she wanted. She'd been jealous and couldn't stand seeing Sam with her, despite the fact that Adele was supposedly happy with Lee. A tear fell from Jade's eye and she closed them. She felt betrayed and humiliated. Adele was definitely not her friend and never would be. The only good thing was that Jade believed Adele would get her comeuppance. After all, she believed in karma.

CHAPTER 6

Sam woke up on a sofa in Steve's sweaty apartment and turned his nose up; the place reeked of alcohol and stale body odour. It was to be expected with three blokes sharing a room, but it never ceased to amaze him how disgusting they could make the room smell. God, it was vile. Sam leaned over, stretching his arm to open the balcony door to let some air in. What happened last night? He must have been drunk if he'd ended up crashing in Steve's apartment. He stayed in a room on his own another five minutes away, but clearly he hadn't been able to make it that far. The sofa creaked as he moved, and he wondered how he'd slept so soundly the whole night through when he couldn't even stretch his legs out.

Sam laid his head back down on the uncomfortable sofa, surprised by how much his temples throbbed when he sat up. He remembered being fairly out of it and doing shots at the bar. Then he remembered Adele; they'd kissed and he was pretty certain she'd tried to persuade him to go back to her apartment to stay with her, but he knew it wasn't a good idea and wouldn't go. Thank goodness he hadn't gone! What on earth was he thinking of, kissing Adele? He had been right; she clearly did still have feelings for him. He would have to tell her when he got the chance that getting back together just wasn't an option, he didn't feel the same as he did all those years back. He couldn't believe he'd even kissed her, but recalled how she'd been all over him and not really given him much choice. She was crazy. Memories of what Adele had said about Jade came flooding back to him. He was so surprised that she was like that and would go round the club snogging random men. And she'd had a threesome? He'd completely misjudged her. That's probably why I snogged Adele, he thought, unhappily. He would never have done it otherwise.

He was disappointed that Jade was like that; he'd really believed she was a nice girl he could have spent some time with. He thought she'd liked him too, but best he knew now, rather than wasting time with her and *then* finding out. Yes, she was single and abroad, but snogging random people in a club was the sort of thing he had done when he was sixteen, not twenty-one. He wondered if she'd seen him and Adele. In a way, he almost hoped she had, then she'd think he wasn't bothered about her either. God, he hated it when girls got to him.

He looked across the bed at Steve who was snoring loudly, and wondered how on earth he had managed to sleep through that racket.

*

The following day, Jade didn't feel much better about the whole situation. She obviously wasn't going to bother with Sam any more, who clearly had some kind of feelings for his evil ex Adele. She also certainly didn't class Adele as a friend in any way, shape or form, and never would. She wasn't really in the mood to go to any lively places to sunbathe, but knew Kelly would want to meet Billy, so she'd have to go.

Kelly was still sleeping as Jade got up, showered and got ready. The problem with Marbella was that you always bumped into people you knew so you had to look your best at all times, even though today she didn't feel like making a big effort. She still needed make-up though, she wouldn't be caught dead without it here. Her face hardly needed it, seeing as she was tanned, but she just skimmed her lashes with mascara, applied some bronzer, eyebrow pencil and Estee Lauder lip gloss and loosely tied her hair in a side plait. She decided to wear one of the new bikinis she'd recently created after they'd gone to the market again. Luckily the market was on twice a week so they hadn't had to wait too long to go back. It turned out that all wasn't lost, because the stall had new and different pieces from the first time they went. Today she chose a pale pink bikini, on which she had sewn sequins and crystals on the top. She had also sewn them in a heart shape on the back of the bottoms. They looked so pretty and eye-catching, Jade thought happily, and was putting on a white fringed kaftan from Zara when Kelly woke up.

'Morning. You look nice,' she said sleepily as she yawned.

'Morning,' Jade replied, picking up her sparkly gold sandals from Dune. They were her favourite, most dressy ones with little crystals on the straps.

'Have you been up long?' Kelly asked, as she stretched her limbs and picked up her mobile.

'About twenty-five minutes,' Jade answered, sitting on the bed.

'How you feeling today? I just can't believe Adele did that last night, you know.' Kelly smiled at a message she'd received, which was obviously from Billy.

'I can. I don't know why, but I had a funny feeling about her from the word go. I felt really awkward about liking Sam from the start; it was the way she made me feel.'

'There are so many men out here, you'll have forgotten

108

about Sam in a week,' Kelly said, getting up and walking to the bathroom to wash.

'Mmm, yeah,' Jade said, hoping that was the case.

Kelly got ready and decided to wear a sparkly black bikini which she'd added a row of fringing to. She also put on her tiny True Religion denim shorts and a hot-pink Wildfox Couture t-shirt which clung to her curves perfectly. Jade and Kelly left their apartment.

'Billy is meeting us at Plaza Beach. Is that okay? He's saved us some sunbeds.'

'That's fine,' Jade replied, honestly, looking up to see a smile plastered on her friend's pretty face. 'You really like him, don't you?'

'Yes, I really do. I don't want to get too excited about it as I don't want to get let down. But, he's so lovely. He told me he really likes me too and I'm the only girl he's met up with more than once since he's been working out here since May,' Kelly grinned, unable to hide her delight.

'Good. You deserve to be happy.'

*

They made their way to Plaza Beach and Jade immediately spotted Adele sitting with Sophie. God only knows how Sophie likes her, Jade thought to herself. She was wearing a red bikini with huge bows on either side, encrusted with silver and red crystals. The crystals were very similar to the ones she'd bought at the market, that she had on her own bikini, Jade noticed. Adele's long, dark hair was down and wavy as normal. She had a pair of oversized Chanel sunglasses on and looked as brown as a berry. Despite everything Adele did to improve her looks, Jade would still never call her 'pretty'. Something just wasn't there – or maybe it was her personality which made her unattractive.

Kelly didn't notice Adele sitting there, and Jade certainly

109

wasn't going to mention she'd seen her, in case she felt she needed to say hello. Adele had definitely spotted them though. Jade saw her head follow their movements as they walked past. They could see Billy, sitting with Jonny and, as promised, he had two extra sunbeds next to them that he'd covered in spare towels. Billy jumped to his feet and hurried over to Kelly when he saw her.

'Morning girls,' Billy said, instantly brightening because Kelly had arrived. He looked so in love, bless him.

'Morning,' they chorused.

Jade wasn't particularly in the mood to talk, so she left Kelly to it and rubbed sun oil into her body, making sure she hadn't missed anywhere. She felt herself relax as she soaked in the rays of the glorious sunshine. She was tired. Sam was right; late nights and alcohol had a way of catching up on you – and they'd only been there just over a week! She felt sure they wouldn't be able to handle going out every single night. Maybe she would just chill out for a couple of nights and go for dinner, watch the sun go down whilst sipping margaritas or even just stay in and read her book? The way she was feeling at the moment, that sounded like a nice evening.

Jade thought about how much her plans had changed since leaving university. Back then, she thought that by now she would have been living in a nice cosy apartment with Tom in Bath, probably working somewhere and looking forward to sharing weekends together. Cooking dinners every evening from cookbooks, spending Sundays being lazy in pyjamas on the sofa, doing the weekly food shopping . . . and look where she had ended up. Yes, she knew that everything happened for a reason and Tom wasn't the person she thought he was, but she had to admit, she loved the security of a relationship and the feeling of knowing, no matter what, that you had someone to go home to. Someone to cuddle and to kiss your tears away when you felt down. Never did she think she'd end up waitressing in Marbella, without a care in the world. Life had a funny way of showing you that you never really know what's around the corner. What's the point of even making plans when your whole world might change tomorrow? It was best to just enjoy everything while you could, taking each day at a time, Jade thought.

The music was blaring out and she could faintly hear Billy and Kelly talking. She smiled. She couldn't explain it, but she just knew that their relationship would end up being serious, even when they got back home. She just had such a strong feeling they would last for a long time. Billy seemed like a really nice boy, and you could tell how smitten he was with Kelly from the moment he first met her.

'Do you want a drink, girls?' Billy asked them, as he made his way to the bar with Jonny.

'Just a water please, babe,' Kelly asked.

'Same please,' Jade replied gratefully, realising actually how thirsty she was now that drinks had been mentioned.

She could see Adele walking their way, so she shut her eyes, hoping she was walking past them to the sea or something. When a figure stood in front of them blocking the sun, she knew when she opened her eyes she would see Adele.

'Alright, girls?' she asked nonchalantly.

'Hi,' they both said, not in their usual jolly voices, which wasn't lost on Adele.

Go away, Jade thought. *Stop pretending to be our friend, you fake cow.*

'God, I was so drunk last night!' she said in her loud gravelly voice, as if this would excuse her behaviour.

'You pulled Sam, didn't you?' Kelly came straight out with it, barely looking up at her.

'Oh God, I know. God knows how it happened, but he was really drunk too I think, and was all over me! Told

111

me he's never stopped loving me and all sorts,' she laughed, which sounded false, and ran her fingers through the ends of her hair.

Kelly nodded, clearly unimpressed.

Adele continued talking into the awkward silence, only making it worse. 'He literally wouldn't leave me alone, saying he's not got over me and wants me back. I only kissed him because I was pissed and kept trying to get him off me. I don't even like him like that any more, plus I'm with Lee.'

'So, you're still with Lee?' Jade enquired, pretending to be shocked, seeing as Adele had been snogging the face off her ex.

'Yeah, he's over there.' She pointed over to her large cushioned sunbed, where Lee was now lying. 'Things are going really well with us,' she said, a little smugly.

'Oh, what if he finds out about you and Sam?' Kelly asked, enjoying the uncomfortable look that appeared on Adele's face.

'He won't.' Adele took a cigarette out of the bag she was carrying and lit it. 'If he does, I'll just deny it.'

Once again, Kelly and Jade just nodded, uninterested.

'Anyway, did you two have a good night?' She exhaled a large cloud of smoke and waved it away with her hand.

'Yeah, it was good,' Kelly said, her face immobile.

Jade simply nodded, looking in the other direction to the sea.

'I'm so tired,' Adele said awkwardly, shifting on her feet. 'Okay girls. Have fun today. See you at work.' Adele walked off, exhaling another puff of smoke as she did so.

'Is she joking?' Kelly said as Adele had reached her sunbed in the distance. They watched as she gave Lee a big kiss on the lips.

Jade was aggrieved, but she closed her eyes trying to relax in the sunshine. 'I know. She doesn't even want Sam.

She just didn't want me to have him. Oh well, to be honest, I just want to forget the whole thing now. I don't like her and never will.'

'Me too,' Kelly agreed.

Jade was secretly pleased about this. Kelly was a very loyal friend, a quality that Adele clearly didn't have.

Two girls they didn't know approached them, interrupting her thoughts.

'Sorry, excuse me. I hope you don't mind me asking, but me and my friend absolutely love your bikinis. Where are they from?'

'Oh thanks,' Jade said, completely flattered. 'This is actually from New Look and then I sewed all the crystals and sequins on.'

'Really? They look wicked. I love the heart at the back. I wish I could sew or had the time to make one. Yours is lovely too,' she said to Kelly, her friend nodding.

'Thanks, babe. I bought mine as it is, but added the fringing.'

'That's what makes it so different,' her friend chipped in. 'I hate having the same bikini as everyone else. At least that way you know you're the only one that'll be wearing it.'

'Hundred per cent, hun,' Kelly agreed, thinking of when it happened to her on the first day.

'Are you girls on holiday?'

'No, we're working here,' Jade informed them.

'You lucky things,' the girl said with a twinkle in her eye.

'I know it's a long shot,' the girl's friend said hesitantly, 'but is there any chance you'd be able to create us one, if we give you our bikinis? We're here on holiday for two weeks and this is our first day. All our bikinis are so boring. We'll obviously pay you.'

Jade was taken aback. They really wanted to pay them

113

to jazz up their bikinis? It was hard to say no, especially seeing as they needed all the money they could get.

'Course, babe!' Kelly smiled, her voice high pitched with excitement. 'I can do one and she can do the other.'

'Thank you!' they chorused, looking thrilled.

'Just tell us what you want done to them and we'll see what we can do,' Jade grinned.

'Our hotel is only over there. Do you mind if we just quickly grab a couple of bikinis each and give them to you now? How much do you charge?'

Jade and Kelly looked at one another, unsure.

'Twenty-five euros a bikini?' Kelly said.

'Great. We'll just go get our bikinis now then!'

The two girls ran off excitedly, leaving Jade and Kelly sitting there, astonished.

'I can't believe we can actually make money this way. I loved customising my ones. It'll be so much fun doing other people's too, don't you think?'

'Yeah, definitely,' Kelly agreed. 'It doesn't even take us that long to do really, especially when we use the stick-on crystals. When you think about how much people pay in the shops for ones like these, it's hundreds of pounds. We could probably even put our prices up if this catches on.'

'Agreed,' Jade said, cheerily. How she hoped that this was the start of something wonderful.

*

They're definitely annoyed with me, Adele thought as she sat on her sunbed. Her plan had worked and she had definitely turned both Jade and Sam off each other. She knew Sam hated girls that got around, it was one of his ultimate turn-offs. Of course he never knew how many men she'd even been with when he started dating her – as usual she had lied and told him only two. All girls lied about that

114

kind of information if it wasn't the answer the man wanted to hear; who would be stupid enough to confess the truth? You just told them what they wanted, it couldn't be simpler.

They'll get over it soon, Adele told herself, as she glanced at Kelly and Jade who were chatting, no doubt about her. It wasn't as if Jade really even knew Sam anyway, they'd only spoken a couple of times, thanks to her mainly. It's not like she'd snogged her boyfriend, for Christ's sake. Jade had a face like a slapped arse when she was over there. She seriously needed to get over it; surely there were other people she liked? I'm doing her a favour anyway, Adele told herself, Sam isn't the kind to want a relationship, he has far too much fun being single.

Adele thought back to the previous night when she had seduced Sam. It had been so easy, just as she knew it would. He'd fallen for her lies straight away about Jade snogging loads of men in the club – as if the goody two-shoes would ever do that! She'd almost had to stop herself from laughing just thinking about it! It hadn't been too difficult getting Sam to kiss her. He'd pushed her away a couple of times, but she knew he wanted her really. No man had ever turned her down, Adele thought arrogantly. She had been very surprised when he'd said no to her offer to go back to her apartment afterwards; she was certain he would have gone. Maybe he was too drunk, Adele reassured herself, remembering how Steve had to help him walk back. She doubted it was because he didn't like her in that way. He'd shown last night that she was still very much what he wanted. Poor Sam; he probably thought she was going to break up with Lee or something ridiculous. No chance. He was just part of her little plan to put Jade in her place and make sure they never got together.

She smiled sweetly at Lee who was lying next to her. He had no idea, bless him. She'd made sure there was no one around that knew her last night and could have told him.

The amount of people that got caught cheating because other people had seen them was ludicrous. Did people not think? Did they not even check or consider who was around them? She had known there was no way that Lee would have seen either, because he'd had a night in to catch up on sleep. She would lie anyway if someone had seen and no doubt Lee would believe her. She already had her excuse planned. She would say that Sam wasn't over her, which was true anyway, and had come on to her and she'd pushed him away.

She'd used some of the crystals on her bikini today that the girls had bought at the market. They looked really good, she decided, as they glittered in the sunlight. She had liked what Jade had done with her bikini bottoms. Perhaps she'd have to try that with her next one. She took out her mirror from her bag and looked at herself, adding some lip balm. She was looking good; no wonder Sam wanted her back.

*

Sam watched Adele say goodbye to Lee near her apartment and figured this was the perfect time to talk to her about the previous night. He felt extremely awkward, but knew he had to say it or it would only get worse. He watched as she rummaged around her beach bag looking for the keys.

'Adele!' he called, before she went in.

Adele squinted in the sunshine, wondering who it was, and then smiling when she recognised him. 'Alright Sam?'

'Yeah,' he stood beside her feeling uncomfortable. 'Can I have a word please?'

'Go for it.' She opened the door, smiling. 'Come in.'

He walked into her apartment and couldn't believe the state of it. There were nail varnishes everywhere, make-up all over the dressing table, fake eyelashes covering every

116

surface and clothes sprawled out all over the floor. Wow, and he thought his room was bad.

'God Adele, has your room been broken into or something?' he joked as he tip-toed round the mounds of clothes piled up on the floor.

'It's Sophie, not me,' she said innocently, with a shrug of her shoulders. 'I'm normally tidy.'

'Well Sophie is a mess then. Anyway, it's about last night,' he said as he sat on the bed, the tidiest part of the room. He took a deep breath. 'That should never have happened and I can't believe it did. I just wanted to say, I'm sorry if you got the wrong idea in any way, but I just want to be friends like normal. I don't have any feelings in that way for you.' He was so awkward he wanted the ground to swallow him whole.

She looked furious, but laughed it off, folding her arms across her chest imperiously. 'Sam, are you kidding? It was nothing, only a kiss; calm down. I don't want to marry you. I'm with Lee, remember? He's everything I've ever wanted in a man and we're really happy together. Trust me, I don't have feelings like that for you either. I was messing around, get over it.'

'Okay,' Sam said, exhaling sharply, relieved. He stood up and faced her. 'Let's just forget about it then. Deal?'

'Yeah whatever,' she said, sounding bored and rolling her eyes. 'Now if you don't mind I need to get showered and ready.' She looked towards the door, as if to say 'now leave'.

Sam nodded and shrugged. 'Fair enough. See you later on then.'

'Bye Sam,' she sang as she shut the front door.

*

What was her problem? Sam wondered as he walked home. There was no need to be so rude about it; he just thought

117

their kiss should have been addressed. He didn't understand women at all; they all had serious issues. She'd been all over him the night before and now she was saying she'd been messing around? Was she serious? She had tried to get him back to her apartment, for God's sake! So was she going to mess around by sleeping with him? It made no sense whatsoever.

He felt pretty guilty about Lee too. Thank goodness it had only been a kiss, he consoled himself. Lee seemed like quite a nice bloke, a bit flash, but he didn't deserve to be humiliated. Not for the first time in his life, Sam realised that his ex was nothing but trouble. He would certainly steer clear of her for the rest of the holiday.

CHAPTER 7

Three weeks later, and Jade was really enjoying working in TIBU, meeting new people and generally having an amazing time. It definitely beat being at home in cloudy old Essex, and she couldn't help but feel quite smug every time she called home and her mum moaned that it had been raining. It certainly hadn't been raining in Marbella – in fact some days Jade actually wished it was a bit cooler, especially in their room, which they could have charged people to use as a sauna. They kept in touch with Lisa, mainly via texting, because they knew their phone bills would cost a fortune. It was strange Lisa not being around too and Jade missed her a lot. There was so much she wanted to tell her but couldn't; often their stories were too long to write by text. It seemed Lisa was bored without them at home and Jade felt sorry for her. Sure, she had Jake, but it wasn't the same as having your two best friends to talk to and go out with, was it?

Adele was still with Lee and had never mentioned Sam again. She still tried to be friends with Kelly and Jade, and they were civil to her, but always declined her invitations to go out, not wanting to be two-faced. Jade had spoken to Sam several times since the night she saw him snogging Adele.

They'd never mentioned it, but it was always in her mind whenever he came to sit with her. It was such a shame, because they got on really well. She'd have to just settle with being his friend though. Yes, he was gorgeous, but he'd happily snogged Adele after saying he liked *her* just moments before. To Jade, this clearly showed he was a typical young bloke on holiday, only interested in one thing, and would end up breaking her heart. There had been a stunning brunette girl waiting for him after work for the last week, and Jade assumed it was a new girl he was seeing.

Kelly and Billy had been getting on like a house on fire, but he'd spent the last week in the UK for his mum's fiftieth birthday and Jade had really enjoyed it just being the two of them once again. She could tell how much Kelly had missed him though, and if she was honest, she was really envious that she'd met someone so perfect for her. Jade had actually got to know Jonny better too, seeing as they were both the tag-along friends, and he was actually really nice and easy to get on with; she felt mean for ever saying he was not at all attractive. In fact, the more Jade got to know him, the more attractive he became and she was surprised that recently she'd been thinking about him when he wasn't there. She loved being in his company – he was so easy to talk to and always had her in stitches. It would be perfect if she got together with Jonny; they could all go out on double dates at home and holidays together. How great would that be? Kelly and Billy were always saying they wished the two of them would get together, while Jade and Jonny just laughed it off, feeling awkward. But she wondered what he really thought about her deep down? For now though, they were friends, and had started to become quite close; it was nice to ask his opinion on what dress to wear in the evening, or if he thought her hair looked better loose. She'd also confided in him about Tom and her past experiences with men.

'You did the right thing,' he'd reassured her, when she said she had left Tom immediately after discovering his infidelity. 'If you'd have given him another chance, he probably would have just done it again, mark my words. You're worth more than that.'

When she told Jonny about how she got her revenge on Tom that night in the theatre, he laughed. 'I can't believe you did that! That's so funny. I bet he went mad! Remind me never to mess with you then.'

He also told her all about his ex-girlfriend who he'd been with for four years. She'd wanted to settle down, get engaged and have a baby and it was then that he realised that she wasn't the one, because he'd felt nothing but claustrophobic and trapped.

'We're far too young to be settling down anyway,' he informed Jade, making her feel better. 'Plenty of time to find "the one" yet.'

It was nice to talk to another man and just be friends, something Jade had never really had before. Since Billy had been home in the UK the last week, Jonny had met up with Jade and Kelly most days when his other friends hadn't bothered to get out of bed. They even had a little game they played where they would each pick someone off the beach they thought would suit the other. Jade was always in stitches laughing at some of the dodgy men Jonny chose for her; he had exceptionally bad taste.

Jade and Kelly had a night off from work, and they were drinking cocktails in a bar. Despite Jade thinking it might be good to have a few early nights, they hadn't even had one so far and Jade was feeling run-down and tired, owing to all the vodka they had consumed every night. Billy was arriving at Malaga airport at seven that evening, so it was a good opportunity for Jade to have a quiet night alone, while Kelly met up with him.

'He texted and said I should stay at his apartment tonight,' Kelly said, excitedly.

'Ooooh. So tonight will be the night then?' Jade teased, raising her eyebrows.

'I suppose so,' Kelly grinned. 'I tried to wait before we slept together, because I like him so much and don't want to ruin it, but when you're with each other every day, it feels like I've been seeing him for ages, not just over three weeks.'

'Just go for it,' Jade smiled, twirling the umbrella round in her cocktail. 'You won't ruin anything, not with him. He knows you're not like the other girls out here on holiday, who drop their knickers if a man buys them a drink. Plus three weeks on holiday is much longer than being at home. You've spent so much time with him.'

'I know,' Kelly took a sip of her drink and paused. 'I feel really nervous though.'

'That's good in a way, as it shows you care.' Jade thought for a second. 'So that's why you put on that pretty matching underwear set tonight and used the heart vajazzle pattern?' she giggled, everything falling into place.

Kelly smirked. 'Oh my God, how funny? You've completely guessed right. I've got my best Agent Provocateur set on for him, so he'd better appreciate it. It's gorge and cost a fortune.' Then she said seriously biting her bottom lip, 'I hope it goes okay.'

'It will,' Jade said confidently, surprised Kelly was so worried. It wasn't as if she was a virgin; she'd gone through a bit of a 'phase', as she liked to put it, when Jade was at university, where she seemed to have slept with quite a few men.

'Have another cocktail and you'll feel better about it,' Jade suggested, passing her the menu. 'Then I'll head back and you can meet him and show him your sexy undies.' She yawned. 'I'm going to have an early night I think.'

After another cosmopolitan each, they parted, and Jade wished Kelly luck as she walked back to their apartment.

*

As she made her way to Billy's apartment, which he shared with Jonny, Kelly felt as nervous as when she had had her first driving test. Billy would have arrived by now and Jonny had gone out, meaning they had the place to themselves. She was excited too; she'd fantasised about spending the night with him for ages and now it was actually happening. It had been a while since she'd been intimate with someone and she couldn't wait, but she just wished her nerves would vanish and she could relax. Why was it when she'd slept with men in the past she hardly knew she didn't care? Now Kelly had found someone who actually meant something to her, and she was petrified. She'd only ever had one boyfriend in the past and that was years ago. She had fallen head over heels in love with him and had told him so after about eight months. He hadn't said it back though, and she instantly knew she'd said the wrong thing. Before saying it, she had been sure he'd felt the same way, but to her horror the next day he had called her up and broken up with her.

'I'm sorry Kelly, it's not you, it's me,' he'd said, all the clichés in the world coming out and hitting her full force. 'Please don't hate me. Let's still be friends, yeah?'

Her heart had been broken and she'd cried for days. He, on the other hand had got over *her* extremely quickly, as just over a week after they'd split, she heard from someone that he was seeing another girl. Ever since then, Kelly didn't trust anyone. The minute they got close she made her excuses, terrified they were going to do the same.

*

123

Kelly reached Billy's apartment and was beaming from ear to ear before he even opened the door. She couldn't wait to see him; she'd missed him loads since he'd been gone. He opened the door with a smile that matched her own.

'Kelly,' he said, taking her in his arms.

She took in the scent of his Hugo Boss aftershave, which she loved. It felt so good to be in his arms again; she could stand there cuddling him all night. She lifted her face to his and kissed him tenderly.

'I missed you, babe,' he said, leading her into his room.

'Me too,' she said, sitting on his bed and gazing up into his handsome face. His tan had faded slightly and his hair looked a bit dishevelled compared to normal, but he was still the most gorgeous man in Marbs in her eyes.

She noticed that his suitcase was on the floor and hadn't been unpacked. 'Want me to help you unpack?' she asked, kindly.

'No, don't be silly. I'll do it tomorrow,' he said, unable to take his eyes off her. 'Thanks though. Now come here and give me a cuddle.'

They chatted about what they'd both been up to over the last week and Kelly felt so comfortable now she was lying in his arms. She felt so safe and wanted; something she hadn't felt in a long time. She wanted the world to just stop, so she could stay with him in his room and be near him. She listened to his heart beating and held him closer to her. She was definitely falling for him, she could feel it deep within her heart. It was a wonderful feeling, but yet again, a terrifying one. As he began to kiss her, she felt herself relax even more. Once this night was over, she knew she'd be even more attached to him.

*

Jade opened the door to their room and as usual the heat hit her instantly, surrounding her like a thick, warm blanket. She had a cold shower and lay on her bed, happy to be alone for the first time in weeks, free to just do as she pleased. It was only eight o'clock, but Jade felt exhausted. She picked up her Martina Cole novel and relaxed as she read, her eyes getting heavier by the second. The shrill of her phone ringing made her jump and she reached into her bag by the bed to answer it. She smiled excitedly as she saw Lisa's name on the caller ID.

'Hello.'

'Hi,' Lisa practically sang, happily. 'How are you two? You having a good time? I thought you might be out so was going to try you in the morning.'

'No, we're not working tonight and I'm having a quiet one. We're both really well and having a really good time, thanks. How are you?'

'Missing you both loads, that's for sure. Not been up to much, just mainly been with Jake. I've been out with my sister a few times but it's not the same as when you're both here.'

Jade's heart went out to her friend. *She* would have hated it if they had both gone and worked away, leaving her at home. 'We miss you too. I wish you were here now actually, as Kelly has met this bloke called Billy who she really likes and she's staying at his tonight, so I'm all on my own. Not that I mind really, I want an early night. Or has Kelly already told you about him?'

'You did text something about some guy she'd met, but that was it. What's he like?'

Jade told her all about Billy and Jonny, then about Adele and Sam, after Lisa asked if she had met anyone she liked yet.

'She sounds like a complete idiot,' Lisa said when Jade had finished the story about how she saw Adele and Sam kissing in the club, 'just keep away from her.'

'I'm trying to, trust me. Hey, can't you come out for a

125

holiday?' Jade asked hopefully. Hearing Lisa's voice made her feel a bit homesick.

'I'd love to, you know I would, but I can't get the time off work. We're working on this programme for Sky at the moment and are really busy,' she said sadly.

'Ah okay.'

'Where are you off to tomorrow? Anywhere nice?'

'We're heading to Ocean Club I think,' Jade told her. 'Some party thing apparently, but we haven't got tickets and everyone else we've spoken to seems to have them.'

'Sounds like so much fun. Good job I called you tonight then, as can't imagine you'll have your phones in the day?'

'No we do, my mum sometimes calls so I have to make sure I have it or she worries, you know what she's like.'

'Sure do. Babe listen, I better go,' she said. 'You know how much they charge for international calls, but take care. Can't wait until you both get back.'

'Okay, no worries. We'll be back before you know it. See you soon.'

Jade put her mobile phone down and thought about how much she did actually miss her friend. Trust Lisa to be the one to worry about the phone bill – she was always so sensible with her money, despite how well-off her parents were. Not like Jade, who could sometimes be careless and would have spoken for another half an hour before the thought of the bill crossed her mind. Jade thought of home and how far away it seemed as she closed her eyes and drifted off to sleep.

*

Lisa hung up and saw Jake grinning at her.

'You're a good liar,' he said, his eyebrows knitting together in a frown. 'Maybe I should be worried about you after all.'

'Don't be so ridiculous,' she said, elbowing him playfully.

'So, have you got everything packed?' he asked, as he ran his fingers through her silky hair.

'Yes, I'm pretty certain I have everything I need. Thank you so much for booking my flights for me; you really are the best boyfriend in the whole world.' She reached up and kissed him on the nose.

He looked round the room. 'You didn't pack all those shoes you had lying out, did you?'

'Yes, why?' she said, knowing what was coming next.

'Lisa,' Jake said, shocked, shaking his head and resting his hands on his cheeks. 'There were about seven pairs of high heels. You're only going for *five* days. What are you going to do, go home halfway through the night and switch shoes, just so you get to wear them all?'

'I don't know what I'm going to wear yet, which is why I need the other two pairs. They all match different outfits,' Lisa defended herself. They always had this conversation when they went on holiday. Lisa just couldn't pack light. It was so hard to know what you wanted to wear each night, which is why she always took back-ups. Then she needed the shoes to match, which is why she always went over the top. How could people plan their every outfit for every night? Other options were always essential, no matter what Jake thought.

'Why don't you just pick five dresses and then five pairs of shoes? But even five pairs are ridiculous. Your case will be over the weight limit and then you'll have to pay.'

'Will you stop being such a worrier? I won't be over the weight limit and if I am, then I'll have to pay extra; it's not the end of the world.'

'Okay, but don't come moaning to me,' Jake jumped up and lifted her case, 'when you get charged extra by easyJet. And judging by how heavy that is, you will.'

'I won't come moaning to you, because it won't *be* over-weight,' she replied smugly.

127

He raised his eyebrows, indicating that he very much doubted it.

Lisa cuddled up to Jake, thinking about how lucky she was to have such a caring boyfriend. She'd been down since Kelly and Jade had gone to Marbella and work had been nothing but stressful, even though she loved her job. Lisa had worked really hard to get to the position she was in. Her aunt had known the director of the TV production company she worked for, and when she'd left college she'd got a job on reception. She had worked extremely hard ever since; she wasn't like the other receptionists there who just waited until the clock struck five and then were nowhere to be seen. There were three of them on reception and she had been by far the most conscientious, always staying late and arriving early to make her boss coffee for when he arrived. Her boss had noticed this, and it had only taken her a year until she was promoted to production assistant, and now she actually got to go on shoots. The other two receptionists, Susie and Karen, were still there and there was no mistaking the cold glares she received from them every morning when she walked past them to her desk. It wasn't her fault she was a more reliable, organised worker that always went the extra mile, Lisa told herself; they were nothing but jealous. She had to admit, the shoots certainly weren't as glamorous as she'd first thought they would be, but she knew she was lucky to be there, seeing as she didn't have a degree. This was almost unheard of in media companies, and she knew she was fortunate that her aunt had helped her get into the organisation in the first place. For one shoot she'd had to be in central London at five in the morning. It had been winter and completely freezing in the old warehouse in which they were filming. She didn't get home until nine most nights during the production of that programme; you couldn't leave until the filming was done and sometimes this took forever. A simple shot would have to be taken five to ten times sometimes, and her hours were anything but normal.

When Jake surprised her with a ticket to Marbella she had nearly cried with delight.

'I've already called your work and arranged your time off,' he'd said, knowing that her first thought would be that she couldn't leave her job for five days.

'Oh Jake, you're so sweet!' she'd screamed, wrapping her arms round him and hugging him as though her life depended on it. He really was too, she thought, knowing that he'd have to go alone to a friend's wedding that they'd been invited to. He'd rather she was happy though, and knew that seeing her best friends for five days should do the trick. She couldn't wait to surprise Jade and Kelly; they would be so shocked when she turned up!

CHAPTER 8

Jade felt someone shaking her gently, and at first she thought she was dreaming.

'Rise and shine, sleepy head,' Kelly said softly, sitting on the edge of her bed.

Jade opened her eyes slightly and then closed them again, slowly waking up. 'What's the time?' she asked in a croaky voice.

'It's quarter to eleven.'

Quarter to eleven? That meant she'd been sleeping for over twelve hours, which showed how much she had needed a good sleep. Jade sat up on the bed and stretched her arms out. 'I had the best sleep ever,' she said, noticing Kelly had perfectly applied make-up. Was she ready to go out today already?

'Why have you got your face on? You stayed at Billy's didn't you?' Jade looked at Kelly's bed, which to be fair she wouldn't know if she'd slept in anyway, because they never made them.

Kelly grinned. 'Yes, I stayed at Billy's and didn't want him to see me without make-up on, so I woke up extra early and went to his bathroom to put some on.'

Jade laughed. 'Kelly that's ridiculous – you don't even need make-up! Plus, you've even got false eyelashes on!'

Kelly laughed at herself. 'I know. I didn't want him to see my real short little stubs for eyelashes, did I?'

'You're hilarious. If things get serious, you'll have to let him see the real you eventually.'

Kelly looked at the floor. 'I'm not so sure they'll get serious.' She added quickly, 'If they did, I'd always set a secret alarm to wake up and put my face on. And hopefully, if he does ever see me ugly and bare-faced, he'll already be in love with me by then and it won't matter.'

'You look lovely all the time, silly,' Jade told her. Why were most girls like that, herself included? You could never see the good things in yourself, but could easily see the great things about your friends. Kelly had beautiful features; huge blue eyes and lovely full, pink lips. With a tan she certainly didn't need any foundation on, like she had now. She still looked gorgeous, but definitely would look better without the make-up.

'I've got loads to tell you,' Kelly said, standing up with a naughty smirk.

'I bet you have,' Jade replied, her eyes sparkling.

'I'm going to have a shower, get ready and then let's go get a fry-up.'

'Sounds good, I'm starving.'

*

The girls sat in the shade at a restaurant overlooking the sea and ordered some English tea, which Jade felt was never the same as at home, a bottle of still water and two English breakfasts. A nice hearty meal was just what she needed after her mammoth sleep, though she doubted she'd eat much else that day after sunbathing around skinny model-like girls. She looked out at the beautiful view in front of her and reminded herself how lucky she was to be here, and not working in a dull job back in Essex. Marbella was

131

not just a playground for the rich and famous, but a stunning place to be. From the impressive marina filled with multi-million-pound yachts, to the amazing beach and rows of designer boutiques selling merchandise so expensive it sometimes didn't even have the price tags on.

Jade poured them both tea. 'Come on then,' she persuaded Kelly. 'Spill the beans. How was your night of passion with Billy?!'

'Mmm, it was okay,' Kelly said, uncertainly as she dropped a cube of white sugar in her cup.

Jade's eyes opened wide in surprise. 'What? Why only okay? Explain all missy, I want details.'

The waitress interrupted them as their breakfasts arrived.

Kelly began to butter her toast as she spoke. 'Well, we were both really nervous because we kind of knew that was the night, you know, and everything was going fine, but then . . .' Kelly hesitated.

'He couldn't get it up?' Jade guessed.

Kelly looked down at the table. 'Well no, not exactly . . . kind of . . .'

'You're not making sense,' Jade said, confused, her eyes glued to Kelly.

'I know, sorry. Okay, I'll tell you bluntly then. He had trouble getting it up at first because he was so nervous, and then when he did, I couldn't even tell . . . I was kind of hoping it wasn't.'

Jade stopped buttering her toast, her knife frozen in the air. 'What do you mean you couldn't tell?'

Kelly kneaded her eyes with her fists. 'Oh, I feel so bad saying this. But he has a really small willy!'

'Oh no,' Jade said, feeling bad for both Kelly and Billy. 'So did you do it or not?'

Kelly looked up with a troubled expression. 'Yes we did. But, it's really small. Like the smallest I've ever been with.'

'How small we talking?' Jade asked, intrigued. She looked

for something to compare it to and then took a huge bite out of her sausage and held it up on the fork. 'Like this?'

Kelly tried not to laugh. Then said seriously after examining it, 'Smaller.'

Jade took another bite, also now getting the giggles. 'This?'

'Smaller,' Kelly said shaking her head.

Jade gasped. She took another bite. 'Okay, well it can't be smaller than this because then there would be nothing left!'

They both burst into laughter and Kelly even spat out a bit of her water, making Jade laugh even harder.

'Stop making me laugh, Jade. It's not funny and I feel awful. Billy is such a nice bloke.'

Jade composed herself, shifted in her chair and said seriously, 'Okay, I'll stop. So, was it bad then?'

'Not so much bad. I suppose I was just a bit disappointed. I really wanted it to be perfect. Why is it I've met men in the past I've hardly even liked and had the best sex ever, and then I meet someone I really do and it's a bit crap?'

'Listen, you really like him. I'm sure it'll get better. It was your first time. Maybe he was a bit cold and it shrivelled a bit or something?' Jade suggested, trying to make her friend feel better and at the same time trying not to laugh again.

'Shrivelled?' Kelly retorted dubiously. 'Are you being serious? His room is hotter than ours!'

'Maybe he'd done drugs?' Jade was sure she'd read somewhere that drugs made a man's penis shrink.

Kelly rolled her eyes. 'Oh yeah, that sounds likely. He smuggled drugs over on the plane and smoked weed on the way to meet me, did he?'

Jade let out her laugh, knowing she was clutching at straws. She looked at Kelly, who was staring out at the sea in a world of her own. Surely this didn't matter *that* much to her? Jade couldn't exactly understand though, as she'd only ever slept with four people in her life and they all seemed to be roughly the same size, which she assumed must be average. 'You do still like Billy, don't you?'

'Yes, I do, but it has put me off a little bit. Think I've been seeing him too much too. Maybe I'll chill with him a bit.' She sipped her drink and exhaled sharply.

'Just because of his small willy?' Jade asked, surprised at the change in Kelly's attitude towards Billy. She felt sorry for him.

'Sex is important to me,' Kelly confided ruefully. 'If it's rubbish, what's the point?'

'He may get better, give him a chance! He may be good at other things?'

'I still think him and me should just chill a bit anyway. We're in Marbella for crying out loud, and we're single. I haven't even given any other men a chance since we've been here.'

'Fair enough. But don't get all upset if lovely Billy meets some other girl that loves him, warts and all.'

'Don't you mean "small dick and all"?' Kelly said with a wry grin, but Jade noticed the smile didn't quite reach her eyes. 'I won't. Now eat up and let's go to Ocean Club Champagne pool party. Everyone is going to be there.'

*

As they made their way to Ocean Club, Kelly knew she'd made the right decision. There was no point in getting attached to Billy any more than she already was and getting her heart broken. It had happened before and she was sure it would happen again, knowing her luck with blokes. She felt terrible telling Jade that made-up story; Billy would be so embarrassed if he knew. He wasn't exactly well-endowed, that much was true, but the sex hadn't been as bad as she made out. She'd just said it as she'd needed a justification to cool things off. They had both been incredibly nervous about their first time together, and she doubted Billy would be raving to Jonny any time soon about how fantastic she was either.

Here they were in Marbella, surrounded by gorgeous women literally everywhere you looked; it was pretty much inevitable that she was heading for a downfall if she got any more serious with him. How could she compete with all those hot girls – not just one night, but for the whole summer? At first she had pictured them seeing each other when they got home, but after thinking long and hard about it she'd worried about whether they'd actually make it that far. Kelly doubted Billy would be able to remain faithful and she couldn't stand the thought of watching him chat to other girls and getting jealous constantly, which she knew she would. And he *would* get girls paying him attention all the time, she mused; he was good looking, friendly and confident. Things would have been different if we'd met in Essex, Kelly thought, just not in Marbella. The best thing to do would be to cool things off; that way she wouldn't get hurt. She was protecting herself and also allowing him to get with other girls at the same time, which was most probably what he wanted to do.

Kelly hated herself for being this way and knew she would probably end up losing a really decent guy, but underneath her bubbly exterior was a frightened little girl, afraid of being let down. The reason she was like this wasn't just because she'd been through a bad break-up, Kelly realised glumly. It was also due to the fact that when she was just eight years old, her dad had left one day and never come back. Her mum had told her he'd had a break-down and moved to Scotland, as far away as possible it seemed, and she'd never heard a word from him since. As she grew older her mum told her the full story, and then

135

Kelly had felt even more abandoned and unwanted. The truth was, he hadn't had a breakdown – he'd had no reason to leave at all, but just packed his bags and walked away. He'd never even sent Kelly a birthday or Christmas card; her mum hadn't heard a word from him since the day he left. As a little girl, Kelly had always loved her dad and recalled nights snuggled up to him on the sofa while her mum made them tea, taking in his scent of cigarettes and Old Spice. How he could have gone and not even said goodbye she would never know. Her mum had been completely torn apart after he went, but she'd held it together for her, and for that Kelly would always be grateful. She was really glad her mum was happy now, especially since meeting Peter seven years ago. He now lived with Kelly and her mum and they all got on so well. Plus, it was a nice feeling to have a bloke about the house. A man like Peter would never have abandoned his family, Kelly thought proudly; he was decent, loyal and loved her mum to pieces, anyone could see that. She was so glad he was in their lives; that's what dads were supposed to be like. It may have worked out for her mum in the end, but Kelly realised it didn't change the fact that she was terrified of getting let down and hurt by men. She always put barriers in the way as soon as she started to like someone and she didn't know how to change. She thought it was easier to just have casual flings; at least that way you knew what you were getting. If she was falling for Billy hard she had no choice but to put a stop to it. Kelly recalled a saying she'd heard many times before, that it was better to have loved and lost than to never have loved at all; she couldn't disagree more.

*

The girls walked towards Ocean Club and were amazed to see how long the queue was. It was at least a twenty-minute wait to get in and it was boiling out in the bright sunshine; standing in a queue sweating their make-up off did not seem appealing to them at all.

'The size of that queue! Are you kidding me?' Jade said, hoping that they weren't going to have to join it.

'Shit,' Kelly said in a whiny voice, thinking the same thing. 'Let's just go over to the security men on the door and see if we can get in that way.'

Jade looked at the huge queue again. The other girls seemed even more dressed-up than ever today, with big, wavy hair and gorgeous summer dresses revealing their glitzy bikinis underneath. She was glad she'd worn one she customised just the day before. It was bright blue and she'd pinned a gorgeous crystal flower brooch in the middle of her bust and sewn a jewelled trim to the bottoms.

They walked over, trying to look confident; Jade standing a little way behind Kelly as she worked her charm.

'Hey,' Kelly said in the sexiest voice she could muster. She played with her long blonde hair seductively. 'We work in TIBU nightclub. Do we have to still queue? I think the manager of this place told us the other day we could get in for free and jump to the front?' she lied.

Jade sighed. They must hear crap like this from girls all day and she didn't feel particularly optimistic.

The men on the door nudged each other, eyeing Kelly up, with their mouths twisting trying not to laugh. Kelly looked at Jade with a confused expression. What was so funny? Okay, so they may have told a slight lie, but how were those men to know that? It wasn't *that* funny and they could have been best friends with the manager for all they knew. Unless . . . Oh shit, Jade thought, maybe one of them really does know the manager? The men were really beginning to laugh now – people were starting to look their way.

'No worries, sweetheart,' the taller one said. 'Come in. Just two of you, yes?'

'Yeah,' Kelly said confidently, strutting towards the entrance, as if she'd fully expected that to happen.

They were given wristbands and then walked straight through behind the taller bouncer, without paying the lady at the desk. This was amazing!

'Thanks,' Kelly said, blowing a kiss as the man waved goodbye.

'OMG! How did we just do that? Well done, Kelly!' Jade shook her head in disbelief.

Kelly was so ecstatic she practically danced on the spot. 'I don't know, babe. So good though! No queuing for us two!'

They were on cloud nine after what had just happened and Jade followed Kelly to the bar.

'Nice tit!' a random bloke shouted at Kelly as she walked past. Kelly looked down and gasped, turning round to Jade, whose mouth also fell wide open in shock. Kelly's right breast had completely come out of her one-piece swimsuit and low-cut dress.

'Fuck!' Kelly swore as she tried to cover herself up, her face getting pinker and pinker by the second. 'Fuckedy-fuck! My boob has been hanging out this whole time!'

They both burst into laughter.

'Maybe no one saw?' Jade said with a smirk.

Kelly turned to her with a disbelieving look. 'You *are* having me on? How could they not see my massive boob just sitting there?'

'At least we got in for free,' Jade said when she got her breath back from laughing. 'All thanks to your boob!'

Eventually the girls stopped giggling and started walking through the party, which was buzzing with people everywhere and music blaring out through giant speakers. They walked alongside the huge pool, looking for a place to sit. Jade spotted Sam on a huge bed with Steve and some others. She noticed, with a stab of envy, he was sitting beside the stunning brunette she'd seen him with lately. She had gorgeous long shiny hair, and was so slim it was sickening. She was wearing a sexy black one-piece swimsuit, which emphasised her dark tan and matched her oversized black sunglasses. The guys waved, and Jade wished they could go and sit with them. I'd hate to watch him flirt with that girl all day though, she told herself, so they carried on looking for somewhere to sit. They also spotted Adele on a bed with Lee and Sophie. Poor Lee clearly had no idea what Adele was really like, Jade thought, knowing how it felt to be made a fool. She looked at Adele's bright orange bikini, which was covered in multi-coloured gems and had something pinned on one of the straps at the top. Her mouth flew wide open when she realised what it was.

'Kel, you're not going to believe this.'

'What's that?'

'Take a look at Adele's bikini.'

Kelly peered over the top of her Ray-Bans and squinted, trying to see what Jade was talking about. 'She has the same sort of brooch that you picked up at the market,' Kelly said, wondering what the big deal was.

'Yes, the brooch we lost because we left it at the beach under the sunbed. Adele was the last one there, remember?'

Jade could see the light slowly dawning on Kelly's face as she finally caught on. She opened her mouth wide in outrage. 'I can't believe this! That cow stole our bags! I even asked her the other night if she'd seen them that day and she said no!'

Jade rolled her eyes, looking again at the brooch on Adele's bikini. 'I actually can't believe it. Not only did she steal our things, but she's even got the cheek to bloody wear them in front of us! That girl has more front than Southend!'

'Let's go over there.' Kelly looked like she was ready

for an argument; she pulled her shoulders back and her chest out, swinging her arms as she began to march over furiously.

'No, let's just leave it,' Jade said, grabbing her arm and pulling her back to stop her. 'Let's just pretend we don't care. She'll never confess anyway. She's so sad! Copying our idea after saying she was too good for the market! I can't stand her.'

'Me neither,' Kelly said, angrily, her eyes narrowing. 'What an absolute cow. Shit, there's Billy.'

Jade spotted him sitting with Jonny on the other side of the pool. Billy noticed the girls looking his way and he beamed a huge smile at them. Kelly gave a casual wave across the pool.

'Shall we go sit with them?' Jade suggested, hoping to spend some time with Jonny.

'No, not today,' Kelly said looking around. 'Let's meet some new people.'

Right on cue, a handsome muscly man with the most defined six-pack Jade had ever seen approached them and introduced himself, offering the girls a place to sit on his bed, which was full of men.

'Hey, I'm Jayden.' He smiled, revealing a perfect row of straight white teeth.

The girls sat with Jayden and his friends and couldn't believe their luck when they were handed glasses of champagne.

'Look at the size of those champagne bottles!' Jade said in amazement. They were so big and heavy she couldn't even lift one when she tried.

'People will spray those everywhere later on,' Kelly said knowledgeably. 'So I wouldn't worry too much what your hair looks like.'

This was something else. Spraying champagne? Jade had never heard of anything like it. It was madness.

'Jayden is hot,' Kelly whispered, eyeing up his body, luckily without him noticing.

Jade nodded in agreement. He was tall, with chocolate-coloured skin and eyes as black as coal. A very handsome guy, but still not as lovely as Sam. Jade cursed herself for thinking that. She needed to stop thinking about stupid Sam who clearly still had feelings for his prat of an ex, and who was also now loved-up with a supermodel by the looks of things.

The champagne went straight to Jade's head. So much so that before she knew it, she was standing on the bed dancing sexily and singing out loud. Kelly joined her and they giggled like schoolgirls as the champagne was constantly topped up by either Jayden or one of his friends. Jade saw Billy looking over and felt slightly sorry for him. Kelly hadn't even said hello to him yet and now here she was dancing on a bed full of men. She saw him walking over and nudged Kelly to warn her.

'You okay?' he said to both of them, his eyes glinting with excitement as he looked at Kelly.

They each kissed him on the cheek and said 'hi'.

'Yeah, we're having such a good time,' Kelly said, fiddling with her pretty beaded Chanel necklace, which matched the beading on her pink bikini perfectly.

'Come and sit with us.' Billy pointed to their sunbed over the other side.

'Ah thanks, babe, but we're okay here for now,' Kelly said, ignoring the hurt in his eyes.

'Okay,' Billy said, defeated. 'Well, shall I meet you later after work tonight?'

'Maybe,' Kelly replied coolly. 'Come see me in the bar when you finish and we'll see. I'm not sure what we're doing yet.'

'Okay.' He went to kiss her on the lips and she turned her head so he got her cheek instead, clearly not wanting Jayden to see. 'Well, I'll catch up with you later then.'

Jade had noticed the shock on his face and her heart went out to him. What was Kelly doing? Why was she being so mean? Of course it was her right to want to cool things down with Billy, but he at least deserved for her to sit down and talk it through with him.

'Come on hun, dance!' Kelly shouted, when LMFAO's *Party Rock* came on.

She would talk to her about Billy later, Jade told herself, but right now it was time to have fun.

*

Lisa unpacked her suitcase. She couldn't wait to get out there in the hot sunshine and surprise her friends. She'd felt extremely nervous on the plane; she hated flying and had never flown alone before. Thank God she got here safely, Lisa thought, a little annoyed with herself for being such a baby.

The hotel was lovely and she had a huge double bed, air conditioning and a large balcony. Maybe she'd ask the girls if they wanted to stay with her one night. Jade had said they didn't have air conditioning in their place; Lisa couldn't even imagine how they slept in this heat. .

She walked out onto her balcony and looked out on the pretty white buildings and the stunning turquoise ocean to her right. This was exactly what she needed. Work seemed like a million miles away now and there was no stress, no deadlines and definitely no waking up at six in the morning! They'd been working on a reality show over the past few weeks and Lisa had really been enjoying it. Dog owners had to teach their pets new tricks each week until there was a doggie winner. There was a gorgeous little chihuahua on the show called Pebbles who Lisa had fallen in love with. He reminded her of Lord McButterpants but was short-haired and a little bit bigger. She'd begged her parents to let her get a dog ever since she was a little girl, but her mum couldn't bear the thought of dog hair all over their carpets. Not that her mum even cleaned the carpets, or anywhere else for that matter; they had a cleaner called Maggie who took care of everything, apart from the cooking. Lisa loved her parents, but they were pretty strict, and she promised herself as soon as she moved out with Jake, which would be soon, she was buying a chihuahua. Jake was very keen to find the perfect place straight away, but as much as she wanted to move out, she wanted to do it in her own time and not feel rushed or pressured. They had already seen two flats, which Lisa hadn't been overly keen on. Jake had thought they were perfect, and didn't understand why she wanted a house when there was only the two of them; but Lisa felt a house was a better investment, even if it wasn't that big. All the house-hunting was a huge step and it was nice to have a break from it all.

She had bumped into Kelly's mum a few days ago in a beauty salon, and when Lisa had told her about her surprise trip, she'd said that the girls were going to be thrilled that she was there. Apparently Kelly had told her mum over the phone that they were both missing Lisa lots. She thought of how Kelly's mum had joined the girls a few times in the pub for drinks; she was such a young, fun mum and was more like Kelly's older sister at times. Kelly often moaned about how her mum had borrowed her tops or shoes and Lisa thought it was hilarious; *her* mum would never go near her wardrobe! Kelly told her mum everything too and always went shopping and on holiday with her. Lisa envied their relationship; her mum was a serious, closed-off person, and Lisa didn't exactly feel like she could confide in her beyond a certain point. Both her parents were workaholics, and had been partners at a London law firm where they had met. They'd always had a good work ethic and had been horrified at first when Lisa told them she didn't want to go to university. She hadn't liked the idea of not earning any money for three more years, and getting into huge amounts of debt with a student loan. Lisa wanted to work so she could be independent, without having to worry. She had always been a hard worker and she genuinely believed she could go far in her career without a degree. As soon as she got her job her parents were happy; providing she was earning money, she was doing her bit as far as they were concerned. Lisa knew she was lucky; her family were very wealthy and as an only child she could have anything she asked for. But she never really wanted anything, not unless she'd paid for it herself. There was nothing like the satisfaction of wearing a gorgeous dress or having the latest phone and knowing that you'd bought it for yourself. Kelly was always calling her mad, openly admitting she would have made her dad buy her a car by now if she were in her shoes.

Lisa put her plain red River Island bikini on and brushed her long dark hair, anticipating the moment when she'd see the girls' faces when she surprised them at Ocean Club. She was up for nothing but chilling out and having fun for the next five days. Home felt like a million miles away and she was glad. This was going to be a holiday to remember, she could just feel it in her bones.

CHAPTER 9

Jade and Kelly were having the time of their lives. They were so drunk that they were completely oblivious to the fact they had to be at work at nine that evening, and were dancing their hearts out near the pool when Adele approached them.

'Alright girls?'

'Fine,' Kelly slurred, pushing her hair back off her brow. 'Nice bikini you have on.'

'Thanks,' Adele smiled, not looking one tiny bit guilty or remorseful.

Jade was so angry she was almost shaking. How did Adele have the cheek to stand there talking to them after having stolen their things?

'That's the same brooch as the one Jade bought from the market the other day,' Kelly said accusingly. The alcohol had definitely made her more confrontational. Jade didn't care though. She wanted Adele to know they were on to her.

'Really? I bought this from a little shop near where I'm staying,' Adele replied casually, feeling it with her fingers as she spoke.

'How convenient,' Jade retorted, the words escaping her

145

lips without her being able to control them. She began to breathe harder and harder.

'What do you mean?' Adele frowned.

'So you *didn't* steal our bags from under the sunbed that day then, no? You were the last one there and it's funny how you now have loads of coloured gems and crystals on your bikini, just like the stuff we bought. Not to mention that brooch.' Kelly was furious, spilling champagne from her glass as she spoke.

Adele was affronted. 'How could you even suggest I'd do something like that? You really think *I* need to steal? Besides, I wouldn't touch all that cheap crap you bought with a bargepole,' she spat haughtily.

Kelly threw the remainder of her champagne straight into Adele's face, leaving her soaking wet and gasping in shock.

'Now *you* look like cheap crap!' she laughed, putting her hand to her mouth.

Jade was astonished and couldn't believe what she was seeing. She grabbed Kelly's arm and pulled her away. 'Come on, we don't want to get into a fight. We've done enough.'

She looked back and saw Adele rubbing her face, her make-up smearing everywhere. *Wow, she looks a mess*, Jade thought as they headed back to Jayden's sunbed. *Still, what's on the outside now matches what's inside.*

'I'm not being funny though, how could she just stand there and lie to our faces! And Jade, we do *not* wear cheap crap and I won't let anyone say that about us.' Kelly's face was glowing with outrage and her eyes flashed with anger.

Jade laughed, holding her glass out as it was filled with more champagne by Jayden. 'I can't believe you just did that! I agree, she needs to know we're not two idiots she can walk all over. How she had the audacity to talk to us like that, I'll never know.'

146

'Babe, I don't know what audacity means. Stop using big words, clever clogs,' Kelly replied with a slight slur.

Jade laughed and began to move her hips to the beat of the music. 'Come on, let's dance again! I love this song. Forget about Adele, the nasty cow!'

Moments later, Jade felt her bag vibrating on the bed where they were dancing and pulled out her phone, surprised to see Lisa's caller ID again.

'Hello?'

'Hi. Where are you?' Lisa asked.

'At Ocean Club pool party. Why?'

'Come to the entrance,' she said happily.

'What? Shut up, don't tell me you're here!' Jade said, practically squealing in excitement.

'Just come outside,' Lisa said calmly, though Jade could hear that she was smiling as she said it.

Jade grabbed Kelly's arm and dragged her outside. She followed, not having a clue what was going on, especially in her drunken daze. 'Trust me, just come with me,' Jade said, almost jogging in her heels. They reached the entrance and there she was. Dressed in denim hot pants that revealed her killer long legs and a pretty vest, Lisa didn't look at all out of place.

'Lisa!' Jade and Kelly yelled in unison. They literally jumped on her in excitement and the three girls laughed happily.

'I thought you said you couldn't come?' Jade asked, her voice high-pitched with joy.

'I was lying! Jake is so sweet. He knew how much I was missing you so he booked and paid for a flight and hotel so I could come.'

'Ah, I love Jake,' Kelly slurred, hugging Lisa once more.

'He's so nice! I'm so glad you're here, I can't believe it!' Jade said, stunned that her other best friend was standing in front of her.

147

'Me either,' Kelly said. 'Where are you staying?'

Lisa pointed in the direction of her hotel. 'Park Plaza Suites. Hotel is gorgeous, you should stay in my room one night.'

'Yes please. Our room is an oven. We've decided that the plus side is that we may lose weight, due to the fact we sweat buckets every night,' Jade said. She took Lisa's hand. 'Come on in, it's so much fun.'

'Looks it. Kelly, you sound smashed already. You do realise it's only two o'clock?'

'Babe, it's cool,' Kelly giggled, her long fake lashes fluttering. 'Come and party with us. We're on a bed of really hot boys. I want either Jayden, Lewis or another one, but I can't remember his name. You can have any of the others.' She hiccupped.

'Did you forget about my Jake?' Lisa giggled, raising one eyebrow.

'Shit,' Kelly thought for a second, as if seeing things clearly all of a sudden. 'I *did* forget about Jake.'

They laughed and then Lisa asked how she was going to get in and whether she had to pay.

Knowing it was expensive and trying to save her friend money, Kelly just walked over to the security guard, smiled and pulled her right boob out again, while Lisa just stared in astonishment.

'What the hell is wrong with Kelly?' Lisa whispered to Jade.

'The champagne has just gone straight to her head!' Jade snorted, raising her arms in the air and dancing to Rihanna's *S & M*, which had just started.

They made their way back to Jayden's sunbed and introduced Lisa to everyone. Like Jade, Lisa had also only ever been to Greece before for a girls' holiday, and Jade could tell by the look on her face she was just as surprised at the difference in Marbella as she herself had been.

'Oh my God, look at all the champagne!' Lisa smiled in delight, stripping down to her red bikini, revealing her toned stomach and long legs. It was nice, but Jade could tell she was also a little gutted she hadn't known about the 'dressy' swimwear that everyone else was wearing round the pool. Though she'd briefly explained it over text messages, judging by her stunned expression, Lisa hadn't quite realised how glitzy the bikinis in Marbella really were.

'Where did you get that bikini from?' she asked Jade enviously, as her eyes flicked from her plain bikini to Jade's pretty sparkling one.

'I made it. Just added this brooch and the crystals. Me and Kelly went to the market and bought them. There is a boutique that sells really nice pieces here, but it's so expensive. I only had flipping Primark swimwear when I got here and Kelly had all this glamorous stuff, so I decided we should make our own. We've made some for a few groups of girls that said they liked them too.'

'Well done, hun. They look so gorgeous! What a good idea.'

'I'll do some of yours if you like? Doesn't even take long.'

'Oh would you?' Lisa replied gratefully. 'Thanks Jade, that's so lovely of you.'

It didn't take long for Lisa to get as merry as they were. Well, as merry as Jade anyway, as Kelly was completely falling-down drunk. All of a sudden it was time to spray the champagne everywhere, and champagne bottles were being lifted, girls screamed, trying to run for cover and boys dived right under the liquid, even managing to drink some in the process.

'How the hell can they waste all this?' Lisa said, slightly shocked that people were just throwing expensive champagne away.

'Hun, chill out, it's what they do here,' Kelly said, laughing. 'It's not called a champagne spray party for nothing!'

Jade smiled at her frugal friend. 'Just enjoy it,' she said, as Lisa downed her newly refilled glass of champagne and joined in the fun. They shrieked as Jayden sprayed a bottle directly at them, and Jade thought it was best to just run and jump in the pool where it was safe. Lisa followed, and they laughed again as they watched Kelly try to dodge the champagne sprays from all directions.

'Just get in the pool!' Lisa shouted to Kelly.

'No way,' Kelly said seriously, ducking down and squealing when a drop of champagne hit her arm. 'My hair will get messed up even more!'

It was a funny sight to see and eventually Kelly admitted defeat and climbed down into the pool, desperately trying not to get her hair wet. Billy, who was watching her from afar, jumped in next to her.

'Hi Billy,' Jade said swimming towards Kelly and Lisa.

'Hi, you alright? Is she drunk or what?' he said, nodding at Kelly, who giggled.

'I'm not that bad, why does everyone keep saying that?' Kelly asked defensively as she lost her balance walking in the pool, her head almost dunking under the water.

Jade, Lisa and Billy looked at one another, desperately trying to keep straight faces, and Jade quickly changed the subject. 'This is our friend Lisa by the way; she came out and surprised us today.'

'Hi,' Billy said, nodding in her direction. 'You working out here too?'

'I wish,' Lisa said wistfully, leaning back on the edge of the pool. 'But my boyfriend would kill me.'

Billy turned to talk to Kelly, so Jade thought it was a good time to speak to Jonny and introduce him to Lisa. He was lying on a sunbed, also soaked in champagne. She introduced them, and when Lisa turned her head Jonny winked at Jade, as if to say Lisa was a bit of all right.

'Already taken,' Jade mouthed back with a stab of envy,

secretly pleased Lisa wasn't single so he couldn't flirt with her. *Why am I thinking like this?* Jade asked herself, confused about her feelings.

'What's wrong with Kelly?' Jonny asked. 'Billy reckons she's been a bit weird since their rendezvous last night.'

Not wanting to get involved or say the wrong thing, Jade acted dumb. 'Really? She hasn't said anything to me.'

'Good, because old Billy boy is definitely in love. Never heard him go on about a girl so much. Kelly this, Kelly that, drives me up the wall,' he joked.

The three of them spoke for a while and Jonny asked Lisa lots of questions, getting to know her. She told him all about her job and Jake and how he'd spoken about them getting married, right before she left for Marbella.

'What?' Jade said, surprised, her eyes opening wider. 'So he asked you to marry him?'

'No,' Lisa said, smiling, her eyes downcast, suddenly coming over all shy. 'He hasn't actually proposed yet, but I do think he will soon. He mentioned that he wants to get married next summer perhaps.'

Jade was incredulous. 'Oh my God, Lisa! Why didn't you say?'

'I was going to,' Lisa grinned. 'This is the first chance I've had. Do you think it's too soon?'

'No! I think do what you feel is right. I'm *so* excited for you!' Jade hugged her friend hard and Lisa clasped her back.

'Don't you think you're both a bit young still?' Jonny asked with a concerned expression, much to Jade's annoyance.

Jade took a step backwards, looking exasperated. 'Jonny, don't say that. You've only just met her and you have no idea how in love they are.'

He shrugged innocuously. 'I don't mean to offend you, I'm just saying, that's all. What's the rush?'

'I see what you mean,' Lisa said. 'I know I'm only twenty-one, well, I'll be twenty-two by the time we get married and he'll be twenty-three, but a part of me thinks age doesn't matter if you're happy and want to commit to each other. You're saying "why rush?" and I think "why wait?"'

'Exactly,' Jade said, looking at Jonny triumphantly, her chin held high. 'And I think you'll be together forever and live happily ever after.'

Billy returned without Kelly, who had gone back to the other sunbed with Jayden.

'Wow, she is seriously hammered,' he said, shaking his head, clearly not very happy.

'You okay mate?' Jonny asked him, looking worried for his friend.

'Yeah, I'm fine,' Billy said half-heartedly.

Jade guessed Kelly had kept up her blasé façade; poor Billy. She looked over and saw her dancing with Jayden and laughing, flicking her hair from side to side, almost slipping over at one point. What on earth was wrong with her today? She knew that deep down Kelly really liked Billy and would be an idiot to ruin things with him. Kelly was just worried she was going to get hurt as usual, like she always did with every guy. Billy was a nice boy, and was completely smitten with her. There is no way Jade could ever see him even looking at another girl while he was with Kelly, but she was being completely unfair and humiliating him after they spent the night together. She saw Kelly kiss Jayden and cringed, hoping Billy wasn't looking.

'I'm going. You coming mate?' Billy announced sharply as he stood up, collecting his bag and getting ready to leave. He'd obviously seen what Kelly was doing and he looked really upset and angry.

Jonny rolled his eyes as he also spotted what was going on, got up and put his t-shirt on too. 'Yeah mate, I'm coming.' He leaned closer to Jade, muttering under his breath, 'Seriously, have a word with Kelly about this. She shouldn't be messing him about.'

Jade nodded in agreement as she gaped over at Kelly who was now being spun round in circles, Jayden holding her arms.

'Bye, girls,' Billy said heavily as he walked off.

Jade and Lisa watched Kelly and were both thinking the same thing; she needed some sleep. She was far too drunk to be out still and had now got to the point where she could hardly stand, with Jayden supporting her in between kisses.

'Come on, let's get her back. She'll feel terrible about Billy in the morning when we tell her what she's done,' Jade said, sobering up almost instantly because she knew she needed to be in control and help Kelly.

Lisa paused while thinking. 'Shit, did you say she's working tonight too?'

'Yeah, don't remind me,' Jade replied as they walked over to Kelly and Jayden.

Jayden started to pour them more drinks as they reached the sunbed.

'Thanks a lot, that's really kind of you, but we're leaving now,' Jade said, gratefully.

'What? You're not going anywhere,' he said, turning Kelly, his arms locked round her waist and kissing her again.

'I'm afraid she is,' Lisa said, pulling Kelly towards them. 'Come on, hun. We're going to get something to eat.'

'Do I have to go?' Kelly garbled. Her eyes were a bit red, one fake eyelash strip was wonky: she looked completely wasted. Then she started to laugh really loudly and Jade thought she'd gone crazy. 'My boob came out earlier didn't it?'

'Yes Kelly, it did. Now come on, we're going.'

Kelly was still laughing like a lunatic as they helped her walk. Holding an arm each, Lisa and Jade waved goodbye to Jayden, but he'd already moved on to another girl and didn't look in the slightest bit bothered that Kelly was leaving.

The girls decided to take her straight back to the apartment and put her to sleep. It would have been impossible to try and get her to eat something when she was this paralytic, and besides, it would have been too embarrassing, walking into any restaurant with a crazy-looking drunk on their arm. They were almost back at the apartment when Kelly staggered to a stop and threw up at the side of the road. Her friends rubbed her back and held her hair, like any best friend would, but both were silently glad they weren't in that state tonight. The girls slowly walked together into the apartment and helped Kelly into bed, but in a second she had bolted to the toilet to be sick again. Eventually she shuffled back from the toilet and climbed straight into bed sleepily.

'We should go and get a pizza for when she wakes up,' Jade suggested.

'Good idea. I quite fancy a pizza myself,' Lisa agreed as she tied her hair back in a ponytail and sprayed it with hair spray. 'We'll be back soon, Kelly,' she said, leaving a bottle of water by the side of the bed.

*

Billy was fuming as he marched back to his apartment with Jonny. Did Kelly seriously just do that in front of him? He'd have been less shocked if someone threw a bucket of ice-cold water over his head. She'd made him look and feel so stupid; he was completely humiliated, and in front of all his friends as well. Why was she acting so differently today? Things had been great the night before and she'd left his apartment in the morning on a really good note, even kissing him goodbye. He was so confused; women were impossible to understand.

The moment he'd walked over to her in Ocean Club he knew she was acting a bit cold towards him, brushing him off like an annoying nuisance. What the hell was her problem? Nothing made any sense. He thought back to the night before when she'd come over to his place. He'd missed her so much when he was back home and he really felt that she'd missed him too. Surely she wasn't faking that she liked him – surely she'd meant all the things she'd said to him? He knew deep down that she did like him, he could feel it, and just knew it wasn't in his imagination. There was a connection; a spark between them that was clear for anyone to see. Billy was really starting to fall for Kelly. He thought about her constantly and couldn't get her out of his head. He was even going to ask if she wanted to officially be his girlfriend, because he couldn't imagine being interested in any other girl now. Plus, the thought of her with someone else made him feel sick, and he'd never been that serious with anyone before. Yes, he'd had girlfriends but never wanted to commit seriously, because he'd never felt like any one of them had been right for him. But he had really felt like he wanted to be with Kelly and make a go of things. Then she'd got so drunk today, treated him like an idiot and snogged some sleazeball, right in front of his face. Didn't she care? What had changed between them? Where was the lovely girl he'd been with last night?

When they'd slept together the earth hadn't exactly moved, but it was only their first time together. He'd been really nervous; he knew it was because he genuinely liked Kelly and actually cared what she thought about him. He'd had his fair share of one-night stands in the past where he couldn't have cared less how he performed, but Kelly was different. He'd wanted to impress her. He'd loved cuddling up to her and falling asleep in her arms; this morning he'd wished he could wake up to her face every day. Never would he have guessed she would have carried on like she did at the Ocean Club this afternoon. He knew she'd been drunk, but in his eyes she knew exactly what she was doing. What on earth had he done wrong? Billy was so angry with her, but also at himself, for caring so much. He was a proud man and wouldn't let her do this to him again; if she thought for one minute he was going to give her a single second of his time, she was mistaken. What he had witnessed today wasn't the Kelly he thought he knew, so maybe he hadn't really known her at all. He was completely gutted, but vowed that when she sobered up and realised she'd made a mistake it would be tough luck. Maybe it was her age? She was a fair bit younger than him and most likely didn't want anything serious, he realised. Billy could just try and make himself feel better by going out and sleeping with random strangers, but deep down he didn't want that – he'd grown out of it. At twenty-eight years old he was definitely past running the risk of taking a few STDs home as souvenirs. He wanted a girlfriend and he wanted to settle down. Marbella was probably the worst place to come for that, he realised now, but maybe Kelly should have a taste of her own medicine and see that there were other girls out there that liked him too.

'You okay mate?' Jonny asked, when they were back in their apartment.

'Yeah,' Billy lied. He'd never been one for talking much about his feelings and always kept everything inside.

'Fuck it, plenty more fish in the sea,' Jonny assured him with a clap on the back.

'You're right,' Billy answered with a forced smile. 'Plenty more fish.'

*

Jade and Lisa found a nice Italian restaurant called Luna Rosa which had pizza on the menu. It was only five o'clock so Jade could relax, as she had ages to get ready for work.

'Do you think Kelly will be okay to go to work later?' Jade asked, worried for her friend.

'To be honest, probably not,' Lisa said, biting her lip. 'I don't feel a hundred per cent myself and I didn't have nearly as much champagne as she did. Not going to stop me partying tonight though.' She sipped her Coke that the waitress had just brought. 'Speaking of tonight, what on earth am I going to do when you're working?'

'Don't worry, you'll be fine,' Jade said confidently. 'We'll just sit you on one of our tables or at the bar and give you free drinks all night. I don't think Jonny is working tonight, actually, so I'll text him and you can sit together.'

'Sounds like a plan.' Lisa's face brightened as she reached for a piece of bread in the basket on the table.

'So,' Jade tore open her roll and smeared butter on it, 'tell me more about what Jake said then, wifey, seeing as we're alone now.'

Lisa smiled. 'He dropped me at the airport this morning, bless him, and we were talking in the car about a wedding we're going to next month, it's one of his friend's.'

'Yeah . . . ?' probed Jade.

Lisa looked in the distance, remembering the conversation. 'Well I was saying I hoped the weather was going to be nice, because it's been nothing but raining in England for the last week, and then I just said that you can never guarantee the weather, even in August.'

'I know, English weather is always crappy.' Jade rolled her eyes.

'That's what *he* said. Then he said he'd like to get married to me next year, somewhere abroad so we'd definitely know it would be warm. I didn't know what to say, so I just said that I'd like that too.'

'So it was kind of like a proposal but not a proper one. That means he'll propose soon!' Jade smiled widely and gave a little laugh.

'Maybe, but I'm trying not to overthink it, babe. Honestly, I know loads of people will say we're too young, but we're happy and I just love him to bits. I can't imagine there is anyone out there I'd want to spend the rest of my life with more than him.' Lisa stared into space and then quickly added, 'I mean, sure, sometimes I wonder whether I should wait a few more years and I suppose I get days when I'm a bit uncertain, but everyone gets days like that though, don't they?'

'Yeah, I'm sure they do,' Jade nodded, chewing a mouthful of bread. 'Ahhh, that's so sweet. I'm so happy for you.' Jade felt a warm, sentimental feeling in her chest. Here was proof that some relationships were built to last. Usually Lisa played down her feelings when they teased her, but it had always been plain to see that she was totally and utterly in love with Jake. She'd fallen for him at sixteen and he was the first and only boy she'd ever slept with. Lisa and Jake rarely argued about anything; they were what Jade would describe as the 'perfect couple'. How exciting if they got married next year! Jade and Kelly could help Lisa plan everything for the wedding! They could go shopping for a beautiful dress and an amazing cake and of course, some hot bridesmaids dresses . . .

'So,' Lisa interrupted her thoughts, 'tell me what's been happening here.'

They chatted as they ate their starters, Jade talking her friend through all the ups and downs of the holiday so far. Lisa said she'd already had enough of Adele, without even having to meet her.

'She sounds like a complete cow,' she said, disgusted, as she pierced a garlic prawn with her fork.

'You're dead right,' Jade had agreed, wolfing down her mozzarella, tomato and pesto salad.

She'd told Lisa all about Kelly and Billy's short history and Lisa agreed that Kelly had been mean, kissing Jayden right in front of Billy. Their pizzas arrived and were completely delicious, so they ate them in no time, and then ordered one to take away for Kelly.

The girls stopped in Astralbar on the way back for a few cocktails, seeing as the sun was still shining and it seemed a shame to waste it by sitting inside a baking hot apartment. Plus, Lisa was only staying for five days so Jade wanted her to make the most of it and really enjoy herself.

Kelly was fast asleep, curled up in a foetal position, when the girls made their way back an hour or so later.

'Should we wake her?' Jade asked Lisa, biting her lip with an uncertain expression.

Lisa glanced down at her watch. 'Yeah, probably. It's seven thirty so she has plenty of time before she has to be ready for work. She can eat her pizza; hopefully that will help.'

Jade shook Kelly, very gently. 'Kel, wake up.'

Kelly stirred, groaning. She sat up, and the girls had to hold back their laughter when they saw her normally immaculate hair, which was now sticking out like a bird's nest on one side and was stuck to her face with sweat on the other.

'You okay, hun?' Lisa asked, biting back a laugh and struggling to keep her voice under control.

Kelly shook her head and then suddenly jumped up, dashing to the bathroom. 'I'm going to be sick again.'

Jade and Lisa walked out onto the tiny balcony and shut the doors so they couldn't hear their friend retching – it would have made them feel just as sick, and there definitely wasn't room for three women being sick in that little bathroom. Jade knew there was no way Kelly would even be leaving their place, let alone going to work. As she thought about how she could cover for Kelly with their manager, she grabbed her mobile and sent a message to Jonny.

159

*Hi, Lisa will be on her own tonight. You're not
working are you? Come to TIBU and sit with her –
free drinks!*

Her phone beeped almost instantly.

*No worries. Will meet her there at ten. JD and
Cokes all night for me please ;)*

Lisa headed back to her hotel so Jade could get ready for
work. Jade looked at Kelly sympathetically – she was snoring
quietly, in a deep sleep. She'd be sorry for how she treated
Billy when she woke up, Jade knew. She thought back to
the first time she had met Kelly at primary school. They
had been put in the same class when they were about seven,
and Jade had been delighted to see Kelly's name card next
to hers on their school desk, which meant they were sitting
next to one another. Something she couldn't explain told
her they would become best friends, and she'd been right.
They'd been inseparable growing up, and had done everything together. If ever Jade got into mischief, Kelly was
always beside her, usually the ringleader. Then they'd met
Lisa in secondary school and she'd become the natural third
member of their gang. Jade had met lots of new friends at
university, but no one had compared to her two best friends
at home in Essex; they had a bond which she believed
would last forever. It didn't matter how long they went
without seeing one another, their friendship always managed
to pick up from where they'd left off, feeling like they'd
never even been apart. People always commented that one
of them *must* feel left out sometimes, after all, three was
supposed to be a crowd, but Jade could honestly say that
it wasn't like that; their friendship was strong and honest.

Jade straightened her hair in the full-length mirror and
studied herself critically. She actually looked quite good,

she thought happily. She had a healthy, golden tan, her hair had been highlighted naturally by the sun and her nails were painted just the right shade of pink. Jade had put on a bit of weight since being in Marbella; the big nights out and fried breakfasts had caught up with her, but on the plus side, her boobs seemed a bit bigger, she thought cheekily.

'I'm off now, Kelly,' she whispered softly. 'Don't worry, I'll tell Joe that you're ill.'

Kelly stirred. 'Okay, thanks,' she croaked, half asleep.

*

It didn't feel the same being at work without Kelly, and for some reason Adele obviously thought it would be a good time to try to speak to Jade, much to her annoyance. She'd rather have talked to anyone rather than Adele. Who knows what kind of conniving she'd get up to tonight? After pretending to be more engrossed with organising the night-club, Jade's luck ran out when she bumped into Adele in the toilet. Jade wondered what she was going to say about the antics at the pool party.

Adele was standing at the mirror applying lip gloss, pouting at her reflection and then running her fingers through her long dark hair, trying to give it volume. In the harsh artificial light, Jade could easily tell Adele's hair was mostly extensions, and clearly not the good quality ones either. It was amazing how convincing they looked from a distance, but up close they looked like plastic Barbie hair.

'Alright, hun?' Adele asked in her rough Essex accent.

'Yes, good thanks,' Jade said as she washed her hands, surprised Adele was even talking to her after what Kelly had done that day.

Adele stared at her. 'Where's Kelly tonight?'

'I was just telling Joe actually; she's not well. She's been

161

sick all afternoon. Think it was something she ate,' Jade lied confidently as she put some MAC lipstick on.

'So it wasn't the champagne then?' Adele asked brusquely with a smirk, shooting Jade a doubtful look. She paused for a moment and then took a deep breath. 'I can't believe she threw that drink in my face because she thought I'd stolen your things. I was fuming, but I knew she was drunk so I let her off. I know she didn't mean it, really. Babe, I swear to God I never had anything to do with it and I would *never* steal from you two. Like I said, I bought that brooch in a little shop. I doubt it's the only one in Marbs! The crystals were already on my bikini too.'

'Just forget it,' Jade replied stonily, not believing a word that came out of her mouth. 'Kelly was drunk and she went a step too far. The reason she's not here isn't because of the champagne either. She ate a dodgy prawn salad for lunch and was sick after that.' Jade knew that if Adele doubted her story, she'd probably 'accidentally' let it slip to Joe that she thought it was a lie. Joe was certain to be annoyed by Kelly missing work due to a hangover.

'Good, I knew you'd understand. Let's be friends again, yeah? How are things anyway?' Adele asked. 'I haven't seen much of you and Kelly lately.'

That's because we don't like you, Jade thought, but instead she said simply, 'Well we've been going out all the time, just obviously not to the same places as you.'

Adele added yet more lip gloss. 'I'm thinking of getting my lips done,' she said, again pouting at her reflection in the mirror.

'You really don't need to,' Jade answered honestly, not a fan of the Essex 'trout pout', which was becoming more and more popular for some unknown reason.

'Mmm . . . I'm not so sure.' She turned and posed in the mirror as though she was on a photoshoot. 'Lee said he loves my lips as they are. I still want them done though.'

Adele was exceptionally vain and the more Jade got to know her, the more she disliked her. She reminded her of one of those mean girls at school that everyone sucked up to; the kind of girl you'd be very wary of because you knew she'd be nice to your face, but not behind your back. Well school was a long time ago now, and Jade couldn't even be bothered to make the slightest bit of effort with a girl she knew wasn't nice deep down inside.

'See you later,' Jade said casually, as she dried her hands and walked out.

Adele was too caught up in her appearance to even notice she'd left.

Jonny showed up with a few friends at ten that night, as promised. The place was empty as people tended to get there a bit later, after hitting the bars first. He would make someone a good boyfriend, Jade thought; very reliable.

'Alright gorgeous?' Jonny winked cheekily.

She smiled at him. He was dressed smartly, wearing an expensive-looking tight-fitted navy shirt, which showed off his athletic body to perfection, and a tight pair of dark jeans with a Hermès belt. 'You scrub up well,' she said.

'Thanks babe. You look lovely too, as always. No Lisa yet?'

'Not yet, she should be here soon though.'

'Well she *is* an Essex girl. I believe they take longer than most to get ready,' he joked.

'Oi you,' Jade laughed, playfully punching his arm. 'JD and Cokes?' she asked them as they sat at the bar.

'Yes please,' they chorused.

'Coming up.' Jade walked away to get their drinks and saw Lisa coming up the stairs, looking drop-dead gorgeous as usual in a little black All Saints dress.

'Hi.' Lisa kissed her on the cheek.

'Hi, how you feeling?' Jade asked. She wasn't feeling that

great herself after all the champagne and hot sun at the pool party.

'I'm actually fine, surprisingly. Ready for more,' she said, her eyes twinkling.

'Then more is what you shall get,' Jade grinned. 'Jonny is over there with some of his mates.' She pointed over at the bar and Lisa walked off to join them. Jade watched them laughing, wishing she could be in Lisa's shoes at that moment without a care in the world. She noticed Jonny gently lean forward, touching Lisa's arm as he spoke, unable to keep his eyes off her, and Jade turned away, wondering why she felt a wave of disappointment. As she watched Lisa throw her head back and laugh at something Jonny had said, while he gazed at Lisa with lustful eyes, Jade froze to the spot. She realised immediately that it was because never once before had Jonny looked at her like that. It dawned on her at that moment that she was jealous.

CHAPTER 10

Jonny had had to stop himself from falling off his chair when he'd seen Lisa approaching the girls in Ocean Club earlier that day. She was exactly his type; tall, slim and dark, she reminded him of his favourite actress, Penelope Cruz. She was the most naturally beautiful girl he'd seen in a long time; shame she had a boyfriend. He wondered if Lisa ever had a wandering eye , and then cursed himself; stealing other people's girlfriends was not his style, no matter how gorgeous the woman was. He hadn't come away to work in Marbella to meet the girl of his dreams anyway – he'd come to have a good time and meet as many women as possible. He might be twenty-seven with a mum that constantly went on about how she wanted grandchildren, but he didn't want that for himself yet, no way. A couple of his mates had already got roped into getting married and one even had two kids; he hardly ever saw those guys any more. Why did people want to rush into marriage and settling down? Marriage was a piece of paper in his eyes, and a very expensive one too.

Jonny thought about how upset Billy was. After they'd got back from the party he'd been quiet for the rest of the day, and then said he wasn't going out after work and was just going to get some sleep. That was unheard of. Billy was usually the troublemaker on a night out, the one who never let anyone go home before dawn. Jonny had offered to stay with him, but Billy was adamant that he wanted to be alone. It was a shame that Kelly had gone off the rails today; normally she had seemed like a really genuine girl. A bit ditzy, but she *was* blonde and from Essex, so it maybe came with the territory. Billy had a soft spot for blonde girls and always had, especially curvy ones like Kelly. The minute they'd met Jade and Kelly, Jonny knew Billy would be all over Kelly like a rash. But he also knew Billy was an extremely stubborn bloke, and since Kelly had bruised his ego it wouldn't be forgotten about anytime soon. Billy had confessed how much he liked her just before they went to Ocean Club, so now Jonny felt even worse for him, after his public humiliation. They were best mates and went back years and it was hard to see all the anger, embarrassment and hurt in Billy's eyes. Oh well, he'd meet someone else to take his mind off it, Jonny was sure; he always did.

'We're going to have fun tonight,' Jonny said with a smile, glancing at Lisa's sexy long legs, which she crossed over elegantly.

Lisa smiled back and pushed her long dark hair away from her face. 'I hope so. That's what holidays are all about, and seeing as I'm out with you tonight, you need to make sure I'm enjoying myself at all times, otherwise there will be trouble.'

Jonny raised his eyebrow. 'Is that so?'

'It most certainly is.' Lisa tried to keep a straight face, but laughed. Jonny couldn't keep his eyes off her.

Jade approached them with their drinks and they thanked her. Jade was a lovely girl, Jonny thought, really down to earth and genuine. He clinked glasses with Lisa. 'Cheers. Here's to making this the best night of your holiday.'

'Cheers,' she replied, as she took a huge gulp of her drink.

*

It wasn't fun working that night as not only was Kelly not there to chat to, but all Jade wanted to do was join Lisa and Jonny for a drink. She felt tired and sluggish due to the champagne she'd been downing earlier and even though she was planning to go out after work, she was looking forward to climbing into her bed later on. Every time she walked past Lisa and Jonny they were laughing, clearly getting more and more drunk on the free booze she was supplying. It was a warm night, with hardly any breeze, and Jade felt irritated and sweaty. Even inside the air-conditioned club she couldn't cool down. She tried her best to be cheery with the men who were paying a fortune for bottles of drink on her tables, but her heart wasn't in it and she wasn't in the best of moods; seeing Sam and the ridiculously stunning brunette again wasn't helping either. The girl literally just perched at the bar all night, talking to Sam whenever he had a spare moment, and Jade was convinced she must be obsessed with him. It seemed that every time she looked over they were engrossed in a conversation, completely absorbed in one another. They made a very attractive couple, she thought resentfully.

When she served last orders to Jonny and Lisa, she noticed Jonny's friends had left, which meant Jonny and Lisa were waiting for her to finish work to go out. Jade couldn't wait for work to be over; it had been a long day.

'We need to clean up now, you two,' she told them as she collected their empty glasses. The club had completely emptied out and Jonny and Lisa were two of the last few people remaining.

'We'll wait for you in Black and White bar,' Jonny said, swaying on his feet a little.

Lisa and Jonny both looked almost as drunk as Kelly had been earlier. What the hell was wrong with everyone today? Perhaps she'd been a bit too generous with those free drinks.

Despite Jade's glum mood, the tips were great that night and Jade took away one hundred and eighty euro. I'll split it with Kelly to help her out, Jade thought. She'd be struggling to pay the rent otherwise. Jade had to admit that this did annoy her a bit though; she'd done all the work while Kelly slept off a hangover. Still, she was sure Kel would do exactly the same for her.

After an hour, they'd finally finished cleaning. Jade had overheard Sam and Steve talking about a girl called Serena and Steve kept telling Sam how stunning she was. She could work out from the conversation it was clearly the brunette who he was always with these days, and Jade couldn't help but envy her. No matter what Sam had done, he was still always in the back of her mind.

'Hey Jade,' Sam called over to her as he was about to leave. 'You coming out tonight?'

'Yes, but I'm not too sure where we're going,' she replied, secretly hoping he ended up in the same place.

'Well, text me and let me know where you lot end up and maybe we'll meet up later.'

Jade nodded. If only he wasn't with that Serena. As much as she wanted to go to the same place to see him, what would the point be if he was with another girl? He obviously didn't fancy her and she just had to face it. He wanted to be her *friend*. Besides, the image of him kissing Adele would never leave her mind.

Relieved that the night was over, she made her way to Black and White bar, expecting to see Lisa and Jonny. When they weren't there, she huffed to herself, annoyed that they hadn't bothered waiting for her. They must have gone off somewhere else, she thought, getting her mobile out and dialling Jonny's number. When there was no answer, she called Lisa. But there was no answer from her either. It's because the music is so loud everywhere, she thought to herself, they wouldn't have just left me behind. Jade sat down on the steps, feeling exhausted and sorry for herself. She called them both over and over again. Thanks a lot, Lisa, she thought angrily, deciding her only option was to go home. She considered texting Sam for a moment to see where he was, but then decided against it. She felt completely deserted by her best friend, who was drunk and having such a good time with Jonny and his friends that she'd forgotten Jade. Alcohol really did change people in a big way, she mused. No way would Lisa ever leave her when she was sober, just as Kelly wouldn't have snogged another bloke in front of Billy.

Back at her apartment, Jade climbed into bed moodily, glancing over at Kelly who was still fast asleep. *She* should certainly feel refreshed in the morning after all the sleep she's had, Jade thought as she drifted off herself.

She woke up the next morning to the sound of tapping and sleepily looked over at Kelly to see her texting away on her mobile. Kelly heard her move and immediately sat up: she was obviously dying for Jade to wake up so she could be filled in on the previous day.

'Okay, so I have a question,' Kelly said, with a serious expression on her face. 'What the hell happened to me yesterday?'

Jade rubbed her eyes, trying to wake up properly. She sat up in the bed to stop herself dozing off again. 'You got totally hammered at the champagne spray party.'

Kelly looked horrified. 'Yes, but what did I do? Seriously, all I remember is meeting that guy Jayden or whatever he was called, dancing on their sunbeds and then that's it! I completely blacked out!'

Jade yawned loudly. 'You do remember Lisa is here, don't you? She came to surprise us.'

'Oh yeah!' Kelly said, happily, her eyes lighting up. 'What else happened?'

Jade explained exactly what had happened the day before, including Kelly throwing champagne in Adele's face and Billy trying to talk to her in the swimming pool.

Kelly's face dropped. 'Did he? Were we talking long? I can hardly even remember seeing him, let alone having a conversation!'

'Probably because you had your tongue down Jayden's throat!' Jade answered, trying to swallow her laughter.

Kelly looked mortified and closed her eyes briefly. 'Oh no! Please don't say I did that in front of Billy?'

Jade grimaced. 'Yes, right in front of Billy and his friends. He was seriously pissed off, I felt so sorry for him. Jonny had said to me just before that how much Billy likes you as well.'

Kelly shook her head, biting her bottom lip and then said breathlessly, 'Oh my God. I'm such a bitch. Why did I do that?'

Jade shot her a sympathetic glance. 'We would have stopped you if we could, but you got straight out of the pool with Billy and went over to Jayden's bed. The next thing we knew, you were snogging!'

Kelly shook her head in disbelief. 'I'm so embarrassed. Billy must hate me,' she said, blushing with shame and looking downwards.

'You definitely have some making-up to do,' Jade said softly.

'What did Joe say about me not going into work?' Kelly asked, panicking suddenly.

'He was fine. I said you ate some bad prawns and he believed me and wished you well.'

'Thanks,' Kelly breathed a sigh of relief. 'I haven't been

170

that drunk since I was about fifteen. Do you remember Lucy Johnson's party when I was sick through my nose? I can't believe I did that to Billy. How was your night anyway? Was Adele alright with you? Did she say anything about me?'

Jade remembered how Lisa and Jonny had abandoned her and ignored her calls. Her mobile was next to her on charge and it wasn't flashing, indicating that she *still* had no messages from either of them. Her anger had now turned to hurt.

'Work was boring,' she told Kelly, rolling her eyes. 'Adele said she'll let you off about the champagne as she knows you didn't mean it and you were drunk. She is still saying she didn't steal from us. Whatever,' Jade said, her eyes narrowing doubtfully.

Kelly was incandescent. 'Lying cow. I knew exactly what I was doing when I threw it in her face. That had nothing to do with being drunk!' she scoffed.

'Jonny and Lisa were supposed to be meeting me after work, but they disappeared and I couldn't get through to them. I think they were meeting Jonny's mates in some club fifteen minutes away so maybe they went there and there was no reception.'

'Really?' A frown wrinkled Kelly's smooth forehead. 'That's well unlike Lisa. I wonder what happened? Maybe she got sick like me and had to go home to bed? I wouldn't take it personally, babe.'

Jade shrugged. 'Mmm . . . I suppose you're right. She did seem almost as drunk as you'd been.' She smiled at Kelly.

'God help the poor girl then!' Kelly laughed. 'She's obviously making the most of it seeing as she's only got five days here. Not sure what my excuse was, apart from the fact that I'm the world's biggest lightweight.'

'You were quite funny,' Jade grinned, remembering the boob-flashing incident.

'Funny or not, I bet I've completely pissed Billy off now and he'll never talk to me again,' Kelly said sadly, the light in her eyes fading.

'I thought you wanted to chill with him for a bit?' Jade asked, confused. Then it clicked and she remembered. Kelly was doing what she always did when she actually *liked* someone. She pushed them away because she was too afraid of getting hurt. She was scared of getting her heart broken; for some reason she had this belief that all relationships ended in disaster.

'Yes, I know, but I didn't want him to hate me,' Kelly said in a small voice.

Jade heaved a sigh. 'Kelly, I know you like Billy. Stop pushing him away like you always do when you meet someone special; he's a lovely guy and is head over heels for you.'

Kelly thought for a second. 'I know. I'm not sure why I always do it when I like somebody. I was so out of order. I just hope I haven't ruined it completely.' Her voice was almost a whisper.

'Tell him you're afraid of getting close to someone because you've been hurt in the past,' Jade suggested. 'Just be honest.'

'He'll think I'm a freak though!' Kelly said, looking up at the ceiling.

'You bloody well are!' Jade joked, trying to bring a smile back to her bubbly friend.

They got ready for the day and then at eleven thirty called Lisa several times.

'She's *still* not answering her phone,' Jade told Kelly, bewildered.

'She's probably asleep. I'm sure she's fine. Call Jonny and see what happened.'

Jade dialled his number, becoming more concerned about them with each ring. Had they been in a car crash? Mugged? What had happened?

'Hello?' Jonny answered to Jade's relief. His husky voice suggested she'd woken him up.

'Hi Jonny, it's Jade. What happened to you and Lisa last night?' she asked.

'Nothing,' he said, sleepily. 'We were just drunk. I walked her back to her hotel and she went to bed in the end.'

Jade sighed with relief. 'Okay. Is Lisa alright then? She's not answering her phone.'

He hesitated. 'Yes, she's fine. She was just too drunk to stay out in the end. She's probably asleep like I was.'

'Okay cheers, I'll try her again and let you go back to bed. You need as much beauty sleep as you can get anyway,' she teased. 'See you later on.' She hung up and then told Kelly, who decided to text Lisa and tell her they fancied a quiet pool day at the PYR Hotel and would meet her there. Jade put on a lovely turquoise bikini with a halter top and cute frilly bottoms, and she'd added a gold bow sequin pattern to both. She put on a small amount of make-up and huge sunglasses. As soon as she had money she was going to start saving for some Tom Ford or Chanel ones. All Kelly's wages went on clothes and accessories and she always looked like a movie star. Jade couldn't wait until she could afford the same. She could feel the old relaxed ways that she'd had in Bath slowly slipping away, as the glitz and glamour of the Essex and Marbella world took hold of her.

*

Jonny yawned and stretched out in his bed. He felt like death warmed up and had no plans to leave his room all day. He was always up first, getting out there in the sun trying to top up his tan, but not today, not when he felt like this. Damn those JD and Cokes, he never wanted to even see the bloody drink ever again, let alone taste it.

His mouth felt as dry as the Sahara desert so he grabbed

the glass next to his bed and took a large gulp, spitting it out when he realised it was a flat, warm JD and Coke from the night before. Why had he left that glass next to his bed? he thought angrily. That was nothing but a recipe for disaster. But as he started to recall the events from the night before, he sighed, knowing disaster was exactly what he'd caused. He didn't know what to do from here or how to act; it was just one big mess.

Jonny wasn't happy with himself and knew deep down he was better than how he'd behaved last night. It always boiled down to having too much drink and not thinking properly – not that that was an excuse by any means. All he knew was that it had been a very surprising night, one he never would have seen happening in a million years.

*

Jade and Kelly lay relaxing by the quiet pool in contented lethargy. Jade even drifted off at one point and it reminded her of their first ever girls' holiday to Malia in Greece, and their peaceful days sunbathing on the beach. Jade had no idea how different Marbella was going to be – the partying, the dressing-up, the amazing bars. She loved it, but it was nice to have quiet days too.

'Hi, sorry to disturb you,' a girl with long dark hair said as she came over with her friend.

Jade sat up and smiled.

'I love your bikini and just wondered where it was from?'

'Oh, thank you,' Jade replied cheerfully. 'I made it.'

The girl looked impressed. 'Really? Wow, it looks gorgeous. That's just the sort of thing I was looking for before I came here. But all the shops have the same stuff – you keep bumping into the same bikinis on the beach.'

'I know,' Jade answered, nodding in agreement.

Kelly looked up. 'Babes, if you want we'll customise your

ones to make them different. We've already done it for some other girls and they loved them. I'm not being funny, but it's *so* embarrassing wearing the same as everyone else.' She sat up, smiled and then whispered, 'Happened to me on my first day here and I almost died.'

The girl's jaw dropped, as though she couldn't think of anything worse. 'How humiliating!'

Kelly frantically nodded, knowledgeably. 'Totes.'

The girls asked Jade and Kelly if they would customise some of their swimwear and they shot a thrilled glance at one another, happy to be getting more customers.

'Enjoy your day.' The girls waved as they said goodbye.

'Thanks. Have a good day too.' Kelly then added, 'Don't worry, you'll have the most gorge bikinis in Marbs soon!'

Jade glanced at Kelly, incredulous. 'That's about the fourth or fifth person to compliment our bikinis so far and the second lot of girls that want us to customise. We should just say it to everyone that asks in future. Imagine the money we could make!'

'I know hun! I'm not being funny but we'd make well good swimwear designers.'

Jade nodded, wishing they could get a job working for a huge swimwear company together. How fun would that be? Kelly's voice interrupted her thoughts. 'There's Lisa,' she said, as she waved and then pointed to the spare sunbed next to them.

Jade watched as Lisa made her way over. She knew instantly that something was wrong. She had enormous sunglasses on covering her eyes, but Jade could still tell by the way her lips were dead straight and her shoulders were slumped that she was unhappy.

'Alright, babe?' Kelly asked, biting her nails with concern.

'Are you okay?' Jade questioned, all her anger from the previous night vanishing as she worried about her friend.

Lisa sat on the end of Jade's sunbed and took her

sunglasses off slowly, revealing watery eyes, which were red and puffy. She looked awful.

'Oh my God,' Kelly said, jumping up and moving closer to Lisa. 'What's happened, hun? Why have you been crying?'

Lisa attempted to speak, but started to cry instead. Jade was totally shocked. Lisa never cried, especially not in a public place, so it must be bad. She leaned towards her and put her arm around her, trying to give her comfort.

'I've done something really awful,' Lisa finally said. She took a deep breath and then said at last, 'I really don't want either of you to think any different of me.'

'Is it to do with Jonny?' Jade asked. She had a feeling she knew what had happened.

Lisa nodded and a tear slid down her cheek, which she wiped away. She sniffed and got her breath back.

'You cheated on Jake with Jonny?' Jade guessed. She saw how drunk they both were the night before and how well they were getting on. Lisa nodded, her eyes looking at the floor guiltily. Kelly sat there staring at her, agog, while Jade gently rubbed Lisa's back.

'Babe, don't worry,' Kelly said softly, pulling herself together and trying to reassure her. She took her hand in her own and rubbed it gently. 'You don't have to say anything to Jake if it didn't mean anything. He'll never know.'

Lisa continued to cry and Jade paused for a moment, memories of Tom and his infidelity flooding back to her. Lisa had met Jake when they were sixteen and Jade remembered that night like it was yesterday. Lisa had pointed out Jake straight away, and he hadn't stopped staring at her either. They finally spoke at the end of the night, had a little kiss and had literally been together ever since. Lisa had been the first one of the three of them to get a serious boyfriend and they'd always envied her happiness, hoping to be in a relationship just as happy one day. Lisa, *cheating*?

It was such a huge shock. Lisa had never so much as glanced at another man before, so why now? And why Jonny? It didn't make any sense. It's not like Jonny is drop-dead gorgeous like Sam, Jade thought, even though she had seemed to develop a little crush on Jonny herself over the past few weeks. She knew now that was all it had been; a silly crush because she felt lonely and missed male company. Jonny was dependable and kind, but he was her friend, and it became clear to her now that she wouldn't want it any other way. What had Lisa actually done? If it was only a kiss then it wasn't *that* bad.

'Tell us exactly what happened. Only if you want to though,' Jade said, not wanting to make Lisa any more upset than she already was.

'We were having such a good night and Jonny was really making me laugh,' Lisa gulped, swallowing back the tears. Kelly passed her a tissue from her bag and Lisa blew her nose. 'Obviously I got very drunk, you saw me,' Lisa said, looking to Jade for affirmation.

Jade nodded, feeling slightly guilty that she'd been giving her countless free drinks. *I was only being nice*, she told herself, *I had no way of knowing this would happen*. But still she felt a tiny twinge of guilt in her stomach.

Lisa continued, shutting her eyes briefly. 'I can't remember everything exactly, but we seemed to be waiting for you to finish work for ages, so Jonny suggested that we go back to his apartment for some drinks, seeing as it was close by. I knew I shouldn't have and I'm so sorry we didn't wait for you, but I was enjoying myself so much and kind of felt like I should be a bit more carefree, like the both of you. I always feel like the boring, sensible worrier in our group and sometimes, I just wish I could be more relaxed, more fun.' She looked up at them sadly.

'Maybe not as relaxed as me,' Kelly said, thinking about the previous day. 'I flashed my boob to security, got ridiculously drunk and danced like a maniac, snogged a stranger in front of someone I really like, threw up on my way home and then couldn't go to work.'

Lisa gave a hollow laugh.

Kelly continued, 'And I wasn't going to tell you this because I was too embarrassed, but seeing as you're down in the dumps, I will. I'm pretty sure I called Billy last night but he didn't answer so I left a voice message.'

Jade gasped in horror. 'What did you say?'

'I have no idea what the hell I said, though I do remember singing.' Kelly put her head in her hands and the girls burst into laughter. Kelly really was hilarious when drunk.

'You're kidding?' Jade said, her mouth curving into a smile.

'Nope. Wish I was. I have this awful feeling it was Kylie Minogue's *Can't Get You Out Of My Head*, because he said she was his ideal celebrity. I'm such a lunatic. No wonder I never have a boyfriend. So Lisa, hun, you're not the only one with regrets from yesterday.'

Lisa didn't look like that thought had helped much. She carried on, 'So I went to his apartment. I didn't think anything of it really, because I just thought of Jonny as nothing more than a friend.'

Jade and Kelly nodded, practically on the edge of their seats in anticipation.

'Then what happened?' Jade asked, wondering at what point Lisa had crossed the line.

She pushed the hair away from her face and sniffed. 'He kept telling me how beautiful I was and how lucky Jake is to have a girlfriend like me. He said I was too young to get married and that we were crazy. I told him proudly I'd only ever slept with Jake and he said he admired that, but asked how on earth I knew if Jake was any good or not.'

'What an arsehole!' Kelly said, angry with Jonny for

making Lisa doubt whether she was making a mistake marrying Jake.

'He didn't mean it how you think. And I seriously doubt he would ever have tried it on with me,' Lisa replied regretfully, twisting the now crumpled tissue in her hand.

'What, so *you* came on to *him*?' Jade asked, stunned that Lisa was the one to make the first move.

Lisa nodded, her face flushing pink. She looked up at the sky and exhaled sharply. 'Jonny was being so nice, but I just kept thinking about what he'd said. I've never been with anyone apart from Jake. That's almost unheard of nowadays. How can I know that Jake is the one when he's the *only* one I've ever been with? So, I kissed him. He stopped, and asked me if I was sure and I said yes.'

'And you slept with him?' Jade knew the answer, but just wanted it confirmed.

Lisa nodded, a tear rolled off the end of her nose. 'It was so strange being with a different person, with a body I wasn't used to. Someone who kissed in a way I didn't know and didn't taste like Jake. After we'd done it, I felt completely numb. He kept kissing me and saying how amazing I was, but I'd sobered up in an instant and I hated myself. He knew I regretted it and kept apologising over and over, saying he wouldn't ever tell anyone if I didn't want him to.' Her voice broke into a sob. 'It wasn't even his fault. I've no one to blame for this but myself. I said I had to go and he wouldn't let me go alone so he walked me to my hotel. I then just went to sleep, hoping I'd wake up and find out it was just a dream. I've got the nicest boyfriend in the world that loves me and wants to marry me, and I've been in Marbella one day and slept with a stranger, pretty much.' Lisa couldn't stop the tears flooding her eyes and she buried her head in her hands.

Jade and Kelly were stuck for words. There was nothing they could say to make her feel better. Jake was the boyfriend everyone wanted; handsome, caring, thoughtful and he would do anything for Lisa, she was his world. Jade knew that Lisa cheating would shatter Jake's heart into a million pieces. How his whole secure life as he knew it would be taken away with a simple sentence. He'd even been the one to book her flights for her, trusting her totally. It would kill him if he knew what she'd done and, like Jade with Tom, perhaps he wouldn't be able to forgive it. He wouldn't see Lisa in the same way ever again; he would see someone capable of being disloyal and hurting him. He would question if he really knew her at all. Yes, some people did get over infidelity and lived happily ever after, but from experience Jade knew that this was easier said than done. Even if you did forgive, not many people could ever forget. By telling him, Lisa would not only be breaking Jake's heart, but her own too. After all, Lisa had wanted to marry Jake and spend the rest of her life with him – but that future would be over if he knew about Jonny.

It was going to be hard to comfort Lisa, as she blamed herself and completely regretted her actions. What was the right thing to do in this kind of situation? Tell the truth? Or pretend nothing had ever happened and live with the guilt? There was no way Jake would ever find out and Jade certainly believed that ignorance was bliss. But on the other hand, Jade knew that Lisa was very honest; she doubted that she'd be able to carry on the relationship as if nothing had happened. The guilt would eat away at her every day.

'What am I going to do?' Lisa asked. She'd stopped crying now but her face was blotchy and her eyes were noticeably rimmed with red.

'Babe,' Kelly said wiping the tears away on her face, 'you've made a mistake. You're only human and he'll never find out. Men do it all the time. I know it's not right, but I wouldn't tell him.'

Lisa thought about this. 'But how will I ever be able to look him in the eye again? What about when he asks if I had a nice holiday? How can I let him touch and kiss me after . . .' She couldn't even finish the sentence, and winced as she recalled the previous night.

'If you tell him, you have to prepare yourself for the fact that he may not want to be with you any more,' Jade said, matter of factly.

Lisa glanced at Jade, knowing her friend had been in this same situation, only she had been on the receiving end of the pain.

'It will destroy us, won't it?' she asked Jade quietly, and then looked away as if she didn't want to hear the answer.

'I'm not going to lie, Lisa, yes, I doubt your relationship will ever be the same again.' Jade didn't want to be cruel, but her friend needed to know the truth.

'Would you tell him?' Lisa asked, staring at Jade. 'If you were me, would you say it?'

Jade didn't know the answer. She shrugged her shoulders. 'I just think you need to do what you feel is right. No one else can make the decision for you.'

Lisa nodded, hands shaking as she fiddled with her sunglasses in her lap. 'I need time to think. I feel like such a cheap slag.'

After an awkward pause, Kelly chipped in. 'Babe, you seriously can't call yourself a slag when you've only slept with two people. What the hell does that make me?'

Jade and Lisa looked at each other and then at Kelly, and started to giggle. It was such a nice sound to hear Lisa laughing again.

Kelly ginned at them and then threw another tissue in their direction. 'Ha bloody ha, you cows!' Kelly stretched out on her sun lounger and then jumped up again excitedly. 'I know what will cheer you up!'

'What?' Lisa questioned, hoping it was the answer to her prayers.

'A vajazzle!'

Jade and Lisa rolled their eyes at each other.

'What?' Kelly said defensively. 'It will!'

*

When Lisa got back to her hotel room she heard her phone beep with a text message. It was from Jake and it made her feel a million times worse all over again.

Hi baby. How are you today? Hope you and the girls are enjoying yourselves. Missing you lots, J xx

Lisa read the text over and over, feeling sick inside. If only she could turn back time and change what had happened. She would never have gone back with Jonny to his apartment and she certainly wouldn't have slept with him. Every time she thought of it, it made her cringe with shame. How on earth was she going to face Jake again, knowing what she'd done? She knew if he'd done that to her she would have been absolutely heartbroken, and doubted that she would forgive him. Why had she thought that it was okay to sleep with someone she'd just met? The thing is, she had really wanted to at the time, she hadn't even thought about Jake once. Did that mean she wasn't really as happy with Jake as she thought she was? And what must Jonny have thought of her? He must think she was easy and so disloyal – which is exactly how Lisa felt just then.

She took a deep breath and texted Jake back like she normally would. She didn't want him to think anything was up.

*Having a lovely time. Weather is boiling. Really
nice seeing the girls too. Hope everything is well at
home and work is okay. Love you lots and miss
you too xxx*

She was such a bad girlfriend. If it had just been a kiss,
perhaps she could have somehow forgotten about it and
just put it down to a one-off mistake, but to have sex with
someone else was just unforgivable. She knew most people
would just go on with their relationship and pretend nothing
had ever happened, but Lisa had integrity and knew she
couldn't live with such a huge lie, that she'd be forever
worrying that he'd find out. Would she rather have to hide
her betrayal and cope with the guilt, or tell the truth and
face the fact he might walk away and never look back?

Lisa climbed in the shower and put her head under the
cold water, wishing it would wash away all her guilt and
shame. Jade had given it to her straight; her relationship
with Jake as she knew it would never be the same again if
she told him. But how could she live with herself if she
didn't?

CHAPTER 11

Kelly and Jade convinced Lisa to go out as much as she could during the rest of her holiday and try to forget about what had happened. What was done was done, and there was nothing she could do about it now. She wasn't exactly herself, but tried to have fun all the same.

A couple of nights later they were in a club called Pangea, sitting on a stunning cream sofa and sipping vodka and oranges. They hadn't seen Jonny or Billy since the eventful day of the champagne spray party, and so both Kelly and Lisa couldn't believe their eyes when they saw the two mates walk through the doors.

'Oh my God, look who's here,' Kelly said as soon as they spotted them.

Lisa looked mortified and extremely uncomfortable as they walked their way.

The boys walked over and sat down at their table. Jonny was acting normally, but Jade noticed that Billy was looking round the club like he was bored and searching for other people more worthy of his attention. It was so awkward and no one knew what to say.

'Alright girls?' Jonny said eventually, breaking the ice.

'All good thanks,' Jade replied. Lisa and Kelly merely nodded.

'You all recovered now then? You were smashed at the pool party,' Jonny said to Kelly with a smile.

'Don't remind me. I hardly remember anything,' Kelly said, looking at Billy and hoping he was listening. She needed him to hear she hadn't meant to do what she'd done and that she was sorry, but he wouldn't even look at her.

They all chatted for a few minutes but Billy literally didn't say a word. He stood up after a while and turned to Jonny. 'Mate, there's Jodie and that lot over there from back home. Let's go say hi.'

Jonny stood up and shrugged at the girls. 'See you a bit later, girls. Enjoy your night.'

'Bye, Billy,' Kelly said, desperately wanting him to at least acknowledge her.

He glanced at her, his face emotionless, and then walked off in silence. They watched as Billy went over to a table full of girls he knew, acting like he normally did, kissing each of them on the cheek and laughing and joking. Perhaps this was worse than Jade first thought; maybe Kelly *had* seriously blown it with him. He was in no mood to talk to her, that much was obvious. He was being overly flirtatious with the other girls and it was clear to Jade that he was trying to hurt Kelly as much as she had hurt him. Why did people play stupid games, Jade questioned – life was too short to waste time like that. Sure, when she'd first met Tom she used to wait at least an hour sometimes before she texted him back as she didn't want to seem too keen, but that was about it. If only Kelly didn't sabotage her relationships out of her fear of getting hurt then she wouldn't be in this mess. Jade was always honest from the start when she liked someone and she wished that Billy wasn't behaving this way. True, he'd been humiliated but Jade really hoped he would just talk to Kelly and let her have her say, rather than trying to get one up on her.

*

185

Billy chatted to Jodie, a girl he knew from home, and flirted with her like he never had before. He knew Kelly would be watching and he wanted her to see him having fun without a care in the world. Jodie was a nice girl, but she was very pretentious and unlike Kelly, didn't have a kind nature. She *knew* she was attractive too, something that ironically he found unattractive. Not that it mattered though; so long as Kelly saw them chatting, that's all he wanted. Jodie was a natural flirt too and was behaving exactly as he wanted her to without her even knowing it; he couldn't have picked a better girl for the part. She kept flicking her hair, laughing out loud and touching his arm. Billy knew girls like her – if he wanted to take her home tonight he could; she was well known round his area for being easy. The problem was he couldn't think of anything he wanted less. He was only concerned about Kelly and whether she was looking at him flirting with someone else.

He'd heard Kelly's explanation that she was really drunk at the pool party – like that was a valid excuse. At least she knows now she's pissed me off, he thought. He hadn't seen Kelly for a few days and he'd been constantly looking around for her, wanting to get his chance to ignore her. It had helped his battered ego to snub her when she'd said goodbye, but she had a long way to go before he'd think about being mates with her again. The only thing she'd done was leave a stupid drunken voicemail the night it happened, singing something so out of tune he didn't even know what the song was. That wasn't good enough as far as he was concerned. Why had she not just had the courage to call or text him and apologise properly?

Jodie interrupted his thoughts. 'Babe, do you want another drink?' she pouted, already pouring vodka from a bottle on her table into his empty glass, along with Red Bull.

'Cheers,' he said, glancing over at Kelly to see if she was looking and then clinking glasses.

'We're going to get some champers soon,' Jodie boasted, running her long acrylic nails through her platinum blonde hair seductively. 'A couple of bottles of Dom P if you want some?'

'I'm fine with the vodka, thanks,' he said, completely unimpressed with her flash ways. 'I don't really like champagne if I'm honest. It gives me a headache.'

'Not Dom P, hun, it's top quality,' she said, as though she was a champagne expert, accompanied by a soft, sexy laugh and a flick of her long hair.

'What are you doing for work now?' Billy asked her, changing the subject. He'd known her from college and as far as he knew she wanted to be a teacher.

'Trying to get into glamour modelling at the moment. Been on loads of shoots attempting to get a portfolio together. Other than that, my dad just gives me his credit card,' Jodie giggled and gently put her hand on his waist, thinking he would laugh too.

He nodded and took a step backwards, even more put off than ever before. Kelly better be watching, he thought as he downed the rest of his vodka. He didn't know how much longer he could stand talking to such an airhead.

*

'Billy one hundred per cent hates me,' Kelly said, looking distraught. 'And he's trying to make me jell.'

Jade took a deep breath and exhaled. 'He doesn't hate you. He's just flirting with those girls to piss you off,' she said, annoyed with the immaturity of it all.

'He wouldn't even say goodbye,' Kelly said as she wiped her eyes. Jade couldn't believe she was actually crying.

'Oh my God, are you okay? Don't worry. Just go over

in a little while and ask to speak to him alone,' Jade suggested.

'Don't cry, hun,' Lisa said, holding her hand. 'It'll all be fine once you've spoken to him. You've bruised his ego, that's all.'

'I'm such an idiot,' Kelly said, getting a compact mirror out of her bag to check her make-up hadn't smudged. 'The minute I meet someone I really like, I ruin it.'

'You're so confusing,' Jade said as she tipped some more ice in her drink. 'After that conversation about his small you know what, I thought you'd gone off him.'

'I just used it as an excuse because I'm a fool. Yes, it's not massive, but it wasn't tiny either. I like him and we were getting on great. I could really see us meeting up when we get home in Essex.'

'Me too,' Jade agreed, feeling sorry for her.

'I can't go over there. I feel so out of order for what I did. I humiliated him and he'll probably do the same to me by saying he won't talk to me, or worse, just blanking me altogether.'

'Then why doesn't Jade go for you?' Lisa suggested, shooting Jade a helpless look.

'I don't mind if you want me to?' Jade said, looking at Kelly.

Kelly's eyes brightened and she smiled. 'Would you, babe? I'd be so grateful. You'll know exactly what to say, you're good at things like that.'

'Of course.' Jade shrugged; she'd do anything to make Kelly happy again.

'I'm all nervous now,' Kelly said, shyly. She glanced at Billy and then back to Jade. 'Go on then, go now. Thanks so much.'

Jade made her way over to the table where Billy and Jonny were sitting with all the girls. Billy was deep in conversation with a blonde girl, so Jade spoke to Jonny first. He looked pleased to see her alone.

188

'I'm glad you've come over,' he muttered. 'I wanted to check how Lisa was and couldn't exactly say it in front of everyone.'

'Well she's not that great,' Jade told him, honestly. 'She feels terrible because she's in a really happy relationship and now she's cheated and she's not sure what to do.'

'I feel so bad,' Jonny said putting his hand to his forehead and shaking his head. Jade could tell that he meant it sincerely. 'I'm sure she's told you what happened. I couldn't help myself and I was drunk; and I know that's no excuse, but when a stunning girl comes on to me, it's pretty impossible to say no. I really like her as well, though I know she's with Jake. I really hope I haven't messed it up for her.'

'Everything will work out like it's supposed to, don't worry,' Jade said, taking a long sip of her drink to cover the fact that she didn't totally believe that herself.

'Just tell her I'm sorry if I've messed things up for her and I hope she's okay.'

'I will. That's nice of you to say that,' Jade replied, tapping Billy on the shoulder. Jonny poured himself another drink as Billy turned around to face Jade.

'Can I have a word?' Jade asked awkwardly as she smiled politely.

'Yeah sure,' Billy said coolly. 'What's up?'

'I'm sure you know why I'm here.'

'Something to do with Kelly? I'm not interested,' he said, but his eyes flicked involuntarily to where Kelly was sitting.

Jade didn't believe him. 'Look, she knows she's messed up. She wasn't herself the other day. I know she was kissing someone else, but she *really* likes you. She's been let down by blokes in the past, and I know it doesn't make sense, but she pushes people away because she's afraid of getting hurt.'

'Well, she's succeeded in pushing me away,' Billy retorted

189

in a low voice. 'I felt like an absolute idiot after the way she treated me.'

'I get that, and trust me, she's really sorry. She didn't even remember anything from that day. *I* had to tell her.'

'That's not exactly the type of girl I'd want to be with; someone who gets so drunk she doesn't even know what she's doing. No thanks. How could you ever trust someone like that?' He stared at Jade.

'That's the thing,' Jade said quickly, desperately trying to stick up for Kelly and turn things around. 'She's never normally like that! Maybe when we were much younger, a couple of times, but honest to God, that's the drunkest I've seen her in years.'

He shrugged and held his hands up. 'What do you want me to do? Just forget it? It's not that easy.'

Jade could see the hurt, as well as the anger in his bright blue eyes. He was very handsome and she could easily see how Kelly had fallen for him. It wasn't just his looks that were lovely, but he had a down-to-earth personality, the type of bloke you would always feel comfortable around. 'Can't you just talk to her and try to patch things up? After all, she's not your girlfriend, is she? It's not like you'd both promised each other you wouldn't be with anyone else.'

Billy thought for a second and frowned. 'I suppose not,' he said at last.

Jade could feel him softening.

'But I wouldn't have done that to her,' he said with a shake of the head.

'Just give her one more chance, Billy, and she'll never do anything like that again. You both like each other so much, it's so easy to see. It would be such a waste if you left things now,' Jade pleaded.

'I'll talk to her a bit later,' he said. 'If she's not snogging anyone else at the time, that is.' He was trying to stay stern but Jade could see his frown was lifting.

'She won't be,' Jade said with half a smile. That was definitely good enough for the time being. He'd forgive Kelly in time; Jade just knew it.

On her way back to her table, someone grabbed Jade's arm. She half expected to see Jonny or Billy again, so was completely shocked to see one of Tom's friends, David, standing there. He had also gone to Bath and Jade had met him at a few student parties when she'd been with Tom.

'Jade, hi!' he said.

'Oh my God, David! What are you doing here? Who are you with?' She looked around quickly, checking Tom wasn't beside him, and was reassured when she didn't see him.

'Just on holiday with some friends from my football team. This place is amazing. You on holiday too?'

'No, I'm working over here in TIBU club.' Jade suddenly realised that everything she told him was going to end up getting back to Tom, so she made sure to say she was having the time of her life and was really happy. So much for not playing games, she thought to herself.

'That's great. You're so lucky to work here,' he said enviously, as he looked around the club with sparkling eyes.

'I know,' Jade boasted, tucking her hair behind her ear. 'I've met so many great people and am having so much fun. I just love it here. Beats being at home, that's for sure. I've met loads of celebrities and even served David Beckham the other night.' That sounds good, Jade thought, happy with her lie. Tom would be so jealous if he thinks I've met him.

David looked confused. 'David Beckham? Are you sure?' he asked, obviously not convinced.

'Mmm hmm,' she nodded, as she sipped her drink, 'about a week ago.'

David frowned, his forehead crumpling, looking at her in a peculiar way, as though she had two heads or something. 'But David Beckham was in California a week ago, playing in a football match. I saw him in the paper. It's where he lives.'

Shit, Jade thought embarrassed, why did I have to say David Beckham? I could have said anyone else. Of course, he lives in America, Posh is always in magazines with her American friends like JLo and Eva Longoria! How could she have forgotten that? She faltered, stumbling with her words. 'Oh . . . well . . . maybe it was a lookalike then. It must have been a really good one.' She forced a smile as she felt her face get hotter. God, David must think I'm weird, she thought.

David changed the subject, not wanting to embarrass her any more. 'Have you spoken to Tom recently?' he enquired.

'No, I told him to leave me alone,' Jade answered. 'I think it's for the best we're not in contact any more.'

He shook his head and then threw it back with a little laugh. 'What you did to him was hilarious. He got the piss ripped out of him for weeks! He actually ended up seeing the funny side in the end, but was really cut up about losing you. He was an idiot for what he did to you, everyone knows that.'

Jade nodded, unsure what to say. It was what she wanted to hear, but it didn't change things.

'He didn't go out for ages afterwards,' David continued. 'I tried inviting him out a couple of times, but he would never come. He's better now, but I know he's still gutted about what happened with you two.'

'So was I,' Jade replied, staring into space.

'Have you met anyone else yet?'

'There's a few people I'm seeing,' Jade fibbed, lifting her chin in a poised manner. 'Nothing serious though. I don't want a boyfriend – I'm enjoying being single too much.'

He clinked his glass with hers. 'Cheers to that,' he said with a smile. 'Let's get a photo.' He handed his mobile phone to a friend to take a photo of them, and Jade tried to do her best smile, knowing that Tom would probably see the image. He showed her the photo after it had been taken and Jade was pleased that she looked pretty good. Her eyes looked piercing because of her tan and her teeth looked so white she could have given Simon Cowell a run for his money.

'It's nice,' she smiled.

'I'm going to send it to Tom now,' he winked. 'Show him what he's missing.'

'No, don't do that,' Jade said quickly. But no sooner had she said the words than she decided it actually might be a good idea. *Yes, why not show him what he's missing? Why not show him exactly what he gave up?* 'Or send it if you'd like, whatever.' She tried to sound like she didn't care either way.

'Sent,' David said, with a grin.

'I'd better get back to my friends,' Jade said pointing in their direction. 'Enjoy the rest of your holiday though, and I'm sure I'll bump into you again soon.' She kissed him on the cheek.

'See you soon. Have fun working out here,' he said as she walked off.

She imagined Tom's face as he received the photo of her and David together. He'd be shocked and jealous, she thought. And he still deserved a little bit more punishment. She didn't even know why she cared; it wasn't as if she would ever get back with him; but she did want him to regret cheating on her and ruining everything. I'll never cheat, she vowed to herself as she walked back to the girls, it does nothing but break people's hearts and ruin relationships. This holiday had shown her that.

CHAPTER 12

It was ten o'clock at night and Tom was watching football in bed when his phone beeped. He couldn't be bothered to move to see who it was; he was comfortable and felt himself drifting off.

He could hear his mum coming up the stairs and hoped she was bringing him a drink. He smiled as she opened his bedroom door.

'Sit up, love. Got you a cup of tea and a slice of Victoria sponge, fresh out of the oven.'

'Thanks Mum,' he said.

Tom sat up and took a bite out of the delicious cake, which was still warm. The sweet raspberry jam and butter-cream went down nicely with a swig of hot tea.

He reached for his phone, wondering if it was the girl he'd met two weeks ago texting him again. Her name was Sophia and he'd been out with her a few times and spent the night with her for the first time recently, staying in a hotel. He didn't really like her that much and had no intention of ever seeing her again, but now she wouldn't stop texting him and it was starting to get on his nerves. It had just been a bit of fun and she seemed up for it, but now, like all the others, she wanted more. *When was he going to see her again?* she constantly asked. *What was he up to?* He didn't understand why she couldn't just accept that it had just been a casual fling and nothing more so he had ignored her messages and calls. He'd had a couple of missed calls from an unknown ID over the past few days, meaning the caller had withheld their number and he would bet his life that it was her. She was clearly checking he hadn't lost his phone and trying to catch him out so he would answer; it was most irritating. He'd got what he'd wanted and now it was over. Seriously, some girls were so bloody stupid. If he liked her, he would call; it was as simple as that. Why they spent hours and hours talking and analysing something men could explain in a few seconds, he'd never know.

Tom was surprised to see David's name on the screen; he hadn't spoken to him for ages. He could do with a boys' night out, he thought, especially seeing as he'd turned so many down when he'd first broken up with Jade. It was getting much easier with time though, and now he wanted to be out on the pull as much as possible. He clicked on the message and his eyes almost popped out his head when he saw the photo of Jade and David on his screen.

She looked glowing, happy and healthy with a natural tan; the best he'd seen her in ages. Why on earth was David with her? Where were they? A feeling of jealousy washed over him like a tidal wave and he had a horrible lonely feeling in the pit of his stomach. Judging by this photo, Jade was well and truly over him; she looked like she was having a great time and here he was, sitting in bed and doing nothing, waiting for his mum to bring him tea. It seemed like a lifetime ago that she was his and he was kissing her, holding her and feeling loved by such a wonderful person. He missed it. He missed *her*. He was such an idiot, leaving that phone where she could find it.

Tom still couldn't believe Jade's revenge tactics, that day in the theatre. It had literally been the worst day of his life.

195

Not only did he lose Jade, but he was found by the whole cast of the play, stark bollock naked. It had been so embarrassing he thought he'd never be able to show his face in public again. He'd spotted Louisa through the crowd that had gathered, and there was a look of horror in her eyes when she realised it was Tom. He'd called for her to help him and had been stunned when her face suffused with colour and she pretended she didn't even know who he was. She was too ashamed to admit she knew him! He still had nightmares about it, and cringed every time the memories came back to haunt him. When he'd finally been freed, which seemed like a lifetime later, he'd been so eager to get the hell out of there that he grabbed the first item of clothing he saw. It was only when he jumped off stage and heard the crescendo of laughter from the waiting audience that he realised he'd picked up a short medieval dress, which only just covered his bum. But despite humiliating him beyond his imagination, he still wanted Jade back. In fact, he realised, it actually made him want her all the more. She wasn't a pushover like he'd assumed her to be.

Tom couldn't take his eyes off the image, the thought of Jade and David together making him sick with dread. If David so much as touches her, he thought, I'll kill him. Though he knew David wouldn't do that to a mate; he knew better than that. As he stared at her amazing blue eyes in the photo, he knew the saying was most definitely true; you never knew what you had until it was gone. Well, Jade was gone alright, but not if he could help it.

He texted David back:

Hi Dave. Nice pic! Haha. Where are you?

He received a reply straight back.

Marbella. It's the bollocks!

Marbella, eh? Tom thought, as he reached for his laptop on the bedside table, wondering how much the flights were.

*

Kelly gathered up all her courage at the end of the night and made her way over to Billy, even though he was still with the blonde girl. She needed to apologise and tell him she wanted things to go back to how they were; she just hoped he would forgive her. Her heart was thumping violently in her chest and she felt embarrassed to be interrupting his conversation, but she had no choice, he'd been with the girl all night and God only knew when he would be alone next.

'Billy,' she said, tapping his shoulder softly. 'Can we talk?'

He looked surprised to see Kelly and casually nodded.

She walked away with him, the blonde girl giving her a cold stare as she did so. 'I'm sorry for the other day,' she started.

He nodded uncomfortably. It was horrible seeing him like this; he was normally so happy and playful with her. She had never seen this serious side to his personality.

She took a deep breath and said in a shaky voice, 'I didn't really like that bloke and don't even remember kissing him.'

Billy looked at her with cold eyes. 'But you couldn't even be bothered to talk to me *before* that. You were acting strange and dismissing me like I was some twat trying to chat you up, someone you couldn't stand,' he retorted curtly.

'I know it makes no sense,' Kelly tried to explain, 'but I get scared when I start to like someone and I got worried you were going to let me down, so I pushed you away.'

He shook his head as though her answer wasn't good enough. 'I wouldn't have let you down, but you'll never know that now.'

Kelly's eyes grew wide. 'Please don't say that. I really

like you, Billy, I just find it hard to trust people,' she said breathlessly.

'You never even gave me a chance,' he said calmly, still acting nonchalant about the whole thing, making her stomach churn with nerves.

She bit her lip, not knowing what to say to make it better. She wanted him to forgive her and just go back to normal, but something told her it wasn't going to be that simple. 'Can you forgive me?'

He looked at her with a frown. 'Kelly, I don't think you realise how much of an idiot you made me feel. Especially after everything I said to you the night before.'

Tears pooled in Kelly's eyes and her cheeks went red as she blinked and started to cry. He wasn't going to forgive her – she'd ruined it. Kelly couldn't blame him for being angry with her; she'd have felt exactly the same in his shoes. She looked up at him and saw his angry look change to concern at the sight of her tears.

'Look, I know I'm not your boyfriend or anything, but what you did was completely out of order. I'm not saying I never want to talk to you again, I just need a bit of time.'

Kelly fought back an excited smile. 'Okay, I understand,' she said. 'Just let me know when you want to talk again.' She walked away with the tiniest spring in her step, feeling it was best to leave on a positive note rather than keep going over the same things. She'd done what she'd done and couldn't take it back. She just had to hope that he could forgive her.

*

Jonny watched Kelly walk away from his mate and went to see if Billy was okay.

'What did she say?' he asked.

'Just that she didn't remember what happened and she was

198

drunk. She doesn't find it easy to trust people and thought I would just let her down in the end, so she pushed me away.'

Jonny shook his head. 'Girls are so messed up at times.'

Billy nodded in agreement. 'I really like her though. She started to cry and it made me feel really bad for her, you know? It's stupid though. I've done nothing wrong and there's me feeling sorry for *her*.'

'Sounds like she's got you wrapped around her little finger already,' Jonny joked, nudging him with a smile.

'I know,' Billy laughed. 'I was adamant not to bother with her after the other day, but seeing her tonight and hearing her say she's sorry, I don't know, I must be weak or something.'

'Mate, I've never heard you talk like this about a girl before. Give her another chance, you clearly want to.'

Billy gave a theatrical sigh. 'I think I need a bit of time first. I'll make her sweat for a bit.'

'Yeah, good idea,' Jonny agreed.

'Things felt well awkward with you and Lisa earlier,' Billy said, remembering the tense moment they'd sat with them.

'I know. I feel so bad, even though it was her that came on to me. To be fair, I reckon she's having cold feet about this long-term boyfriend of hers or something. Did you know she thinks he's going to propose to her – and she's only twenty-one! She admitted she's only ever slept with him and then I came along.'

'She obviously couldn't resist your charms,' Billy joked. 'Must have been your nose that did it for her.'

'Alright, don't take the piss,' Jonny smiled, covering it with his hand; his nose was the butt of all jokes because it was on the large side.

Billy put on a girl's high-pitched voice. 'Sorry, babe, I met Gonzo on holiday and always wanted to sleep with a celebrity.'

Jonny laughed, slapping him on the back playfully.

'You're such a mug. Sort your own issues out first before you start to wind me up.'

Billy was about to reply when Jodie tugged his arm.

She fluttered her long fake eyelashes. 'Babe, what car do you reckon I should get when I go home? Gemma reckons a Merc convertible but I want either a Range or a Porsche. My dad says I can have whatever I want, so money isn't an issue.'

Billy and Jonny glanced at one another, both thinking the same thing; she was definitely not classy in any sense, bragging about cars that her dad was going to buy her.

'None,' Billy replied with a lopsided grin. 'Get what I've got and save your poor dad some money. A Hyundai W-reg hatchback. Only cost two hundred quid.'

The look on Jodie's face was priceless. Who cared about what car you had? As long as it took you from A to B and you didn't have to use public transport, it was good enough for Billy. He wasn't into material things and hated girls like Jodie, showing off to everyone about her dad's wealth. It was so embarrassing. He hadn't known her very well at college; if he had, he certainly wouldn't have picked to speak to her tonight, to make Kelly jealous. She obviously didn't like his answer because she gave him a dirty look and turned her back on him, talking to her friends.

'Come on Jonny, I'm off,' he said, nodding in the direction of the exit. He'd well and truly had enough of Jodie; she was so superficial and it made him appreciate how sweet Kelly was even more. He couldn't believe Kelly thought he'd let her down; once he was in a relationship, he was serious. It was the first time in his life he could honestly say he wanted to *be* serious too. He wanted to get married and have kids in a couple of years; he'd be thirty then after all. He felt like he'd met the right girl for him, finally. His only issue with Kelly was that she was quite young and wasn't sure she'd want the same things. He wasn't going to worry about that now though, he'd cross that bridge if they ever came to it.

Billy saw Kelly watching as he left and felt a little unkind. Maybe he should have said goodbye? It was too late now though and besides, he couldn't forgive and forget that easily, otherwise she'd think he was a doormat.

It was two thirty a.m. by the time he and Jonny crawled into bed; an early night for them. As Billy started to fall asleep he wondered how long he could last without caving in and going back to normal with Kelly; he was going soft, that was for sure. He missed being with her already.

*

Sam was drinking on his balcony with a few of his friends and started to feel weary. He needed to go to bed, but it was his room they were in and he didn't want to spoil the fun. He was relieved when Serena was the one to say she was tired.

She yawned loudly and then smiled. 'Guys, I'm off to bed. I need to go to sleep now. Feel exhausted.'

Steve chuckled, shooting Serena a disappointed look. 'You're not as hard core as Sam, seeing you're his cousin. I had high hopes for you as well.'

She flashed him a smile. 'Sorry to disappoint.'

'Come on you lot, you better leave now,' Sam said as he collected the empty glasses and bottles of beer. 'Serena won't be able to sleep if we're out here talking.'

'I'll read her a good night story,' Steve offered, raising his eyebrows in a suggestive way.

Sam laughed, knowing his friend had the hots for his cousin. He'd done everything he could to get with her, but she wasn't interested in anyone at the moment. 'Leave my cousin alone and find someone else to stalk,' he joked.

'What?' Steve asked, acting innocent and lowering his voice. 'I think she likes me,' he whispered so she couldn't hear. 'She will do soon anyway. Give me a couple more weeks and we'll be dating.'

'In your dreams sunshine,' Sam smirked knowing as usual Steve was trying to wind him up. 'Night everyone,' Sam called as they reached the front door. He walked back into his room. Sam wasn't keen on sharing so he'd found a really cheap small room with a single bed, small kitchenette, TV and sofa bed, just for him. He'd stayed in the same place the year before so made sure he came back first thing in May to get the room again before it got booked up.

He looked at Serena who was asleep already on his sofa. He'd been so shocked when his mum had called to say Serena was coming out to see him because she desperately needed to get away. Serena was a bit older than Sam, being twenty-seven, but they'd always been very close. They'd grown up together and she actually felt more like a sister to him. She'd been happily engaged to a man named Stuart when Sam had left for Marbella, but she'd broken things off because she'd found him doing drugs one night when she came home early from work. When she confronted him, he admitted he had a huge coke problem and was in loads of debt. She decided she had to leave; she'd been planning their wedding for the past six months and was completely devastated that she'd been deceived by him. Sam would never have believed that Stuart was into drugs, apparently so much so that he even felt like he had to do a few lines before he went to work every morning.

'I can't be married to a coke head,' she'd told Sam firmly when she got there. 'I can't believe anything he says any more. To think we've been trying for a baby as well.'

'You've done the right thing by leaving him,' he'd replied sympathetically. Poor Serena really hadn't deserved to be lied to, and in his opinion, Stuart was a complete idiot and would never find anyone as nice as his cousin. It was clear Serena had been upset when she first arrived though, suggesting she still had feelings for him, so Sam had tried to remain upbeat and positive for her sake. 'Who knows, maybe if he gets help you could work things out?' Sam had said to her.

She'd shaken her head in disagreement. 'No Sam, I couldn't go back; he's lied to me for far too long and I couldn't trust him now. It's definitely over.'

He was glad when she said that. Sam hated drugs with a passion and had never once tried them himself. When he was sixteen he had a really good friend that had gone to a London nightclub, tried an ecstasy tablet and died. He'd always thought that if he'd gone out that night maybe he could have stopped him. That maybe things would have been different. But there was no point in thinking that way, because who knew what would have happened if he had have gone out that night. Maybe Sam would have tried a pill himself? He could never be sure.

Serena hadn't said how long she was staying. He knew she was enjoying herself though, so that was the main thing. He'd introduced her to a few girls he knew and she'd become friendly with them, which had done him a favour. She was looking for an apartment, and was going to see one the following day with a girl she'd recently met, who had decided she didn't want to go home after a holiday. He was glad about this as sharing his room was a bit of a squeeze; he loved his own space and always had since he was young.

Brushing his teeth, Sam considered that this would probably be his last summer working in Marbella. He'd had fun, but he wanted to go home and sort out his career now; he couldn't keep running away every summer and trying to escape the real world. He wished in a way he'd gone to university. If he'd studied something he'd at least know which path to take now. Plus, it was supposed to be fun. Hadn't Jade said that she had the best years of her life at uni? He thought about how he'd seen Jade and Kelly a lot lately, always with those two blokes who worked for News Café bar. He knew Kelly was with one of them, Billy, and he assumed Jade must be with the other one. And maybe other people as well, if what Adele had told him about Jade was true, he thought sadly. It was a shame, as in every other single way she was a lovely girl. If Sam was honest with himself, he was still disappointed about what had happened in the club that night. He thought he'd felt a genuine spark between them; something real, something that could go somewhere. But he'd obviously been mistaken, maybe just a bit too drunk, and now he had to put Jade out of his mind. It was hard when he saw her at work, and out and about on the beach and in clubs. His eyes just wanted to follow her around, even though his brain told him they shouldn't. Adele had saved him from some potential heartbreak there, so maybe he should just be grateful for having good friends and move on. Jade certainly had. Sam shut his eyes, trying to blot out images of her being kissed by random blokes as he fell into a weary sleep.

CHAPTER 13

'What do you mean you're going to Marbella?' Tom's mum asked him in shock. They were in the kitchen and Tom was sitting at the dining table, waiting for his dinner to be served. 'When did you decide this? And who will you go with?'

'It's fine Mum, please stop worrying. I know someone out there on holiday and I'm going to stay with him.' Tom put his head in his hands, wishing his mum would stop with all the questions. He just wanted to go away for a week, that was all; anyone would think he'd told her he was going to join the army.

Tom's mum exhaled sharply, waving around a tea towel in her hand as she spoke. 'Well, have you told work? How can you just get up and go?'

He stared at her, beginning to get impatient. 'I haven't taken *any* holiday this year, that's how. I decided yesterday actually, just thought that a holiday would do me good. I thought you'd be glad I was going to enjoy myself, especially after everything that's happened to me this year.' He pulled a sad face, wanting some sympathy. He'd lied to his mum when she asked him why he'd broken up with Jade, saying that she'd dumped him because she wanted to live in Essex again.

'I knew she wasn't good enough for you,' his mum had said at the time. 'Let her go back to Essex; it's her loss. She won't find anyone like you out there, mark my words.'

Then she'd fussed over him for weeks, which was exactly what he'd wanted. Now though, he just wanted to go away and bring Jade back with him. He'd made up his mind – he wanted her back. She'd had a lot of time on her own now and surely she was missing him. She must have forgiven him for cheating by now too; it was ages ago, and everyone deserved a second chance.

Luckily there was an extra bed in David's room. He still had another week and a half of his holiday left, and Tom planned to spend his last week with him. Apparently Jade was working over there in some club, which was meant to be really good. David said all the girls that worked there were all gorgeous and wore these sexy little outfits. He was so angry when he heard that, imagining blokes chatting Jade up every night. He felt sick with jealousy just thinking about it, and promised himself he would put a stop to it as soon as he could.

'I suppose you do deserve a break,' his mum answered, patting him on the head gently, after thinking for a bit.

He knew he could win her round. His mum was such a worrier; it didn't matter how old he was, being the youngest child, he was still her baby. She'd miss him being there to wait on too; she loved nothing more than making his breakfast, lunch and dinner.

'It'll be great for me to relax and see some sunshine,' he said. 'Everyone needs a holiday, Mum.'

'Well, make sure you wear factor thirty and no lower,' she warned with a serious expression. 'My friend Joan was only saying the other day how her friend's son, who's only forty would you believe, just found out he has skin cancer. People don't realise just how strong the sun is. And take a cap too to protect your face, you don't want to end up with wrinkles like me.'

'You don't have wrinkles,' Tom said sweetly, his mouth curving into a smile.

'Don't be so ridiculous,' she said, dismissing him with her hand, but clearly flattered.

'I'm leaving next Monday. My flight is five in the afternoon.'

His mum opened the oven, checking to see if the dinner was ready. 'Okay darling. I'll get the suitcase out from the loft and help you pack. I'll give you my medical kit as well to take; you never know what you'll get wrong with you on holiday and it's got everything you can think of.'

'Thanks,' Tom said, as she handed him his favourite pie and mash dinner.

'I'll give you a lift to Bristol airport as well, save you paying for a taxi; it would cost you a fortune.'

'Great. Thanks Mum.'

He was looking forward to getting to Marbella now. Maybe he'd go on the pull for a few nights before he went looking for Jade; after all it would be better to get it all out of his system before he had a girlfriend again.

*

It was Lisa's last day in Marbella, and the girls were at Buddha Beach, eating chicken salads in the sun. Kelly was wearing a large stylish Missoni hat with her huge oversized sunglasses and lips coated in gloss. Lisa was looking pretty in her new black bikini Jade and Kelly had added embellishments to. Jade had also made an effort; her hair had been blow-dried big and bouncy and she was wearing a black monokini with flowers on, another of their creations.

'It was so nice having you here, Lisa,' Jade said, her eyes shining because she was sad that her friend was leaving in

207

a few hours' time. The five days she'd been with them had gone so quickly. Jade didn't mind it being just Kelly and herself again, but it was so much better when it was the three of them together.

'Ah thanks,' she replied in between sips of Coke. 'Apart from the obvious awful first night, I've really enjoyed myself.'

'Who's getting you from the airport, babe?' Kelly asked.

Lisa rolled her eyes. 'Jake is. I'm so nervous to see him I feel sick. I'm a terrible liar and will probably go bright red when he asks me if I've had a good time.'

Jade then noticed that Lisa had hardly touched her food and was just pushing it around the plate. She was clearly really worried.

'Have you decided what you're going to do yet?'

'No, I've tried not to think about it.' She took a small mouthful of chicken. 'He's being so nice to me. He called me this morning and said how he can't wait to see me and that he's taking me to a really nice restaurant in Loughton tonight. Part of me thinks "just don't say anything" and the other half thinks I just have to tell him. My head is so messed up.'

'See how you feel when you see him,' Jade suggested, adding some more caesar dressing to her bowl .

Lisa swallowed hard. 'I'm not looking forward to going back to work, either.'

'God knows what I'm going to do when I get home,' Jade complained, dreading the fact that she was going to have to go back to searching through job adverts online. It was so soul-destroying. She'd applied to so many and hardly ever even heard back. There were so many people after the same jobs and she had no experience, so who would want to employ her?

'I'm fed up of being a beautician, as well. I used to love it, but I've lost all my enthusiasm,' Kelly joined in.

What Jade really wanted, she realised, was to start her own business and be her own boss. How much fun would that be? Especially if it was doing something that she loved. Maybe they should really go for it and sell bikinis to make money! Marbella had showed them how popular they were and every day girls complimented them on their original swimwear.

'Kelly, why don't we start up a bikini business?'

'Babe, that is the best idea ever! OMG, I can't believe we didn't think of it before. When we customised those girls' bikinis they loved them!'

Jade gazed into the distance dreamily. 'It would be amazing. We could buy bikinis and mono . . . whatever they're called, one-piece costumes, and then customise them with tons of different designs.'

'Completely bling them up!' Kelly said animatedly, clapping her hands together.

Jade was so glad they'd thought of it. There was certainly a gap in the market, because she'd never seen swimwear like the girls wore in Marbella in any high street shops, or even any UK websites. Kelly had had to buy all her blinged-out bikinis from websites in the States, so what a brilliant idea to design their own unique swimwear and sell it to girls in the UK! Their hobby could become their careers!

'We could buy all the swimwear in bulk and get a whole-sale price on the pieces. Then we can sew bits on like we've done to ours and make them look . . . well . . . Essex!' said Jade, excited.

'I love it,' Kelly said, her voice high-pitched with enthusiasm.

'It's a good idea,' Lisa agreed with a little nod. 'Just make sure you give me a discount,' she joked.

'What can we call it?' Jade asked. 'We want a name that says exactly what we are.'

'What about "Bling Bikinis"?' Kelly suggested.

'Mmm . . . not sure,' Jade replied, biting her lips as she racked her brain for names.

'"Don'tbejellofmybikini.com"?' Kelly reeled off.

Jade laughed; she actually quite liked that. 'What about "Essex bikinis"?'

'Yeah, that's not bad. People associate Essex with being reem and glamorous, so that could be good. Though, it's a bit plain. I'm really excited to start this now.' Kelly's eyes lit up and her curls bounced as she jiggled around in her seat.

Jade felt excited too. It was a great feeling to think that she could go home now and have something to focus on. They would have to start off small but she could always get a part-time job, and Kelly could continue with her beauty as a sideline. Back at home, her family had an office in their house that Jade's dad used when he occasionally worked from home, so they'd be able to use that.

'My cousin is a web designer,' Lisa said. 'He'll put together your website for you for a fair price.'

'Wicked,' Jade said, nodding happily.

It was going to be such a fun job, and who knew, it might really take off. They could advertise on Facebook and Twitter and other social networking websites. Plus, Jade knew someone who worked in public relations, so would be able to give them some contacts for magazines and newspapers for publicity coverage. Perhaps Lisa may have some TV contacts she could pass their way? Jade couldn't wait to get started when she got home and she was so happy they'd thought of it.

A wasp buzzed round them all of a sudden, making the girls jump up in fright. Jade screamed, terrified. As the wasp landed on her salad, she got her napkin and shooed at it, picking her plate up and walking away as the wasp landed where she had been sitting.

'Don't be silly,' Lisa said, waving her napkin at it. 'Come and sit down!'

Jade hated wasps with a passion; they were the most annoying, creepy things when you were trying to eat. As another buzzed round her plate she screamed and almost dropped it, while Kelly and Lisa tried not to laugh. She walked off even further, eating her salad as she did so. She could see someone looking at her and glanced to her left, horrified to see Sam standing with his supermodel girlfriend. He looked at her with a confused face, and her cheeks started to burn as she realised how strange she must look walking on her own, carrying a huge salad bowl and eating as she went.

'Jade, what are you doing?' Sam asked, shooting her an odd look.

'What?' she said, as he stared. She added quickly, 'I like to walk and eat. Burns the calories off quicker.'

Why did *he* have to be the one standing right there? And why did she pretend that she ate standing up? She was too embarrassed to say she was running away from a wasp, it was ridiculous. He would have to be with his gorgeous girl again too, wouldn't he, Jade thought cringing inside. Those two looked very happy and comfortable together and were probably both thinking how weird she was. She noticed his girlfriend murmur something and then walk off to a group of girls. Jade turned, about to head back to Kelly and Lisa, when Sam's friendly voice startled her.

'Jade, you still enjoying it here?' he asked, clearing his throat.

She walked back closer towards him, thinking how painfully good looking he was. His body was to die for; it wasn't too pumped-up and over the top like some of the men here, but just beautifully toned and muscular, with an enviable dark tan shown off to perfection in his pale blue Vilebrequin swimming shorts. Jade flicked her caramel-coloured hair behind her shoulders. 'Yes, still enjoying it. What about you?'

'Yeah,' he said with a twinkle in his eye. 'I'm trying to organise a night out soon. You know, get everyone together and go for dinner, drinks and then a club or something. You should come.'

'Sounds like a good idea,' she smiled with a hint of embarrassment. She wondered what the brunette girl would think if she turned up on their night out? Would she be the jealous type? *Not when there is nothing to be jealous of*, Jade told herself.

'Obviously you can bring Kelly or whoever,' Sam continued.

She gave a brittle laugh and then said breezily, 'Yes of course. Just let me know.'

He scratched his head. 'It won't be easy that's for sure. Getting everyone together is hard work, but hopefully a night can be planned soon, before everyone starts to leave for England.'

Jade nodded and then remembered she was still carrying her salad bowl. 'Cool. I'd better go and finish my lunch. See you soon, Sam.'

He waved her off. 'Speak soon.'

She really thought Sam was nice, but ever since the night he snogged Adele he just confused her. She wondered why he wanted her to go out with him and his friends if he had a girlfriend; it was so odd. Perhaps he was just getting as many people together as possible? He only saw her as a friend anyway, Jade told herself. He'd probably invited Adele along too, but there was no way she was going anywhere with that weirdo, so she dismissed the thought of a night out straight away.

*

Lisa kissed her friends goodbye and got into the taxi. She felt so down and exhausted. She had drunk far too much

212

alcohol in Marbella and it did nothing but make her feel awful and depressed the next day. A detox for a few weeks should make her feel better again, but it wouldn't shift the heavy lump of guilt in her stomach.

Lisa was looking forward to getting home and being in her own bed; the worst part of every holiday was travelling home as it seemed to take forever. Especially seeing as she was alone too. If only you could just click your fingers and be at your front door.

She felt nervous and shaky at the thought of seeing Jake. She still couldn't believe she'd slept with someone else. It made her feel sick just to think about it now. Would it be obvious that something was up the minute he clapped eyes on her? She felt like she had a huge tattoo on her forehead saying 'I've cheated.' Lisa tried to imagine her life without Jake, even though it was hard. She imagined not seeing him after work, meeting up at weekends and going out to parties, the cinema, and restaurants. Not cuddling up to him again or laughing and joking together. He was all she had ever known, how could he not be in her life? She didn't want to be single and start again. She had no interest in dating; it terrified her. It was always 'Lisa and Jake' and she didn't want it any other way. But why had she cheated? Surely if she was a hundred per cent satisfied with Jake, she wouldn't have slept with Jonny? Maybe a part of her agreed with Jonny; she *was* too young to settle down. But the thought of being without Jake brought a hard lump to her throat that she just couldn't swallow. She needed him so much, he was all she'd ever known. She was so confused.

Lisa fell asleep the moment she sat on her seat on the plane and was over the moon when she woke up due to an announcement saying they were about to land. Before she knew it, she had collected her suitcase and was on her way to meet Jake outside. He'd texted her saying where he would be waiting and she saw his white van as soon as she

213

walked outside. She was so excited to see him, but also felt so guilty she could cry. He got out the van as he saw her approaching, with a huge smile on his face.

'Hello,' he grinned as he hugged her close to him and kissed her lips.

'Hi,' she smiled, feeling uneasy. It was strange; she was usually so comfortable in his arms and now she felt like he was a stranger.

'You look gorgeous,' he said, admiring her tan. 'Can't believe you got that dark in five days.'

Lisa opened the car door and sat in the passenger seat. 'Well, my dad *is* Spanish, kind of helps I suppose.'

He picked her suitcase up and put it in the boot of his car.

'So, did you have to pay extra then? Was your case overweight?' Jake asked as he sat down next to her and started the ignition.

'No,' she lied, looking out the window. 'It was fine.' She'd had to pay twelve pounds extra but what was one more secret now?

'Lucky,' he said with a jokingly suspicious look that made her stomach flip.

She waited for more of his questions, concentrating on acting completely normal.

'So, tell me all about it then. Did you have a good time?'

She paused trying to think of her answer. 'Yes, it was great. Really sunny and the girls are having such an amazing time over there too.'

'Good,' he said, and then asked a few more questions about what she got up to and what Marbella was like. 'I really missed you,' he said after a while.

'Ahh . . . I missed you too,' Lisa replied, her stomach doing somersaults with remorse. She never knew she'd feel this bad about herself. She hated herself so much for what she had done it was all she could think about. Clearly some

214

people were just not cut out to cheat and she was definitely one of them. How did people have full blown affairs for years? How did they ever relax? She'd be constantly on edge, looking over her shoulder and worrying every minute that he was going to find out. It simply wasn't worth it to her. If she continued to feel like she did at that moment, she just knew she would have to tell him. She couldn't let him look at her with such love in his eyes, when it was all a lie. He was worth more than that.

When they were in Chigwell, to Lisa's surprise, Jake drove past her road.

'Where are we going?' she asked him.

'Thought I'd treat you to a meal in Sheesh,' he said, glancing at her with affection.

'You're so sweet,' she said, feeling worse and worse about herself by the second. Sheesh was a stunning Turkish restaurant in Chigwell, and one of her favourites.

'Well, you're worth it,' he said, squeezing her knee.

Why on earth is he being so wonderful? Lisa asked herself. Of all the days, why now, when I feel this low? She didn't deserve anything. She just wanted to go home and sleep, forgetting all about Jonny and Marbella. It was only when she was asleep that she didn't think about what she'd done.

'Thanks babe, but I'm kind of tired.'

'Oh come on, I haven't seen you for five days. And they do the best moussaka in the world. I haven't stopped thinking about it all day.'

'Okay,' she caved in. How could she say no?

'Stay at mine tonight too,' he said meeting her eye with a suggestive glint. 'You have work clothes in my wardrobe and my mum and dad are away in Norfolk. I've been lonely in bed without you.'

She felt like the guilt was eating its way through her insides, giving her a dreadful hollow feeling that she'd never experienced before in her life.

Lisa sat through the meal, trying to be her normal self, but all she could think of when she looked him in the eye was that she'd been with Jonny. She'd allowed another man to make love to her and it was wrong. It was disgusting. How on earth could she now climb into bed with Jake tonight, knowing that? She was a good person; she didn't know if she could act forever. The alternative was too painful to think about though. Jake seemed so happy to see her; so grateful to have her home with him again. She'd only been gone for five days and he couldn't get enough of her. Throughout the meal he held her hand and she asked herself if she could ever really let him go.

As they pulled up outside his house, he turned to her with a serious look on his face.

He knows something is up, Lisa thought, *he can tell I'm acting weird.*

'Okay, can you do me a huge favour and not ask any questions?' he said, his voice a little shaky.

Lisa held her breath and nodded, not knowing what was going to come next.

'Just wait here for a few minutes and then when I come to the front door and wave, come in the house.'

'Okay,' Lisa said weakly, frowning and wondering what on earth was going on. He was acting strange and it was unnerving.

As promised, a few minutes later he appeared and she got out of his car and walked towards the front door. What was he doing? She was so confused. He disappeared into his house and as she reached the front door, her heart stopped as she heard their favourite song playing; *Make You Feel My Love* by Adele. There were red rose petals laid out in a path with candles each side, and as she walked along them, she knew in her heart what was coming. Lisa felt like she wanted the ground to swallow her whole. As she reached the front room where the path led to she stood there breathless, as she read the words made from petals.

Marry me?

Two tears fell from her eyes and then it was like a water-fall of emotion had been unleashed, and she couldn't stop them from falling.

'You're not supposed to cry!' Jake said, welling up himself and half-laughing, half-crying. 'I want to say that I love you so much, Lisa. You're the love of my life and I know you're the only person I want to grow old with. I could search the whole universe and I would still only want you. You make me happier than I ever thought I could be. You're my best friend, soul mate and lover all wrapped into one. Will you marry me?'

Lisa shook her head. 'Please stop,' she cried, rubbing her eyes and smudging her mascara. She couldn't believe this was happening; it was all she'd ever wanted. Hadn't she dreamt about this moment for years?

He cried too then and looked up at her smiling. 'Well, what do you say?'

'Yes,' she said, kissing him hard on the lips, trying to block out the voice inside her, shouting that this was all wrong. 'Yes Jake, I'll marry you.'

CHAPTER 14

Tom reached the hotel in a taxi and called David to tell him he'd arrived. The air was thick and suffocating with heat; he couldn't wait to get into his room and have a cold shower. Then he planned on going out and getting very drunk. He hadn't had a boys' holiday since before university; Jade would have hated it if he had told her he was going away with all his friends when they'd been together, just as he would if she'd said the same. He honestly believed you should only do it if you were single. He couldn't wait to meet some good-looking girls who were looking for a good time and nothing more; hopefully he wouldn't bump into Jade until he was done having fun. He would find out the nights her club was open and go and win her back then. It was all planned out. Have fun for the first three or four nights, then get Jade back towards the end of his week. Perfect.

An hour later, he was washed and ready for the night. Tom couldn't believe his eyes as he walked through the bumpy, winding little roads that led to Lineker's Bar. This place was amazing! Everywhere he looked there were beautiful women; it was like a dream come true. He felt like a child in a sweet shop, surrounded by temptation everywhere.

Why had he never been here before? Why had he never even heard of Marbella? He couldn't believe that Jade had been working here while he had been moping about at home. He didn't even want to think about what she'd been up to. The girls looked like the kind of women who were up for exactly what he wanted; a casual bit of fun.

'Wow,' he said to David with a broad smile. 'Fit girls everywhere.'

'Tell me about it, mate. It's brilliant, isn't it?'

When they arrived in Lineker's Bar it was packed. Luckily David had booked them and his friends a table and they ordered a few bottles of vodka to start their night off. Tom felt amazing. Girls looked over at them like they were royalty, clearly wanting to be on a table rather than on the dance floor with everyone else.

There were a group of girls on the table next to them and as he glanced over, he noticed that at least four of them were good looking enough to pull for the night. Maybe a few of David's mates weren't fussy, they weren't exactly oil paintings themselves. He nudged David and glanced over, and he understood immediately what he was saying.

'Not bad, Tom. Let's call them over in a bit and see if they want to join us.'

There was one girl in particular that caught his eye. She wasn't the prettiest of the bunch but kept staring, a sure sign that she fancied him. She'd do just fine. After a couple of his chat-up lines she'd be like putty in his hands.

*

Kelly was feeling tense. Billy had texted her asking to meet for dinner so they could chat and she needed to look amazing.

'My outfit is like the most important thing ever tonight. I need something that says "I'm sorry and you have to forgive me because I look so sexy",' Kelly said, flipping through her rail of clothes. 'I'm going to wear my clip-in hair extensions too so I look extra glamorous.'

Jade grinned; her hair was naturally so thick already that extensions were the last thing she needed, but she knew Kelly would never believe her. She could put a potato sack on and still look like a knockout. Besides, Billy wouldn't be one bit interested in what she was wearing; he'd fallen for her because of who she was inside.

'Okay, so what about this?' Kelly said, pulling out a tiny silver Jovani sequin dress, which was made from nude mesh material, with thin spaghetti straps and a sexy sweetheart neckline. The sparkling sequins were scattered all over the dress, leaving some parts see-through; it was incredible, but not suited to the occasion at all.

'Kelly, no way!' Jade gasped.

'Too much?' she said, raising her eyebrows and holding it up to her in the mirror.

'Far too much just for dinner. Though I'd love to borrow that for the Nikki Beach party.'

The Nikki Beach party was a night where girls dressed completely OTT – even more than normal. Lots of them wore flowing maxi gowns which were often embellished with sequins and crystals, and either low-cut or backless. An array of colours filled the club; sparkly metallics, feminine pinks, striking greens and sexy reds. Girls seemed to save their best dresses for this night and Kelly said the last time she'd been she had recognised stunning garments by designers such as such as Sherri Hill, Ruth Tarvydas, Scala and Forever Unique. It was a fantastic night they'd been looking forward to for ages.

'Course you can, hun, try it on when you like. What about this?' Kelly asked, holding up a little leopard print dress.

'I love that. But maybe it's a bit too short. You don't want everyone to be able to see your knickers.'

'Mmm . . . you're right. This?' Kelly said, pulling out a stunning cream backless catsuit from Reiss. It was classy, sexy and sophisticated; perfect for the occasion in Jade's eyes.

'Yes that's the one,' she smiled with a nod. 'That always looks gorgeous on you. Billy won't know what's hit him.'

'Ah thanks hun. I'll wear it with my Swarovski crystal peep-toe Louboutins,' Kelly announced, going to the mirror to apply her make-up. 'That will brighten up my outfit, don't you think?'

'They would brighten up any outfit,' Jade agreed, admiring the jaw-dropping heels that were sitting at the bottom of the wardrobe. Every inch of them was covered in sparkly crystals and it made the iconic red sole stand out when Kelly walked. It was a good job she was always complimented on them, because Jade knew they'd cost her an arm and a leg to buy.

Kelly swung round and looked at Jade, in-between plucking her eyebrows. 'Then you have to help me with what bag to take. I'm not being funny but bags are more important than people give them credit for. At the end of the day they can make or break an outfit. I'll go through my collection and make a shortlist, so when I'm ready you can tell me which one looks best.'

When Kelly was ready, Jade thought she looked gorgeous and just knew that Kelly and Billy would be happy together again before the night was out. She, on the other hand, was meeting up with Jonny for a few drinks. She didn't want to drink much; she was saving herself for Nikki Beach in a few nights' time. They'd probably get something to eat too. It was nice that they were friends; she could clearly see now that any feelings she thought she had towards him were simply because she had been feeling a bit lonely. Jade wondered how Lisa was, and what had happened with Jake. She'd call her tomorrow and find out. Lisa had texted saying she'd landed safely, but that was the last she'd heard from her. Jade hoped she was okay and that somehow she and Jake would last. If they couldn't make it work then who could?

She had to admit, she was feeling a bit down lately. She was happy for Kelly, but couldn't help but feel slightly envious that she'd met someone she really liked. When would *she* meet someone? She spoke to handsome men every night as part of her job, but apart from the odd couple of snogs here and there, nothing ever happened. She was fed up of men always being after one thing too; the minute you kissed them they wanted to take you back to their apartment. They may as well just have said, 'Oh by the way, I only want you for sex, and after tonight you'll never hear from me again.' That wasn't what Jade wanted; she'd never been that way. Fair enough to the people that could have one-night stands and happily enjoy them, but she always got attached and couldn't shut off her feelings. When would she find a boyfriend? The way things were going she could see herself being single forever. She knew there was no rush and she hadn't even been single for long, but she couldn't help but miss the nice bits about having a boyfriend. Some people were happy being single, but she was definitely more content being with someone, even if it wasn't a serious relationship straight away. She sighed; she'd have a good moan to Jonny tonight about it.

*

Billy watched Kelly walking towards him and had to catch his breath. Her figure looked amazing in the all-in-one suit she was wearing and it was low enough to show a glimpse of her ample cleavage. He couldn't believe she even liked him; he must be the luckiest man on the planet! He was waiting outside the Restaurante Regina, which he'd been to before and loved, so decided to take Kelly there. It had an open kitchen where you could watch the flames flickering and the chefs bustling round, their passion for food clear to see as they created stunning, intricate dishes. It was a sophisticated restaurant too, where they were unlikely to bump into other workers or people they knew; Billy wanted Kelly all to himself tonight.

'Hi,' she said, as he kissed her.

She smelt good enough to eat, forget about dinner, he thought, as they made their way through the restaurant to where they were sitting.

They were a little awkward with each other at first and Kelly wasn't her usual bubbly self, but it wasn't long before they both relaxed. Billy felt like he should just bring up what happened so they could clear the air and move on.

Billy took a deep breath and looked at her with a serious expression. 'Kelly, I'm not going to lie, it hurt me a lot to see you all over that bloke at Ocean Club and I really thought I'd never speak to you again. But there's something about you I like a lot; it's hard to describe. Like I told you that night we spent together, I've not felt this way in a very long time.'

'I can't explain how sorry I am,' Kelly said, nervously fiddling with her napkin.

'I want to just forget about it now and make it clear that I want to be with you,' he looked into her big blue eyes and added, 'only you.'

'You don't know how glad I am to hear you say that. I thought I'd ruined it all.' Smiling, Kelly reached for his hand across the table. 'I only want to be with you too and I promise I won't so much as look at anyone else, on my Louboutins' life.'

He smiled, slightly embarrassed by all this emotional stuff and then said, 'So . . . does that mean you're my girlfriend?'

223

'I hope so,' she beamed, 'if you'll have me?'

He sat up and reached across the table to kiss her. He'd missed those lips so much; they tasted sweet like honey and he wanted to drag her back to his room and never let her leave his bed.

'What are you having for starters?' he asked her, happy they'd sorted everything out at last.

She picked up the menu and studied it. 'Don't know yet. You?'

He read from the menu, 'A Duo of Fish *Carpaccio* served with a delicate sauce.'

Kelly was bemused. 'What does that mean? Isn't *Carpaccio* a coffee?'

He couldn't contain his laugher. 'No you doughnut, it's fish.'

'Really? Never heard of it,' she said puzzled, swooshing her hair back.

'Do you like salmon and tuna?'

'Yes,' she answered.

'It's both of those, but raw. Delicious, you should try it.'

'Okay, I will then,' she said, telling the waiter when he came over a few moments later.

Despite feeling head over heels for Kelly again, something weighed on Billy; he'd had a phone call that had shocked him to the core. He hadn't told anyone about it but it really felt like Kelly could be the one he could talk to. He knew now he could definitely trust her with this. He was scared; more than he'd ever been in his whole life. So scared that he wanted to run away and never go home.

'You okay babe, you look like you've seen a ghost?' Kelly asked, noticing his tormented expression.

Billy shook his head.

She gazed into his eyes with alarm. 'What's up? You can tell me.'

He could see the concern in her eyes and knew that now

224

was the time to let it out. It had been eating him up inside for days. 'I got a phone call last week,' he said sadly, his breathing getting harder and harder. 'It was from my mum.'

'Right . . .'

Billy looked down at the table awkwardly, not able to raise his eyes. 'Basically, about two years ago she had breast cancer. She went through hell, you know, having chemo-therapy and all that. Lost all her hair, she did, and it was like living in a nightmare seeing her so ill and haggard. She was fine on her birthday when I went home, though she did say she had to go and visit the doctor about some-thing. Anyway she called me last week and . . .' He couldn't finish the sentence without welling up and had to take a deep breath.

Kelly grabbed his hand and squeezed it. She wanted him to know she was there.

'It's come back again . . . the cancer. They checked if it was in her lymph nodes and it was. She has to go through chemotherapy again and now radiotherapy as well.' There, he'd said it; finally admitted it out loud to someone that his mum was in trouble. He had wanted to ignore it and pretend it wasn't happening, but knew he couldn't. He had to face up to the terrifying fact that his mum might die. Wasn't it funny how you just always assumed your mum would be there? He thought of all the times he'd upset her during his teenage years and all the ways he could have helped her round the house and hadn't. He'd just taken her for granted and the thought of losing her was so painful he couldn't bear it. Life was so cruel. What had his poor mum ever done to anybody? Why her? But then again, why not her, he thought miserably, good people got sick every day. His whole family would fall apart if anything happened to her; they would all be in pieces, especially his younger sister who was only sixteen.

'Oh my God, babe, I'm so, so sorry,' Kelly said, shocked

at his news, her eyes glistening. 'Have you thought of going home to be with her?'

'Yes,' he said, 'but I'm too scared to face her. I know I need to go back and help her get through this, but she made me promise I wouldn't because she wants me to be happy and enjoy myself here. I told her no way could I be happy in Marbella, knowing that she's sick again, but she told me she has my dad and sister looking after her and there is nothing I can do at home. She said she'll beat it again, but how can she be so sure?'

Kelly looked at him sympathetically, her voice soft and gentle. 'It's so awful, Billy. I don't know what I'd do if my mum was sick, but I do know I'd be going back home in a heartbeat. She's being positive saying she'll beat it, though, and that's a good sign, surely? People beat cancer every day. Don't one in three beat it or something?'

He shook his head and corrected her. 'No, Kelly. One in three people *get* cancer.'

Kelly's cheeks turned pink and she put her hands on them, clearly mortified. 'Shut up! Are you being serious? Sorry, babe. I suppose a one in three chance of beating it wouldn't be that good anyway, would it? Forget I said that.' She bit her lip.

He nodded and squeezed her hand, knowing she felt terrible. She came out with the daftest things. He wished he could be as positive as she was though. It was bad enough his mum having cancer the first time round, but finding out it was back *and* in her lymph nodes was keeping him up at night. He wasn't a doctor, but he sure as hell knew it was a bad sign. Billy wanted to go home, knew that he should go. His mum meant absolutely everything to him and he would gladly take the cancer from her body and instead have it himself.

'I'm going to get a flight and go home next week,' he said. 'I doubt I'll come back again this year. The only thing that's important is being with my mum.'

Kelly nodded, understanding completely. 'I think that's the best thing you could do. You'll just be worrying otherwise.'

'You're right. And we'll meet up when you get home?' he asked, not entirely happy that she'd be in Marbella without him.

She rubbed his hand tenderly. 'Of course we will. I doubt I'll want to stay much longer if you've gone home.'

'Don't be so stupid,' he said; the last thing he wanted was for her to go back home to Essex just because of him. 'You stay out here and enjoy yourself until the end of the season. It's what you came to do and you should.'

'I'll miss you though,' she said sadly. Then she nodded in satisfaction. 'Your mum will be fine, I just know it.'

The waiter interrupted them by delivering their starter. Billy watched as Kelly took a bite out of her salmon and pulled a disgusted face.

'Babe, I think there is something wrong with this salmon. Surely it's gone off?' she said, swallowing it very reluctantly and turning her nose up.

'No it's not, it's nice,' he said, confused after trying a mouthful of delicious fresh fish.

She shook her head, pushing her plate away with a grimace. 'Well, I've never tasted salmon like that before.'

'It's raw,' he informed her. 'That's what *carpaccio* is.'

'I just thought it would be like the smoked salmon you get in bagels or tinned tuna or something,' she said, completely miffed.

He bit back a laugh. She always made him laugh – it was one of the things he loved about her. Now they were officially a couple, Billy had a feeling he would need her there to help him smile a lot more in the not so distant future.

*

Tom had just seen Jade walk out of a bar with another bloke and was furious. He had been so shocked he almost screamed. Just seeing her after all this time was bad enough, but the fact that she'd clearly already met someone else made him even more determined to get her back before it was too late. How could she have replaced him already? Tom had been dying to call her name when he saw her, but had just frozen to the spot. It was so strange to see her in Marbella and she looked so different, lovelier than he ever remembered. Far too much make-up, but that was because she'd been hanging around with Kelly, and he could easily change that again. Had she really had that fantastic body when they were dating or had he just not noticed it? The guy she'd been with was certainly not on Jade's level; *he* was much better looking than that guy, Tom thought smugly, and was certain everyone else would agree. Jade had looked so happy, with no cares in the world, laughing as she left. Had she ever been that happy with him? Tom hoped so; he wanted her back now more than ever. So much so that he wasn't sure what he'd do if it wasn't an option. They were made for each other, he was sure of it now.

He was supposed to be going to TIBU the following night to casually 'bump' into her. He and David had booked a VIP table there, asking for Jade to serve them. Tom had pretended to David he just wanted to catch up with her as friends, and he'd believed him. She'd be so surprised when she clapped eyes on him there.

If he was honest, Tom hadn't thought much about Jade since he'd arrived; until he'd seen how beautiful and happy she looked, that was. He'd been far too busy chatting up anything in a skirt. So what though? He was young, free and single at the minute – *and* good looking. He'd met a girl on the first night in Lineker's and slept with her back at her hotel; it had been fantastic and she hadn't held back by any means either, pulling out a pair of handcuffs as soon

228

as he got in her room. Obviously he'd been a bit nervous at first due to his *last* experience with handcuffs and there was no way he would have let her use them on him, but he'd had plenty of fun tying her hands together. She didn't seem at all bothered the next day when he said he was going to breakfast with his friends and would maybe 'see her around'. That was exactly the kind of girl he was after. Until he got back with Jade, anyway. The girl hadn't been that bad looking. She was from Essex too, unsurprisingly, as Marbella seemed to be the Essex of Spain, pretty much.

If Jade was happy with some other bloke, then he certainly wouldn't hold back when it came to pulling girls tonight. What Jade wouldn't know wouldn't hurt her.

CHAPTER 15

Lisa woke up with a splitting headache and looked at the clock on the wall. It was five forty-five and she'd have to get up in fifteen minutes for work. Why was it that she always seemed to wake up just before her alarm? She was so tired. At the weekend she still woke up at six and could never get back to sleep. It was so annoying! She would kill for another two hours in bed today. She cuddled up to Jake who was fast asleep – he didn't have to get up until eight. It had been two days since he'd proposed, and she had thought about nothing else since. The man that she loved more than anything had asked to spend the rest of his life with her; was it the right thing to say yes? How could she have said no at that point, when he'd gone through all the effort and built himself up to ask her? She *wanted* to marry him, that was the problem. But perhaps they'd met each other at the wrong time in their lives. Lisa wished she could freeze time and meet him when she was twenty-five and definitely ready to settle down, but lately there had been a voice telling her she was too young and their relationship was a bit of a habit. There was so much she wanted to do before marriage and kids, but she felt like that was all Jake wanted. She couldn't stop thinking about how she'd betrayed him in Marbella with Jonny. There was no way she would be able to walk down the aisle with this huge secret eating away at her, bit by bit. It was impossible to even imagine breaking the news to him though; she was trapped in her own terrible mistake. Jake was so excited now they were engaged and had clearly spent so much money on the huge beautiful diamond ring. He'd sent her links all day yesterday to various wedding locations he liked, even some that were abroad. Jake wanted her to have the perfect wedding day and had told her outright that nothing was too much. With every generous thing he did, her heart felt heavier and heavier.

She kissed Jake on the cheek when her alarm eventually went off, climbed out of bed, and went into the bathroom for a shower. Tomorrow night Jake had planned a meal to get their parents together to tell them their news. He'd called her mum himself and arranged the whole thing. Lisa's mum had called her at work the day before, asking her what the news was and saying she hoped it wasn't that Lisa was pregnant. Trust her mum to assume the worst.

Lisa had no idea how she could avoid the whole thing and at first told Jake she might be working late, but then he offered to call her boss and explain how important the dinner was, if that was the case. She hadn't wanted him to think something was up, so had agreed to the dinner in the end. But how could she sit there in front of their parents and tell them she was getting married, while carrying around this awful secret? And when she wasn't sure Jake would even want her after she told him the devastating truth? She had to come clean soon, but when was there ever a right time to break your boyfriend's heart? She should have told him the moment she left Arrivals; then he wouldn't have proposed and she wouldn't be in this mess. The whole thing was making her unbelievably stressed and she felt ill with worry. A headache had pounded behind her eyes ever since

Jake had got down on one knee and Lisa desperately wished that she could just go back in time and change the past.

When Lisa arrived at work, she decided to wait until nine o'clock to call Jade. It would be ten in the morning in Marbs and a good time to catch her. She had to tell someone what was happening; she needed help.

Jade answered almost immediately. 'Hey Lisa, I was going to call you today.'

'Hi, you okay babe?' Lisa asked, wishing her friend was at home more than ever.

'Yes, I'm fine. Alone in the apartment, about to get ready to go sunbathe. Kelly stayed with Billy last night; think things are finally back on track with those two now, which is good. How are things with you?'

'Not good,' Lisa replied, her voice cracking.

Jade exhaled sharply. 'Did you tell him?'

'No,' Lisa sighed. 'He proposed to me when we got back from the airport and I said yes.'

'What? Oh my God, you're engaged!' Jade gasped, not sure whether in this instance to be happy or not.

'Yes, but I need to tell him the truth. I can't live like this for much longer, it's killing me. I feel dreadful every time he kisses me and tells me how much he loves me. He should know what a bitch I am. But I'm so scared of breaking his heart.'

'You're not a bitch,' Jade said calmly. 'You just made a mistake. It's not like you're having an affair with another man and are running off with him to have his baby.'

'What?' Lisa said, feeling the blood instantly run to her face.

'I just said it's not like you've been having an affair,' Jade repeated.

Lisa didn't know what to say; the words wouldn't come out of her mouth. She hadn't used protection with Jonny, had she? She wasn't on the pill either, as it gave her terrible

232

mood swings, so she and Jake had always used condoms. What if she were pregnant? She pushed the thought from her mind; they'd only had sex that one time. 'I better go, Jade, I'm at work and someone is coming,' she lied.

'Oh . . . okay,' Jade said, disappointment and doubt in her voice.

'I'll call you in a few days and let you know how I'm getting on, yeah? I'll have told him by then.'

'Yes, call me anytime you need to. I'm here for you.'

'Speak soon. Take care.'

'Bye, Lisa, and good luck,' she replied.

Lisa ended the call and quickly got her diary out of her bag. Her period was due in four days' time. She was usually regular as clockwork, every twenty-eight days. She'd just have to wait; she would be fine. But what about STDs? She didn't know Jonny at all; he could have slept with hundreds of girls for all she knew. Why had she been so stupid and irresponsible that night? What was wrong with her? Lisa felt anger at herself burn in her heart. She quickly typed 'Essex clinics' into Google; she would go and get herself checked as soon as possible.

*

Kelly woke up next to Billy and smiled, remembering the night before. Sex had been so much better this time round and they hadn't gone to sleep until about four in the morning. Billy had texted Jonny asking him to stay elsewhere for the night and luckily he had, no questions asked. Kelly was blissfully happy and definitely wasn't going to do anything to ruin things ever again. She had a boyfriend! It felt so strange to think that, because she'd *always* been single.

Kelly watched him as he slept, thinking how gorgeous he looked. She could watch Billy's peaceful handsome face all day. She wanted to kiss him and wake him up, but didn't feel brave enough. She was honoured he'd chosen to tell her about his mum and her heart went out to him. Losing her own mum was one of her biggest fears and it made her eyes well up just to even think about it. She'd miss Billy so much, but he needed to go home and be with his poor mum. It wouldn't help to just run away from it all and bury his head in the Marbs sand. She knew that once he'd gone home, she'd probably want to go back too, but that wasn't fair on Jade; they'd planned to stay the whole summer and so they would. Kelly wasn't going to be one of those girls who disappeared and never saw her friends again just because she had a boyfriend.

Lifting her mobile phone from the side of the bed, Kelly looked at the time. It was eleven and she bet Jade wanted to kill her for being gone so long. Jade wouldn't be on her own for long anyway, she considered, with Billy going back to Essex soon. She quickly texted her mate to let her know she wouldn't be too long and would meet her by the PYR hotel pool again. That way, she'd be fine sunbathing on her own as it was very quiet and chilled most days there.

Sorry hun, only just woken up. Won't be too long, maybe a couple of hours. Meet me by PYR hotel pool. Loads to tell you xxx

Jade replied straight away.

Okay, no worries. See you there x

Kelly reached into her bag, which was on the floor beside the bed, and took out her compact mirror as quietly as possible. *Oh dear Lord*, she thought, as she looked at her reflection in the mirror, *I look a state!* She crept into the bathroom with her bag and applied foundation, blusher, eyeliner, eyeshadow and mascara. It would be too obvious she'd put make-up on this morning if she used her fake eyelashes too. Billy had laughed last night when one had fallen out into the bed.

Kelly put toothpaste on her finger and rubbed her teeth with it and then took a large swig of mouthwash and attempted to gargle silently – it wasn't easy. Much better, she reflected, as she gave herself the once over and sneaked back into bed with him.

Billy stirred as she pulled the sheet over her. 'Morning gorgeous,' he grinned.

'Morning,' she said kissing him, glad he'd finally woken up.

'It's nice to wake up without a hangover,' he said, then looked at her affectionately, 'and with you of course.'

'About last night,' she started, running her fingers through his hair, 'thanks for trusting me with the stuff about your mum. I won't tell anyone.'

Billy's smile faded a little and he took Kelly's hand. 'Thanks for listening. You can tell Jade, it's fine. I'll have to tell Jonny too. I decided before I went to sleep last night that I want to leave as soon as possible. I'm going to book a flight back today.'

'Do you want me to come with you to book it?' she offered.

'No that's fine,' he said. 'You can do me one favour though,' he said in mock-seriousness.

'What's that?' Kelly looked at him, her eyes open wide with anticipation.

'Get your sexy little arse over here,' he said, dragging her on top of him as Kelly let out a throaty giggle.

*

Jade waited for Kelly, a bit annoyed that she'd been left on her own all morning. She couldn't help feeling frustrated; she had made an effort today, after customising a red bikini with colourful feathers, and wanted to go to Plaza Beach to show it off. She understood that Kelly was happily falling in love, but she'd been waiting for ages and it was now one o'clock. There was hardly anyone round the pool at the PYR hotel and half of it was in the shade so she had to keep shifting places to stay in the sun as it moved.

Ten minutes later she saw Kelly approaching. About bloody time, Jade thought, getting up, folding her towel and putting it in her beach bag.

'Hi,' Kelly smiled cheerfully, walking with a spring in her step. 'Sorry I'm a bit late.'

'That's okay,' Jade replied, but not exactly meaning it. 'Though I have been on my own for ages. I've been *so* bored. I take it you're back together now then?'

'He asked me to be his girlfriend,' Kelly beamed, lifting her chin in the air proudly.

Jade couldn't help but smile. Kelly looked happier than she'd ever seen her. She couldn't be too annoyed for being left to her own devices for just one evening and morning. Besides, she could have met up with Jonny and his friends if she'd wanted to, but had decided she wanted to read her book instead and wait for Kelly.

'You won't be left on your own for long anyway, babe,' Kelly explained. 'Billy is going home.'

'Why?' Jade asked, mystified. He and Kelly had just sorted things out, so why on earth would he be going home now?

'I'll explain all on our way to . . . where are we going?'

'Plaza?'

'Okay, hun.'

Jade was very saddened to hear about Billy's mum, and thought how scared he must be. Jade had lost her nan to cancer of the bladder two years ago, and it had been so upsetting watching her slowly disintegrate week by week. She wasn't sure how she'd cope if her mum had to go through the same thing. Poor Billy, she thought, hoping his mum got well again.

Jade slicked on a coat of Clinique lip gloss before they reached Plaza Beach and Kelly asked to borrow some.

'You look gorgeous today, babe,' Kelly said, noticing Jade had made a real effort. Her old Essex ways were definitely back now; fake tan, eyelashes and nails were back in Jade's life once more.

'Thanks,' Jade smiled happily. 'Some of us still need to make an effort to impress. We don't all have sexy boyfriends, like you,' she joked.

They walked through the centre of all the large cream sunbeds, which were already full because it was so late in the day, when Jade heard someone call her name. She looked round and felt a wave of panic rush through her body – it was *Tom*. Was she seeing things? Why on earth was Tom here? She saw David next to him and knew then that it wasn't in her imagination.

'Oh my God, shut up! Tom is here!' Kelly gasped, her mouth wide open.

'I can't actually believe this,' Jade said, making her way over to him shakily. He was lying on one of the sunbeds, smiling at her like butter wouldn't melt. He did look good, she had to give him that, but it didn't change the fact that he was a lying scumbag.

'Hey,' he said, reaching forward to give her a kiss on the cheek.

Jade felt herself stiffen and pulled back, uneasy. 'What the hell are you doing here?' she asked, still amazed he was sitting in front of her. She'd come here to get away from him and now here he was, acting like it was completely normal!

'I came for a holiday,' he said nonchalantly, lying back down and gazing up at her. 'I'd already booked it before I knew you were here. That's okay with you, yeah? You look

237

like you've seen a ghost. Or is it because the last time you saw me you had tied me naked to a bed on stage?' He looked behind her and smiled. 'Hi Kelly.'

'Hi,' Kelly said blankly, not moving forward. She'd never be friendly with him after what he did to her best friend.

'You deserved what you got, Tom. And of course it's okay with me that you're here,' Jade said brusquely, annoyed by his arrogance. Marbella was a big place and he could do what he liked for all she cared. She sighed and shrugged her shoulders. 'It's your life; you can go where you want. I'm really not bothered.'

'You look amazing,' he said, eyeing her up and down. 'Seriously . . . amazing.'

'Thanks.' She felt her face go hot but kept her voice cool. 'How long are you here for?'

'Only have another three nights left,' he said, staring at her and pushing his hair back. 'We're going to that TIBU club tonight or something. David has booked us a table.'

'Oh, has he now?' Jade said tightly, not believing a word. Tom knew that was where she worked, she would put money on it. 'Well I'll see you there then, because I work there.'

'David couldn't remember if you'd said that to him the other night or not,' Tom answered coolly, rubbing his sunglasses with a little cloth. 'You know what he's like after a few drinks. I didn't think it would be a problem anyway. What happened between us was a long time ago now and I'm sure you're over it.'

'Yes, I am,' she retorted firmly, shocked he was being so blasé. It was really annoying.

'Good,' he nodded, putting his shades on. 'I'll catch up with you later then; will be nice to have a little chat if you get the chance.'

'Maybe. We do get very busy,' Jade answered quickly.

Did he seriously think he could just show up here, snap his fingers and she'd want to waste her time chatting to him?

'Okay, cool.' He gave her a little nod. 'Enjoy the rest of your day. Nice tan by the way.'

'See you later maybe,' she said, rolling her eyes at Kelly as she turned round. It took her a few seconds as she walked away to realise she was trembling. She felt pumped with adrenaline; seeing him had been the shock of her life and brought back lots of feelings she'd suppressed for so long. How was she going to be able to work tonight without talking to him? Tom wasn't supposed to be here, this wasn't the plan. And what was with the compliments and eyeing her up like he had a right to? He made her so angry. Jade had thought she was over him and had been for months, but now he was here she had to admit that along with her anger, she had a very odd feeling of excitement. Did she still care about him a little bit? Jade *knew* she would never get back with him – she wasn't that stupid – but the hurt he'd caused had gone, and it was nice to have some complimentary attention. Behind his cool façade was someone very much not over his ex-girlfriend; she knew him well enough to know that. Why would he come here otherwise? Marbella was definitely not his kind of place.

'Oh my God, I can't believe Tom is here! He *so* still fancies you!' Kelly said as they found two free sunbeds. 'I'm not being funny but he blatantly couldn't stop staring. It was hilare. So obvious!'

Jade was exasperated. 'Why on earth has he come here? David sent him that photo of us the other week, so it's obviously because he knew I was here. He reckons he'd already booked his flight by then, but I don't believe that for a minute.'

'Me either.' Kelly nodded.

Jade couldn't relax after seeing Tom. She just couldn't believe he was in Marbella and kept wondering if he was watching her as she sunbathed. She couldn't help but feel slightly flattered that he'd come here because of her. He obviously wasn't over her and if she was honest, she was glad. Girls always wanted their ex-boyfriends to regret losing them, didn't they? It didn't mean she still had feelings for him, just that she was glad *he* still liked *her*.

A short while later Billy and Jonny arrived, putting their towels down on two empty sunbeds next to them. They said hello and then Jade watched as Billy kissed Kelly firmly on the lips. Kelly couldn't stop smiling when he arrived; they were like two lovesick puppies. Jonny was hungover and didn't say much, in fact he was asleep within five minutes of laying his head down.

'How are you, Billy?' Jade asked, shooting him a concerned expression, wondering if he had any more news on his mum.

'I'm okay thanks. Booked my flight a minute ago.' He looked at Kelly.

'Oh. When do you go?' Kelly tried to hold back her pout.

'Four days' time,' he answered, rubbing her knee affectionately.

'Oh babe, I'm going to miss you,' Kelly said, getting up and sitting on his sunbed to kiss him.

Well, this isn't too awkward, Jade thought to herself as they continued to kiss for ages; *where am I supposed to look?* She understood that they weren't going to see each other for a while, but seriously, why didn't they just save it for the bedroom? Yes, she was happy for Kelly, but she did feel like she was being completely forgotten about. She wasn't used to her mate having a boyfriend and it was strange. In a selfish way, she was kind of looking forward to Billy leaving, so Kelly would be back to normal.

Jade looked over at Tom and he waved. Great, she thought, I look like a complete Billy-no-mates with no one talking to me. As much as she was happy Kelly had patched things up with Billy, she hated feeling left out and like a gooseberry. Still she couldn't be too angry, it wasn't as though Kelly did this all the time; usually she was single. Jade closed her eyes and tried to relax, hoping that tonight wasn't going to be too awkward with Tom.

*

Jake had chosen Smith's Brasserie in Ongar to announce their engagement and, knowing it had a reputation for having rich clientele, Lisa wore her best black Herve Leger bandage dress. She'd got it in the sale at Liberty London for two hundred and fifty pounds and Kelly had nearly had kittens when she told her she had bought the last one, because they were normally at least five hundred pounds. The dress had looked stunning on though and, seeing as it was plain black, she'd told herself it would never date and would last for years.

As she waited for her parents to get ready, Lisa heard the taxi sound its horn and felt butterflies in her stomach. She was so nervous. Her parents made their way down the stairs. Her mum looked attractive in a knee-length cream dress and jacket, and her dad very smart in black trousers and a shirt. They must have guessed what the night was in aid of, but they didn't say.

'You look beautiful,' her dad said proudly.

'Thanks Dad,' Lisa said, slightly embarrassed and looking away.

All she ever wanted was to make her parents proud. Would they be proud of her and look at her the same if they knew she'd had a one-night stand with a relative stranger on holiday? She knew the answer to that. They loved Jake. Everybody loved him. The truth would shock them all. Why had she still not told Jake? This night was such a ticking timebomb.

241

When they arrived at the restaurant, Jake and his parents were already in the upstairs bar. They had a drink before they sat down at their table and Lisa made sure she ordered a large glass of white wine; it was going to be a long night.

'You look absolutely stunning,' Jake said when he saw her, wrapping an arm around her waist and giving her a gentle squeeze.

'How are you, Lisa?' Jake's mum asked her, giving her a huge smile to reveal her perfect white veneers. 'Did you have a lovely time in Spain?'

'Yes thanks. How was Norfolk?' she asked, changing the subject quickly. Jake's mum, Susan, was a really lovely woman, but very much a typical Essex housewife. She was always going on about Botox parties and even trying to get Lisa to attend, even though she was only twenty-one! Lisa still got asked for ID everywhere she went, so she doubted she needed Botox. Susan had also had a boob job and her nose done; Lisa had been amazed when she saw her old photos, she looked like a completely different person! Jake's mum and her own mum were like chalk and cheese. Her mum was all about her career and dressed her forty-five years of age; whereas Susan was obsessed with all the latest brands and fashions and hadn't worked since she'd had her kids. She reminded Lisa of Kelly's mum in a way and she thought that if they were introduced would get on like a house on fire. She listened as Susan told her all about Norfolk, and thought about how much she would miss Susan, if she and Jake split up. That was the problem; she wouldn't just be losing Jake, but his family too. Just the thought of it stung.

A waitress came over and led them to a circular table downstairs. Jake squeezed her hand as he sat down beside her and smiled. She forced a smile back, but all she wanted to do was pick up her bag and run out the door.

The food was amazing and after the starters, Lisa's

stomach flipped over as Jake banged his glass quietly with his spoon to get everyone's attention. She felt sick. This was it; this was the big moment.

He cleared his throat and then finally spoke. 'I just wanted to say that I know you're wondering why we've brought you here tonight.' He turned and smiled at Lisa, then held her hand. 'Obviously Lisa and I have been together for quite a few years now, and I love her with all my heart. After I picked her up from the airport the other day I asked her to marry me . . . and she said yes.'

'Congratulations!' they all chorused.

'That's fantastic news,' Susan said, grinning from ear to ear.

'I couldn't be happier,' Lisa's dad said as he shook Jake's hand. 'Lisa couldn't have chosen a better man.'

'This calls for some champagne,' Lisa's mum said, smiling, signalling for their waitress to come over.

'When are you planning to get married then?' Jake's dad asked.

'Next year, hopefully,' he replied.

'You had better get a move on then!' Susan answered, unable to stop smiling. She shot Lisa a look of excitement. 'You'll need to go shopping for a dress soon, Lisa.'

She nodded, wishing that she was invisible. What was she going to do? This was supposed to be one of the happiest moments of her life and she wanted to disappear. Should she tell him? Or could she live with what she'd done? After all, he would never find out otherwise. It would make life a hell of a lot easier if she could bury it deep down. Maybe she wasn't too young to get married? She needed time to think. Lisa was so confused about everything. Shopping for wedding dresses was the last thing on her mind. This was all getting too much and happening too quickly. Jake hadn't stopped talking about going away for the weekend to Italy to see possible wedding venues. She felt the panic rise inside her and, feeling hot with the guilt and stress, excused herself to go to the toilet.

Lisa sat in the cubicle and forced herself to take deep breaths. Her eyes filled up with tears and she furiously blinked them away. This was a not a good time to cry, she thought; she needed to hold it together. She could tell him tonight and get it over with. Maybe he would forgive her? All she knew was that she was carrying a huge weight around on her shoulders and it was about time it was lifted off.

*

When they were alone in his room later that night, Jake turned to her, wrapping his arms around her waist.

He breathed in the scent of her and kissed her head. 'Well, everyone seems really pleased, don't they?'

'Mmm . . .' Lisa said, sighing and taking a step back as she removed her diamond Tiffany's necklace. She couldn't drag this on any longer. Jake wasn't engaged to the girl he thought he was.

Jake sat on the edge of the bed, throwing his shoes off. 'I hope you don't mind, but my mum asked me to ask you if she can go wedding dress shopping with you. With your mum too, of course. It's just she never got to go with my sister because she was in Australia and she always feels like she missed out.'

'Yeah . . . maybe.' Lisa turned away from him as she unzipped her dress.

'What's up? Do you not want her to go? Just say and I'll tell her. She was only asking.' He walked over to her with a concerned frown.

Lisa gave an irritated sigh. 'Nothing is up. She can come. I'm just tired,' she said, batting him off as he tried to get close to her.

'Something *is* up. I can tell. You can talk to me. You're not getting cold feet already are you?' He laughed.

'No,' she snapped. 'Just leave it. Nothing is up . . . I just . . . oh I don't know.'

Jake looked really worried now. 'You just what?'

She took a deep breath. 'Look, I just think it's all happening so fast,' she started.

'Nothing is happening fast, we haven't even organised one thing yet! You do want to marry me, don't you?' His eyes were wide and shiny with fear.

Lisa hesitated, not able to look him in the eye. 'Yes . . . it's just . . .'

He took her hands in his and held them firmly, looking her in the eye confidently and as he spoke calmly. 'Look, I love you more than life itself. I want you to be my wife! There is nothing to worry about. It might feel like things are happening fast, but we need to organise the wedding now if we want to get married next year abroad. There are lots of things to do. I thought you'd love organising your wedding?'

She nodded feebly. 'I'm . . . just tired. I need to sleep.'

He kissed her. 'Go on then, sleeping beauty, go to sleep. You'll feel better about it in the morning. Planning a wedding can seem scary, everyone says it, but I'm here to help too, remember.'

'Thanks Jake,' she said sadly. She climbed into bed with a heavy heart, knowing she probably wouldn't sleep a wink that night. When was she going to get the courage to tell him?

CHAPTER 16

Adele didn't feel great when she arrived at TIBU that night; she had a splitting headache and really needed a good night's sleep. She thought it was best to at least show up to work though and make the effort, even if she probably wouldn't stay. She was pretty bored of working now, despite the fact it was only three nights per week. She'd been doing it since May and the novelty had well and truly worn off. It didn't help that Lee had quit his job and was now just having a holiday; she always felt so jealous of his free time.

'Hi girls,' she said merrily, as she caught up with Jade and Kelly.

'Hi,' they replied unenthusiastically. Their faces seemed to drop as she approached them.

They'd never been the same with her since the night she kissed Sam and always kept their distance. Adele wasn't too fussed, they still spoke to her at work and she was sure they'd eventually get over it. She was bound to bump into them at home in Nu Bar or Faces and who knew, maybe they could all go out together one night? It was convenient for her because they lived so close. Sophie lived two hours away so it wasn't like Adele would be meeting up with her very often. Kelly may have thrown a drink in her face, but Adele supposed she did deserve it, really. And she was sure they'd be back to normal soon.

'How have you both been? I haven't spoken to you properly for ages,' she said, as they walked up the stairs to work.

'Good, thanks,' Kelly answered, uninterested.

'Love your shoes, babe,' Adele told Jade, trying to compliment something to get in her good books. Seeing as she was wearing the TIBU uniform, this was the only thing she *could* say she liked.

'These are old,' Jade said, looking surprised and suspicious. They were only a cheap pair of plain black heels; nothing special whatsoever. 'Thanks though.'

Adele forced a smile at her. 'How are your love lives going?' she asked, ignoring their lack of response.

Kelly's face changed into a slight smile. 'I have a boyfriend now. He works here in Marbella too, he's called Billy.'

'Really, hun? I think I've seen him talking to you in the bar before. He's hot. What about you, Jade?'

She shook her head. 'No one really.'

No thanks to me, Adele thought happily, and then pushed the thought from her mind. She needed something to impress them, and thought back to the other night when she had managed to pull the most handsome guy she'd seen in a long while.

She flicked her hair over her shoulder. 'Oh my God, the other night I went out with the girls to a few bars. Pulled this amazing bloke, like, literally the fittest one I've seen in ages,' she announced, smugly.

Kelly's eyes narrowed in disapproval. 'So you're not with Lee any more then?' she asked.

'Oh no, I'm still with Lee,' Adele laughed awkwardly, with a slight wave of her hand. 'It's just this guy was to die for, totes hot, trust me. If you'd seen him you wouldn't have blamed me.' She was slightly annoyed that they were looking at her with disgust. What the hell was their problem? So what if she cheated on Lee? He was probably doing the same to her, no doubt. All men cheated and so she did too. It's not like she was harming anyone and Lee didn't find out, so why did they care?

'Oh, right,' Kelly said, raising her eyebrows and looking extremely unimpressed.

Jade had already walked off to arrange the tables.

'We'll have to go out together when we get home.' Adele turned to Kelly, trying to leave things on a good note. 'We'll swap numbers and that, meet up for some drinks in The King Will or Sugar Hut, yeah?'

Kelly merely nodded and turned away to get a cloth which was behind the bar. 'Yeah, maybe. We'll take your number before we leave at the end of the season.'

Adele replied enthusiastically as she followed her, 'Wicked, babe. I'm buying my own flat soon down Manor Road in Chigwell, you know, the really nice ones. Trying to get the penthouse. My dad has put an offer in for me. If I do, it will be amazing. Has two big balconies, massive front room, ensuites, the lot. You can stay over and we can have drinks at mine and then even go up London or something?' They'd want to go out with her now, Adele bet. The place her dad was trying to buy her was out of this world and she would always be having parties there.

'Sounds good,' Kelly said looking behind her at the tables that needed cleaning. 'We'd better start working before Joe gets here.' She walked off to help Jade.

They were getting friendlier with her already, Adele thought, thinking everything would be fine and forgotten about when they all got home. She didn't have many girl-friends that she could truly count on. She loved going on nights out at home and always thought it was good to have as many back-up friends as possible in case she found herself at a loose end. Kelly and Jade were perfect for that; they were both fun, pretty and the three of them would draw lots of attention from men. She'd make sure that she got the most blokes though; no one stole the limelight from her.

Adele saw Joe walking up the stairs and walked over to him, giving a fake little cough as she did so.

'Hey,' he said, 'problem?'

Adele shook her head and looked at him innocently, opening her eyes as wide as possible and making her voice even huskier than usual. 'Joe, I'm really not feeling great tonight, I don't think I can stay.'

'What's up?' he asked, not looking at all pleased.

'Terrible headache.' She put her hand on her forehead and coughed again for good measure. 'Maybe it's the flu?'

'Try a paracetamol, we have them in the back office,' Joe said dismissively, about to walk off.

She stopped him in his tracks by adding quickly, 'No honestly, this is serious. I think I have a migraine coming on.'

He raised an eyebrow dubiously. 'It's not a hangover, I hope?'

She lowered her voice. 'No, I promise. I'm not like Kelly, who had to throw a sickie after getting smashed at Ocean Club.'

'First I've heard about that,' Joe said, annoyed by this bit of news, but also that Adele was a grass. Even though he wasn't happy, he wouldn't say anything to Kelly. After all, it was weeks ago now and he was actually more irritated that Adele was so transparently trying to manipulate him. Weren't girls supposed to stick together? He sighed. 'You better go home then.'

Her mouth curved into a smile. 'Thanks Joe. Sorry, but I'll be no use at all to you tonight.'

He waved his hand at her and walked away.

Brilliant, Adele thought, happy that she now had the night off. She'd take a headache tablet and then go and see

Lee for the night. She certainly didn't want to be serving drunken customers all evening. Hopefully Kelly would get in trouble too. That would teach her for throwing champagne in her face that day. No one crossed Adele.

*

'You won't believe what that nutter has just said to me.' Kelly turned to Jade who was lighting the candles on the table.

'What?' Jade looked up at her, wondering what on earth Adele could have said now.

Kelly was incredulous, her voice high-pitched with astonishment. 'That we can all go to her flat when we get home to have drinks and then go out for the night together.'

'Nothing surprises me with her,' Jade said, shaking her head in disbelief. 'When will she just realise that we're not cool with what she's done and we're not up for being friends?'

Kelly shrugged.

Jade was getting fed up with Adele and her fake friendliness. Seriously, why did she think they'd want to know about her getting with some guy the other night? She was a complete egomaniac.

Jade was scared of seeing Tom again tonight, and she hoped that he wasn't sitting at one of her tables. That would be so embarrassing; waiting on the man that had broken her heart. Jade hadn't been able to get him out of her head all day since she'd seen him. She used to believe that Tom was the person she couldn't live without; that he was the person she could completely be herself around; someone she could tell all her innermost thoughts to. Today when she'd seen him it had been like meeting a stranger. And the way he'd acted so casual had infuriated her.

Her worst fears were confirmed when Tom arrived with

David and his friends and were shown by a waitress to one of the tables she was serving. *Why me?* she thought angrily, wondering if she could ask if they could be moved. Jade then realised it would only look like she was bothered if she did say something, and that was the last thing she wanted Tom to think. She walked over to them and smiled sweetly. 'What can I get you?' Jade asked in the most self-assured manner she could muster.

Tom looked her up and down, exactly how he had on the beach earlier that day. 'Loving your sexy little outfit,' he said, as the others laughed.

She felt exposed and vulnerable standing in her tight black skirt and tiny red vest but carried on coolly, ignoring the comment. 'Would you like vodka? Gin? Whisky? The menus are on the table, so when you've had a look let me know.' She turned on her heel, flicked her hair and walked away. She would not let him beat her tonight and would act confident, even though she didn't feel it. Tom had this way of making her go all flustered when he spoke to her, and he stared like he was undressing her with his eyes. Why couldn't he just leave her alone? He'd made a real effort tonight with his appearance she noticed; he was looking very hot indeed.

After serving them two bottles of vodka and mixers, Tom stopped her as she was about to walk away.

'How are you, Jade?' he asked.

She smiled tightly. 'I'm good, thank you. Just fine. Having a wonderful time here,' she said, about to walk away.

He grabbed her wrist as she turned. 'I've missed you,' he said breathlessly, glaring into her eyes and making her heart ache. It was what she'd always longed to hear. His eyes told her he was hurting still; that he wasn't over their break-up. She always wanted him to regret it and now he was showing her he did. Even after she'd set him up in the theatre, embarrassed him, he still wanted her.

'Look, I have to get back to work,' she replied, brushing him off. There was no way she'd ever give him the satisfaction of telling him she'd missed him too; she had far more pride than that. So why did she still feel a longing towards him? She wanted him to pay her attention and she didn't know why. It was said that girls always loved a bad boy and she knew now how very true that was.

'Are you going out afterwards?' Kelly asked her as they crossed paths.

'If you are?' Jade replied.

'Apparently everyone is going to a club called Olivia, it's about five minutes in a taxi, so let's go there. Billy is meeting me after my shift.'

Jade nodded. *So Billy is going too*, she thought. That meant they'd be all over each other, leaving her on her own as usual or with Jonny, who she knew deep down would prefer to be chatting up other girls. Jade wanted Kelly to be happy, she really did, but she always ended up as the spare part. *Would I have been any different though if things had worked out with Sam?* she asked herself. Probably not, but it still didn't make her feel any better.

Tom kept his eyes firmly fixed on Jade all night, making her feel very self-conscious. She made sure she flirted with as many men as possible so he could see, which clearly made him angry. She could now see why Billy acted the way he did with those girls in Pangea that night, Jade thought, as she realised she was behaving in the exact same way.

'You going to Olivia tonight?' Sam asked her when she went to the bar to get some drinks for a table of giggling girls.

She shrugged. 'I'm not too sure yet. Are you?'

'Yeah, why not?' he replied with a smile that still melted her heart. He was shaking a cocktail as his eyes flicked up at her. 'You should go. It's massive and really good.'

'Hopefully I will,' she muttered as she placed the drinks on a tray he handed her across the bar.

'Yeah, hopefully,' he said warmly, holding her gaze and making exhilaration bubble inside her. *Stop being so pathetic and hold it together,* she ordered sternly. *He just wants to be friends.*

Jade sighed when she saw Billy arrive alone, going straight over to Kelly and kissing her. Why was Jonny not even out tonight? It would be so awkward if it was just the three of them.

'No Jonny?' she asked him, when she got the chance.

'Not tonight, he's being boring, went straight home after work,' Billy explained, lifting his eyebrows.

'Don't worry, we won't leave you out,' Kelly said, putting her arm round her shoulder and making her feel stupid.

'I'm not sure if I'm going to go to be honest,' Jade said touchily, extremely irritated that she was being left on her own again.

'Why?' Kelly asked, her voice strained, unable to hide her disappointment. 'Oh please come, I promise I'll be with you all night. Billy knows other people going.'

'I just don't feel like it,' Jade said stubbornly. She knew Kelly meant well, but she was also sure that Billy wouldn't be leaving her side all night either, and the thought of standing there like a gooseberry, especially in front of Tom *and* Sam, wasn't one bit appealing. She walked away in a sulk and began to clear away. The bar was emptying now and people were starting to leave. She noticed Tom and the others standing up, about to do the same.

'Where are you going after?' Tom asked her.

'I'm not,' Jade said moodily, as she collected more empty glasses on her tray.

The smile on his face disappeared in a flash. 'How come?'

She was pleased he looked disappointed. At least someone cared. 'I'm tired and it's late. I'm not really up for it.'

'Do you want to go for a quiet drink somewhere, just us two?' he asked hopefully.

Jade felt her heart flip. She wanted that more than anything, but how could she say yes after what he did to her? How could she act like he'd done nothing wrong and give him the wrong impression? She'd come so far in getting over him and couldn't allow herself to go back to square one. She wiped down the table with a cloth and then looked at at him, finally answering. 'Mmm . . . I don't really think it's a good idea,' Jade said softly, her eyes downcast.

He nodded, looking frustrated and giving a theatrical sigh. He folded his arms, his shoulders slumped and the light faded from his eyes. 'I understand. It was a long shot anyway. We're off now, but hopefully I'll see you again before I leave.'

Tom kissed her cheek, slowly, then he walked down the stairs where his friends were waiting for him. That was it; he was gone.

Jade set to work cleaning the bar and club, feeling sorry for herself but also pretty proud that she had been so strong.

'Babe, please come tonight,' Kelly tried again with a sweet smile.

'Kelly, I really don't feel like it. Please don't worry about me. Just go out with Billy,' she answered stubbornly.

'If you're sure you don't mind?' Kelly said, looking unsure. She quickly added, 'It's just that he's only got a few nights left and then he goes home.'

Jade carried on pretending she was fine with the situation, when really she was annoyed. Angry with Kelly for leaving her and then angry with Tom for coming to Marbella. She knew she was being stupid in not going out when she wanted to, but all her frustrations were making her snappy and stubborn. Jade knew deep down she was the only person that would ultimately lose out, but she was still lashing out, trying to make some kind of point to her friend.

Kelly asked her one more time to go, then left with Billy when Jade declined again. *Another early night on my own*, Jade thought miserably. She had had a great time in Marbella, but if she was ever to come back in future she would definitely make sure there were at least three friends together. It was no good being in a two when one of you fell in love. She walked down the stairs to the entrance and began the journey home. When she heard Tom's voice she turned round in surprise.

'Jade?'

'Tom, what are you doing here?' she asked in confusion, though she could tell he must have been waiting for her.

'I needed to see you.' His voice was serious.

'Where are your friends?' Jade looked round, expecting to see David and the others.

'They've gone to a club. I didn't want to go without you. Where are you going now, home?'

'Yes,' she replied, her insides turning to jelly.

'Then please let me at least walk you back?' Tom asked, the desperation clear in his voice.

She nodded, feeling flattered that he'd blown his mates out to be with her, even if it meant only walking her back to her apartment. It felt good to be around someone she knew; someone that cared about her. It was wrong to be with him now, she knew that, but she simply couldn't help it. Tom was being so loving and sweet and that was exactly what she wanted.

'How was it moving back home?' he asked, after a few seconds' silence.

'It was strange,' Jade replied. 'I wasn't sure if I'd fit in again. I changed so much going to university and . . . being with you. I wasn't sure if I *could* go back to living in Essex.'

'But you're happy now?' His head turned to see her response.

'Yes, I got used to it again pretty quickly and it kind of

255

felt like I'd never left after a while.' She didn't want to tell him how difficult she'd found it at first. He didn't deserve to know that she used to lie awake some nights, wondering where it all went so wrong.

'It was hard for me when you left,' he said forlornly, staring at the floor as he walked. He looked wistful as he remembered how gutted he had been when Jade had left his life. 'Everywhere and everything reminded me of you.'

She didn't know what to say. Didn't he think it had been harder for her, having to move back home after being humiliated and heartbroken?

'Everyone told me I was such a fool,' he continued, 'and I know I was . . . am. I lost the only thing that mattered to me in my life.'

'I don't really want to talk about it,' Jade said sharply. She didn't want to go over what had happened any more; it was all she had thought about for weeks on end before she'd come to Marbella and she was sick of it.

'Fair enough,' he said, shrugging his shoulders as though he didn't blame her. He changed the subject quickly. 'So what's your place like?'

Jade pictured their tiny, sweaty apartment covered in clothes and make-up and laughed. 'It's terrible. You'll see in a minute. Kel and I are a nightmare together because we're so messy.' She knew Tom – used to a super tidy home – would hate it, and she was looking forward to seeing his reaction. When she'd been his girlfriend he was always telling her off for having any mess in her university room and she used to try to keep it extra clean for his sake.

They reached her apartment after a few minutes and Jade felt extremely awkward. Did she invite him in? Or did she just say thank you and goodnight? Kelly wouldn't be back tonight; she would obviously go back to Billy's again. Jade felt lonely and hated herself for wanting Tom to come in and be with her.

'So, are you going to show me what a state your room is then?' he said in a lame attempt at a joke, when they reached the door.

'I wasn't lying when I said it was bad,' Jade replied with a giggle, opening the door and cringing at the state of the place.

'Whoah,' Tom said, looking at the mess with an astonished expression.

'Well it's not really our fault,' she tried to quickly explain, 'the room is too small for two girls but it's all we could afford and . . .'

'Shh,' he said, placing his fingertips gently on her mouth and looking at her lustfully. 'Your secret is safe with me.'

Her lips tingled even after he took his hand away and she felt herself blushing from the contact. Jade knew then that she didn't want Tom to leave that night. She wanted to spend one last night with him; not to get back together, but to feel that affection once more, something she hadn't had for a long time. She realised how much she missed the physical presence of a man in her life. It was more than just sex, it was being close to someone; feeling loved and comforted. Even just to cuddle would have felt great. Jade knew she couldn't get attached to him, because there was no trust there any more, but despite herself she felt a burning desire rush along her skin, inside and out, and she ached for him to come closer when he sat on her bed.

'Jade,' he said seriously. 'You look stunning, you know. I haven't been able to take my eyes off you all night.'

She wanted him to lean forward and kiss her, make the first move, but wasn't brave enough to say so.

He shook his head. 'Honestly, I know you probably think I'm just saying this,' he continued, 'but you're the perfect girl for me. Believe it or not, I haven't been with anyone else since you. Not a single girl.'

She didn't care what he had to say, it made no difference. She wanted him with an urgency she didn't even know existed. Jade leant forwards and pressed her lips against his and felt his response instantly. As he ran his fingers through her hair, she bit his bottom lip, craving every part of him. She started to unbutton his shirt but he stopped her.

'Are you sure you want to do this?' he asked as he caught his breath back.

Jade didn't reply; just continued to remove his shirt, revealing his muscular chest. Her fingers skimmed down the smooth skin of his back. Once again she found his lips, kissing him hungrily. Her need for him was greater than ever before and she groaned as Tom pushed her back on the bed forcefully, and arched her back as he lifted her vest over her head and unhooked her bra. She closed her eyes as he began to pull down her black mini-skirt and then he paused.

What now? she thought, impatiently.

His voice was high-pitched. 'Jade, what the hell is this?'

She looked down and realised he was staring at the few remaining crystals of her vajazzle, which had been a red crystal design in the shape of lips. Kelly had done it for her almost two weeks ago and it had come off minus three crystals, which she realised as she looked down did look rather odd. It had been so low down she hadn't really thought about it. She exhaled sharply, putting her hand over her eyes. 'It was vajazzle, don't worry about it,' she said with an embarrassed laugh. She'd forgotten it was there.

'A what?'

'Vajazzle. It looked a lot better before, it's nearly all come off now.'

'Whatever you say,' he replied, confused. But it didn't delay him for long.

*

Tom was woken the following morning by the powerful Marbella sunshine beaming through the windows. He looked at Jade sleeping soundly next to him and smiled as memories of the previous night came flooding back. She'd been all over him as soon as he got in her room, he mused. To think he'd even worried for a minute that he couldn't get her back; it had been easier than he thought.

Last night had been outstanding, maybe even their best sex so far, he thought, recalling Jade's wild ways. He didn't know what had got into her, but he liked it.

He laid his head on the pillow and watched her. She was so beautiful, and now, once again, she was his; he had another chance. He wouldn't ruin it this time, and he would try his best to remain faithful to her. Hopefully she'd get a flight back with him in a few days' time, when he left. After all, she couldn't expect to stay in Marbella now they were back together; he wouldn't like that idea at all and would let her know straight away. When they got home she could move back to Bath and they could go house hunting; he'd already seen a few properties online that seemed perfect. Or maybe they could wait a little bit so they could save enough to buy somewhere instead. He didn't like the idea of renting; it was money down the drain, but they would want to live together sooner rather than later so it was a discussion they'd have to have soon.

Tom was thankful that it hadn't been a wasted trip to Marbella. He'd had his last bit of single fun and now he'd got exactly what he came for. He had clearly been wrong when he thought she was seeing some other guy, after seeing her with him a few nights back. Obviously they were just friends. He wasn't sure how he would have taken it if she'd met someone else.

Jade's eyes opened and he felt a wave of excitement. Maybe she'd be up for a repeat performance of last night, he wondered, kissing her. She gently pushed him away and groaned.

'Give me a chance, I've just woken up,' she said, groggily getting out of the bed and padding to the bathroom.

He watched her walk away in her underwear and imagined peeling it off again when she got back in bed. She had a great little figure and her breasts were just as he liked them; small and pert. He hoped she'd got over her whole boob job phase; he hated fake breasts with a passion. That had been a part of the Essex girl coming out in her, but when they were together again he'd soon put a stop to all that.

'I'm so tired.' Jade returned and sat on the edge of the bed. She had put some shorts and a top on, which disappointed Tom.

'That's because you kept me up till God knows what time,' he smirked as he sat up in bed, folding his arms and leaning his head on his hands.

She laughed, slightly uncomfortably.

'Come here,' he said in a low voice, patting the bed next to him.

Her face dropped. 'I can't. I have to get ready to go out. I'm meeting someone.'

He nodded, but it stung and Tom wondered why she was being cold towards him. 'No worries,' he said. 'Shall I meet you as well? Where are you going? I'll go back and get ready.'

She paused and then answered finally. 'It'll be a bit awkward because I'm meeting someone that needs to speak to me about something.'

'Okay,' he said, swallowing his irritation and trying to be understanding. He didn't want to push it; he'd only just got on the good side of her. 'Are you going to Nikki Beach tonight?'

She swallowed hard. 'Yes, we are.'

'Jade,' he took her hand gently, gazing into her eyes seriously, 'when we get home, I want you to move back to Bath with me. We can start looking at a few places to rent. Though if you'd prefer to live at my mum's for a while so we can save to buy . . .'

'Tom, what are you talking about?' Jade looked discomfited, her forehead creasing into a frown.

'Where we're going to live when we get back home.'

She pulled her hand away, making him flinch. 'I'll be living in Essex,' she replied, bemused.

He was perplexed. 'What do you mean? You love Bath and you know Essex is inconvenient for me for several reasons.' He was becoming impatient now, as she sighed and looked in the other direction, standing up.

'Look, Tom, I think you've got the wrong idea. Last night was great, but it doesn't mean I want to get back together with you. I'm sorry if you thought otherwise,' Jade said, avoiding eye contact with him.

Tom wanted the ground to swallow him up. 'So what was last night then? Did you just use me?' He was incredulous; eyes staring at her accusingly.

'Come on Tom, don't be so dramatic!' Jade said, rolling her eyes. 'You wanted it as much as I did. It was just a bit of fun, nothing serious. It's not like we haven't done it before.'

She was acting so casual about it that it made him even more exasperated. 'Funnily enough, Jade, we're not all like you; sleeping around for the *fun* of it,' he retorted curtly, eyes narrowed into angry slits. 'I've been willing to forgive you for what you did to me in the theatre that day and this is how you treat me? It wasn't exactly fun, you know, being laughed at for weeks! They even made a Facebook group about me!'

'I'm sorry,' she said, biting the inside of her cheek to prevent herself from laughing; his indignation was bordering on funny, considering how he'd treated her in the past. Then she turned to him, affronted, speaking firmly. 'But I *don't* sleep around, so get your facts right before you say them. That's pretty rich coming from you, as well.'

'Whatever,' he replied tersely, jumping out of bed and throwing his jeans and shirt on in a flustered manner.

She breathed out sharply. 'You're being ridiculous.'

He ignored her, and then turned around before he opened the door. 'Last night meant something to me. If you weren't so stubborn you would get over the past and give me another chance, like I know you want to deep down.' His tone was scathing.

Jade shook her head with disbelief at the turn of events. 'Tom, I'm sorry, but you've got the wrong idea. I don't want to be with you. You lied and cheated and I won't ever forget that. Please, just leave.'

'Don't worry, I am!' he shouted furiously, slamming the door behind him as he went. He couldn't believe what had just happened. What on earth was the matter with her? It was obvious she wanted him back; she just had too much pride to say it. Well, she'd lose him this time for good now; he wasn't going to wait around for her any longer. How dare she make him look so stupid? Jade was just trying to get him back for what he did in the past, but this time she would end up the loser. He was going to enjoy the rest of his holiday now and forget all about her. Tom was going to sleep with as many girls as possible – and make damn sure she knew about it!

CHAPTER 17

Jade was finishing her eye make-up when Kelly opened the front door.

'Hey,' she called out as she walked into their room.

'Hi,' Jade replied, walking out of the bathroom to tell her what happened. 'How was your night?'

'It was really good, you should have come. The club was amazing.'

Like I really had a choice, Jade thought. 'You'll never guess who came back here last night,' she said guiltily.

'What? You had someone back here, you little hussy?' Kelly teased. Then her face dropped. 'Oh please don't tell me it was Tom!'

Jade nodded, abashed. 'But before you have a go at me, it was a one-time thing. Closure. I promise I'm not getting back with him or anything like that. I just felt a bit lonely.'

Kelly shrugged her shoulders. 'Then you should have come out with us, not slept with that loser!'

'How do you know we slept together?' Jade's eyes narrowed.

Kelly eyed her suspiciously. 'Well, did you?'

'Yes, but like I said, it was for closure.' Jade brushed her hair in the mirror on the dressing table.

'I really hope so,' Kelly said earnestly as she sat on the edge of the bed, took her heels off and rubbed the soles of her feet. 'And?'

'Pretty amazing, seeing as it's been such a long time for me; I was almost beginning to feel like a born-again virgin. Then this morning he was like "Oh so when we get back home you'll have to come move back to Bath."'

Kelly was affronted. 'Is he for real?'

'I know. I can't believe he thought he was totally forgiven and we could just go back to how things were! I told him no way, it was just a bit of fun.'

'Good,' Kelly replied, her eyes flashing with anger. 'How could he think he could just walk back into your life like that?'

'One more thing,' Jade said, cringing as she remembered. 'What?'

'I was basically the hairiest person alive. You were supposed to wax me yesterday, but never got round to it. It was *so* embarrassing! It's like a bloody forest down there.'

Kelly burst into laughter and fell on the bed holding her stomach as tears ran down her face.

'Glad you find it funny,' Jade said with a giggle.

'That's the funniest thing I've ever heard. Absolutely hilare!' Kelly said as she tidied up her hair again. 'I'm going to call you Kate Bush from now on.'

'Or George Bush,' Jade added, laughing as she took some fake eyelashes out the packet and fiddled with the glue.

'Who's that?' Kelly asked with a baffled expression.

'The ex-president of the United States, you dope. You know him. He's short, grey hair, bit slow on the uptake . . .'

Kelly frowned. 'Sorry, Miss Smarty Pants, but I don't even know the president of our country, let alone the United States.'

'You mean Prime Minister? It's David Cameron, and before that it was Gordon Brown. Remember?'

Kelly giggled, throwing her head back. 'I thought Gordon Brown was that chef off the telly!'

Jade burst into a fit of laughter and rolled her eyes. 'That's Gordon Ramsay! Right, stop talking before you say something else totally ludicrous.'

'Right hairy Mary, I'll quickly get ready, and then we'll go to the beach or something. I said to Billy I'd meet him if that's okay?'

Jade nodded, secretly angry that once again she had to spend the day with Billy and Jonny. Did Kelly not realise how boring it was for her? Why couldn't she just wait until she got home to see him? No doubt he'd be going to the Nikki Beach party as well that night, she thought grumpily.

What a morning she'd had. She couldn't believe that Tom had seriously thought everything was okay between them just because she'd slept with him. He'd reacted so childishly too, slamming the door when he left. It wasn't *her* fault she didn't trust him and couldn't ever get back with him. She couldn't believe he'd made that dig about her sleeping around too! What was he on? That was seriously hypocritical.

It had felt good being with someone so familiar, but when she'd woken up she had just wanted him to leave. The lust from the previous night had completely disappeared and she felt no choice but to lie and pretend she was spending the day with someone she needed to talk to confidentially. She almost felt sorry for Tom at first, but then he'd become angry, which only showed her she was making the right decision. She'd never regret sleeping with him one last time – she had needs after all, and he'd been the perfect person at the time to fulfil them. Jade had hurt him though; she'd seen it in his eyes, and despite everything he'd put her through she hadn't wanted to do that. She'd got him back enough that day in the theatre. Jade walked over to their wardrobe to see what she could wear for that evening.

The silver sparkly dress was to die for. It had the most gorgeous glittery silver sequins sewn on nude mesh material with cut-out transparent parts. The built-in cups on the top would even make it look like she had a decent pair of boobs. It was incredibly daring to wear it, because it looked so sexy, with glimpses of flesh revealed in between the scattered sequins. She'd try it on and hopefully it would fit. Kelly wouldn't mind her borrowing it, they were always swapping clothes. Kelly always had the best dresses: tight mini body-con dresses, stunning sequin and jewel encrusted numbers and a corset dress that pushed her boobs up so high they were practically under her chin.

Jade had always been a shopaholic before university, often going to Bluewater, Lakeside or the West End with Kelly, but when she'd moved to Bath she'd changed. Tom never approved when she bought anything new, always telling her she had plenty of clothes in her wardrobe already that she never wore, so eventually she didn't go shopping for anything unless she really needed it. Why had she listened to him? What had it been about him that always made her feel like she was striving for his approval? She promised she'd never change herself for any man ever again. Looking through Kelly's clothes made Jade realise how much her wardrobe needed an update. She couldn't wait to go home, get a job and be able to afford dresses like Kelly had.

She slipped the dress over her head and zipped it up. It fitted perfectly. Wow, she thought as she studied herself in the mirror, the dress did amazing things for her figure. Kelly came out of the bathroom wrapped in a towel and gasped.

'Babe, you look fantastic! Seriously beauts!'

'Do I?' Jade said, smiling as she twirled.

'You one hundred per cent *have* to borrow that for tonight. You look like you've been vajazzled all over!'

Jade laughed. 'You and your bloody vajazzles!'

Later that evening the girls were glammed up and standing outside Nikki Beach nightclub, waiting to go in. Jade felt fantastic in Kelly's dress and was pleased to see a few men admiring her as she walked past them. She had clip-in extensions tonight and decided that when she got home she was going to get real ones; it felt great having twice the amount of hair, curled to perfection. She felt like a film star.

As they walked through to the club, Jade couldn't believe how busy it was already. Girls swarmed the dance floor wearing long embellished maxi dresses, and she even noticed a couple of reality TV stars. This was definitely the place to be tonight, Jade thought happily, as she spotted a group of attractive men eyeing her and Kelly up.

'Let's stand near those men,' Jade said excitedly, heading in their direction. 'They're all gorgeous and haven't stopped looking over.'

Kelly barely glanced at them before saying 'Babe, Billy is over there. I said we'd sit on his table. They have free drinks and everything. Come on, it'll be fun.'

Jade was fuming. Couldn't they just have half an hour on their own any more? Kelly had spent all day with Billy, why did she have to be with him all night too? Did Kelly ever consider that it might be a bit boring for Jade? Ever since she'd met Billy all Kelly did was worry where he was and want to meet up with him; it was driving Jade crazy!

Jade rolled her eyes. 'Whatever,' she replied.

Kelly frowned and shook her head, her long hair bouncing as she did so. 'Don't be like that, Jade, he'll be going home soon.'

'We won't be here for that much longer either though, Kelly, and you *will* see him again, you know,' Jade retorted sarcastically.

'Yes I know that,' Kelly said huffily. 'It's up to you what you do, but I'm going to sit with Billy.'

Jade exhaled loudly. 'And obviously I have no choice but to do the same,' she said to herself as she followed in Kelly's footsteps.

'Hi girls,' Billy beamed as he saw them approach, grabbing two glasses and filling them with ice and vodka.

Kelly kissed Billy and whispered something in his ear, making him laugh.

She's leaving me already, Jade thought, feeling more and more annoyed.

Two other girls joined their table and Jonny began to chat to one of them, leaving Jade feeling completely isolated. Kelly noticed and called her over.

'Come stand with us,' Kelly said.

Jade stood and tried to join in their conversation but it was no use. They were too loved-up to notice she was even there and were constantly making private jokes, talking about things she wasn't involved in. She felt the frustration and anger rise inside her. Kelly was completely out of order. Why couldn't she spend some time away from her boyfriend?

After a few more vodkas and not feeling any better about the situation, Jade noticed Tom on a table a bit further along from them and he signalled for her to go over to him. Despite the fact she really didn't want to talk to him, she thought it would be nice to talk to *someone* at least and not be standing by herself like a loner, so she made her way through the crowd to his table.

'Hi,' he said with a serious expression.

'What's up?' Jade asked nonchalantly.

'Can I talk to you a minute?' Tom looked to the part of the club which was outside, where it was quieter.

Jade nodded and followed him, wondering what on earth he was going to say to her.

He stopped and turned to her, looking completely out of his comfort zone. He put his hand on her shoulder gently.

'Look,' he said. 'I apologise for what I said earlier, but you have to understand where I'm coming from.'

'Yes, I know. I'm sorry for giving you the wrong idea,' Jade replied, glad he wasn't too angry now.

'I was upset because being with you last night brought back so many memories. I'm not over you and I'm not interested in any other girls.' He relaxed a bit and looked at her with his big puppy dog eyes.

Jade nodded but bit her lip, unsure what she should say. He still didn't get it, did he?

'I still love you,' he said, staring into her eyes and making her feel awkward. 'I'm willing to forget about how you've acted this morning and give you another chance. After what happened I decided I wasn't going to speak to you again, but today I couldn't stop thinking of you. I think we should get back together – and make it work this time. We're so good together, you know we are. Please stop being so stubborn; you've punished me enough now. Just admit that you feel the same?' he pleaded confidently with a lopsided grin, rubbing her cheek lightly with his hand.

Jade couldn't believe her ears. *He* was going to give *her* another chance! What a nerve! She didn't want him to. He was the last person on earth she'd ever want to be with.

She gently removed his hand from her face, holding it for a few seconds before letting go. 'Tom, I'm going to say this for the last time. I *don't* feel the same as I used to and I never will. Do you really think I could just get back with you and act like nothing has happened after what you've done? I would never trust you again. I'm not being stubborn, I'm being honest.' She saw him flinch and when a flicker of anger appeared in his eyes again, she knew it was best to leave him. 'Look, I'm going to head back . . .'

'We *can* make it work, Jade, you know we can,' Tom said desperately, reaching out for her hand.

'I'm sorry . . .' She took a step back from him.

'You're not fucking sorry though, are you?' he exploded out of nowhere, his face turning puce with rage. 'How do you think this makes me feel? Maybe if you'd have wanted sex a bit more than once a bloody week in Bath I wouldn't have had to go elsewhere!'

Jade was so shocked that she slapped him round the face. She quickly turned to walk away, stunned by her own actions, when Tom grabbed her forcefully and yanked her backwards towards him, breaking the strap on Kelly's dress.

'I'm not finished with you!' he scowled, his face contorted in anger.

Jade was furious and stared him in the eye fearlessly. 'Well, I'm finished with *you*! Now leave me alone, I don't ever want to see or speak to you again!'

'Is everything okay here?' Sam appeared, shoving Tom out of his way and standing in front of Jade to protect her. He gave Tom a baleful look and there was a steely edge to his voice. 'Why don't you just leave her alone? It's clear she doesn't want to speak to you. I just see you've already had one slap and if you're not careful you'll get another.'

Tom looked at him coldly, obviously livid, shaking his head as if he no longer cared. 'She's all yours, mate. Have her.'

Sam turned to face Jade with a concerned expression. 'Are you okay?'

Her eyes were hot, brimming with tears and there was a lump in her throat, which meant she couldn't even answer. She was shaking with adrenaline and fury as she strode away, holding the strap of the dress. It had completely snapped and she doubted it could easily be sewn back on. How dare Tom grab her like that? One minute he was the nice guy and then when he didn't get his own way he turned! Jade never wanted to see his face again as long as she lived. Tears started to stream down her cheeks and she brushed them away, furious that she was getting upset over such a pathetic bloke. It was nice of Sam to intervene, but she'd never felt so embarrassed in all her life. Kelly would understand; she really needed some sympathy right now. But as she made her way over, Kelly's mouth flew open.

'What the hell has happened to my dress?' she asked angrily.

'It was Tom,' Jade said, thinking Kelly would soon change her tune when she knew what had happened. 'I went to speak with him and he pulled me back and ripped the strap. I'm so angry with him. You'll never believe what he sa . . .'

'Oh my God,' Kelly interjected, devastated as she touched the strap and looked at the material to see if it could be fixed. 'That dress cost me three hundred quid! It took me ages to save for that! It's completely ruined! Thanks Jade.'

Jade's mouth opened wide. 'Sorry, but it was *Tom*. He was being so horrible to me. He started saying he was going to give me another . . .'

Kelly interrupted before she could finish the sentence. 'Jade, for God's sake, when are you going to learn that the guy is a complete prick? He's a snobby, womanising cheat and I can't believe you even fell for him in the first place. Why did you bother wasting your time going to talk to him?' she asked crossly, folding her arms.

Jade's face darkened. 'Well maybe it's because my best friend does nothing but leave me all the time. Do you really think I want to stand here all night on my own while you snog Billy's face off?'

Kelly's eyes opened wide with shock. 'What? How can you say that? I'm constantly trying to include you, but you just act so miserable when he's around. To think of all the times I've been there when you've had a boyfriend or met someone you liked. You're just well jell,' she said, narrowing her eyes and shaking her head.

271

'Jealous of you? *Please*, do me a favour,' Jade replied, just as nastily as Kelly had, nearly spitting out her words. 'I've never left you alone every night for weeks. Maybe the odd night out, but come on, it's getting a bit of a joke now. Some friend you are.'

'You can talk! You've just ruined a brand-new dress that cost me three hundred quid and you're not even sorry! I have to work to afford nice things, Jade. I didn't just pack my bags and run off to uni to get four days off a week and a student loan,' Kelly fumed, flicking her blonde hair back over her shoulders.

'I said sorry, didn't I? And who are you to slag off going to uni? At least I could actually get into one!' Jade was exasperated, her blue eyes getting bigger and rounder by the second.

'That's low, Jade, really low. After everything I've done for you!'

'Like what?' Jade challenged her, shrugging her shoulders.

'I was the one who helped you look normal again. Do you realise how pale you first were when you came home. *Do you*?' Kelly said sharply.

Jade threw her eyes to heaven. 'So what? You lent me fake tan! Big deal!'

Kelly was affronted. 'It wasn't just the fake tan. I helped you get back to your old self; inside and out. I helped you realise that the old Jade was the *real* one. The one we love. I helped you see that you were willing to change into some kind of frump to please that bastard Tom!'

Jade showed Kelly her palms and lifted her shoulders. 'I said sorry about the dress. What else do you want me to say?'

'Yeah, you really looked like you meant it when you said sorry,' Kelly answered sarcastically, shaking her head with disappointment. 'I'm getting a drink.' Kelly turned and walked back towards Billy.

'That's right!' Jade called after her. 'Go back to Billy, you *have* been apart from him for two whole minutes, you're probably missing him like crazy by now! However have you coped without him by your side?'

Jade stormed to the toilet, desperate to get away. Now what was she supposed to do? This whole night had been nothing but a disaster. She *did* say sorry to Kelly about her dress – how was it her fault if her psycho ex-boyfriend had ruined it? If Kelly wasn't with Billy every single second then Jade wouldn't have spoken to Tom in the first place! She was so angry. Jade was angry with Tom for being so arrogant and aggressive and now she was angry with Kelly, for not realising how much she left her on her own all the time. Her eyes welled up with tears and she ran into the toilet cubicle so she could cry in private. Kelly didn't even care about her. She was all alone, away from home. Maybe she'd had enough of Marbella, she thought as the tears smudged her make-up; perhaps it was time to go home soon. Back to nice home-cooked meals and her warm bed. She would even welcome the colder weather, if it meant getting a warm welcome from her family and being around people that really wanted her there. She'd give herself another few weeks and then she was going to book her flight home. Kelly would probably be over the moon when she told her, as she'd get to see Billy all the time. Maybe Jade *was* a little envious of their relationship; she wasn't jealous though, like Kelly said. Deep down Jade was happy for her best friend, but she couldn't help being fed up playing the spare part all the time. Surely Kelly would have felt the same had it been the other way round?

Jade wiped her eyes and got out her compact mirror from her bag. She didn't look too bad, she supposed, despite the ripped dress. She decided she was going to leave the club and find a taxi to take her home; she'd definitely had enough tonight. She wouldn't bother telling

Kelly she was going; she doubted she'd care anyway, and she'd probably be staying at Billy's tonight anyway. Another day of waking up alone, Jade thought miserably. Maybe she'd just find a nice quiet spot on the beach and sunbathe alone tomorrow.

As she left the toilet she walked over to the huge mirrors to wash her hands, and sighed as she saw Adele leave another cubicle behind her. Just when I thought my night couldn't get any worse, Jade mused.

'You alright, babe?' Adele asked her brightly with a huge grin.

'Good thanks,' Jade lied, wanting to get away as quickly as possible.

Adele pouted at her reflection and took bronzer out of her bag, applying it to her thickly coated, chocolate-coloured cheeks. 'Nice dress.'

'Thanks,' Jade murmured, looking down. 'Shame it's ruined.'

'How do you know that guy you were chatting to earlier?'

Jade frowned and stared at her. 'What guy?'

'You were having a conversation – the one that broke your dress,' Adele said as she turned to face her, her back to the entrance of the toilets just a few feet away. Jade saw Lee approach the door. He stood there waiting for Adele, without her realising. 'Tom, is it?'

'Tom?' Jade's forehead creased up as she wondered why she was asking about *him*. 'He's my ex-boyfriend. We broke up not long before I came here,' Jade replied, perplexed.

Adele looked ecstatic, flapping her hands up and down as she spoke. 'Oh my God, babe, you're joking. I met him the other night at Lineker's bar and he came back to mine! All over me, he was. He's been texting me ever since,' she said proudly, a smug look on her face.

Jade saw Lee's mouth open in shock and thought it would be a good idea to get some more details for him to hear.

Adele deserved it, after all. 'What, you slept with him? You slept with Tom?'

Adele nodded. 'Yeah. What a small world,' she said with a giggle.

Jade cringed, wincing as she said the words. Not only because the thought made her feel sick, but because she knew Lee was at the door and had heard every word too.

'Is that so?' Lee said loudly, his face red with fury. He raced off through the club and Adele ran after him.

'Lee!' she wailed. 'Wait!'

Jade rinsed her hands under the taps, wishing she could rinse away everything that had happened that night too.

*

Adele chased after Lee, terrified that he wouldn't forgive her. What could she say? How could she deny it? He'd just heard her boasting to Jade that she'd slept with her ex-boyfriend the other night; she'd been caught red-handed. Why was he waiting for her outside the toilet when she said she'd meet him back at their table? And why hadn't she just kept her big mouth shut? He'd never forgive her, she just knew it. She couldn't believe she'd been caught. *Think*, Adele thought to herself, *think of something you can say*.

She chased after Lee, who was almost jogging now, and called after him again as he reached the front of the night-club to leave. 'Lee!'

He turned around with a face like thunder. 'What the hell do you want? Just leave me alone,' he said, heading for the taxi rank.

'Can you at least let me explain?' Adele said breathlessly, not even sure what she was going to say. She felt sick with desperation.

'Okay, go for it. What do you want to explain?' he asked

coldly, standing still as he glared at her. He shrugged when she didn't answer right away.

'I didn't sleep with that bloke the other night. I was just saying it to piss her off. I know you won't believe me, but I swear it's true,' Adele lied, putting on her best innocent voice and a doe-eyed expression.

'Bollocks, you were lying,' he glowered, looking at her like she was a speck of dirt on his shoe. 'I heard every word you said. You were showing off, and you *weren't* lying. You went to Lineker's the other night and how the hell do I know where you stayed or who stayed with you? Just do me a favour and fuck off,' he spat furiously.

'What, so that's it then?' Adele said sniffing, letting the tears fall down her face and hoping he would have some sympathy for her. He'd never seen her cry.

Lee turned away from her, uninterested. His voice was calm as he said, 'Funnily enough, yeah, that is it.'

Adele pulled his arm, turning him round to face her. 'Are you seriously saying we're over because I made something up to Jade? I don't understand why you won't believe me?'

'Wipe away those crocodile tears, babe,' he said. 'They don't suit you.'

'Please, Lee!' she shouted, as he climbed into a taxi.

He ignored her, staring straight ahead, and she watched, heartbroken, as the taxi sped away.

She'd really messed things up this time, hadn't she? Even *she* couldn't get herself out of this one. Adele thought back to the night she'd met Tom. The minute she saw him she'd fancied him and knew he'd be the one that would be accompanying her home that night. He hadn't exactly been hard to get, she remembered. After he'd stayed that night she thought she wouldn't even see him again; he lived nowhere near her Essex home and was only there on a holiday. She'd lied about her name as well, as she didn't want it to ever get back to Lee. She had told Tom she was on holiday too, worrying if she'd told him she worked at TIBU he might have been some lunatic that showed up to see her again. Adele couldn't believe her eyes when she'd seen Tom talking to Jade; she knew there had been something between them because of the way they were acting. Tom had looked really upset and there was no denying the love in his eyes for Jade. He certainly hadn't looked at Adele that way.

When she'd seen Tom rip the strap on Jade's pretty little dress, she'd laughed out loud. *Gutted, Jade*, she'd thought, *your dress isn't looking so good now, is it?* She couldn't wait to tell her that she'd slept with him and followed her to the toilets. She wanted Jade to know she could have *anyone* she wanted; that she was just as pretty as her and Kelly, and could have any man either of those two had. She saw the shock on Jade's face when she told her and had loved her reaction, but when she heard Lee's voice her blood had run cold.

Adele didn't know where to go. Should she go home, or round to Lee's to try and amend things? There was no point tonight, she acknowledged, he was totally angry and she wouldn't get anywhere with him. She'd let him calm down and sleep on it and that would also give her time to think of a really good story. Of all the people she'd cheated on him with, she never thought she'd be caught out with Tom. That was supposed to just be a one-night stand with a fit guy, not the end of her relationship with Lee. Plus, she'd only just discovered that Lee had really wealthy parents. Maybe she wouldn't have been so quick to cheat on him if she'd known that before. He'd told her that he lived in Woodford Green when she met him, so she assumed he must have a big house seeing as it was such an expensive area, but it was only a few days ago that he started reeling off all the places that his parents had places abroad. They even had one in New York! That had been a huge bonus and she had to stop herself from asking when *they* were going. Adele had always been dying to go to New York since becoming hooked on *Sex and the City* years ago, and she had pictured Lee whisking her off on a first-class flight to take her shopping in Saks Fifth Avenue. She imagined the type of present he would have bought her for her birthday. Maybe diamonds or a Chanel handbag? She was going to fight tooth and nail to get him back; she'd always wanted a rich boyfriend and now she had one she wasn't going to lose him just because of this stupid incident. If only she could think of a good reason why she'd said she slept with Tom, Adele thought, as she walked over to the nearest taxi.

*

Kelly looked round the nightclub and noticed that Jade was nowhere to be seen. She's probably left without even telling me, she thought angrily. She couldn't believe she'd ruined her dress and didn't even seem that bothered about it. She'd only ever worn it once herself and loved it. It had taken her ages to save for it too. All Jade seemed to care about was her stupid ex-boyfriend, who frankly Kelly didn't understand why she was even giving a second of her time to. What was wrong with Jade? Yes, she'd been spending lots of time with Billy, but surely Jade understood that he was leaving soon to see his sick mum and she wouldn't see him again for ages? Why couldn't Jade just be happy for her? Kelly took another sip of her drink and sighed. Usually they never argued, in fact, she couldn't even remember the last time it happened. No doubt if Jade had met someone too they wouldn't have even had cross words. Well, Kelly wasn't sorry that she'd met Billy, or for spending time with him. Jade should just accept that, like any good friend would.

'You okay, honey?' Billy asked, kissing the top of her head.

'Yeah, just a bit pissed-off that Jade's gone home without even letting me know.'

He looked at her with a concerned expression. 'Do you want to go back to your apartment and make things up with her? Maybe check she got back okay on her own?'

She exhaled wearily. 'No, it's fine. She's a big girl now and she's the one who should be coming to find me to say sorry, not the other way round,' Kelly answered stubbornly. Besides, she wanted to spend the night with Billy. He wouldn't be around much longer and Kelly was going to miss him so much. Kelly was at the stage in their relationship where she knew she was in deep enough to get hurt; it was a scary place to be, yet absolutely thrilling at the same time. She couldn't get enough of him and knew he felt the same. It was hard getting out of bed in the mornings when she stayed at his apartment, she could lie in Billy's arms all day, but knew she couldn't leave Jade on her own, even when they were in such a mood with each other.

Kelly's mum had been even more excited than she was when she'd told her she had a new boyfriend on the phone the other day. *Mum will be on about marriage and grandkids in no time*, she thought fondly; she was always going on about how much she couldn't wait until Kelly had children. Kelly was in no rush for all that though; she was far too young and wanted to have a career before she properly settled down. This new bikini business that she and Jade had thought up sounded like a great idea. She'd already been studying women in their swimwear for the last few days and thinking up some sexy new creations in her head that she couldn't wait to make a reality. How amazing would it be to run your own business; to have no one else to answer to and to be the one to make all decisions? She did work for herself now, Kelly supposed, but freelance beauty wasn't exactly the same. It didn't completely fulfil her and she wanted more from life. Who would ever have guessed she was entrepreneurial? Everyone just thought of her as Kelly; the girl who was nice, but a bit thick. She couldn't really blame people for having that impression of her though; she'd hated school and exams, and didn't exactly have the best common sense in the world. She always remembered when her mum was going to KFC and had said she was getting a pound of wings.

'But pandas don't have wings,' Kelly had said, bemused.

Kelly was always the butt of everyone's jokes and didn't mind half the time, because she liked making people laugh, cheering them up. Even if it was *at* her and not *with* her. But sometimes she did want people to take her seriously. She hoped that their business was a success, so it would make people view her differently.

Kelly had one last look around the club and checked Jade hadn't come back.

'She's definitely gone?' Billy asked her as she reached him, waiting by the entrance.

Kelly nodded, checking her phone once again to see if Jade had at least texted her. There was still nothing.

'Let's get a taxi then, babe, she must have left for sure.'

As she cuddled up to Billy in the taxi, Kelly felt a slight feeling of guilt creep up inside her. Maybe she should have spent a bit more time just with Jade? Maybe, if she'd given her a chance, her best friend would have apologised about the dress? She hated rowing with Jade, and felt even worse that she'd gone home all alone late at night in a foreign country. Her mum would kill her if she knew! She couldn't believe that Tom had actually ripped the strap on her dress; what on earth was wrong with that boy? She did feel a bit bad not checking if Jade was okay, but she just couldn't see why she had gone over and spoken to Tom in the first place when Jade knew how nasty he could be already. Kelly was tired of always being the one to apologise and back down first so maybe for once, she would let Jade do the running. Jade was in the wrong, so surely she would anyway? They couldn't both stay in Marbella not talking to each other. As she closed her eyes in the back of the cab, she hoped they could sort it out soon. How would she cope if they didn't?

CHAPTER 18

Lisa felt sick with worry as she made her way back to her desk after lunch. She didn't even care about the dirty looks and fake smiles she received from Karen and Susie as she walked past reception. Normally she felt hurt every time they snubbed her, but today she had far more important things to worry about.

She had four new emails and her heart sank when she saw that two were from Jake, sent from his BlackBerry. She knew it was going to be about the wedding; it was all he ever emailed her about recently. He was worse than a Bridezilla, she decided, and she was playing the role of the laid-back groom, something she never thought she'd do. There was a reason why though, and every time she thought about it, it made her panic. She clicked on the emails and saw he'd sent yet more links to wedding websites in Italy and France. Seriously, did he think of anything else all day apart from the wedding?

Lisa ignored the emails, including the other two work ones, picked up her bag and made her way to the toilet. Hands shaking slightly, she reached into her bag and quietly opened the pregnancy test she had just bought. She said a silent prayer. She couldn't believe she was two days late:

she was never late! At first, she'd tried not to think about it, willing her period to come and constantly trying to convince herself she had stomach cramps, even though she didn't. But not being able to think of anything else, she felt she'd had no choice but to buy a test and put herself out of her own misery. But what if she *was* pregnant? She didn't believe in abortions, but surely she couldn't keep the baby? She hardly even knew Jonny; the last thing she wanted to do was raise a child with him. Lisa had so much she wanted to do before she had children, not to mention her parents would go utterly ballistic if the test was positive. She would have to deal with it alone, she decided. If she was pregnant she would get rid of the baby and not tell a single soul. She wouldn't ever be able to admit she'd gone through with it.

Lisa had been so embarrassed buying the test in Tesco on her lunch break. She felt like the cashier knew her dirty little secret and was judging her, although that was impossible. She'd bought some make-up remover and a few magazines that she didn't even want as well, just so it wasn't only the pregnancy test to scan through. There was a security box around the test which the cashier took ages to remove, making Lisa feel even more flustered. She'd made sure a colleague wasn't in there at the same time buying their lunch before going to the till; if anyone had seen her with the test she would have died.

Lisa took a deep breath as she got ready to pee on the stick. She would be fine. She had to be.

Why did they make it so difficult to wee on the stick? How on earth could you do it so it didn't touch your skin? It was impossible! Her hand was all wet so she wiped it on some tissue and put the test on her lap, breathing slowly and trying to calm her nerves. It seemed to take forever to show the result, but it was clear to see. She wasn't pregnant! She felt like screaming with happiness and joy, but also cursed herself again for being so irresponsible. Lisa sat for a moment and wasn't surprised when tears formed in her eyes. She blinked them away, furious at herself for crying yet again. It's all she'd done recently and she was sick of it. She'd made her bed and would have to lie in it; everything that had happened was her own fault and she deserved it. She just wished that Kelly or Jade was around. She needed her friends more than ever at the moment, and it wasn't the same speaking over the phone for a few minutes before one of them panicked about their phone bill.

Lisa wondered why her period was late if she wasn't pregnant, but she'd read somewhere that stress could cause your periods to be irregular. Some people didn't have them at all when a trauma happened in their life. She'd been extremely stressed over the past few weeks so it made perfect sense.

I can't handle this any more, she thought, as she made her way back to her desk. The constant talk and planning of the wedding, the guilt she felt every second of every day, the lies she told Jake about how she couldn't wait to be married when he asked her if she was excited; it was all too much. She needed to come clean. The pregnancy test was the last straw. She *had* to confess everything to Jake. He needed to know what she'd done and she hoped with all her heart that when she told him he would still be there. But somehow she doubted it very much.

She sat at her desk and her phone rang.

'I have Jake on the line for you,' Susie said in a flat voice.

'Thanks, put him through.'

'Hello, how's it going?' Jake asked.

Terrible, she wanted to say. *I've just had to do a pregnancy test because I slept with someone in Marbella.* 'Yes, busy as normal. What's up?'

'Just wondered if you had a chance to look at those links yet? My mum was saying that Lake Garda in Italy is amazing. She went to a friend's place there years ago. I think you'll love it. The Amalfi Coast looks beautiful, too.'

'Babe, I'm really busy at the minute with work. I'll look when I get a chance though, sounds lovely.' Lisa took a deep breath and closed her eyes, concentrating on doing the right thing and not being a coward. 'What are you doing after work tonight?'

He paused for a moment as he thought. 'Mmm . . . said I'd go for a quick pint with the others, but nothing after that. Why, what are you thinking?'

'Do you fancy meeting for dinner when I get in? I'll get off the tube at Loughton and we can go to Loch Fyne or somewhere. There are some things we need to discuss.'

'Yeah, sounds perfect. About six thirty?'

'Yes, I'll text you if I'm going to be late.'

'Okay. Try and have a look at those links so you can tell me where you'd prefer. Then maybe we could have a short weekend there and go and view some venues. easyJet flights to Italy are dirt cheap for October, I've been having a look.'

'I'll check them out,' she said to placate him. 'I'd better go. I'll see you a bit later on.'

They both said goodbye and Lisa hung the phone up, feeling more pressure than she'd ever felt in her whole life.

She clicked on the rest of her unread emails and sighed as she read one from her boss asking her to carry out various mundane admin tasks. She had so much on her mind that concentrating was difficult today. She preferred it when they were out on a shoot rather than in the office, even if it meant she worked more hours. That way she was completely distracted and hardly thought about her problems. She had to be brave tonight and do what was right – she just prayed she had the strength to do it.

Later that evening, she sat in Loch Fyne with a glass of wine to calm her nerves. Jake had just called to let her know he was running five minutes late. Lisa looked around the restaurant, glad that she had been seated in a quiet area with no one else around. She looked at the menu, not feeling in the slightest bit hungry. How could she eat when she was about to ruin both their lives? Lisa had thought about asking him to go to her house for dinner, but didn't want her parents overhearing. She felt safer telling him in a public place.

Jake made his way round to their table. He'd gone home to change after work and looked so handsome in his white shirt and jeans, his hair slick in a side parting.

'Hello babe,' he said, kissing her on the lips with a huge grin before taking his seat. 'I'm starving.' He picked the menu up, eyes scanning his options eagerly. 'Do you know what you're having?'

'I'm not that hungry so I think I'll just get some mussels.'

'I might get oysters,' he said, raising an eyebrow and giving her a cheeky smile.

She laughed, despite feeling completely dreadful inside. Jake always managed to make her smile.

The waiter came over and they ordered. Lisa ordered another glass of wine and gulped the rest of her first glass nervously. When should she bring it up? When was a good time to tell him? Jake chatted about work that day and Lisa just nodded, not really listening to what he was saying, only thinking about what she had to tell him.

'So, did you take a look at the locations? What do you think?' he asked her, finishing off his herb-crusted cod.

'They're both lovely,' she said quietly, knowing that now was the time to say it. She took a deep breath and looked at him sadly.

'What's wrong?' he asked, frowning in concern.

Tears formed in Lisa's eyes and she dropped her head. This was it, she couldn't go back now. 'I need to tell you something.'

He shot her a frightened glance. 'Please just come out with it, you're scaring me.'

'Before I do, I want you to know that I love you so much and I would never do anything to purposely hurt you,' she said as the tears ran down her cheeks.

'I love you as well,' Jake said. 'Just tell me what's wrong, Lisa.' He sounded almost frantic with worry.

'When I was in Marbella, I slept with someone else.' The second the words escaped her lips, Lisa felt like a huge weight had been lifted from her shoulders. She looked at him and saw his face completely crumple. He took in two deep breaths and stared at her, obviously trying to hold his tears back.

'Who?'

Lisa was really sobbing now; it was as though all the feelings she'd bottled up for weeks were finally being released. 'I'm so sorry. I swear to God, it didn't mean a thing. I'd had too much to drink and I just did it. I'm so, so sorry, I didn't mean it and I've felt dreadful ever since.' She tried to hold his hand across the table, but he pulled it away. Suddenly Jake seemed to become calmer and in control.

His eyes widened and he glared at her, the irritation in his voice clear. 'Why did you agree to marry me knowing that you'd cheated?' he demanded.

'Because I love you,' she replied quickly. 'When your boyfriend, who you love, asks you to marry him, you say yes. It's always been my dream. I made a mistake and I could never have gone through with the wedding without telling you,' she sniffed and saw that his hands were shaking, like her own.

'I can't believe it,' Jake said shaking his head and then resting it in his hands. He suddenly looked up at her furiously and hissed, 'How could you do that to me? How could you sleep with someone else?'

Lisa's tears choked her as she looked at the disgust on his face.

'I respect you for telling me, but you know this means that I can't be with you any more,' he said firmly in a flat tone, his face set.

It would have hurt less if he'd picked up his knife and stabbed her. 'Please don't say that. Maybe it's just not the right time for us? I love you so much, Jake. Please don't go. I can't live without you,' she said desperately, trying once more to hold his hand. Jake let her this time and when she felt his skin, which was rough from working, she wanted never to let go.

'Don't make this harder on me, Lisa,' he whispered as his voice cracked with emotion. He pushed his chair back, making a loud scraping sound. 'I have to go.' He took a wad of notes out of his pocket and placed it on the table before walking off.

'I'll pay!' she called after him, but he was gone.

It had been worse than she'd ever imagined and she sat in the restaurant with her head in her hands, crying her eyes out, not bothered if anyone saw her. He didn't want to know her and how could she blame him? Lisa had hoped so much that he'd forgive her and tell her it was all okay, but he hadn't. Jake no longer wanted her to be his girlfriend and it was a terrifying thought. She'd been with Jake since she was sixteen and loved him with all her heart. He was all that Lisa knew. How was she going to live her life without him?

CHAPTER 19

After her eventful night out, Jade had spent a nice peaceful
day on the beach alone, and when she'd bumped into a
few girls she knew from TIBU, she took them up on their
offer to have dinner together. As she made her way back
to the apartment later that night, she wondered anxiously
if Kelly would be there. Jade had gone out early that morning
and Kelly hadn't returned from the previous night, which
hadn't surprised her in the slightest. She had obviously
stayed at Billy's, not caring one iota if Jade got home safe
or not. Kelly hadn't even texted her all day.

Jade was still shocked at the events from the night before.
She couldn't believe what had happened with Adele. Tom
had clearly been lying when he'd said he hadn't been with
any other girls. She was so gullible; maybe the only good
thing to come out of this was that she wouldn't be so naïve
in future. Jade wondered what had happened afterwards
with Adele and Lee. Surely she couldn't have got herself
out of that one? She hoped not; Adele deserved to be alone.
She was nothing but a spiteful, manipulative cow. In fact,
Jade thought wryly, Adele and Tom would make the perfect
couple.

She looked at her watch and was shocked to see it had

just gone eight p.m. She didn't have to work tonight, but she didn't really fancy going out, though she was glad she had the option to meet up with the girls for a few drinks if she fancied it. She was sure that Kelly would want to be with Billy again, so it was nice to have an alternative plan. Besides, she doubted Kelly was even talking to her. Jade did feel bad about the dress and she supposed she could have been more apologetic at the start, but Kelly really hadn't given her a chance. Jade promised herself she'd buy her a new one as soon as she got home. Maybe she had overreacted by leaving last night without even telling her, but it wasn't as though Kelly had seemed bothered about her. She could see a light on in their apartment and opened the front door, to see Kelly sitting on her bed reading a magazine. She half expected to see Billy there as well and was relieved when he didn't appear.

'Hi,' Jade said, feeling tense as she walked in the room.

'Hi.' Kelly's eyes flicked up briefly, and then she went back to her magazine.

Jade sat down on her bed opposite Kelly, unsure what to say. It was strange that there was an uncomfortable atmosphere between them; normally they would be laughing and joking already by now.

'Why didn't you tell me you were leaving last night?' Kelly asked, finally turning her face to Jade. She looked hurt.

'I'm surprised you even noticed,' Jade replied sulkily as she twisted her hair round her index finger.

'Don't be so ridiculous.' Kelly rolled her eyes.

Jade's phone beeped signalling she had a text message. As she read it she gasped.

I told Jake what happened and he's finished with me. I'm completely devastated though deep in my heart I think it may be the right thing. Can't talk

about it at the moment because I'm too upset. Will
see you when you get back. Lisa x

'What's happened?' Kelly asked, concerned by Jade's stunned expression.

'Oh my God. It's Lisa. She told Jake and he's split up with her!' Jade told her hastily.

'Oh my God!' Kelly said, biting her bottom lip.

'Poor, poor Jake. I bet Lisa's in bits.' Jade shook her head, staring at the message on her phone.

Kelly nodded, dumbfounded.

'I never ever thought they would break up. I feel like we should be there for her,' Jade said, biting her nails.

'Me too.'

Jade moved closer to Kelly and spoke softly. 'Listen, about last night. I'm so sorry about your dress. I promise I'll get you a new one. And this whole thing about you and Billy; I'm happy for you.'

'Babe, please, I'm the one who should be saying sorry. I know you're not jealous of me. I've been spending so much time with him; I don't blame you for getting annoyed at times. I know you didn't mean to damage the dress either. I was just pissed off at the time. Alcohol makes things seem worse.'

Jade nodded in agreement. 'Friends?'

'Friends,' Kelly said warmly as she moved to hug her. 'You're my favourite Essex girl, remember that. We'll always be best mates.'

Jade told Kelly the whole story about Adele, Tom and Lee. She was gobsmacked.

Kelly's eyes flashed with anger and her voice rose several octaves. 'I can't believe Adele! She cheats on him all the time! And what were the chances of it being with Tom? I hope Lee sees her for what she really is now; a big, fat, cheating cow.'

'Well, she's not exactly fat,' Jade laughed, picturing her size ten figure.

'I know,' Kelly smiled. 'But saying it made me feel better.'

'I'm not going to lie. I'm missing home now,' Jade confessed hesitantly.

'I know what you mean, hun,' Kelly murmured thoughtfully. 'I miss my mum and Lisa and I could really do with a cuddle from Lord McButterpants.'

Jade smiled at her. 'I feel like Lisa needs us too; we should be there for her. Shall we see if we can get a flight back in a week or so?' she suggested.

'Yeah. I've loved every minute of Marbs, but I feel like if we stay too much longer it may get boring and we'll ruin what's been the best holiday of my life. It's best to leave now while it's still a hundred per cent reem.'

'It's settled then,' Jade said, feeling relieved, but also sad that their trip was coming to an end.

'Shall we go for a few drinks? I've told Billy already I'm spending the night with you tonight. I'm seeing him tomorrow before he leaves and the boys are treating him to his last night out.'

Jade smiled, gratefully. 'Thanks. Let's make the most of Marbs while we're still here then!' She went over to the fridge and poured them two generous measures of vodka.

*

Lisa hadn't slept all night. Her head was pounding and she had a lump in her throat that felt like the size of a golf ball. The previous night when she'd got home she'd gone straight up to her room. She didn't want to face her parents just yet and had said she wasn't feeling too well when they came up to see her this morning. What would she say when they asked why she and Jake split up? Lisa desperately didn't want the truth to come out, she'd be mortified.

Everyone would be so shocked. Would they all think she was a complete tart?

There was no way she could go to work today, she thought, as she sat up in bed. She was exhausted and felt completely drained. She'd actually made herself ill because she was so upset.

Lisa had always believed that everything happened for a reason. As heartbroken as she was, there was a part of her that thought she *had* been too young to settle down, she knew that now. She hadn't experienced enough of life yet. Lisa wanted to travel, go places, meet people. Would she really have been able to do that if she'd married Jake? Perhaps she'd slept with Jonny because what he said had hit a nerve; questioning how she knew Jake was 'the one' when she'd only ever been with Jake. How many other girls her age could say that? How did she truly know that he was her soul mate if she'd never even been with anyone else? What she had done was wrong and she did regret it, but perhaps she'd subconsciously done it because she wasn't certain marrying Jake was the right thing. If she was really honest, their relationship had become a comfortable routine. It didn't make it any easier though. It still hurt like hell.

Lisa had texted Jake when she'd got home saying how sorry she was for everything, and how cheating on him was the biggest mistake of her life. She added that she knew she'd probably never meet anyone like him again and would never forgive herself for hurting him. He hadn't replied, and Lisa had to prevent herself from picking her phone up and throwing it out of the window in hysterics. She couldn't bear the silence that told her he hadn't texted back so, eventually, she had switched it on silent mode, hoping that maybe if she left it for a few hours, she'd look at her phone and suddenly see a reply. When the reply never came, she began to despise her phone and switched it off and threw it into her bedside drawer in anger. Jake always replied to her messages; even when they argued, he would still text her back. Ignoring her was the worst thing he could do. She wanted him to be angry and to shout at her. To tell her how much of a bitch she was, anything. But no, he obviously hated her that much he thought she wasn't even worth replying to. She'd never experienced a feeling like it; overwhelming regret and a pain that hurt so much inside, she didn't know if she'd ever be the same again. At the moment, the thought of being with another man made absolutely no sense. When she pictured her future, it was always Jake she saw. Was there any way that they could eventually be friends, at least? She couldn't imagine him not in her life in some way, even if it was just as mates.

But Lisa knew she'd done the right thing by telling him; she could never have lived a lie for the rest of her life, and Jake deserved so much more.

Lisa glanced at the clock on her wall. It was still only six forty-five; too early to call work and let them know she wasn't coming in. She laid her head on her pretty Cath Kidston pillow case. She loved Cath Kidston and remembered telling Jake that when they moved in together she would be decorating their bedroom in the signature pretty floral patterns. He'd laughed, saying there was no way he was having such a girly room, but then when he saw the disappointment in her face had said she could have whatever made her happy. He'd been the loveliest boyfriend she ever could have asked for and Lisa didn't know how she was going to cope without him; she missed him already.

But the last thing Lisa wanted to do was to mope around feeling sorry for herself; she wasn't that kind of person. She had to accept what had happened and concentrate on her career instead. This was the only day she was going to have off from work, she told herself. She hated calling in sick, even when she genuinely couldn't work, like today. Her company were shooting a new show next week and that was exactly what she needed to take her mind off Jake. Her hours would be long and she simply wouldn't have time to keep thinking about him and checking her phone. Unable to stop herself, she took the phone out of the drawer and turned it on, her heart thumping loudly in her ears. She felt sick. How could doing such a simple, mundane thing make her feel this way? Lisa thought of the hundreds of times she'd seen Jake's name flashing up on her phone. It didn't mean anything to her at the time and it was strange that something so little would make her so happy now. Her heart sank when she turned her phone over to see absolutely nothing. If only she'd told him before she went away that she wasn't sure about their future. It would have hurt him still, yes, but she wouldn't have cheated. But had she known she was having doubts back then? She'd still been happy, hadn't she? A wave of anguish swept through Lisa and she sobbed her heart out silently into her pillow.

CHAPTER 20

Jade took one last look around their apartment, making sure there was nothing left behind.

'I can't believe we're leaving,' Kelly said. 'I feel like I've been here for ages. I've had such a good time.'

'Me too,' Jade agreed, dragging her suitcase to the door. 'I'm looking forward to getting home though. Can't wait to start our new business either.'

'Yeah, we'll make it so good, babe. We need to save as much money as possible first, buy the stock, create amazing designs, get the website done and then think about advertising and that.'

'I'm going to see if I can get some temping work in an office for a few months to save,' Jade said happily as they walked out of their apartment. They stood by the door together and looked around. 'Bye, room,' Jade said.

'Ah, I feel sad leaving,' Kelly said, the light in her eyes fading. She turned to the mirror on the wall. 'I totes need to wear sunglasses seeing as it's so sunny as usual, but my make-up looks too good today to cover up.'

Jade laughed and rolled her eyes. 'Don't wear them then.'

Kelly put them on. 'I'm practically in mourning though and may get tearful, so I have no choice. Marbs is over.'

'You'll be seeing Billy soon and you won't be sad then,' Jade reminded her, knowing that Kelly couldn't wait to see him again. She'd missed him more than she'd let on, Jade was sure of it. They'd been texting non-stop since he'd left over a week ago, and Jade always knew when it was him because of Kelly's permanent grin. It was nice seeing Kelly so happy for once.

One thing Jade was glad about was that she wouldn't have to see Adele any longer. After the night at Nikki Beach last week she'd been really quiet and had hardly spoken to them. She'd heard from the other workers that Lee had broken up with her and apparently she was really upset about it. Jade had no sympathy for her whatsoever though; Adele was nothing but trouble in her eyes.

The taxi driver helped them put their cases in the boot and the girls sat in the back.

'Have you heard any more from Lisa?' Kelly asked as they sped through the town.

'Not since the other day, no,' Jade replied, thinking about when she had called her, even though Lisa had said she didn't want to talk. She had seemed very depressed and was just about to get on the train after work so had to cut the call short. Jade had texted her subsequently, saying if she needed to talk to her or Kelly at any time of day to just call.

Now that her time in Marbella was over, Jade had to admit she missed having a boyfriend. She'd had a few random snogs over the summer and obviously her disastrous night with Tom, but apart from that she hadn't met anyone she partic-ularly liked, apart from Sam. They got on so well and had become quite good friends. It was just a shame he had a new girlfriend who he was always with. She had to admit that they made a good-looking couple, even if the sight of Sam still made her heart flutter. Oh well, she thought, it obviously wasn't meant to be. Jade was a strong believer in fate.

The taxi pulled up at the airport and the girls split the fare. As they pulled their suitcases along, Jade caught a glimpse of her reflection in the window. She couldn't believe how much first Essex, and now Marbella, had changed her. When she'd been living in Bath she was always dressed casually; never making too much of an effort with her appearance. It had always been about being comfortable and natural. But now, even only going to the airport, she had curled her hair and brushed it to give it a slight wavy look, had opted for a pretty floral playsuit and put a fair amount of make-up on. Kelly had done the same too, even wearing her false eyelashes because Billy was picking them up from the airport back home.

'Do I look okay?' she'd asked Jade, as she climbed into a tight white dress that showed off her gorgeous glowing tan.

'Kelly, you look lovely,' she'd replied honestly. Billy was going to think all his Christmases had come at once when he saw her.

The girls groaned as they saw the huge queue to the easyJet desks.

'Look who's in front of us,' Kelly whispered as they reluctantly joined the back.

'Who?' Jade questioned, trying to see who she was talking about.

'Sam. He's there, see?' she said as she pointed to him.

'Oh yeah,' Jade answered, wondering if he had his girlfriend with him. She couldn't see her, but maybe she'd gone home on a different flight or was staying in Marbella longer. She didn't say anything else though, as she didn't want Kelly to think she was still interested in him. What was the point, when Sam didn't like her in that way?

The girls sat drinking cappuccinos and reading magazines after they made their way through security.

'She's definitely had Botox,' Kelly said, pointing to a photo of Kylie Minogue.

Jade agreed. 'Without a doubt. She still looks about twenty-five! In fact, her eyes look very cat-like, maybe she's had a facelift?'

'I'm so getting that done soon,' Kelly announced.

'Not a facelift, surely?' Jade couldn't believe her ears.

Kelly laughed and looked at her as though she'd gone mad. 'Don't be so ridiculous. I meant Botox.'

'Kelly, are you being serious? You're only twenty-one! Like you need Botox!'

'You have to have it young, babe, before it gets too late. Then it won't work, trust me. My mum always says she wished she'd had the chance to get it done when she was young. I want it in these lines on my forehead.' She frowned to show where she meant.

'You're being stupid.'

'Frown then,' Kelly demanded.

Jade pushed her eyebrows up and glanced at Kelly for her reaction.

'See, you get the lines too,' Kelly said smiling, pleased with herself.

Jade took a compact mirror out of her hand luggage. 'Where?' she said, pulling the face again. Then she saw them. Completely normal. In fact, she wouldn't be able to move her forehead without them!

'They do Botox parties in this boutique in Shenfield. Come with me next time and we'll buy some nice new dresses and speak to the doctor about getting it done maybe. My mum goes and I think Jake's mum does too.'

'Mmm . . . I'll think about it,' Jade replied, going back to the story in her magazine.

'You'll be jell if you don't, when I come back with my face as smooth as a baby's bum.'

Forty minutes later and Jade wondered if their flight had been delayed. 'Kelly, are you sure it doesn't say our gate or anything yet? Does it say we're delayed?'

Kelly, who was closer to the screen with the flight details on, walked up to it once again. 'No, babe, says nothing,' she shrugged.

Jade looked at her watch. It was three o'clock in the afternoon and their flight was taking off at three thirty. It couldn't be possible to not have any information on the screens. 'Kelly, you *are* looking at the three-thirty flight going to Stansted, aren't you?'

Kelly started anxiously. 'Shit! I thought we were going to Luton? I've been looking at the flight for Luton!'

Jade's heart skipped a beat as she panicked. 'You're kidding? Quick, let's go!'

The girls grabbed their bags and quickly ran back to the screen to discover what gate they were at. The last thing they wanted was to miss their flight. Typical Kelly, Jade thought, as they ran past people with puzzled looks on their faces, trust her to be looking at the wrong departure. They raced through the airport and joined the back of the very short queue of people going through the gate.

'At least we won't have to queue now,' Kelly said sheepishly.

'That's one good way of looking at it. Forget the fact you've almost given me a heart attack,' Jade replied, wiping the sweat from her forehead. 'We probably won't be able to sit together now. We're the last people getting on the plane. We've only just made it.'

'Awww I hate sitting on my own.'

'Kelly, you fall asleep as soon as you sit down, how can you say that? You wouldn't even know if you were sitting next to Brad Pitt!'

'Trust me, if Brad Pitt sat next to me, I'd manage to stay awake!' Kelly gave her trademark throaty giggle.

They handed their boarding passes over to the air hostess as they made their way onto the plane.

'There is one seat here at the front,' she said to them, 'and there is another at the back.'

Kelly was in front so she took the first one.

'See you soon,' Jade said unhappily, as she made her way to find the other empty seat. She walked down the plane, feeling fairly self-conscious as hundreds of faces watched her. As she saw the empty chair she felt a thankful moment of relief, but then in the next breath almost died as she saw who she was seated next to. It was Sam. She felt flustered as she tried to put her large hand luggage into the overhead locker.

'Do you need help?' Sam asked.

'No,' she laughed nervously. 'It's fine. Thanks.' Jade gave her bag one almighty thump and sighed with relief as it fitted into the small gap. She was boiling hot and wiped her brow again, using her magazine as a fan as she sat down. Was this some sort of joke? Did she seriously have to sit next to Sam for the whole journey? She was almost shaking with excitement and nerves. She couldn't wait for Kelly to see; she'd never believe it. Out of all the people on the plane, he was the person with the empty seat next to him. Sam looked amazing in a black Hugo Boss polo top, which was fairly tight and showed off his toned physique, golden tan and green eyes.

'Hey,' she said, a little awkwardly.

'Hi,' he smiled, coolly. 'I didn't realise you were leaving. Your last night at work must have been the same night as mine,' he said, sweeping his hair away from his face.

Jade nodded. 'We just kind of miss home really. There is only so much sun and alcohol we could take.'

'Agreed. I told you the novelty wears off after a while. I'm not drinking for ages now.'

'Me either. Lots of water, fruit and vegetables for me for a while I think. Can't wait to get back into the gym too.'

'What gym do you go to?' he asked, interested.

She gave a little shrug. 'I haven't got a membership

anywhere just yet. I went to Fitness First when I was at uni in Bath, but need to join somewhere when I get home.'

He paused. 'You live in Chigwell, right?'

She nodded. 'Yes, fairly close to The King William pub.'

'You should go to David Lloyd. I live in South Woodford, so not too far from you, and that's the one I go to. It's a really nice one.'

She tucked her hair behind her ears. 'I'll look into it when I get back. I may have to just go jogging for a while to start with because I need to save as much money as possible.'

He stared at her. 'Oh right, what's that for? You moving out or something?'

'No, not yet,' she said shaking her head. 'I wish I was though. Me and Kelly are going to try to start a new business. We're going to customise swimwear.'

He raised his eyebrows. 'Sounds like a great idea. The holidaymakers in Marbella will love it, not to mention Ibiza and Vegas. All you girls love to dress up for the pool,' he laughed. 'Not that I'm complaining. My old school-mate works for a women's magazine. She might be able to help you when you want some publicity.'

'That would be great,' Jade replied gratefully.

'You'll have to text me when you get it up and running and I'll speak to her for you.'

The next few hours vanished in a flash. Jade loved talking to Sam and getting to know much more about him. How could she have even felt the slightest bit uneasy with him before? He was so easygoing and friendly.

'I'm starving,' Sam said as the pilot announced they were landing. 'Can't wait to go home and get a home-cooked dinner. Though I must admit, I would love the ribs and chips they do in Billy's restaurant in Puerto Banus right now.'

'I don't think we ate there. Always used to see it, but never went.'

302

'What? You didn't go Billy's? You've missed out big time,' he said, shaking his head. 'Me and Serena went there practically every night one week.'

'Is that the brunette girl you were always with? Your girlfriend?' Jade asked timidly.

'What, Serena?' Sam laughed. 'God no, she's my cousin! She went home last week actually; she never planned to stay for as long as she did.'

'Oh . . . I thought she was your girlfriend because she was always with you,' she muttered.

Jade tried to hide her delight as Sam explained the story. So he didn't have a girlfriend after all? That didn't change the fact that he'd snogged Adele though, she remembered glumly.

'So what about you? Seeing anyone? Meet anyone you like? Apart from that charming bloke that ruined your dress in Nikki Beach of course,' he said sarcastically, before looking at her sympathetically.

Jade felt her face get hot. 'God, don't remind me. Crazy ex-boyfriend. Thanks for trying to help that night by the way, it was really kind of you. I was too embarrassed and upset to talk to you, sorry. In answer to your question, I didn't meet anyone I liked. I had quite a quiet summer in the relationship department, to be honest.'

Sam laughed and looked at the view out the window. 'Okay, if you say so.'

Jade frowned. 'What do you mean by that?'

'Nothing, sorry,' he replied, flushing with embarrassment.

'Tell me. You can't just say something like that and not back it up.' Jade was so confused. What did he mean?

'It's nothing to be ashamed of; you're single, after all. Adele told me that night I was speaking to you that you were snogging loads of blokes in the club, that's all. Oh and something about a, um, *threesome* with a couple of guys that worked there?'

303

Jade was livid. 'She said *what*?'

Sam looked awkward. 'I shouldn't have said anything. Just forget it.'

Jade was so horrified she could feel the blood pulsating round her head. 'No, I won't forget it. That's a complete lie! There is no way I would have a threesome. And I didn't kiss anyone that night. I was with Kelly the whole time and then went to find you and you were snogging Adele's face off!'

Sam's forehead creased into a confused expression and he gently ran his fingers through his hair. 'Why did Adele tell me that then?'

Jade shrugged her shoulders angrily and narrowed her eyes. 'Because she was jell, clearly. She obviously had a problem with the thought of us together. I knew it from the moment I told her I fancied you she didn't like it.' Jade couldn't believe she'd just let that slip out; she was mortified. Then again, she reminded herself, it wasn't like he didn't know it anyway.

'Oh, that kind of makes sense then,' Sam said digesting the information. 'What is Adele's problem? I know she doesn't even have feelings for me in that way.'

Jade exhaled and folded her arms. 'Don't even get me started about Adele. She's a very manipulative troublemaker in my opinion. Sorry, I know she's your ex, but I'm really not keen on her. I can't believe she would stoop so low and make up lies about me.'

Sam's eyes widened. 'Don't apologise! I feel the exact same way. God knows what I was thinking that night when I kissed her. Trust me; I have no feelings for that girl whatsoever. I was actually on my way to find you when she approached me.'

'Really?' Jade smiled.

'Yeah,' Sam said and their eyes met.

Jade was ecstatic. She felt like she was in a dream. All

she wanted to do was kiss him, there and then. Those perfect pink lips that she knew would taste divine. She couldn't believe Adele though. What an absolute cow! If she ever saw her again it would be too soon. After pretending to be helping Jade, she had done everything she could to keep her and Sam apart. Well, she thought happily, it didn't work in the end.

As they arrived into Stansted airport, Sam walked alongside Jade, even offering to take her suitcase. Kelly was waiting ahead for her, and was grinning when she saw the two of them, even more than Jade was.

Sam waved to Kelly and kissed Jade on the cheek. 'I'm going to dash and quickly get my bag. My dad is here already waiting for me. I'll text you and we'll go out soon, yeah?'

'Yeah, sounds good. Speak to you later.'

Fate had brought them together again on this flight, Jade was sure of it.

EPILOGUE

'Happy birthday, dear Billy. Happy birthday, to you!' They sang, cheering and clapping as the waiter brought over the cake, covered in candles.

He blew them out with a grin. 'Thanks, everyone.'

'Make a wish!' Jade reminded him.

They were in Zizzi's in Loughton and had just finished their meal. It had been a month since they'd come back from Marbella and the first time they'd all been able to meet up again.

Billy blew out his candles.

'Open my present now,' Kelly said excitedly, thrusting several gifts under his nose.

He unwrapped a couple of jumpers and a pair of jeans. 'They're lovely, babe, thank you so much,' he said, kissing her on the lips.

'There is another one as well,' she said, picking it off the table.

Jade and Sam tried to not laugh as he opened it, but Kelly had told them the other day what she was getting him and they thought it was hilarious.

'Errr . . . what is it?' Billy asked with a baffled expression.

'It's a pajazzle, silly,' Kelly replied.

Jonny snorted. 'What the hell is a pajazzle?'

'Vajazzle for men,' Jade told him with a smirk.

Jonny took the crystal pattern out of Billy's hands. 'Oh my God. Please put that on, Billy! I can't wait to see you blinged up like a girl. That photo is going straight on my Facebook!'

'Piss off,' Billy said, embarrassed.

Jade, Sam and Sam's friend, Steve, sat there laughing.

Kelly wagged a finger at him. 'Jonny, do not take the mick out of Billy's pajazzle. I think they're sexy and they're not girly either! I got him the man's one. It's a cross.'

Jonny laughed so much he was almost crying and Kelly ended up laughing with him.

'That reminds me, Kelly. I have the perfect name for our company,' Jade told her.

'What?' Kelly said as her eyes widened in wonderment.

'Vajazzle My Bikini.'

'That's totes perfect! Well done, babe!'

Luckily, Jade had found a temping job the second week she got home, so they were both saving as much money as possible to get a website built and to buy some stock. Lisa's cousin had already agreed to design it and with a discounted price too, which was a result. It wouldn't be too long before they started, Jade thought, happily.

'I have a little present for you as well,' Jade said to Kelly, who looked surprised. 'It's not even my birthday though!'

'Just open it.' Jade handed her a parcel, wrapped in glittery baby pink paper with a fuchsia-coloured bow on top.

'The wrapping is beauts!' Kelly gushed, as she tore open the paper to find a brand-new silver Jovani dress, just like the one that Tom had ruined. Jade had luckily found one on eBay that was brand new with tags and just one hundred and fifty pounds.

'A new Jovani dress! Oh thanks honey!'

'Hi everyone,' Lisa said as she made her way over to

their table. 'Sorry I'm so late. Happy birthday, Billy.' She kissed his cheek and handed him a card.

'Thanks, Lisa. We're going for some drinks now in Nu Bar. Have you eaten?'

'Yeah, I ate something at work because I was working so late. A drink sounds good though. Just what I need,' Lisa said, taking a seat and saying hello to everyone round the table.

Jade glanced at her friend and wondered if she was going to feel weird being around Jonny. She'd had a tough time at first after splitting up with Jake. He hadn't taken any of her calls or answered any of her messages; it was like he had vanished into thin air. But lately, she started to feel like herself again and she'd confided in Kelly and Jade that she really did believe that it was for the best. Lisa wasn't ready to be anybody's wife and needed some time to herself being single. She was out more than ever now, especially as there was a new girl that had started at her work who was also single and into nights out. Jade was so happy Lisa was enjoying herself; she seemed so carefree and laid back now. Yes, she had always been happy with Jake, but Jade had agreed with her when she confessed she felt their long relationship had become a bit predictable. It had been the same old routine and the excitement had gone. In the end, Lisa had said they were more like friends. She'd said she'd loved Jake with all her heart, so as much as it had been painfully hard to let go, it was the best thing to do for both of them. Jade hoped that one day they could speak again, as it was such a shame after such a long relationship to lose all contact. Who knew, maybe they would in a few years' time?

'Let's pay the bill and go to Nu Bar then,' Jonny said, getting the waiter's attention. 'Let's take the cake with us, unless anybody wants a piece now?'

'I'm stuffed,' Billy said rubbing his stomach, and they all agreed.

Sam put some money on the table and ran his fingers through Jade's hair affectionately, while the others were paying on their cards.

'Mind my hair extensions!' Jade warned.

'I didn't even know you had them in,' Sam said, surprised.

'They're only clip-ins. I'd like real ones though.'

'You don't *need* extensions. You're beautiful to me as you are,' he said, kissing her deeply.

Jade sighed. Men just didn't get it. She was getting proper extensions as soon as she had the money. It wasn't about needing them: it was about making herself feel good and looking her best. It was about not being afraid to stand out and make an impression. The meek girl from Bath uni who let someone else tell her how to behave was well and truly gone. Jade had read an article the other day, saying that girls that came from Essex were more likely to have hair extensions than girls from any other county. Well, she was Essex and proud.

What was it they said? You could take the girl out of Essex, but you couldn't take Essex out of the girl.

JADE'S GUIDE TO ESSEX

The best Essex bars and clubs

Nu Bar, Loughton

Nu Bar is one of my favourite places to go before a club: Kelly, Lisa and I love it! It may be small, but it's always buzzing and is also a celebrity hot spot so keep your eyes peeled and get your cameras ready.

www.nubar.co.uk

Sugar Hut, Brentwood

A great nightclub for a Saturday night out! Sugar Hut has various rooms playing different music, so there is something for everyone. Your friends will be well jell if you go there . . .

www.sugarhutbrentwood.com

Faces, Gants Hill

Put on your highest heels, your biggest lashes and your favourite dress before you hit Faces! The girls and I love it here, too. It's closer to where we live in Chigwell than Sugar Hut and often has celebrity hosts and special party nights.

www.facesnightclub.co.uk

The Brickyard, Romford

The Brickyard is a gorgeous place to go for dinner before you dance, with its stunning a la carte menu. We often enjoy drinking a few glasses of wine in the upstairs bar before heading downstairs to party in the club. Quite simply, it's reem!

www.the-brickyard.co.uk

Restaurants

Sheesh, Chigwell

Sheesh is the perfect and most glamorous place to dine in Essex and the Turkish menu is delicious! I love getting glammed up and going there with the girls or Sam (we've been twice already since we started dating!).

www.sheeshrestaurant.co.uk

Alec's, Navestock Side

If you love fish, then Alec's is the place to go. It has stunning views, spiral staircases (be careful in your heels!) and spacious dining rooms. You're certain to enjoy your meal here.

www.alecsrestaurant.co.uk

Shopping

Lakeside, West Thurrock

Lakeside shopping centre has all our favourite high street shops under one roof; you'll be spoilt for choice! It's nice to have lunch along The Boardwalk too on a sunny day, looking out at the lake.

www.lakeside.uk.com

My Celebrity Dress, online

This is a great website based in Essex, with the very best

glam, sparkly, unique dresses around! The designer dresses are available to hire and many have even been seen on *TOWIE* cast members.

www.mycelebritydress.com

Debra, Chigwell
A small boutique in Chigwell with some of the loveliest dresses for sale. Head there for an outfit for your next big night out!

www.debrachigwell.co.uk

Hair

Barry Graham, Woodford
If you're after the perfect highlights or the trendiest cut, then Barry Graham is the best place to go! Kelly loves getting her big bouncy blow dries done here!

Tel: 0208 504 4949

Spargo, Brentwood
Another hair salon you'll be 100% happy with is Spargo, situated down Brentwood High Street. Get your hair done here before heading to Sugar Hut further down the road!

www.spargo-hairdressing.co.uk

Crown and Glory Extensions
For some beautiful Essex hair extensions, visit www.crownandgloryextensions.com, run by Kirsty in Essex who is a mobile hair extensionist and has the best quality hair extensions around.

Email: info@crownandgloryextensions.com.

Dog boutiques

Diva Dogs, Chelmsford

The best place to buy everything from dog clothes and luxury pet beds to pet jewellery and carriers, Diva Dogs has everything your furry pal could need, including a pet grooming section.

www.divadogs.co.uk

Puppy Kit Pet Couture, Buckhurst Hill

If you love nothing more than to pamper your pooch, then head straight to Puppy Kit Pet Couture. Lord McButterpants gets spoilt rotten here.

www.puppykit.co.uk

Beauty salons

Sparkle, Gidea Park

When Kelly is busy, I just love this beauty salon as it offers everything an Essex girl could ever dream of at really reasonable prices! The name says it all; you will truly be sparkling after a visit here. Enjoy a whole pamper day and get a big bouncy blow dry here too.

www.sparklebyholliejane.com

Amy Child's Salon, Brentwood

Take a trip to *TOWIE* star Amy Childs' salon, down Brentwood High Street. Excellent for massages, manicures and pedicures and a stone's throw away from Sugar Hut. Great for that all-important vajazzle too!

www.amychildsofficial.co.uk/salon

For Essex styling tips, exclusive content
and more information about
author Laura Ziepe,
visit her Facebook Fan Page:
facebook.com/EssexGirlsBooks
or follow her on Twitter: **@lauraziepe.**

Follow Avon on
Twitter@AvonBooksUK
and
Facebook@AvonBooksUK

For news, giveaways and
exclusive author extras

Read on for an *exclusive* extract
of Laura's next book, *Made in Essex*,
available from Avon in January 2014.

CHAPTER ONE

'Open your eyes after three. Ready?'

Jade squeezed her eyes shut and nodded, excitedly. 'One, two . . . three.'

Her hand flew to her mouth and she gasped loudly in amazement as Kelly strolled into the room coolly wearing the very first bikini in their new collection. It was amazing seeing something that they'd actually designed themselves as a finished product, and it looked far better on than she'd ever imagined.

'How hot is this bikini, babe?' Kelly beamed from ear to ear. 'Just picture how good it would look with a dark tan and blue vajazzle as well.'

'Oh my God! You look unreal,' Jade admired, her eyes wide. It was a bright petrol blue colour and had a glittery effect, which sparkled in the light and would look even better in the sunshine. The girls had decided to replace the simple tie strings on the bottoms with a row of three gold chains and then inserted some pretty gold dangling charms in between the two cups on the top. It was simply done and looked incredible on Kelly's killer figure. 'It looks easily as good as the expensive ones you buy from America, Kel. It's beauts!'

'I know! I love it!' Kelly said as she glanced at her reflection in the mirror. 'What are we calling this one?'

Jade thought for a moment. 'I like the name "Essex Show Girl"' she decided. 'What other colours can we get for this design?'

'Caitlin said she also has gold and hot pink, hun.'

Jade jotted it down in her notebook happily. Those colours would also look great. She had a feeling that the 'Essex Show Girl' bikini was going to be very popular indeed.

She was thrilled to be starting her own swimwear business, Vajazzle My Bikini, with her best friend and couldn't wait until everything was up and running. They'd been on holiday to Marbella the year before and when Jade had realised she was the only one with ordinary, plain swimwear on her first day she'd almost been in tears. After finding a boutique that stocked similar glitzy and glamourous bikinis to everyone else's, she'd been horrified at the expensive prices and had decided they should make their own instead. It had been fun visiting the Spanish market for jewels and beads to customise their swimwear, and when they were constantly stopped by girls wanting to know where they'd purchased their costumes from, Jade had realised they were on to something. Kelly was still working as a freelance beautician and Jade had been temping in mundane office jobs to save money for their website. They'd finally saved enough now, and while their friend Lisa's cousin, Tony, was designing and creating their website at a reduced price, they were making the swimwear and planning their collections. They'd found a lovely lady online called Caitlin, who ran a swimwear company in America and sold them bikinis in bulk at discount prices so they could then customise them. So far everything was working out perfectly.

Jade inspected the bikini and looked closely at how well

Kelly had made it; she was impressed. Kelly was fantastic at sewing, whereas she was better at sketching the designs on paper, so they could share the workload. They were going to split the administration and had decided that Jade was going to take all the calls and deal with customer queries.

Kelly looked round the room blankly. 'When can we arrange the office properly?' she enquired.

Luckily Jade had an office in her home that was big enough for the two of them. It was Jade's dad's, but he never used it for more than one day a month. She paused. 'What do you mean? All we need is another chair. We'll just go out and buy one.'

Kelly arched a perfectly neat eyebrow. 'Mmm . . . I was thinking we could change it a bit as well, you know, make it our own?'

'By doing what?' Jade asked in bewilderment, looking round at the perfectly practical and tidy oak wood office.

'I've brought some bits with me in my car, hun. I hope you don't mind, but I'm not really feeling it in here. I read online the other day that you need to feel comfortable where you're working to be able to do your best. The workplace is an important environment, babe. You go and get yourself a snack or something and come back in about thirty minutes. Just let me have a little move around with the furniture,' Kelly told her wisely.

Jade gave a little nod and surrendered, 'Okay, whatever you think. Just don't touch any of my dad's work in the bottom drawer, or he'll kill me.'

'Cross my heart.' Kelly smiled, getting changed back into her clothes and making her way downstairs to her car.

Thirty minutes later, Jade heard Kelly calling her so she made her way upstairs, wondering what on Earth was wrong with the office in the first place. As she entered the room she was greeted by fluffy pink pens in sparkly pen holders, pink and white flowers in a silver mirrored vase, decorated photo frames with their holiday snaps, hot pink feathered cushions and a white furry rug, replacing the plain brown one.

'Ta-dah!' Kelly sang as she twirled round on the spot, pleased with her work. 'What do you think?'

'I think it looks like Barbie and Sindy have decorated the room!' Jade snorted with laughter. 'What is my dad going to think?'

Kelly giggled. 'Oh come on, old Jimbo will love it,' she said with an amused smile.

'I can't imagine my dad appreciating you calling him Jimbo,' Jade joked.

Kelly swivelled round on the spot, looking at her work. 'Do you not like it?' She pouted.

'I'm sure I'll get used to it,' Jade replied, knowing Kelly could never work in an office without a bit of sparkle. If it inspired them to create the best swimwear then the sparkle would stay. It did make the office a bit more girly and personal too, she admitted, spotting a photo of her and her boyfriend, Sam, in one of the frames, unable to contain her grin.

'That's such a gorgeous photo of you two,' Kelly said, when she saw Jade looking at the photo, 'I just a hundred percent *had* to put that one up.'

'Thanks,' Jade said, flattered, as she picked up the frame. The photo had been taken at Kelly's boyfriend, Billy's, birthday last year in Nu Bar. They both still had a slight tan from Marbella where they'd met and it made their teeth look amazingly white. They looked so happy, and luckily they still were.

'You two make such a sweet couple,' Kelly grinned. 'I'm so glad that Sam's become good friends with Billy too. I love going out just us four.'

Jade nodded. She had to agree it was great that they all

got on together so well. If only Lisa had a boyfriend too though, she thought, remembering her other, single best friend. Not that Lisa minded being single one bit. Ever since she'd split up with Jake, her long term boyfriend, the year before she'd been having the time of her life. It was difficult for her and Kelly to even get a minute of her time because she was always going out. She had been in a relationship since she was sixteen though, Jade reminded herself; Lisa was simply making up for lost time. She was constantly on dates with different guys and it was impossible to keep up! Jade didn't blame her, and she was happy if Lisa was; that was the most important thing. She had really thought that Lisa would have married Jake a year ago and they'd even been engaged, but after Lisa cheated on him with Billy's friend, Jonny, in Marbella, Lisa had realised she hadn't been as happy as she'd always thought. Thank goodness Lisa finished it, Jade thought, otherwise she would have been divorced in her early twenties!

Kelly interrupted her thoughts. 'So what are the categories going to be on the website?'

Jade opened her red notebook. 'We decided on the places where all the best pool parties are, didn't we? So we have the Essex section, which is going to be our most over the top, blinged up swimwear, the "No Carbs Before Marbs" section, the "What Happens in Vegas" section, the "Romantic Getaway" section, which will be a bit more toned down for when you go away with your boyfriend or husband, and the "Ibiza Zoo Project Section", which will be all animal print.'

'Love it.' Kelly beamed, running her fingers through her thick blonde hair. 'It's going to be so much fun naming all the bikinis. I just love this job already!'

Jade felt the same. 'Me too. We need to meet with Tony tomorrow at six o'clock to go over the web designs, so make sure you're free. I'll meet you straight from work.'

Kelly nodded and there was a long pause. 'I *so* need a diary.'

'You need one of these,' Jade said, waving her red notebook in front of her, 'diary and notebook in one.'

Kelly poked her tongue out cheekily, 'Alright, Little Miss Organised!' She took a package out of her bag ebulliently. 'I forgot to show you some of the sequins and beads that got delivered to my house this morning. They're gorge.'

'Wow, they're great.' Jade agreed, as she watched her pulled out various colours of sparkling sequins and pretty beads from the package. She couldn't believe how good they looked when they were so cheap to buy. It filled her even more with excitement and ideas for new bikini designs were flying around in her head.

'I know,' Kelly sighed, 'although I'm going to have to call the company up we bought them from and complain about something.'

'What?'

'Well, look here at the receipt,' Kelly pulled out a piece of paper received in the package, 'it says flat shipping rate £3.99.'

Jade squinted as she read it. 'So?' she asked, bemused.

Kelly looked at her with a surprised expression, as though Jade had missed something. 'I don't live in a flat, so why should I have to pay that? The package was delivered to my house!'

Jade laughed. 'Kelly, flat shipping rate doesn't mean they've charged you because they think you live in a flat. That just means standard shipping rate, you dope!'

'Oh,' Kelly said sheepishly, packing the sequins away again, 'well, they shouldn't call it that then, it's confusing; a simple mistake. Anyway, I must dash as I have a client coming at seven for a spray.'

'Why? What's the time?' Jade asked in a panicky voice.

'Quarter to seven,' Kelly replied.

'Oh shit!' Jade said slapping her hand on her forehead. 'Sam is going to kill me! I was meant to meet him at 6.30 for dinner!'

Kelly pulled a face. 'Oh dear. You did the same thing last week, didn't you? Just call him, babe, don't worry.'

Kelly kissed her goodbye and left.

Jade sighed, biting her bottom lip. The problem was she couldn't just call him and let him know that, once again, his girlfriend had simply been too busy working and forgotten she was meeting him. What could she say? She looked at her appearance in the mirror and quickly added some Mac lip gloss and kohl eyeliner. She threw on the first pair of skinny jeans she found, texted Sam she was on her way and ran out of the front door.

'Come on,' Jade said to herself moments later as she was sitting in traffic feeling stressed. Why were all the cars in front of her going so bloody slow tonight? She could hear her phone ringing in her bag and the fact that she knew it would be Sam wondering where she was made her even more anxious. She needed to make something up. She had been extremely pre-occupied with the website recently and forgetting about Sam was becoming a regular occurrence, much to his frustration.

Ten minutes later she was almost running through the doors of The Bluebell restaurant in Chigwell. She saw Sam's unimpressed expression as soon as she walked in.

'Hi, babe,' she kissed him hard on the lips, hoping to ease his annoyance at her being over forty minutes' late.

'Where have you been? Why are you so late?' He asked petulantly.

'I'm so sorry,' Jade said as she sat down, 'it's just we had some issues with the new website and I had to sort them out with Tony.'

Sam nodded and the look on his face told her he'd heard it all before. 'You could have called earlier to tell me, you know, so I didn't come here and have to sit alone for over half an hour. You did the same thing last week too.' He looked offended as he sipped his glass of water.

'I'm sorry,' Jade said gazing into his eyes to show she truly meant it, 'please don't be annoyed with me. Let's have a nice evening, yeah?' She grabbed his hand and held it across the table.

Jade noticed his expression soften and felt relieved.

'So, how's it all going anyway with the website?' He asked a few moments later, genuinely interested. She knew he found it attractive that she was taking a risk and running her own company with Kelly. He was proud of her.

'It's all coming together now.' Jade grinned. 'Kelly put on the first bikini in our collection today and it looked amazing. We know exactly what we want on the website, which is nearly done, and then just need to make the rest of the swimwear, have a photo-shoot so it all looks professional and then the website can go live. I can show you some of the categories we're putting the various bikinis in,' she said, getting her notebook out of her bag and passing it across the table to Sam.

'That's great,' Sam said browsing through the pages. He laughed, 'You take this red notebook everywhere.'

'It's in case I think of new ideas,' Jade told him, smiling warmly. 'I write everything down.'

He looked at her lovingly. 'You look nice tonight, by the way.'

'You're joking? I've got hardly any make-up on and got ready in about two minutes! I'm as pale as a ghost!'

'I like you looking natural, you know that,' he said.

Jade smiled. Sam always said the right thing and made her feel good about herself. Thank goodness he was nothing like her awful ex-boyfriend, Tom, who not only used to constantly make jokes about her being from Essex, but also cheated on her. She was so happy with Sam; he meant everything.

325

'Anyway, there are some good films on at the moment at the cinema. Fancy it tomorrow night?'

'Yeah that'll be great,' Jade said, her eyes bright. Then she remembered something and her face fell. 'Oh no, I can't tomorrow night, sorry, we have another meeting with Tony about the website design. I don't know how long it's going to go on for.'

She could tell Sam was trying to hide his disappointment. He lowered his voice and fiddled with his phone. 'No worries.'

'What about Saturday night though? We may be meeting Tony again in the afternoon but I can meet you in the evening?' Jade suggested cheerily.

Sam nodded. 'If I didn't know better, I'd be worried about you and Tony.'

Jade's jaw nearly hit the table.

'Only joking,' Sam added when he saw her shocked expression. 'Saturday night sounds good to me.'

Jade hoped he really was only joking. She couldn't handle him starting to get jealous, especially about Tony. She thought of Tony and his dark hair and hazel eyes. She supposed he was quite good looking in a rough-round-the-edges kind of way, but she didn't look at him like that. He was just Lisa's cousin: their web developer. She didn't want anyone else and wouldn't dream of ever even looking at another man when she was with Sam. Why would she when he was pretty much perfect?

'Sam, I'm sorry I've been so busy lately. I promise you: it's just work, nothing else.'

'I know,' he reassured her, 'it's fine.'

Ey 3/13

mischief

Naughty by Nature

Mischief is a new series
of erotic fiction.

We publish the sexiest stories
with the hottest modern, historical
and paranormal fantasies.
Available in ebook.

Read Mischief whenever and
wherever you want.

Check our website for special offers
www.mischiefbooks.com